The [illegible]ggar Maid

Dilly [illegible] grew up in North-east London and began her career in television, writing scripts for commercials. She is married with two grown-up children and four grandchildren, and now lives in Dorset on the beautiful Jurassic Coast with her husband. She is the bestselling author of nineteen novels. She also writes under the name of Lily Baxter.

Also by Dilly Court

Mermaids Singing

Born into poverty and living under the roof of her violent and abusive brother-in-law, young Kitty Cox dreams of working in a women's dress shop in the West End.

The Dollmaker's Daughters

For Ruby and Rosetta Capretti, life in the slums of the East End holds little promise. Despite their humble background, Rosetta is determined to work under the bright lights of the music hall and Ruby longs to train as a nurse.

Tilly True

Dismissed from her position as housemaid under a cloud of misunderstanding, Tilly True is forced to return home.

The Best of Sisters

Twelve-year-old Eliza Bragg has known little in life but the cold, comfortless banks of the Thames, her only comfort the love and protection of her older brother, Bart.

The Cockney Sparrow

Gifted with a beautiful soprano voice, young Clemency Skinner is forced to work as a pickpocket in order to support her crippled brother, Jack.

A Mother's Courage

When Eloise Cribb receives the news that her husband's ship has been lost at sea she wonders how she and her children are ever going to manage.

The Constant Heart

Despite living by the side of the Thames, eighteen-year-old Rosina May has wanted for little in life. Until her father's feud with a fellow bargeman threatens to destroy everything.

A Mother's Promise

When Hetty Huggins made a promise to her dying mother that she would look after her younger sister and brothers, little did she know how difficult this would be.

The Cockney Angel

Eighteen-year-old Irene Angel lives with her parents in a tiny room above the shop where her mother ekes out a living selling pickles and sauces, whilst her father gambles away what little money they do manage to earn.

A Mother's Wish

Since the untimely death of her husband, young mother Effie Grey has been forced to live on a narrowboat owned by her tyrannical father-in-law Jacob.

The Ragged Heiress

On a bitter winter's day, an unnamed girl lies dangerously ill in hospital. When two coarse, rough-speaking individuals come to claim her, she can remember nothing.

A Mother's Secret

When seventeen-year-old Belinda Phillips discovers that she is pregnant, she has no option other than to accept an arranged marriage, and give up her child forever.

Cinderella Sister

With their father dead and their mother a stranger to them, Lily Larkin must stay at home and keep house whilst her brothers and sisters go out to work.

A Mother's Trust

When her feckless mother falls dangerously ill, Phoebe Giamatti is forced to turn to the man she holds responsible for all her family's troubles.

The Lady's Maid

Despite the differences in their circumstances, Kate and Josie have been friends since childhood. But their past binds them together in ways they must never know.

The Best of Daughters

Daisy Lennox is drawn to the suffragette movement, but when her father faces ruin they are forced to move to the country and Daisy's first duty is to her family.

The Workhouse Girl

Young Sarah Scrase's life changes forever when she and her widowed mother are forced to enter the notorious St Giles and St George's Workhouse.

A Loving Family

Eleven-year-old Stella Barry is forced into service when her family find themselves living hand-to-mouth.

The Beggar Maid

Dilly Court

arrow books

Published by Arrow Books 2014

2 4 6 8 10 9 7 5 3 1

First published in Great Britain in 2014 by
Century
Random House, 20 Vauxhall Bridge Road,
London SW1V 2SA

www.randomhouse.co.uk

Addresses for companies within The Random House Group Limited can be found at:
www.randomhouse.co.uk/offices.htm

The Random House Group Limited Reg. No. 954009

A CIP catalogue record for this book
is available from the British Library

Typeset in Palatino by Palimpsest Book Production Limited,
Falkirk, Stirlingshire

Printed and bound in Great Britain by Clays Ltd, St Ives plc

For Ruth May and Steve Pardoe BDS,
two of my favourite people

Chapter One

Threadneedle Street, London 1887

'Can you spare a copper, mister?' Charity held out her hand to the gentleman in the city suit who was hurrying towards the imposing colonnaded entrance of the Bank of England. He ducked his head down, eyeing her warily beneath the brim of his bowler hat as he quickened his pace and strode past her. 'A half-penny, then,' she shouted after him. 'Blooming old miser.' She shivered as a bitter east wind whistled between the buildings, picking up bits of straw and scraps of paper and flinging them about like a naughty child having a tantrum.

She cupped her mittened hands around her mouth and blew on them in an attempt to bring back the feeling. Her fingers and toes were numbed by cold, and hunger gnawed at her belly. She had eaten nothing since the previous evening, when supper had consisted of a crust of dry bread and a cup of ice-cold water from the communal pump. Duck's Foot Lane, where she and her grandfather lived in a basement room in a dilapidated terraced house, was not the sort of area where anyone would want to venture in daylight, let alone after dark. The damp cellar with fungus growing from the walls and water seeping through the flagstone floor at high tide offered the most basic shelter to a constantly changing assortment of itinerant Irish, immigrant Jews and anyone who could afford to pay the landlord for a night's lodging. It was the last stop before living rough underneath railway arches, or facing the final indignity of the workhouse.

Charity had grown hardened to the privations she suffered daily, but her rebellious spirit refused to accept that this was the way it would always be. She supported her ageing, alcoholic grandfather as best she could, and had done so since the age of eight when begging on street corners evoked some sympathy in the hearts of passers-by. Now, at sixteen, she was only too well aware that men looked on her in a different way. The offers of money she received were rarely unconditional, and she had to choose the time and place where she importuned the better-off with great care. The bustling world of finance in the City was as safe as any area, and safer than most.

She spotted an older man as he emerged from the Monument station with a leather document case under one arm and a tightly furled umbrella in his hand. His greying beard and air of respectability made him a likely target, and she sidled up to him with an appealing smile. 'Good day to you, sir. Would you have a halfpenny to spare for a cup of tea? Please,' she added hastily when he stopped and gave her an appraising look. 'I ain't used to begging, sir, but misfortune has come upon my family, and I'm an orphan with an ailing grandparent to support.'

The gentleman frowned thoughtfully. 'There are charities that will help such as you, young lady.'

She could see her chance slipping by and she managed a weary smile. 'That's me name, sir. Charity is me name, but I seen little of it since me dad passed away.'

'And your mother?'

'Died giving birth to me, sir. My grandpa is the only one left.'

The gentleman put his hand in his pocket and took out a handful of change. He selected a silver sixpence and gave it to her. 'I hope you've been telling me the truth, young lady. Don't go spending it on a new bonnet or such fripperies as young women are so fond of.'

She drew herself up to her full height. 'You can't eat fripperies, sir. It will feed Grandpa and me for three days, if I'm careful. God bless you, your lordship.' She could hear the small change clinking in his pocket as he walked away, and for a brief moment she wished she had learned to dip like the street arabs who roamed the East End. She had been brought up to be honest and God-fearing, and only in the direst of circumstances had she overcome her scruples and stolen a loaf of bread or a meat pie. Before the lure of jigger gin had stolen his health and loosened his grip on reality, Grandpa had instilled morality into her young mind, and she had learned how to read, write and do basic arithmetic at the Ragged School. She tucked the coin into the top of her stays with a wry grin. Not that learning had been much help to her on the streets, but at least she could add up her takings for the day, and she knew when she was being cheated over the price of a fish supper or a dish of jellied eels.

She looked round for another likely benefactor, but

the clerks in their cheap suits with frayed cuffs and leather patches on their elbows were not worth bothering with. They worked long hours for low wages and their grey faces etched with worried frowns suggested married men with families to support, and neat little suburban houses to maintain. She suspected that the brown paper packages clutched in their hands held their lunch, which they would take to St Paul's churchyard at midday and devour in seconds before returning to their dingy offices and dusty ledgers.

The minutes were flying by and soon the streets would be all but deserted as the business of the day commenced. There would always be one or two latecomers scurrying to work, their features pinched with cold and the fear of instant dismissal, but they would as soon trample her underfoot as waste another second and were best avoided. She had learned early in her life that philanthropy was far from the minds of ordinary people whose day to day existence was hard enough, without worrying about the poor and needy.

A hansom cab drew up at the kerb and a gentleman wearing an expensive cashmere coat with an astrakhan collar climbed down. He tossed a coin to the cabby and was about to walk off without demanding change when Charity barred his way. 'Can you spare a copper, sir?'

He came to a halt, giving her a speculative look, and for a moment she thought she had struck gold, but then she realised her mistake. He shook his head. 'My dear girl, what you need is gainful employment. You should not be begging on the streets.'

'I know that, sir,' she said humbly. 'But you see I have an aged grandpa to care for and . . .'

He laid his hand on her shoulder. 'Even more reason for you to find honest work. How old are you?'

'Just sixteen, sir.'

'And what is your name?'

'Are you a cop?'

He smiled. 'I am not a policeman, and I believe I have your best interests at heart.'

'I'm not that sort of girl,' Charity said, backing away.

'I can see that,' he said slowly. 'And I wasn't propositioning you. I merely asked your name, but you don't have to tell me if you don't want to.'

There was something in his tone of voice and an earnest expression in his dark eyes that convinced her he was speaking the truth. 'Me name's Charity,' she said reluctantly. 'Charity Crosse. Now you know, so push off and leave me to earn a crust.'

'Charity,' he said slowly. 'It seems apt.'

'I only beg because we've fallen on hard times, and I can't find work.' She glanced down at her soiled and ragged skirts. The uppers of her shabby boots had parted from the soles, exposing her bare toes which were ingrained with dirt and blue with cold.

'So you took to begging on the streets. Not perhaps the best way out of poverty.'

'What would a gent like you know about how the rest of us lives?' she said angrily. 'Who'd take me on looking like this? I've tried knocking on doors, asking for work of any sort, but they was always slammed in me face. No one wants to employ a girl like me.'

'You would make an interesting case history.'

'I ain't no one's whatever you said. I'm off.' She was about to walk away when he caught her by the sleeve.

'Don't be frightened, Charity. I mean you no harm.'

'They always say that. I know your sort.'

He shook his head. 'No, you've misunderstood my motives. I am an academic and a lecturer at University College. You must have heard of it.'

It was her turn to look baffled. 'No, sir. Like I said, I'm off, so kindly let go of me sleeve or I'll have to call a copper.'

'I'm conducting a study on social anthropology. Your case interests me.'

'I got no idea what you're talking about,' Charity said, wrenching free from his grasp. 'And I ain't a case. Now if your lordship will excuse me, I'm moving on.'

'Where will you go now?'

'Not that it's any of your business, but I make me way towards Fleet Street, and if there's no profit to be had there, I go to Covent Garden. Sometimes I can pick up a few flower heads and sell them as buttonholes, but you got to watch out for them flower girls. They'll pull your hair out by the roots if they think you're queering their pitch.'

'Fascinating,' he said, falling into step beside her. 'Tell me more.'

She stopped. 'What's it worth?'

'How much do you earn an hour, Charity Crosse?'

'You are a cop,' she said, narrowing her eyes. 'I knew it. You want to bang me up for soliciting.'

'No, indeed I don't. I told you, I'm a professor of

anthropology, and I would genuinely like to have someone like you to tell me first hand about life in the gutter.'

She recoiled angrily. 'Hold on, guv. Who said I live in the gutter? Me and Grandpa live in a room. We pays our rent and that's what I'm trying to earn, so sling your hook and let me get on with it.'

'I'll give you my visiting card and you will see that I'm telling the truth.' He slipped his hand into his pocket and took out a small silver case. He paused, staring at her with twin furrows on his brow. 'I don't suppose you can read . . .'

'I can read and write, guv. Just because I'm poor don't mean I'm ignorant. I can add up and recite me times tables with the best of 'em.'

'I'm sorry.' He managed a faint smile. 'I stand corrected, but that just shows how much I'm in need of your guidance. My card, Miss Crosse.' He handed it to her with a curt bow.

She tucked it into her stays next to the silver sixpence. 'I'll think about it. Now I'll be obliged if you'll let me go on me way.'

'Sixpence an hour,' he said hopefully. 'If you will come to my house in Doughty Street, I'll pay you that for each hour or part of an hour.'

'And what do you expect from me?'

'I just want you to talk, and I'll make a note of what you say.'

'And that's all?'

'It is.'

'And no funny business?'

'Certainly not. I told you, I'm an academic. I'm Professor Wilmot Barton.'

Charity shrugged her thin shoulders and walked away, but the temptation to look over her shoulder to see if he was watching her was too great. She turned her head, and saw him striding off in the opposite direction with a feeling of pique. 'So much for the professor,' she muttered. 'Didn't trust him anyway.' She set off in the direction of Cheapside and St Paul's, where she often lingered on the steps, hoping that a pious worshipper might take pity on her. Flakes of snow had begun to flutter from a pewter sky, but by the time she reached the cathedral people were scurrying for shelter and she might as well have been invisible. She wrapped her shawl around her head and shoulders and continued on her way. Fleet Street was buzzing with activity as reporters hurried into the newspaper offices, clutching their notebooks in a race to be first with the latest story to hit the headlines. Covent Garden market was busy, although the first rush of the day was over, and the flower girls long gone. The few crushed blooms that lay wilting on the cobblestones glistened with lacy snowflakes, but their diamond brightness would soon fade, leaving them slimy and unrecognisable. There was no profit to be made here.

A sudden wave of nausea washed over her and she felt faint, but she managed to stagger into the shelter of the colonnades. She leaned against one of the pillars, taking deep breaths until the world righted itself. It was only when the warm aroma of baked potatoes assaulted her nostrils that she realised she must eat or collapse with hunger. She peered through the lace curtain of falling snow and saw a man with a handcart who was selling baked potatoes served with a generous dollop of butter, and mugs of tea. She had intended to use the sixpence to pay the arrears in rent, but she knew that she would never make it back to Duck's Foot Lane in her present state. She hooked the coin from its warm hiding place and made her way across the slippery cobblestones to the stall.

A burly young porter stood in the queue beside her. 'Care to join me, love? I'd share my murphy with you any day.'

She managed a weak grin. 'Ta, mate, but you got nothing that interests me.' She held her money out to the vendor. 'Baked tatty, please, and a cup of split pea.'

The young porter tipped his cap to the back of his head. 'Come and sit with me then. I promise to keep me hands to meself.'

'Ta all the same, but I prefer to eat on me own.' She took her change and counted it carefully, despite the trader's protests that he was an honest man.

'Mistakes happen,' she said tersely and walked away, carrying the potato wrapped in newspaper and the mug of tea to the church on the far side of the piazza. She thought at first the young man might follow her, but he had gone to join his mates, leaving her to eat her meal in peace. She sat on the cold stones, sheltering from the snow beneath the portico, and munched the hot, buttery flesh of the potato with relish, savouring each mouthful and trying not to feel guilty. Grandpa would be hungry too, and he would be desperate for a tot of gin. It was all very well for people to tell her not to give him money for drink, but it was the only thing that stopped the terrible tremors which affected his whole body, turning him into a gibbering mass of humanity who could hardly string two words together. A jigger or two of blue ruin would stop the shaking and he would be able to function again, albeit in a limited way. His use of the harsh spirit had wreaked a terrible revenge on him, taking away the power of rational thought and robbing him of memory. It took more and more of it to settle him down these days and he often became violent. He had never struck her, but sometimes, when he returned from the pub very much the worse for drink, she was afraid of him. The drunken stranger who inhabited Joseph Crosse's body would start fights over the most trivial matters, and had to be restrained by the men who shared their lodgings. The humiliation of seeing her grandfather carted bodily into the yard and having his head held under the pump was not something she cared to witness, but it happened all too often these days.

Fortified by the hot food and sweet tea, Charity stood up and stretched. She took the battered tin mug back to the stall and started on the long walk back to Duck's Foot Lane, hoping to pick up a penny or two on the way. But the weather was not such that it made people feel generous and she was largely ignored. On a couple of occasions she received a mouthful of abuse, and as she drew nearer to her destination she had a sudden and terrible premonition that something was wrong.

It was late afternoon and already dark by the time she reached Upper Thames Street. The snow was thick underfoot and beginning to freeze, and as her feet crunched its brittle surface the ice penetrated the holes in her boots, stabbing her toes and causing her to yelp with pain. Above her head snowflakes danced dizzily in the yellow gas light, and the sounds of the river filled her ears as she neared the place she called home. The hoots of steam boats and the creaking of wooden masts were almost drowned out by the grinding and groaning of cranes as ships discharged their cargoes onto the wharves. The great River Thames never slept, nor did the denizens of the tightly packed buildings that crowded its banks. Narrow alleyways threaded their way from the main streets to the wharves at the water's edge. These dark and dangerous conduits were lined with warehouses, manufactories, pubs, brothels and tenements housing workers and their families, as well as the dispossessed. Communal cellars often filled with water and sewage during a particularly high tide, and rats the size of cats lived alongside the human occupants in the most unsanitary conditions imaginable.

Duck's Foot Lane was just wide enough for a horse and cart to squeeze through, leaving little room for error. The tall buildings leaned towards one another at crazy angles, and were linked by overhead walk-ways. Steel hoists protruded from the walls high above street level, and vicious-looking hooks dangled idly from ropes awaiting deliveries of raw materials next day. From dawn until dusk whole cargoes of imported goods, baled and tied or transported in wooden kegs, would be hauled skywards and dragged into the upper floors of the buildings by men who worked at dizzying heights with nothing to save them should they slip and fall. Accidents were common and fatalities occurred too frequently.

Charity had grown up in this undesirable neighbourhood, but she had fond memories of her early years. Before her father died they lived in a neat terraced house in Chelsea. Her grandmother had looked after her and Pa and Grandpa left early each morning to catch a horse-drawn omnibus to the City, where Grandpa worked as a clerk in a shipping office and Pa followed the time-honoured profession of law writer. She remembered the distinctive smell of Indian ink that clung to his stained fingers when he returned home in the evening, and the lines of fatigue drawn on his face by an invisible pen that would not wash away. Tired he might have been but he always found time to take her on his knee and tell her about his day, or to read her a story from her favourite book. Early on in her life she had learned to love the sound of words and the rhythms and patterns of speech. Story books led her into an enchanted land of imagination like no other, and an escape into worlds that she would never otherwise have known.

She quickened her pace. It had stopped snowing and the wind had veered round, bringing with it a strong smell of malt and hops from Barclay and Perkins' Brewery south of the river, with just a hint of acidity from Potts' Vinegar Works, and something much less pleasant from the tannery in Bermondsey. She plunged into the dark canyon of Duck's Foot Lane. It was relatively quiet in the early evening, but it would grow noisier as the night progressed and seamen of all nationalities thronged the pubs and brothels, or sought solace in the opium dens. The snow had been trodden underfoot and churned up by horses' hooves and cart wheels, turning it to filthy slush, and she picked up her skirts, treading carefully as she approached the tenement building where she and her grandfather lived.

The front door was never locked as the landlord left security to each individual tenant, which meant that there was none. People came and went as they pleased and as long as the rent collector was paid his dues he did not bother to count heads. Charity almost fell over the prostrate body of a drunken woman who was slumped at the foot of the stairs. It was a common occurrence and not one to cause her any concern. What worried her more was the sound of raised voices emanating from the cellar. The door was open and she went to investigate.

In the dim light of a single oil lamp she could just make out the shape of two men who seemed to be pinning her grandfather to the ground. She only knew who it was who was flailing his arms and legs by the sound of his voice as a torrent of abuse left his lips. When sober, Joseph Crosse never swore when there were women present, and Charity knew that he would be mortified when he sobered up, but she realised quickly that this was no ordinary fit of drunken rage.

Her grandfather was plainly terrified and was fighting off some nameless beast, and the men who held him down were attempting to calm him. She hurried to his side, stepping over a couple of shapeless mounds sleeping soundly beneath piles of newspaper, cardboard and rags despite the commotion. 'Grandpa.'

'Get back, girly.' One of the men lifted his hand and pushed her out of the way. 'The old codger's gone mad.'

'Leave him alone. You're hurting him.' Charity tried to pull him away but he was a big man and muscular.

'He tried to kill me,' he said breathlessly. 'Went for me with a chiv.'

'No,' Charity cried fiercely. 'He would never do such a thing. Get off him, please.'

The second man glanced over his shoulder. 'You ain't helping, miss. Stand back or you'll get hurt. I seen this happen before. The drink has addled his brains. He's been seeing things what aren't here.'

'He's lost his head, all right. The best thing you can do for him is call a constable. Your granddad needs locking up for his own safety and yours.'

'Aye,' his companion said gruffly. 'The Bethlehem Lunatic Asylum is where he should be.'

'No, please.' Charity moved closer. She was horrified to see her grandfather's features twisted into a rictus grin and his face was turning blue. 'Let me deal with this. I know how to handle him.'

Suddenly, Joseph relaxed and went as limp as a rag doll. The men released their hold and sat back on their haunches. 'He's passed out,' the younger man said, wiping the sweat from his brow. 'Thank God for that.'

'I ain't so sure.' His friend leaned over and felt for a pulse. He shook his head. 'Sorry, love. I think he's a goner. Must've had some kind of fit.' He scrambled to his feet. 'Let's get out of here, mate. We don't want to be mixed up in this.'

Charity fell to her knees beside her grandfather. 'Grandpa, speak to me.' She chafed his hands and laid her head on his chest, but she could not hear a heart-beat. She looked up and found herself alone except for the ones who were dead drunk or under the influence of opium and had slept through everything.

She sat for a moment, too stunned to cry and too frightened to move. She had seen dead bodies often enough in the street, but this was different. This lifeless corpse had once been her much loved grandparent. He was her last link with her family and now she was alone and very scared. She was suddenly eight years old again, and had been told that her father had succumbed to the dreaded disease of cholera only a few hours after it had claimed her grandmother. She leaned over and shook her grandfather, uttering a cry of horror as his head lolled to one side and his sight-less eyes gazed blindly into space.

Before she realised what she was doing she found herself outside in the street, retching and gasping for breath. The cold air filled her lungs and her head began to clear. The enormity of what had happened filled her with horror and she went in search of help.

The doctor lived in Old Fish Street and to her relief

he was at home, having his supper. His housekeeper refused her admittance but her cries of distress brought the doctor himself to the door.

'I only got fourpence, doctor,' she said breathlessly. 'But I'll work until I paid off your fee. It's me grandpa. I think he's dead.'

'Then it can wait,' the housekeeper said firmly. 'Do you know how many times Dr Marchant has been called out today?'

'It's all right, Mrs Rose,' Dr Marchant said, slipping on his overcoat. 'Keep my dinner warm and I'll be back before you know it.' He put on his top hat and picked up his medical bag. 'I seem to remember you, young lady. Didn't I treat you for mumps not so long ago?'

'Yes, sir.'

He placed his hand on her shoulder. 'I remember now. Duck's Foot Lane, and you live with your grandpa. It's not a good place for a girl like you, Miss, er . . .'

'Crosse, sir. Charity Crosse, and I think Grandpa's dead. He had some kind of fit . . .'

'We'll see. The quicker we get there, the better.'

Charity waited in the narrow hallway while the doctor examined her grandfather. It did not take long. He returned moments later and guided her out of the building into the street. 'I'm afraid he has passed away,' he said gently. 'I'll make the necessary arrangements.'

'What did for him, sir? Was it the drink?'

He nodded his head. 'Without a doubt, Charity. I've seen it all too often.'

'I can't pay you the full amount, and I got no money

for the undertaker. My grandpa will have a pauper's funeral.'

'You need not worry about my fee, but as to the latter I'm afraid there's no alternative, unless you have relations who would help.'

'I got no one, sir. Grandpa was all I had.'

'Have you any friends who will take you in?'

'None, sir.' Charity met his anxious gaze with a defiant lift of her chin. 'But I'll be all right. I've lived by my wits since I was a nipper. I don't need no one to look after me. I can manage on me own.' She hunched her shoulders against the cold and started to walk away.

'Miss Crosse – wait.'

Chapter Two

Charity glanced over her shoulder. 'Yes?'

Dr Marchant hurried to her side. 'You've had a terrible shock, my dear. I insist that you come home with me. Mrs Rose will look after you – just for tonight, you understand.'

'There's no need, sir. I'll be all right.'

'I can't allow a young girl like you to roam the streets in weather like this. I wouldn't get a wink of sleep if I let you go now.' Dr Marchant took her firmly by the arm. 'Mrs Rose has a brusque manner, but beneath the hard shell beats a heart of gold. She'll find you a bed.'

'You can sleep there, under the kitchen table.' Mrs Rose folded her arms across her ample bosom. 'Dorrie lies down by the range and that's her place. I don't expect to come down in the morning and find any different.'

Charity shot a wary glance through the open door which led into the tiny scullery. Dorrie, who could not have been more than eight or nine years old, was standing on a box struggling to cope with the washing up.

'Do you understand?' Mrs Rose demanded angrily. 'Or have your wits gone begging too?'

'I understand, and I'll be off first thing. You won't need to be bothered with me any longer than necessary.'

Mrs Rose took a step closer, staring at her with narrowed eyes. 'I know exactly how much food there is in the larder and I count the cutlery every morning, so don't think of taking anything that doesn't belong to you. I've warned the good doctor about his charitable actions, but he has a soft heart and people take advantage of his good nature. If you abuse his trust I'll have the law on you so quick that your head will spin.' Mrs Rose waddled across the room to stand in the scullery doorway. 'Hurry up, Dorrie. Make sure you dry the dishes properly and put everything away. I'm going to my bed now but you'll be for it in the morning if I come down to a mess.' Taking the oil lamp with her she stamped out of the kitchen, closing the door behind her with a thud.

Charity took a spill from the jar high up on the mantelshelf and lit a candle, placing it on the kitchen table. The fire in the range had been banked up for the night, but the kitchen was warm and the aroma of mutton stew lingered in the air. For all her faults, Mrs Rose was a good cook, and it was obvious that the kindly doctor was well cared for. Charity had eaten well for the first time in months, although nothing could take away the pain of bereavement and the shock of seeing her grandfather breathe his last. She was physically exhausted, but she doubted if she would be able to sleep. The fact that she would be lying on the cold, hard floor did not come into the equation. She had slept on worse, and at least it was warm and dry in the doctor's kitchen, unlike the damp cellar in Duck's Foot Lane.

She walked into the scullery and was just in time to catch a plate as it slipped from Dorrie's fingers. The child was half asleep and in danger of falling into the stone sink where a thick scum of grease floated on the surface of the rapidly cooling water. Charity patted her on the shoulder. 'Wake up, little 'un.'

Dorrie opened her eyes and blinked. 'I'm doing it, miss. I'm working as hard as I can.'

Charity lifted her from the box and was shocked to feel how little the child weighed. 'You're soaked to the skin. Have you got a change of clothes?'

'Who are you?' Dorrie eyed her suspiciously. 'You ain't gonna take me back to the workhouse, are you, miss?'

'Certainly not. I'm only here for tonight because I've nowhere else to go, and in the morning I'll be gone. But that's neither here nor there – you need to get out of those wet things and go to bed.'

'She'll skin me alive if I leaves a mess. I got to finish the dishes and put everything away. You heard her. She's a terror when she's roused.'

Charity rolled up her sleeves. 'I'll do the dishes, and I'll put them away. Now do as I say or you'll catch your death of cold.'

Dorrie backed away. 'I dunno. You're not going to steal stuff when me back's turned, are you? One of the doctor's charity cases took six silver spoons and an egg cup.'

'I'm not going to do anything of the sort. Now go to bed like a good girl. You need your beauty sleep. That's what my granny used to say to me.' Charity's eyes filled with tears as she thought of her old home and she turned away quickly. 'Go on, Dorrie. Do as you're told.' She busied herself washing and drying the remaining dishes, and when she took them into the kitchen to put them away she found Dorrie curled up on a crocheted rug by the fire and already sound asleep.

Having made certain that everything was as it should be, Charity glanced at the space under the table where she was supposed to make her bed and decided instead to sit in the rocking chair by the range. She knew it was where Mrs Rose chose to sit, but she had no intention of sleeping on the bare tiles. Tomorrow she would be gone, and in the morning she would face the world on her own. She sat down and took off her boots. Her feet were filthy and it was at least two weeks since she had treated herself to the public baths. It was only now that she was away from the foetid stench of her old lodgings that she realised there was a distinctive and unpleasant odour emanating from her person. It was little wonder that Mrs Rose did not want her to sleep in one of her clean beds. Shame and humiliation added to her raw emotions. She was tempted to leave the doctor's house and disappear into the night, but the fact was that she had nowhere to go. And even worse, her grandfather would now be lying on a cold stone slab in the dead house, awaiting the coroner's verdict before he could be interred. At the very worst, his lifeless body might have been taken illegally and sold to a medical school for anatomical dissection. The thought of that happening made her feel sick, and made it all the more important for her to remain at the doctor's house until she knew what arrangements had been made to give her grandfather a proper burial, even if it had to be in an unmarked pauper's grave.

She slept at last, only to be rudely awakened by someone shaking her by the shoulder. 'Get out of my chair. What did I tell you about where you had to sleep?'

Charity opened her eyes and found herself looking into Mrs Rose's irate face. She slid off the chair and stood up. 'I'm sorry – I must have dropped off.'

The cold light of a snowy dawn filtered through the kitchen window and a gust of icy air blew in through the scullery door as Dorrie struggled into the room hefting a bucket of coal. 'Shut the door,' Mrs Rose ordered in stentorian tones. 'And get the fire going, you stupid child. You should have been up half an hour ago.' She turned her attention back to Charity. 'As for you, miss. I have to say it – you smell. And your clothes are filthy. Take them off now.'

Charity shook her head. 'I got nothing else to wear.'

'The doctor is known for his work amongst the poor and needy and there are generous people who donate clothes for the missionary barrel.'

'I ain't going to the women's refuge, if that's what you're thinking,' Charity said, sticking out her chin. 'I got me pride, ma'am, and I ain't no pauper.'

'But you are happy to take from others by begging, so I see very little difference in your station in life. You and your kind are a burden to society.' Mrs Rose took a step towards her. 'Now either take those filthy clothes off, or leave this house and don't return because the door will be slammed in your face.'

'But I got to know what happened to Grandpa. The doctor promised me he'd see to everything.'

'It's your choice, Miss Crosse.'

Charity knew when she was beaten. She could not let her grandfather down now. 'All right,' she said slowly. 'But at least give us a blanket or something. I ain't standing here naked for all to see.'

A triumphant smile lit Mrs Rose's grim features for a second and then was gone. 'At least you have some sense of decency.' She wagged a finger at Dorrie. 'Hurry up and get the fire going again, and fill the kettle and the largest pan with water. Miss Crosse is going to take a bath. I'll fetch a towel and a change of clothes.' She fixed Charity with a hard stare. 'Cleanliness is next to godliness – always remember that.'

She bustled out of the room, leaving Charity to undress.

'I'll get the fire going and it won't take the water long to heat up,' Dorrie said with a shy smile. 'Ta for what you done last night. I won't forget it in a hurry.'

'It was nothing. Anyway, it's too much work for a youngster like you.'

'I'm eight, miss. Or at least I think I am. That's what they told me in the workhouse.' Dorrie riddled the embers and added more coal to the fire. She took the bellows and pumped them until flames shot up the chimney. 'Tell her you can bath yourself,' she said in a whisper. 'If she gets the loofah to your skin you'll end up red raw, and don't let her pour neat vinegar over your head. It don't half sting your eyes.'

'I haven't got nits,' Charity said firmly. 'I'm not a guttersnipe, even if she treats me like one. I'm only putting up with all this because I want my grandpa to have a proper send-off. Otherwise I'd be out of here like a shot.'

'Would you really?' Dorrie picked up the kettle and hurried into the scullery. 'I'd come with you if I could. I hates it here, and she hates me. I can't please the old besom no matter how hard I try.' She staggered back into the kitchen, slopping water on the tiles in her efforts to put the kettle on the hob.

'Let me help you. After all, it's for my benefit.' Charity snatched a pan from the shelf and took it into the scullery. 'I'll do what I can for you while I'm here, but I'll be gone by tonight.'

Dorrie stood in the doorway, watching her. 'Where will you go, miss?'

'You don't have to call me miss. My name is Charity.'

'Where will you go, Charity?' Dorrie grinned, revealing a missing front tooth.

'I haven't the faintest idea, but it won't be the workhouse. Maybe the old besom is doing me a favour with all this palaver. I might find work if I look clean and tidy.'

Scrubbed until her skin glowed and with her hair washed and towel-dried, Charity peered at her reflection in the fly-spotted mirror above the mantelshelf. The clothes that Mrs Rose had selected from the missionary barrel were not meant to enhance her looks, but at least they were clean and in good condition. The navy-blue linsey-woolsey skirt was faded and the hem slightly frayed, but it was a reasonable fit, and the white cotton blouse was on the large side but there was plenty of wear left in it, as Mrs Rose was quick to point out. A grey hand-knitted cardigan that came down almost to Charity's knees completed the outfit, and what it lacked in style it made up for in warmth.

'You'll have to make do with your own boots,' Mrs Rose said, standing back to admire her handiwork. 'But you'll do.' She reached out and lifted a strand of Charity's hair, allowing it to run through her fingers. 'Such dark hair, and yet you have blue eyes.' She frowned. 'You're not Irish, are you?'

'I'm as English as you or the doctor,' Charity replied, stung by the implied insult. The only Irish she had ever met were itinerant navvies who had a reputation for drinking and brawling, although in her experience they mostly kept to themselves.

'Well, it's an unusual combination. Your looks will get you into trouble, Charity Crosse. You will have to take care or you'll come to no good.' She dragged the damp curls back from Charity's face. 'That's better. I'll find you a scrap of ribbon so that you can tie it back and look tidy. When you're done I'll take you to the doctor's study. He has something to tell you.'

Dr Marchant looked up from his desk where he was writing something in what looked like a diary. The book-lined study and clutter of files and correspondence reminded Charity of the house in Chelsea. She had been allowed into her father's tiny study on infrequent occasions, as he seemed to spend all his spare time writing papers on what she had considered to be a very boring subject. As a diversion from work he liked to pore over books on archaeology, and had tried to explain his fascination for ancient Egypt, but she had been too young to understand. He had taken her to the British Museum, but she had been scared by the huge stone statues, and soon tired of peering at artefacts in glass cases. She hung back, waiting for Mrs Rose to speak.

'Miss Crosse is here, doctor.'

'Thank you, Mrs Rose. That will be all for now.'

Mrs Rose opened her mouth as if to argue, but a look from the doctor silenced her and she swept out of the room with a disgruntled twitch of her shoulders.

Dr Marchant took off his spectacles, gazing at Charity with a smile of approval. 'You look rested.'

'Yes, sir. Thank you for taking me in, sir.'

'It was the least I could do, my dear.' He picked up a slip of paper. 'I received this by messenger this morning. Your grandfather's body has been released for burial. It seems the coroner was satisfied with my diagnosis of death from natural causes.'

Charity blinked back tears, swallowing hard. 'Thank you, sir. What happens now?'

'An undertaker will do the rest, and I'm afraid it will be a pauper's funeral.'

'Can I see him, sir? I never had a chance to say goodbye.'

'I'm not sure that's a good idea, Charity. Wouldn't

you rather remember him as he was before the drink destroyed him?'

'He was all I had in the world. I got nothing now, and I would like to see him.'

Suddenly businesslike, Dr Marchant closed his diary with a snap and stood up. 'Very well. We'll pay a call on the undertaker before I take you on to a place where I think you might find gainful employment.'

'It's no good, sir. I tried to find work round here and they all turned me away.'

'Not now, I think. Mrs Rose has done you proud, and I will stand by you. Can you read and write, Charity?'

'Yes, sir. I know me tables too. Granny was very particular about learning.'

'In that case I think my good friend Mr Dawkins might take you on, although I can't promise anything.'

'Who is this cove, sir?'

'Jethro Dawkins owns a bookshop in Liquorpond Street. He struggles to look after himself and his shop.' Dr Marchant gazed at her thoughtfully. 'I think you two might be good for each other.'

'In what way, sir?'

Dr Marchant glanced out of the window. 'It's snowing again. You'll need a shawl and bonnet, and gloves.' He reached over and rang the bell. 'I'll ask Mrs Rose to go through the missionary barrel again, and then we'll set off.'

The undertaker's office was as gloomy as Charity had imagined. Tucked away down a side street it was sandwiched between a pawnbroker's premises and a second-hand clothes shop, where shabbily dressed women sorted through piles of garments that were little better than the ones they were wearing. Dr Marchant turned to a girl who accosted him, begging for a copper to buy milk for her baby, but when he demanded to see the needy infant the girl backed away, shouting obscenities which were taken up by a couple of women who had been arguing over a moth-eaten shawl. Dr Marchant hurried Charity into the undertaker's office, closing the door to shut out the stream of abuse. 'Poor souls,' he said, shaking his head. 'Life is hard and they have so little, but we must not allow them to intimidate us.'

A man dressed in black emerged from a door at the back of the room. His ingratiating smile broadened when he recognised the doctor, and he shook his hand. 'Good morning, Dr Marchant.' He glanced through the grimy window. 'You seem to have upset the locals, sir.'

'I'm up to their tricks, Mr Wiggins, and they know it.'

'So what can I do for you, sir?'

Dr Marchant laid his hand on Charity's shoulder. 'This young lady lost her grandfather last evening. I believe you have him here.'

'What is the name of the deceased?'

'Joseph Crosse,' Charity said in a small voice. 'I'd like to see my grandpa, if you please, sir.'

Mr Wiggins gave her a searching look. 'Are you sure about that, young lady?'

'I'm sure, sir.'

'Then come this way.' Mr Wiggins ushered her into a dimly lit back room where an open coffin rested on a bier.

Charity approached slowly, bracing herself for what she might see, but the shrouded figure looked like a wax effigy. The person lying in the coffin had her grandfather's features but his spirit had gone, and for the first time in years, he looked peaceful. He had fought the battle with the demon drink and he had lost, but she could not in all conscience wish him back to continue the struggle. She leaned over and dropped a kiss on his cold brow. 'Goodbye, Grandpa. I love you.'

Dr Marchant put a comforting arm around her shoulders. 'Come along, Charity. Your grandfather's trials are over.' He turned to Mr Wiggins, lowering his voice. 'When will the interment take place?'

'We've got several clients for the Necropolis Company railway to Brookwood cemetery, leaving from Waterloo at midday. These trains are always packed and I wouldn't advise the young lady to accompany the coffin.'

'But I can't let Grandpa make his last journey alone,' Charity protested.

Dr Marchant met her anxious gaze with a gentle smile. 'He won't be alone, my dear. I'm sure he knows that you will be with him in spirit, and the last thing he would want is for you to suffer more distress.'

'Besides which, I doubt if you have the return fare,' Mr Wiggins said pointedly.

Charity looked from one to the other. 'No, I suppose not.'

'Your grandfather would want the best for you, Charity,' Dr Marchant said softly. 'The most important thing now is to find you paid work and somewhere to live. Will you trust me to guide you in this?'

She nodded silently. 'Forgive me, Grandpa,' she said in a barely audible whisper.

'Come along, miss.' Mr Wiggins' voice had a sharp edge which brought Charity back to reality with a sharp jolt. 'I'm sure that the good doctor has much to do today.'

Dr Marchant held out his hand. 'Come,' he said briskly. 'I'll take you to Liquorpond Street.'

'I ain't too sure about this,' Charity said doubtfully.

'It won't hurt to have a look, my dear. Anyway, Mr Dawkins ordered a book for me some time ago and it should be in stock by now.' He paused in the doorway. 'You'll find him a little odd at first, Charity, but don't judge a man by his outward appearance. Jethro Dawkins is a good fellow at heart and in dire need of someone to help him.'

Charity would have questioned him further but her benefactor was already out on the pavement, flagging down a passing hansom cab. 'Dawkins' bookshop please, cabby. Liquorpond Street.' Dr Marchant climbed into the cab, holding out a hand to help Charity negotiate the iron stirrup that served as a step, which was a considerable feat for a girl wearing a long skirt and a red flannel petticoat. She sat beside him and he closed the half doors to protect them from the worst of the weather. The cabby flicked his whip and they were off.

Travelling in a cab was a luxury that Charity had not enjoyed since she and her grandfather had been forced to flee from their old home, but the image of him lying cold and stiff in the cheap pine coffin filled her thoughts, spoiling any pleasure she might have experienced while being driven in such style. His send-off would not include a glass-sided hearse pulled by plumed black horses, and there would be no engraved headstone to mark the place of his burial. She gazed out at the city streets but her vision was blurred by tears. She was suddenly a frightened eight-year-old, travelling into the unknown with a much older man, only this time it was the kindly doctor and not her beloved grandfather.

'We're here, Charity.'

She blinked and dashed her hand across her eyes, realising with a start that they had come to a halt outside the workhouse in Liquorpond Street. She turned to Dr Marchant in horror. 'I'm not going in there. I'd sooner freeze to death on the pavement than put a foot inside that place.'

Dr Marchant shook his head. 'I wouldn't do such a thing.' He pointed to the buildings on the other side of the street. She peered through the thin veil of snow that had begun to fall again in tiny flakes.

'Reid's Brewery?' The name stood out in bold letter over the arched gateway.

Dr Marchant climbed down to the ground, holding out his hand. 'Not there either.' He helped her down from the cab and tossed a coin to the cabby, who tipped his cap and drove off. 'See there, tucked in between the shop selling exotic birds and reptiles and the ale house.' He led her across the road, coming to a halt outside a bow window filled with an untidy jumble of leather-bound books. 'Come in out of the cold.' He opened the door and somewhere deep inside a bell clanged.

Charity stepped over the threshold and her nostrils were assailed by the musty smell of old books, dry rot and the acrid odour of burnt toast. Outside the world was dazzling white with snow but the interior of the shop was dark, like stepping into the underworld. Then, out of the gloom, a horrific figure lumbered towards her. His head seemed too large for his misshapen body and he walked with a pronounced limp, dragging one leg. His pale face seemed to glow in the dark and his features had been affected by some cruel palsy that gave him a lopsided appearance. She stood, frozen to the spot, too terrified to scream and unable to run.

Chapter Three

'Jethro, my dear fellow, how are you today?' Dr Marchant rested his hand on the man's shoulder.

'Your book's here.' Jethro's voice was gruff and seemed to come from deep within his twisted torso. He shot a suspicious glance at Charity. 'Who's this?'

'This young lady is Charity Crosse, and she recently lost her only living relative.'

'Why bring her here then? Has she come to mock a poor cripple?'

Dr Marchant let his hand fall to his side. 'Now then, Jethro, that's not the way it was at all. Don't go frightening the poor child. She's had enough to bear without you adding to her troubles.'

Charity backed towards the door. 'This is a mistake, doctor. I ain't staying here.'

'Who asked you to stay, young lady?' Jethro turned his back on her. 'I don't need anyone, least of all an orphan child.'

'I'm not a child,' Charity said with dignity. 'I'll have you know that I'm sixteen and I've been supporting both myself and my grandpa for years.'

Jethro limped over to the counter and snatched up a heavy tome. 'That will be half a crown, doctor. Pay up and take the girl away. This is no place for the likes of her.'

Dr Marchant put his hand in his pocket and pulled out a leather purse. He placed a silver half-crown on the counter. 'When did you last have a decent meal, Jethro Dawkins?'

'What's that got to do with you?'

'Just as I suspected.' Dr Marchant beckoned to Charity. 'This man can't even toast a slice of bread without burning it, as I think you'll have guessed from the smoke and the smell coming from the back room.'

'An unfortunate slip of the toasting fork,' Jethro said defensively. 'I know you mean well, doctor, but I haven't got the time or inclination to take in a young female.'

'But you do need someone to help you.' With a sweep of his hand Dr Marchant encompassed the untidy state of the shelves and the books spilling onto the floor. 'Charity can read and write and she needs a roof over her head. She is eager to improve herself and you have a wealth of learning here in the shop. You might be able to help each other.'

'Hold on,' Charity said sharply. 'I haven't said I'll stay here. He doesn't want me and I think I'd rather go back to begging on street corners than live in a hole like this.'

Jethro took a step towards her, squinting myopically. 'She says what she thinks. I like that. What else have you got to say, girl? Spit it out. Tell me why you don't want to live here.'

'You want me to say it's because you've got a

hunchback and there's something wrong with your face,' Charity said angrily. 'I think you enjoy scaring people and making out that you're a mean old man, but Dr Marchant says you've got a good heart, although I don't see much of it showing. No wonder people avoid you, if this is how you always behave.'

A sharp intake of breath from Dr Marchant brought her to a halt. 'I won't apologise, sir. I've dealt with worse than Mr Dawkins in my life, and I'm not afraid to speak my mind.'

Jethro stared at her blankly for a moment and then a growling noise in his belly suddenly erupted into a loud guffaw. He staggered and clutched at the counter for support as his laughter echoed off the book-lined walls. 'She's a one!' he gasped breathlessly. 'I like her, Henry. I haven't laughed like that for years.'

Dr Marchant stared at him in overt amazement. 'Well, I never did!'

'Is he all there?' Charity asked in a whisper. 'Is he all right in the head?'

Jethro clutched his hands to his chest, drawing deep breaths. 'I'm as sane as anyone in this shop, but you've tickled me pink, young Charity. I would be happy to give you work and a roof over your head.' His smile faded into a scowl and he wagged a finger at her. 'But you'll earn your keep, young lady. Make no mistake about that. I'm not a rich man.'

'There,' Dr Marchant said with a sigh of relief. 'That sounds like an offer you can't afford to refuse, Charity. What do you say?'

She looked round the dingy shop. Dust hung heavily

in the air, coating the shelves and the piles of books that littered the floor. Cobwebs festooned the beams and the floorboards that were visible to the naked eye were ingrained with dirt. But a quick look outside at the wintry scene, where the snow lay ankle deep and the sky was heavy with the promise of yet more to come, was enough to convince her that she had little choice. At least she would have somewhere to stay until she found something better and there was obviously plenty to do. She hardly dared imagine what state the rest of the rooms were in, and she did not ask. She nodded her head. 'All right. I'll give it a try but if I don't like it I'll leave. I'm not afraid to live on the streets.'

Dr Marchant turned to Jethro. 'You will pay her a wage, won't you? And you must promise to treat her well.'

'I'll pay her four shillings a week, all found.'

'That sounds fair enough.' Dr Marchant took Charity aside. 'Use this opportunity to improve your education, my dear. There is a wealth of knowledge on these shelves and Dawkins is an honest and trustworthy fellow. You've obviously got his measure and you can see that he needs someone to look after him, as do you yourself.'

'I'll be all right, sir.'

'I believe you will.' He held her hand, squeezing her fingers. 'But if you ever need help in the future you can always come to me. I'm a regular customer anyway, so I'll see you again quite soon.' He picked up his book, tucking it under his arm. 'Goodbye, Jethro. I've no doubt that I'll be back to browse your shelves in the very near future.' He opened the door and a gust of cold air blew in from the street creating eddies in the dust, and then he was gone. Charity was left alone with the crippled bookseller.

She was tempted to rush after Dr Marchant, who was the last link with her old life, but she fought against the urge to run away. She turned slowly to find Jethro staring at her with a baffled look on his face, although his deformity was such that it was almost impossible to read his expression accurately. For all she knew he might be deliriously happy or incredibly sad. She peeled off her mittens and laid her shawl over her arm. 'Where would you like me to start, Mr Dawkins?'

His mouth worked soundlessly and then he cleared his throat. 'Can you make toast?'

She nodded.

'The kitchen is out there.' He jerked his head towards the back of the shop, which was shrouded in darkness. 'Come to think of it, that's all the accommodation there is. I don't know where I'm going to put you, girl. I'm beginning to think this is all a big mistake.'

Charity had a sudden vision of herself turned out into the cold, and the thought of regular meals, a warm bed and four shillings a week was too tempting to give up easily. 'I can sleep under the counter, if there's nowhere else,' she said stoutly.

'Under the counter,' he repeated. 'Yes, that would be all right, I think.' He retreated behind it and picked up a book, opening it and holding it in front of his face. 'I'd like some tea and toast. You can have some too, but not too much. I'm a poor man and you will have to be frugal.'

'I'm used to that,' Charity said as she made her way towards the back of the shop, stepping over the books that were strewn about like autumn leaves. She opened the door and entered the kitchen, half expecting to find it was also filled with stock from the shop, but apart from the odd sock or two the floor was bare and there was no work of literature in sight. Cold grey light filtered through a grimy window at the rear of the building and a door opened into a tiny scullery with a stone sink and a wooden draining board. The half-glassed back door opened into a walled yard cluttered with crates, boxes and empty bottles. A narrow pathway had been cleared in the snow, and this led to a brick-built privy and a rusty pump. Two flights of rickety wooden steps clambered up the back of the building, and judging by the sound of raised voices and crying children it seemed that the upper floors were fully occupied. They would no doubt all share the facilities but Charity had noticed a cold tap in the scullery, which meant she would not have to go outside to pump water for cooking and washing. She closed the door and went in search of a kettle.

A desultory fire burned in the rusty iron range and she added a few lumps of coal, heeding Jethro's instructions on economy. She could see by the sparsely filled shelves on either side of the range that he lived a monk-like existence. There was a partly filled tea caddy and a crock in which she found the remains of a stale loaf. Mould had started to sprout from the crust, but she shaved the affected bits off and sliced the rest, ready to toast when the coals gave off enough heat. She put the kettle on to boil and went to the dresser to look for cups and plates, selecting the least cracked and chipped items and placed them on the pine table. She noted with a wry smile that there was only one chair – they would have to take turns to sit at the table or someone would have to perch on the single iron bedstead that stood against the far wall. It had been abandoned, unmade, and the ragged quilt lay in a tangled heap together with sheets that might once have been white, but were now stained and grey.

She found a toasting fork in one of the dresser drawers, mixed up in a jumble of sealing wax, scissors, brown paper and string. She sat patiently toasting the bread by the fire as she waited for the kettle to boil, but there did not seem to be any butter and there was a little milk in the bottom of a jug but it had set into a solid mass and was sour. She took a plate of dry toast and a cup of tea into the shop. 'The milk was off and there is no butter or jam. Is this how you live all the time, Mr Dawkins?'

He looked up from the book he was reading, staring at her in astonishment as if he had forgotten her existence. 'Toast is all I need. Butter and milk cost money.'

'But you aren't so very poor,' she said reasonably. 'Surely you can afford to eat properly, or are you a miser like Mr Scrooge?'

He was suddenly alert. 'You've read *A Christmas Carol*?'

'Not exactly. My grandmother read it to me when I

was a child, but I would like to read it myself if I had the book.'

A crooked smile curved Jethro's lips. 'It's there on the shelf, girl. What is your name – I've forgotten it already.'

'It's Charity, Mr Dawkins, and I will read it when I have time, but there is a lot to do and I, for one, can't work on dry bread and tea without milk or sugar. I can sit and read and do nothing, like you, or I can have a decent meal and clean this place up. What's it to be?'

He seemed to shrink into his oversized black tailcoat. 'What do you want?'

'A few pennies to purchase necessities, Mr Dawkins. We need food, and some soap would be a help if I'm to clean properly.'

'I knew this was a mistake,' he muttered, picking up a metal cash box. 'You'll bankrupt me before the week is out.'

'Nonsense,' Charity said firmly. 'If the shop is better organised you'll get more customers and sell more books.'

He took a bunch of keys from his pocket and unlocked the box. 'I'll give you sixpence, but I want change.'

She took the coin and tucked it into her bodice. 'I won't be long.' She put on her mittens and wrapped her shawl around her head and shoulders. If Mr Dawkins paid her a wage as promised she would buy herself a proper winter coat and a velvet bonnet. She had noticed a dolly shop on the corner of the street, and she intended to make full use of it when she received her pay. With this thought in mind she stepped out into the icy cold and made her way to Gray's Inn Road. She called in at the grocer's shop and bought a bar of carbolic soap before going on to the dairy and then the bakery. She purchased milk, bread, butter and a meat pie, and was on her way back to the shop when she spotted a street vendor selling baked potatoes. She bought two potatoes and a bunch of watercress, which would go down well between two thick slices of bread and butter. Her mouth watered as she hurried on her way, arriving at the shop flushed and breathless but with change in her pocket which should satisfy her new employer.

Jethro Dawkins snatched the three farthings with a grunt of dismay. 'I knew you'd ruin me, you stupid girl. Sixpence would feed me for three days at least.'

Charity stood her ground. She was used to outbursts of temper from her grandfather when he had had too much to drink and was unmoved. 'No wonder you're pale and thin, guvner,' she said calmly. 'You need some good vittles inside you.' She marched into the back room without giving him a chance to argue, and set her purchases down on the table. She took off her mittens, hung her shawl over the back of the chair, and set to work to find plates, knives and forks. Minutes later she carried the food into the shop and slapped it down on the counter. The soft fluffy inside of the potato glistened with melting butter that oozed onto the plate making a golden pool around the slice of pie. The savoury aroma wafted into the air and Jethro put his book down, staring at the plate and salivating. 'It ain't Christmas Day,' he muttered, snatching up the cutlery and attacking the food like a hungry hound.

Charity watched him shovelling the pie into his mouth with a satisfied smile. 'There's more if you want it,' she said, trying not to sound smug. 'I'll bring you a cup of tea with milk and sugar.'

'You'll be the ruin of me,' he said through a mouthful of hot potato.

'I'll prove you wrong.' Charity left him to finish his plateful and went to fetch the tea before settling down to enjoy her meal.

It was easier to work with a full stomach and she started in the kitchen, sweeping the floor before going down on her hands and knees to scrub away the grime and grease that had built up over the years. She would have liked to wash the bedding but that would have to wait for a good drying day, and having dusted the dresser and washed the dishes she made a start on the shop.

'What are you doing?' Jethro grumbled when she began pulling everything off the wide shelf in the window. 'Leave things alone.'

She turned on him with a derisive snort. 'For one thing the glass is filthy and no one can see in, and a higgledy-piggledy pile of books isn't going to tempt the passers-by to come in and look round.'

'I don't want people barging in who aren't interested in buying. My customers come from the university and the medical school. Professors and students buy my books, not the hoi polloi.'

Charity picked up a copy of *Treasure Island*, waving it in front of his nose. 'My granny used to read this to me when I was only seven or eight years old. I wasn't a professor or a student, but I loved to hear about Jim Hawkins and his adventures on the *Hispaniola*. You're missing an opportunity to sell to all sorts of people, Mr Dawkins.'

He snatched it from her and clutched it to his chest. 'Don't tell me how to run my business, girl. You've only been here five minutes.'

She reached out and prised it from his fingers, dusted the cover and set it on its end in the middle of the window. 'And I'll prove you wrong before I've been here much longer. Please don't stop me now. The light is beginning to fade and I'd like to get the window finished before it's too dark to see.'

He backed away, muttering beneath his breath, but made no further attempt to hinder her. She worked with a will, dusting the covers and arranging the books in some semblance of order so that the titles were clearly visible to anyone looking in from the street. She stepped outside several times to check her work and managed to complete her task just as the last glimmer of daylight faded into an inky dusk.

'You might as well lock up,' Jethro said sulkily. 'We won't get any customers after dark.'

'You would if you installed gaslight,' Charity said eagerly.

'I can't afford to do that. It costs money.'

Charity locked the door, taking a last look out into the street. The lamplighter was doing his rounds and as each lamp flared into light the world outside began to come alive again. 'It would be worth it,' she said softly. 'You'd get people who were on their way home from work and students who had attended lectures and wanted to study the things they'd been taught that day.'

'You're talking rubbish.' Jethro picked up the cash box and tucked it under his arm. 'I suppose you want supper tonight as well as that big meal midday.'

Charity followed him into the kitchen, matching her pace to his shambling gait. 'You promised the doctor that I'd get all my meals as part of my wage. It's not too much to ask, and I've worked hard all afternoon.'

He stopped in the doorway, turning his large head slowly from side to side. 'What have you done? There's a strange smell and everything's been moved.'

She pushed past him. 'The strange smell is cleanliness, Mr Dawkins. I've scrubbed and cleaned and tidied until my hands are red raw, so don't you dare grumble.' She stared pointedly at his bed. 'I'll wash your sheets when the weather improves.'

Jethro sank down on the wooden chair, staring round the room with his lips trembling. 'I don't like change.'

Charity hurried over to the range and moved the kettle to the hob. 'You'll feel better for a nice hot cup of tea and some cold pie with watercress and a slice of bread and butter.'

He eyed her warily. 'I don't want you in here when I go to bed. You'll sleep under the counter in the shop, and not come in here until I rise in the morning.'

'We've already agreed to that,' Charity said mildly. She took the loaf from the crock and cut two thick slices. 'I don't want to sit in here with you, but I'll need a candle so that I can see what I'm doing out there.'

'If you must,' he said grudgingly. 'I'm not sure this is going to work, but I'll give you until the end of the week. If I'm not satisfied you can go back to the doctor and tell him you don't suit.'

'Fair enough,' Charity said, pouring the tea into two clean cups. 'And it works both ways. If I don't like it here I'll be off anyway, so you'd better watch your tongue, Mr Dawkins.' She put his meal in front of him. 'I'll wash the dishes in the morning.' She lit another candle and took it into the shop, returning moments later to collect her food. 'Goodnight, Mr Dawkins.' She did not wait for his response but she had the satisfaction of seeing him tucking into his supper as she closed the door.

She was alone in the shop. The candle flickered in the draught that whistled under the outer door and through the ill-fitting windows, and it was bitterly cold. The bookshelves and stands, which looked ordinary enough by daylight, loomed above her taking on sinister shapes, and she had the feeling that she was being watched. She retreated behind the counter and sat down, placing the candlestick on the floor at her side. Suddenly the dank, overcrowded cellar seemed a much friendlier place than the lonely bookshop.

As she ate she could hear a strange rustling, scratching sound emanating from the other side of the counter and an unpleasant smell assaulted her nostrils. She snatched up the candle and rose to her feet, hardly daring to look but needing to know what it was that disturbed the night. She held the candle high and the sight that met her eyes made her cry out in horror. The floor was a heaving, moving mass of cockroaches that had seemingly come from nowhere, and as the light fell on them they scattered and were gone, leaving behind their ghastly stench.

Although she was accustomed to all manner of insects and vermin, Charity had never seen cockroaches in such a vast horde and she felt physically sick. They did not seem to like the light and so she set the candlestick down on the top of the desk. In the morning she would take on the task of clearing the floor and cleaning the place so that it was fit for habitation, but in the meantime she would have to try to sleep in the cramped space under the counter. Jethro had somewhat reluctantly parted with a filthy blanket that smelled of horses and might easily have come from the stable attached to the neighbouring brewery. Perhaps it had been given in part exchange by a scholarly drayman, she thought with a wry smile as she cocooned herself in its coarse folds. She curled up on the floor, but even though she was exhausted it was some time before she fell asleep. The sudden death of her grandfather had been a terrible shock, and she wished she could have accompanied him on his last journey to the cemetery at Brookwood. Even though she knew that he was beyond pain and the problems that afflicted the living, she could not help feeling guilty for deserting him at the last. And then there were the cockroaches. Every small sound, even the rustle of her own clothing, brought her out in a cold sweat. She could imagine a whole army of them marching over her while she slept. She would have to stay awake all night to ensure that did not happen. She pulled the blanket over her head.

She was awakened by the sound of heavy horses pulling a dray, and pounding of booted feet on the icy surface of the cobblestones as men went to work in the brewery. She was cramped and stiff and her clothes were damp with sweat, even though the temperature of the shop could only have been a little above that outside. The horse blanket had done its work and she had slept soundly, despite a series of nightmarish dreams. She scrambled onto her knees and stood up, stretching and taking deep breaths in order to clear her head. It was still dark but the light of the street lamps filtered through the windowpanes. For a moment when she first opened her eyes she had not known where she was, but now the reality of her situation hit her with full force. This was to be her home for the foreseeable future, and there was little or no choice for a girl from her background, as she knew to her cost.

She shook the creases out of her second-hand skirt, lifting it above her ankles as she walked round the counter, her gaze fixed on the floor. But to her relief there was no sign of the cockroaches that had appeared so suddenly and then vanished. 'Well,' she said out loud, 'I'll soon sort you out, you little brutes. I'm going to turn this place upside down today and woe betide any of you that get in my way. I'm going to scrub and clean every corner of this shop.' She made her way towards the kitchen, stepping carefully over the obstacles in her way. She opened the door quietly and, as she had suspected, the lumpy shape in the bed was snoring loudly. Jethro was still asleep. She did not want to wake him, and she crept through the scullery and let herself out into the back yard.

What she had not anticipated was the long queue for the privy. The occupants of the upper floors stood in line, shivering with cold, some of them still half asleep, and others mumbling to each other in hushed tones. Above them the sky was still inky black with no sign of dawn, and the snow and sludge had frozen overnight to a crisp coating that crunched underfoot. Charity was in two minds as to whether to stand in line or go indoors and wait until everyone had relieved themselves, but just as she was about to retreat someone caught her by the hand. She peered into the darkness and saw a friendly face smiling at her. 'You're new here. What's your name?' The girl, who Charity guessed was roughly the same age as herself, looked pale and ethereal in the pre-dawn gloom, but her eyes shone in the reflected light of the snow, and she was very pretty. Charity warmed to her at once.

'Charity Crosse. What's yours?'

'Violet Chapman. I live up top.' She pointed to a small attic window. 'There's ten of us lives in one room so as you can guess it's a bit crowded. Me dad works at Reid's Brewery, like most of the men round here, and me mum does the washing for the brewmaster's wife, which leaves me to stay at home and look after the nippers. That's me, so what's your story?' She shivered, clutching her thin shawl around her slender body.

'I only came here yesterday,' Charity said through chattering teeth. 'I'm working for Mr Dawkins in the bookshop.'

Violet pulled a face. 'Not him? The monster, we calls him. He's ugly enough to scare the bogeyman.'

'That's not fair. He can't help the way he looks.'

'He's a miserable geezer.' Violet shuffled on a couple of paces as a man emerged from the privy, shrugging on his jacket and pulling his cap down over his eyes. 'That's me dad. He's a drayman at Reid's.' Violet turned away as her father strode past them and he ignored her, which Charity thought odd, but maybe there had been a falling out in the family.

'Hurry up in there.' A woman's voice rang out across the yard, echoing off the high walls. 'Some of us ain't got all day.'

'That's Mary Spinks. She lives on the second floor too, and she's a cook at the workhouse. Keep out of her way. She's got a fearsome temper and she'll clock you one as soon as look at you if the mood takes her, but her daughter Maisie is a good laugh if you keep on her right side.'

'Isn't there anyone it's safe to talk too?'

Violet smiled sweetly. 'There's always me, Charity. I could do with a friend.'

'And so could I,' Charity said wholeheartedly. 'I lost

me grandad the day afore yesterday. He's to be buried in a pauper's grave and I won't be able to find him, even if I saves up enough of me wages to go to Brookwood. It was the drink that did for him in the end.'

Violet slipped her arm around Charity's shoulders and gave her a hug. 'You poor thing. I know how you feel. There's three of my baby brothers and sisters buried in unmarked graves. It's only the toffs what can afford headstones and horses with plumes.'

Charity was about to answer when she heard a shuffling noise behind her. She turned to see Jethro skidding across the ice. 'Look out,' he shouted. 'I can't stop once I get going.'

'It's always like that.' Violet leapt out of the way and the line of people parted as Jethro careered along towards the privy, almost knocking down the startled man who was coming out, doing up his trousers. Jethro plunged into the brick building and the door slammed shut.

Charity felt embarrassed for him and also for herself as all eyes turned upon her.

'Are you really going to work for him?' Violet stared at her in disbelief.

Chapter Four

Charity was in the shop alone. Jethro had gone to an antiquarian book sale in Aldgate and left her in charge. During the six months she had been working for him they had come to an uneasy truce. He was still suspicious and his temper was easily roused, but although getting money out of him for necessities was still an uphill struggle, he was not as parsimonious as he had been in the beginning. Charity felt sorry for him, and she had been quick to realise just how difficult life was for a man with disabilities that left him in constant pain. She had discovered early on that he relied on laudanum to help him sleep, and she had learned to keep out of his way when he was having a particularly bad day.

She could not say that she liked him or that he was a kindly employer, and she still slept under the counter in the shop, although Jethro had given her the money to buy a flock-filled mattress, which made sleeping easier. The cockroaches had seemingly left the building or had made the journey to the upper floors due to Charity's obsession with cleanliness. She swept and scrubbed the floors daily, and there was not a speck of dust or dirt to be seen in the living accommodation or on the shop floor. The bookshelves were immaculate and she had begun to catalogue the volumes on sale. She took pride in window dressing and many more customers came through the door as a result. Jethro was slow to praise but Charity had the satisfaction of seeing the takings increase, and it was largely due to her efforts.

The weather was hot and oppressive at the approach of autumn. She had wedged the shop door open in an attempt to cool the air, but had been forced to close it in order to shut out the smell of seething sewers, horse dung and the fumes from the brewery. Trade was slow due to the fact that the students and their professors would not return to the university until the autumn term. She undid the top button of her cotton print frock, which she had recently purchased from the dolly shop in Gray's Inn Road, and went to sit on the high stool behind the counter, picking up a copy of *A Thousand Miles Up the Nile* by Amelia Edwards. She was already halfway through the fascinating account of the intrepid lady's travels in Egypt, and it had fired her with a desire to see such wonders for herself. Of course that was an impossibility, but it was wonderful to dream of an exotic country with fascinating glimpses into a past civilisation. She was so intent on reading that she only realised that the door had opened when the bell jangled noisily on its spring. She closed the book with a snap and sat upright. 'Good morning, sir. May I be . . .' She stopped midsentence, staring at the elder of two gentlemen who had entered the shop. 'Mr Barton?' she said tentatively. 'Is it you, sir?'

He came closer, staring at her curiously, and then a slow smile spread across his handsome features. 'It's

Charity, isn't it? I remember you very well. It was outside the Old Lady of Threadneedle Street that we met, wasn't it?'

She shook her head. 'I dunno about any old lady, sir. But it was outside the Bank of England. I knows that for a fact.'

Barton's companion, a much younger man with a mop of unruly fair hair and hazel eyes, chortled with laughter, but a look from Charity silenced him and he blushed. 'I beg your pardon, miss. I didn't mean any offence.'

'What's funny?' she demanded angrily. 'You shouldn't mock the way I speak – it ain't polite.'

'Quite right.' Wilmot Barton nodded in agreement. 'Remember your manners, Daniel my boy.'

'I'm sorry, sir.'

'You'll have to forgive my nephew, Charity. He's a raw lad up from the country and has yet to learn the ways of polite society.'

Daniel grinned sheepishly. 'Hold on, Uncle. I haven't got straw growing out of my ears. Just because I grew up in Devonshire doesn't mean that I'm a yokel.'

'Of course not,' Wilmot said equably, 'and that's my point, Dan. Just because Charity lacks a little polish doesn't mean that she's a lesser person.'

Charity cleared her throat to remind them of her presence. 'I ain't deaf, sir.'

'And I'm being just as impolite as my young nephew.' Wilmot treated her to a disarming smile. 'You didn't take up my offer. Why was that? Were you afraid that I had ulterior motives?'

'My grandpa died, sir. I had to find work and a place to live.'

'I'm sorry for your loss.' Wilmot eyed her curiously. 'What was it that brought you here to Dawkins' bookshop?'

'Dr Marchant brought me here because I had nowhere else to go. He thought I would suit this type of work.'

Wilmot nodded his head. 'A wise gentleman indeed.'

'And he's very kind and caring. He came here a few days ago making the excuse of ordering a book, but I think he wanted to make sure I was all right. I can't think of many professional men who'd bother with someone who used to scratch a living by begging on street corners.'

'I say, did you really?' Daniel's eyes opened wide in astonishment. 'Wasn't that terribly risky for a girl like you?'

'I suppose it was, but I learned how to take care of myself.'

'You look as though a puff of wind would blow you over.' His cheeks burned with colour. 'I say, I'm frightfully sorry. I seem to say all the wrong things.'

'Think nothing of it, sir.' Charity turned to Wilmot with a polite smile. 'How may I help you?'

'I came to browse through Jethro's collection of antiquarian volumes. Occasionally I find something of interest.' He gazed round at the neatly labelled shelves. 'I can see that you've been busy.'

Charity accepted the compliment with a nod of her head. 'I can't bear a muddle, and books should be treated with respect. I just think of the work that someone has had to do putting all those words together and it's little short of a miracle.'

'I wish my students were as appreciative as you.' Wilmot walked over to the stand where Charity had stacked the rarer editions. He paused, turning to his nephew. 'You might find something on the shelves that will keep you amused while you're staying with me in Doughty Street, Daniel my boy.' He chuckled and began to browse.

Daniel shrugged his shoulders. 'I'm more of a doer than someone who is happy to take everything from the pages of a book.' He picked up the book that Charity had been reading and his eyes lit up with interest. 'Now this is a good read. Are you interested in Egyptology?'

'I ain't sure what that means exactly,' Charity admitted grudgingly. 'But if you mean reading about Egypt and Pharaohs and such, then yes I am.'

He pulled a face. 'I apologise again if I offended you.' He opened the book and flicked through the pages. 'The study of ancient Egypt interests me too. I'm an archaeology student and I hope one day to visit the Valley of the Kings and see the ancient wonders for myself. Doesn't Miss Edwards' account of her experiences make you want to follow in her footsteps too?'

'I dunno. It never crossed my mind. I'm as likely to fly to the moon as travel abroad.'

He leaned forward, fixing her with an intense gaze. 'But that's where you're wrong. Look at the women who've achieved amazing things in science and medicine, and those who campaign for women's suffrage.'

'I dunno about all that either. The only women I know have to do what their men tell them or they get a black eye for their trouble.' Charity had seen the bruises on Mrs Chapman's face often enough to know that her husband had a violent temper. Maisie Spinks had warned her about his wandering hands and lewd suggestions, and it was obvious that Violet was afraid of her father. There were plenty of men who ruled by the fist, especially when drunk on jigger gin or too many pints of ale.

Daniel ran his finger round the inside of his stiff white collar and looked away. 'I believe that does occur in some quarters,' he said slowly. 'I'm sorry.'

'What for? You done no wrong so far as I can see.'

'Shall we start again, Charity?' He held his hand out to her. 'My name is Daniel Barton and I'm studying archaeology at University College.'

She shook his hand. 'I'm Charity Crosse and I work for Mr Dawkins. I'm teaching meself, I mean myself, by reading as much as I can. I'm pleased to make your acquaintance.'

'Now we're friends we can speak freely. What was it my uncle wanted you to do?' He smiled apologetically. 'Forgive me for being nosey, but I'm curious.'

'You mean you can't think what an educated toff like Mr Barton would want with an ignorant girl like me.'

'That's not what I meant. Do you take pleasure in putting me in the wrong?'

She suppressed a giggle. 'You do that without any help from me.'

'I've never met anyone like you, Charity Crosse. I don't know whether to be amused or . . .' he hesitated, 'or cross.' His eyes danced with merriment, and Charity found herself laughing with him.

'I can't help my name or the way I am.'

'And I've never met a girl who could make me laugh. You're quite different from the young ladies I meet in the normal course of things.'

'Are there many girls at the university?'

'I don't know the exact numbers, but there are quite a few. You would enjoy attending lectures if you had the chance.'

Charity sighed. 'That's not for the likes of me. I've got all the learning I need. I know how to cook and clean, and how to keep Mr Dawkins in order.'

'You know, you should take my uncle up on his offer. I'm assuming it was to do with his work on social anthropology, and he must have thought you could make a valuable contribution. You can trust him.'

'He might have changed his mind, and anyway I'm very busy with the shop.'

Wilmot, apparently overhearing her last remark, strolled over to the counter with a book in his hand. 'Of course my offer is still open, although it might not sound as attractive now that you're settled in work.' He laid the leather-bound book on the counter. 'I'll take this now, please. I've another on order so perhaps you might like to deliver it to my lodgings in Doughty Street when it comes in, and we could discuss my project then.'

Aware that Daniel was watching her closely, Charity

smiled and nodded. 'Yes, sir. Of course.' She glanced at the price written on the inside of the front cover. 'That will be five shillings, please.' She waited while he counted out the coins. It would take her over a week to earn such a princely sum. Mr Barton must be a rich man to be able to afford such a luxury. She locked the money away in the metal cash box.

'I look forward to seeing you soon, Charity,' Wilmot said, doffing his bowler hat. 'You must come in time for tea. My landlady makes the most delicious muffins and chocolate cake.'

'I can vouch for that,' Daniel said enthusiastically. 'Do come, Charity. She only brings out the cake when someone special comes to tea, and it's my particular favourite.'

'I never go out after the shop closes, but I'll come if Mr Dawkins lets me.'

'Make sure he does,' Wilmot said solemnly. 'Dan will see you safely home.' He tucked the book under his arm and headed for the door. 'Come along, old chap. There are other customers waiting.'

Daniel hurried after him and it was only then that Charity realised there were two more people waiting to be served. She turned to the pinch-faced woman who was tapping her foot impatiently on the floor-boards. 'How may I help you, madam?'

After supper that evening when Jethro settled down in his chair to read the newspaper and smoke his briar pipe, Charity stepped outside into the yard to get a breath of air. It was a hot and sultry evening, with the threat of a thunderstorm hanging like a cloud above the steamy city streets. Flies settled in heaving masses on scraps of fat that had been tossed carelessly from upstairs windows, and the stench of the privy was all but masked by the smell of boiling hops and malt from the brewery, but it was marginally cooler outside than in the stuffy confines of the shop and kitchen. Charity leaned against the rough brickwork, marvelling at the tenacity of a dandelion that somehow managed to grow and thrive in nothing but dust. That's me, she thought dreamily. I'm like the weeds that fight their way through concrete and survive against all odds. She smiled to herself as she realised that her feeling of optimism was due to a chance meeting that morning with Mr Barton and his young nephew. She had not taken to Daniel Barton at first, but there was something about him that made her want to get to know him better, and he had taken the trouble to talk to her. Despite his initial rudeness he had seen her as a person in her own right, unlike the majority of the customers who came into the shop, to whom she was virtually invisible.

'A penny for 'em.'

Charity turned with a start and saw Violet coming down the stairs. 'You made me jump.'

'You was miles away.' Violet leapt the last three steps, landing cat-like on all fours. She straightened up and wiped her hands on her grubby pinafore. 'And you was grinning. What's so funny?'

'I wasn't grinning.'

'Yes you was. I bet it's a bloke. It always is. I seen

it often enough with me eldest sister, Betsy. She used to smile like that after she'd been with the butcher's boy and he got her in the family way afore she was fifteen. They live in Brixton over the shop and she has three nippers and another on the way.'

'It's not like that, Vi. I'm just feeling more cheerful, that's all.'

Violet sidled up to her. 'What's his name then?'

Charity could see that she was not going to be put off no matter what she said. 'All right, I did chat to a young man this morning. His uncle came in to buy a book.'

Violet squatted down on her haunches, pulling Charity down beside her. 'Go on.'

The cobblestones were warm beneath her buttocks and the brick wall released the heat of the sun that it had absorbed during the day, making her feel warm and relaxed. Suddenly she had the need to confide in someone. 'I met this cove when I was begging on the streets. He said he was a professor of something or other, and he wanted me to go to his lodgings and help him in his work.'

'Oh yes, we've all heard that one.'

'No, I don't think he meant it like that. He seems a really nice man and he still wants to see me – just to talk, nothing else.'

'If you believe that you'll believe anything. Men are all the same, Charity, love. You can't trust 'em, and you can't believe a word they say. Ma's drummed that into us girls again and again, since Betsy got caught out. Mind you, it don't always work for the best. Me cousin Sukey's nearly twenty and she's said no so often that the fellers have given up. She'll be an old maid if she ain't careful.'

Charity scrambled to her feet. 'There must be more to life than marrying the first bloke who comes along just to keep a roof over your head.'

Violet shrugged her thin shoulders. 'That's life, my duck. What choice have we got?' She stood up and stretched. 'I'm going to the Jockey Fields with Maisie Spinks. Are you coming?'

'Not tonight. I've got some reading to do.'

'You won't get much of a laugh from a dusty old book.'

'Maybe not, but at least I won't get into any trouble.' Charity gave her a cheerful wave as she retraced her steps across the yard.

'And you won't have no fun neither,' Violet called after her as Charity opened the scullery door.

'I can do without that sort of fun,' Charity murmured as she went inside.

Jethro was still sitting at the kitchen table but he had abandoned the newspaper and was poring over a ledger. She cleared her throat. 'Ahem, Mr Dawkins, may I have a word with you?'

He looked up, scowling. 'What d'you want? Can't you see I'm busy?'

'It won't take a moment, sir.'

'Very well. Make it quick.'

'Mr Barton has a book on order. I wondered if I might deliver it myself?'

'Why would you want to do that?' Jethro eyed her suspiciously.

'Because he's interested in me as a subject for one of his lectures.'

'I never heard it called that before,' Jethro said, curling his lip. 'I'll send it by messenger as usual. You keep away from men like him.'

'It would be quite proper,' Charity protested. 'His nephew would be there and his housekeeper. I've been invited to have tea with them.'

'I'm not paying you to socialise. You work here on my terms and if you don't like it you know what you can do.' He bent his head over the columns of figures, dismissing her with an impatient wave of his hand. Charity realised that it was futile to argue when he was in this sort of mood and she retreated to the shop and immersed herself in the travels of Miss Amelia Edwards.

The order arrived from the warehouse two days later but Jethro was adamant, insisting that Charity remain in the shop and that a messenger be sent to Doughty Street. She wrote a brief note explaining why she had not come in person and slipped it inside the cover, hoping that Mr Barton would understand. She handed it to the messenger with a feeling of acute disappointment. Her chance to visit another world, quite different from her own, had slipped from her grasp.

'There is something you can do for me.'

She turned with a start to see Jethro standing behind her with a book clutched in his hand. He thrust it at her with an attempt at a smile which only served to emphasise the paralysis of one side of his face. 'Dr Marchant's order,' he muttered. 'It needs to go to Old Fish Street today. You must take it.'

'Me? But I thought I wasn't allowed to leave the shop.'

'You are if I say so.'

'I don't understand why it's all right for me to go all that way when you wouldn't let me make the short trip to Doughty Street.'

'I don't pay you to think – I pay you to do as you're told. Dr Marchant is a friend as well as a valued client, so put your bonnet on and take this to him now. I expect you back before closing time and I don't want any excuses.'

'Of course I'll go, but it would be quicker if I had the cab fare.'

'I'm not made of money. Selling books pays your wages. If you want to go by cab you can pay for it yourself.' He thumped the book down on the counter and turned his back on her. 'Go now, before I change my mind.'

Charity hooked her bonnet off its peg and picked up the book. She left the shop and started off on the long walk to the doctor's house. The sky was overcast when she set out, and the atmosphere humid. In the distance she could hear the rumble of thunder which rolled closer as she neared the river. She quickened her pace, hoping to get to Old Fish Street before the rain clouds broke and soaked her to the skin, but large drops began to fall as she reached St Paul's and the air was thick with a sulphurous glow. A sudden gust of wind tore at her bonnet and careered down the street like a runaway horse. The city skyline was illuminated by a sudden sheet of lightning followed by a resounding crash of thunder. She started to run, making her way across the busy street and narrowly escaped being run down by a startled horse which reared in the shafts of a hansom cab.

Blinded by the sudden downpour, she sought shelter beneath the colonnaded portico of St Paul's Cathedral. She took off her straw bonnet which was soaked and ruined. The colours in her cotton print frock had run, and trickles of blood-red dye stained her wrists and hands. Even worse, the brown paper wrapped around the doctor's book was soaked with rainwater. She peeled it off, uttering a heartfelt sight of relief when she saw that the leather binding was damp but undamaged. She huddled up, wrapping her arms around her knees and shivering despite the muggy heat. There was nothing she could do other than sit and wait for the storm to pass.

Mrs Rose opened the front door. 'Well,' she said, shaking her head. 'You look a sorry sight, Charity. I thought you were well set up with Mr Dawkins, but just look at the state of you.'

'I brought the doctor's book,' Charity said through chattering teeth. She was wet through, and although the sun was now shining from a peerless blue sky she was chilled to the bone.

'Come inside.' Mrs Rose ushered her in and closed the door. 'You look in a worse state than you did last winter when you turned up in a snowstorm. Go through to the kitchen.'

'I sh-should g-give the doctor his book first.'

Mrs Rose snatched it from her. 'He's out on a house call, but I'll put it on his desk. Now do as I say, and don't argue.'

The kitchen was warm and the aroma of roasting meat made Charity's stomach rumble with hunger. 'It's you. You've come at last.' Dorrie abandoned the task of shelling peas and flung her arms around Charity's neck. She stepped back, pulling a face. 'You're soaking wet.'

'She is indeed.' Mrs Rose bustled into the kitchen, carrying the now familiar missionary barrel, which spilled over with garments. She dumped it on the table. 'Take off those wet things, my girl. I'm sure we've got something to fit you and that dress is all but ruined.' She fingered the wet fabric, shaking her head. 'Cheap material and badly made. You bought this in a dolly shop, I should imagine. Well, whatever you paid for it you were robbed, Charity my girl. Now take it off and pick something from the charity box.' A grim smile lit her normally humourless features.

Dorrie chuckled. 'I see the joke, Mrs Rose. The box is called a charity box and Charity needs a new frock.' She bit her lip, blushing. 'I'm sorry, Charity. I weren't laughing at you.'

Charity slipped off her wet clothes and selected a clean cotton shift and a grey poplin dress. 'It's all right, Dorrie. No offence taken.' She dressed quickly and immediately felt more comfortable. 'I can pay for the clothes. I'm earning a wage at the bookshop.'

Mrs Rose picked up Charity's discarded garments and laid them over the back of a chair. 'There's no need. All were given freely by people who are far better off than you or I. Dorrie will wash these and put them in the box for the poor and needy. No one will be any the wiser.

'Ta,' Charity said doubtfully. Mrs Rose might think she was one of the poor and needy but in her own mind she had risen above that now. She was a working girl, employed in a respectable trade. 'When do you expect Dr Marchant to return? I have to get back to the shop.'

Dorrie clutched her hand. 'You can stay for a while, can't you? I wants to hear all your news. You mustn't go just yet.'

Mrs Rose opened the oven door and a gust of fragrant steam billowed out. 'The doctor will be home for his midday meal, especially as it's collops of lamb with mint sauce and roast potatoes, which is his favourite. You must stay and eat with us, Charity. He would be very put out to think I'd sent you away with an empty stomach.'

Charity eyed the meat and her mouth watered in anticipation. 'I should be getting back, but I have to collect payment. Mr Dawkins made that very clear.'

'Then you'll stay and eat with us.' Mrs Rose closed the oven door. 'Have you finished shelling the peas, Dorrie? I'll need to get them on soon, so hurry up you stupid child.'

'I'll help.' Charity took a seat at the table.

'I think I heard the doctor's key in the lock.' Mrs Rose hurried from the room leaving Charity and Dorrie to finish their task.

'How are you?' Charity asked in a whisper. 'She's not working you too hard, is she?'

Dorrie's bottom lip trembled. 'I shouldn't complain. I got a bed and a full belly. What more could a workhouse girl expect?'

It was mid-afternoon when Charity left the doctor's house. She had eaten well and enjoyed every last morsel of Mrs Rose's excellent cooking. Dr Marchant had been pleased to see her and had questioned her at length about her situation at the bookshop. She had found herself telling him about Wilmot Barton's interest in her background and his offer to pay her for helping him with his research.

'It's not uncommon,' he had said at length. 'There are men with conscience who wish to make the lives of ordinary working people better, and for that they have to understand the way they live. I don't know Barton, but if he's a professor at University College, then I imagine he is a respectable fellow with your best interests at heart.'

'So you think I ought to accept his offer?'

'It would be worth further investigation. I think Dawkins is afraid of losing you, and that is why he was so adamant in his refusal to allow you to accept Barton's invitation.'

'But I can't go against him, Dr Marchant. I'd lose everything and be out on the street.'

'I might be able to persuade him. Next time I visit the shop I'll have a word.' Dr Marchant had then placed two silver crowns on the table. 'That is what I owe

Jethro. Take it to him now and tell him I'll be back very soon. Books are my one weakness, as you will realise.'

Charity quickened her pace, and the coins in her pocket clinked together, keeping time with her long strides. She hoped that the doctor would remember his promise to speak to Mr Dawkins and persuade him to change his mind. It was not simply the thought of earning sixpence an hour that made Wilmot Barton's offer so attractive, it was the opportunity to further her education. Working all day with books crammed with information had excited her imagination and made her even more eager to learn. She had been born into a middle-class family and her father had been an educated man: it was misfortune and the frailty of her grandfather that had dragged her down to the gutter. Now she was clawing her way up and she was determined to better herself and regain her rightful situation in life. Education was the way out of an existence dominated by toil and servitude, and who better to help her than a university professor?

She walked on with her head down as she grappled with the problems that beset her. She realised that compared to young Dorrie she had an easy life, despite the restrictions placed upon her by Jethro Dawkins. Maybe sleeping beneath the counter was not ideal, but it was better than bedding down in a damp cellar or under the railway arches. She was about to cross Verulam Street when a gang of ragged boys appeared seemingly out of nowhere and surrounded her. 'She works for the hunchback.' The biggest of the youths, who seemed to be the leader of the gang, picked up a stone and threw it, narrowly missing Charity's head.

'Stop that,' she said angrily. 'Go away and leave me alone.'

'Give us your money.' He advanced on her with fists clenched and a menacing look on his face. 'Give us your purse and you won't get hurt.'

'Go away. I've got nothing.'

'Then what's that clanking sound every time you take a step?' He grabbed her by the arm, and the rest of the pack surrounded her, chanting abuse.

'Let go of me, you young villain.' She struggled in vain, calling for help, until a blow on the head sent her spiralling into a pit of darkness.

Chapter Five

'Charity.'

She could hear her name being repeated over and over again. They don't know who I am, she thought dazedly. She opened her eyes. 'What happened?' She blinked and found herself gazing up into Daniel Barton's anxious face.

He helped her to a sitting position. 'You were attacked by a gang of street arabs. Are you all right?'

She struggled to her feet. 'Yes, I think so. I must have fainted.'

'Have they taken anything?'

She put her hand in her pocket. 'The money is gone. Mr Dawkins will go mad when he finds out. He'll blame me and it wasn't my fault.'

'You've had a nasty shock. I'm taking you back to Doughty Street. Uncle Wilmot's housekeeper will look after you.'

'No. Thank you all the same, but I'll have to face Mr Dawkins sooner or later. I'm all right now and it's not far to Liquorpond Street.'

'I'm coming with you. Old Dawkins won't make too much of a fuss if I'm there.' Daniel tucked her hand into the crook of his arm. 'Lean on me. You look a bit groggy.'

Charity could see that it was useless to argue. Despite her brave words, she felt shaky and was glad of his supporting arm as they made their way slowly towards the shop.

Jethro was perched on the high stool behind the counter, and his expression was that of a malevolent goblin. 'Where've you been?' he demanded. 'It's nearly closing time and you've been gone for hours.' He glared at Daniel. 'Why are you here?'

Charity took a deep breath. 'I was robbed, Mr Dawkins. I was set upon by a gang of hooligans and they took your money. Daniel just happened to be passing.'

'And it's lucky that I was close by,' Daniel said without giving Jethro a chance to speak. 'I was on my way here as a matter of fact, Mr Dawkins. My uncle asked me to find out if Charity had considered his request, and I saw the youths attacking a young woman. I chased them off and then I realised it was Charity who was lying on the pavement. Luckily she wasn't hurt.'

'I've lost a lot of money, thanks to her incompetence.' Jethro climbed down from the stool and rounded the counter in two ungainly strides. 'You can go back to your uncle and tell him that Miss Crosse isn't interested in his social studies. She's got plenty to do here and I can't spare her. I'm running a business, which is something that you academics don't understand. You've done your bit so you can just sling your hook and take that message back to Mr Barton.'

'I'm so sorry, Daniel,' Charity said in a low voice. 'Thank you for walking me home.'

'I'm glad I was able to help.' His expression hardened.

'As to you, sir, you ought to be ashamed of yourself for treating a young girl in such a cavalier fashion. She could have been seriously hurt by those young ruffians, and all you can think of is the money you've lost. Had you sent Charity to Doughty Street as my uncle requested, none of this would have happened.'

Jethro's misshapen jaw protruded at an ugly angle and he gave Daniel a shove that sent him staggering towards the door. 'Get out and keep away from her in future. I know your sort and you've only got one thing on your mind when it comes to a pretty face.'

'That's not fair, Mr Dawkins.' Charity stepped in between them, fearing that Daniel might retaliate, but it was Jethro who swung his fist, catching her on the side of her head and knocking her to the floor.

'That's what you get for insolence.' He barred Daniel's way as he rushed to Charity's aid. 'I told you to get out. Do you want me to report your behaviour to the Dean? I could blacken your name so that he would have to send you down and that would put an end to your career. You'd end up digging graves for the newly dead instead of grubbing round in the earth for ancient bones.'

Charity struggled to her feet. She staggered to the counter and leaned against it, focusing her eyes with difficulty on Daniel's stricken face. 'I'm all right,' she murmured. 'Please go. You'll only make things worse.'

He wrenched the shop door open. 'Get your things, Charity,' he said angrily. 'I'm not leaving you here with a brute like Dawkins. Only a complete coward would strike a helpless girl.'

'I'm all right, really I am.' Charity felt far from well, but she did not want to make the situation worse.

Jethro turned his back on Daniel. 'Get back to work, girl. I'm hungry and I want my dinner,'

'Don't do it, Charity,' Daniel said urgently. 'Come with me. Uncle Wilmot will take you in, or at least he'll find you another position where you're not treated like a slave.'

Charity's head ached and her limbs seemed to have turned to lead. Her first instinct had been to walk out of the door and go with Daniel, but experience warned her against putting her trust in impulsive pledges. Her grandfather had lived his life making promises he could not keep and she suspected that this might be the case now. Daniel meant well, of that she was sure, but he was an impecunious student and she was by no means certain that she would be received on a permanent basis in Doughty Street. 'Thank you for your concern,' she said in a low voice. 'But you'd best go now, Daniel. I can look after myself.'

He shot a look of pure loathing at Jethro. 'I don't want to leave you with this brute.'

'I've been called worse.' Jethro shambled towards him.

'I'll be back tomorrow, Charity.' Daniel stepped outside into the street. 'I won't rest until I know you're all right.'

'Good riddance.' Jethro slammed the door and put up the *Closed* sign. 'Get on with it, girl, or you'll feel the back of my hand for a second time today.'

Charity retreated to the kitchen, slamming the door

behind her. Jethro had been harsh in his treatment of her but he had never lashed out with his fists as he had today. There was no one in authority to whom she could go for protection – the law would be on the side of her employer. She was a humble worker and he was entitled to chastise her as he saw fit. Men had been getting away with violence against women for centuries and there was little or nothing they could do to protect themselves. She doubted if either the doctor or Mr Barton would want to get involved. Daniel was an idealist and he was young, but she suspected that he too would realise the futility of trying to help her when he had had time to cool down. She set about preparing a meal despite her aching head and bruised body.

When she put his food in front of Jethro that evening he kept his gaze lowered as if afraid to look her in the eye. 'You wasn't wearing that frock when you left here this morning,' he said suspiciously. 'Did you spend my money on new duds and make up the story about being mugged by a street gang?'

'I most certainly did not.' Stung by the unfairness of this accusation, Charity forgot to be humble. 'How dare you suggest such a thing? This dress came out of the missionary barrel at the doctor's house.'

He shot her a sideways glance. 'And why would the doctor give you a new dress. Did you ask for less money in order to get on his good side? Have you been cheating me, miss?'

'You sent me all that way without the cab fare and I got caught in a thunderstorm. I was soaked to the skin and my dress and bonnet were ruined. Mrs Rose took pity on me and gave me a change of clothes, the same as she did when I first went there last winter. My name is Charity and I'm a charity case, as she pointed out.'

'So where did my money go?'

'I was set upon and robbed on my way back to the shop, as I told you. I'm not a liar, Mr Dawkins.'

'The money you lost will come out of your wages,' he muttered. 'And if that young fellow comes sniffing round I'll carry out my threat to report him to the authorities at the university. You'll keep away from young men while you're under my roof. Do you understand?'

'I've no interest in Daniel Barton,' Charity said firmly. 'But if you lay a finger on me once more I'll walk out of that door and you'll never see me again. I work hard and you need me, so don't think you can bully me and get away with it, Mr Dawkins.'

He met her angry gaze with a vicious snarl. 'You'd better learn to hold your tongue, young lady. I'm not a violent man, unless roused beyond endurance.'

'I'll stay for now, but don't count on my loyalty forever.'

Jethro's misshapen torso rose and fell as he struggled to catch his breath. His dark brows drew together in an ominous frown and he clenched and unclenched his fists, flexing his fingers as if preparing to strike again. 'You'll do as I say or you'll get a taste of my leather belt around your skinny backside. That's the last time I let you out of my sight, girl. From now on you won't go anywhere without my say-so. D'you understand?'

Charity could see that he was beyond reason and acknowledged his harsh words with a brief nod as she took her plate of pease pudding into the shop, closing the door on his continued ranting. She sat on the floor under the counter and attempted to eat, but she had no appetite and she left the food untouched. She was trapped. She knew enough of the hardships in the outside world to understand the value of a roof over her head and regular meals, however meagre. She had seen poverty at its ugliest and she knew that there were few choices for a young woman who had neither family nor friends to protect her. She had seen fresh-faced girls, little more than children, who had been forced to sell their bodies in order to survive. In a few short years they would be old before their time, dependent upon the use of opium and cheap spirits to dull the pain of their futile existence and the disease that raddled their bodies. She could run away, but she might end up in a far worse situation; at least here, in Dawkins' shop, she had found an escape in books, and if she were to better herself it would be through education. If she had learned one thing in the past few months it was that the world was there for all to discover in the written word.

She waited until it was dark and she could hear Jethro's loud, laudanum-induced snores before going into the kitchen to clear the table. She left the dirty dishes soaking in cold water, and she went out into the back yard. The privy was in its usual disgusting state and she spent as little time as possible in its stuffy, evil-smelling confines. The smoky air outside seemed fresh in comparison and she made her way to the steps where she sat down, allowing the cool night air to caress her bruised face. She would have a black eye by morning and she would have to explain that away with the time-honoured excuse of having walked into a door. No one would believe her but they would be too polite to enquire further.

It was unusually quiet in the moonlit yard. The only sounds emanating from the upper floors were a baby crying and the occasional shout of laughter, but for once there were no raised voices to corrupt the serenity of the night. The click of the latch on the back gate made her suddenly alert and she shrank back into the shadow of the building, breathing a sigh of relief when she realised that it was Violet who sashayed down the narrow pathway between the piles of rubbish. She was holding out her patched skirts as if she were on a ballroom floor, dancing to music that she alone could hear. She looked unreal and ghostly in the moonlight, and she was smiling. 'Violet, it's only me,' Charity said softly, trying not to startle her friend by suddenly making her presence known.

Violet came to a halt, peering into the shadows. 'Charity?'

'Yes. I didn't want to scare you.'

'I've been out with Maisie and the boys,' Violet said dreamily. 'We had such a laugh. You ought to come with us next time.' She moved closer. 'What's up with your face? You've got a real shiner coming.'

'Nothing,' Charity said, instinctively raising her hand to cover her bruises. 'I walked into the door.'

'I heard that one before.' Violet flopped down beside her. 'The hunchback's got a reputation for using his fists, that's why he can never keep anyone for long. They all pack up and leave in the end.'

Charity stood up. Her whole body ached and she was overcome by weariness. 'Well, I haven't got much choice, Violet. So I think I'll be here for quite a while yet.'

'I'm so glad.' Violet leapt to her feet and gave her a hug. 'You really must come out with us one evening. You need a bit of fun.'

Charity eyed her curiously. 'How do you manage it, Violet?'

'Manage what? I dunno what you mean.'

'The back gate is always padlocked at night. How do you get in and out so easily?'

Violet slipped her hand into her pocket and produced a small key. 'I use this to let meself out, and climb over the gate if it's locked when I get back. One of the boys we meet is an apprentice locksmith. He's keen on me and he was only too happy to make a duplicate. Me and Maisie can get in and out without anyone knowing. You could too, if you had a mind to.'

'Thanks. Maybe I will one day, but I'm dog tired so I'll say goodnight, Violet.' Charity made her way slowly and painfully into the scullery where a pile of dirty dishes awaited her.

Next morning she was in the shop alone when the door opened to admit Wilmot, followed closely by Daniel. 'My dear girl.' Wilmot studied her face with an angry scowl. 'Daniel told me what happened last evening. Where is the scoundrel?'

'It's nothing, sir. I'm all right.' She looked away, conscious of the livid bruise on her cheek and a black eye.

'I want a word with Dawkins,' Wilmot said angrily. 'I abhor violence of any kind, especially when used on women and children. I intend to tell him so.'

'Please don't make things worse, sir.' Charity laid a restraining hand on his coat sleeve. 'He's still very angry with me for losing the money and you'll only make things worse.'

'I know what I'd like to do to the wretch,' Daniel muttered. 'But as long as you're not feeling too bad, I suppose we ought to let it rest for now.'

Wilmot handed a small, deckle-edged card to Charity. 'This will remind you of my address. It's not far from here. When might I expect you?'

'I'm not allowed out,' Charity said sadly. 'I'm afraid I can't come.'

'Surely he can't keep you after hours?' Wilmot's frown deepened. 'I must speak to him. This is unreasonable behaviour.' He took a step towards the back of the shop but Charity moved swiftly to bar his way.

'I beg you not to say anything, Mr Barton. I have nowhere else to go and I would be in a far worse state if I lost my job.'

'She's right, Uncle,' Daniel said reluctantly. 'We might make things worse if we try to interfere.'

Wilmot looked from one to the other, shaking his head. 'This is a sorry state of affairs.' He was silent for a moment, stroking his chin thoughtfully. 'Very well. It goes against all my better judgement, but I'll leave it for now.' He patted Charity on the shoulder and strode out of the shop.

Daniel gave her a sympathetic smile. 'We'll find a way round this. Do you think you could meet me on the corner of Gray's Inn Road after dark?'

'He locks the shop up at night and keeps the key about his person. I'm not allowed out.'

'What about the back yard? Isn't there a gate into the alleyway?'

'There is, but that's locked at night.' Charity had a sudden vision of Violet dancing home after an enjoyable evening out, and she smiled. 'But I know someone who has a key.'

'Nine o'clock this evening,' Daniel said in a low voice. 'Meet me on the corner.'

In the soft buttery glow of gaslights the tree-lined elegance of Doughty Street was like stepping into another world when compared with the commercial bustle and ugliness of Liquorpond Street. The terraced four-storey Georgian houses, with discreet basement areas protected by gated iron railings, exuded a confident aura of respectability and gentility from a bygone age. Charity had vague memories of the street in Chelsea where she had lived as a child, and although their house had been little more than a cottage it had been built in a similar style and roses had clambered over the porch in summer. She could recall the scent even now and she experienced a sudden and overwhelming feeling of homesickness.

Daniel, however, seemed to take it all for granted

as he mounted the front steps and knocked on the door.

'It's very nice here,' Charity said in a hushed tone. 'Is this where you live too?'

'Right now I'm supposed to be at home in the country, but I did rather badly last term so I'm here to do some swotting.'

'And are you?'

He grinned. 'Sometimes, but I'm more interested in working in the field than writing long theses on archaeology. I'm not an academic like my uncle.'

The door opened before she had a chance to comment and a maidservant ushered them inside. 'Thank you, Biddy.' Daniel flashed a smile in her direction, and Charity was quick to notice that the girl blushed to the roots of her hair before scuttling off towards the basement stairs.

'Do you have that effect on all the girls?'

'Of course,' he said modestly. 'All except one.'

'If you mean me, you're wasting your time, Daniel Barton. I'm not interested in romance.'

'Who said it was you?' He tweaked a lock of her hair that had escaped from beneath her bonnet. 'Come upstairs. Uncle Wilmot's rooms are on the second floor. You will stay for supper, won't you?' He bounded up the stairs without giving her time to answer, and she followed more slowly in his wake.

Daniel opened a door on the second landing which led into a large room furnished with an eye to comfort rather than style. A mahogany desk set against one wall was littered with papers and writing materials.

In the middle of the floor was a saggy, well-worn sofa and there were two armchairs, neither of which matched the other. The alcoves on either side of the chimney breast were crammed with books, some of which had overflowed onto the floor, while others were piled up on the small dining table and the three chairs which surrounded it. Faded blue velvet curtains had been drawn across the windows, and the room was lit by a gasolier which fizzed and popped occasionally, emitting a yellowish light. The walls were hung with framed watercolours of seascapes and sailing ships, and the whole atmosphere was decidedly male, cluttered and comfortable. She could imagine Wilmot and Daniel seated on either side of the fire on winter evenings, reading or talking over the events of the day.

'Welcome.' Wilmot rose from a leather chair at his desk and came towards them holding out his hand to Charity. 'I was afraid you might not make it, but you're here now and that's splendid.'

Charity took off her bonnet and shawl and laid them on a chair.

'Sit down, my dear,' Wilmot said, smiling. 'Would you like a glass of sherry wine? I've asked my housekeeper to send up a light supper and coffee.' He chuckled. 'Actually, Mrs Bragg is my landlady and not my housekeeper – a title which suggests that I own the premises or at least rent the whole house. I do not, of course; I am merely a lodger here.'

'My uncle is always precise,' Daniel said, grinning. 'But we are very comfortable and well fed.'

'You are a great deal too comfortable for your own

good.' Wilmot tugged at the bell pull by the fireplace. 'You should be off on a dig somewhere, instead of lounging about and enjoying yourself. Term starts in a few weeks and you'll have to buckle down to some hard work.'

'I know it, Uncle, and I promise that I'll do my best.'

Charity sat down on the edge of the sofa, folding her hands in her lap as she waited for someone to tell her exactly what was expected of her. She could not imagine that she had any useful contribution to make to Wilmot's work, but she was here now and she might as well enjoy her brief time away from Dawkins and all that he stood for. She sat in silence, listening to their banter until the maid brought in a tray laden with plates of cold meat, bread and butter and a dish of pickles.

'Thank you, Biddy,' Wilmot said, nodding in approval as she placed the tray on a table, taking care not to disturb the books. She blushed, and it was obvious to Charity that Daniel was the only person in the room as far as Biddy was concerned. She walked past him slowly, swaying her hips, but he seemed oblivious to her charms.

'Put the poor child out of her misery, and tell her you're not interested,' Wilmot said when she had left the room. 'She has a fondness for you, boy. Heaven knows why.'

'She's a servant,' Daniel protested. 'And Mrs Bragg would beat me with her rolling pin if I dared to flirt with her daughter, which I would never do.'

Wilmot took a seat at the table, pushing aside a pile

of books. 'Come and sit down, Charity. Have some supper and then we can sit and talk. Daniel will see you home, so don't worry about the time.'

Daniel rose to his feet and held out a chair for Charity. She murmured her thanks, wondering if this was how a gentleman treated a lady, or whether Daniel was simply trying to put her at ease. She sat down and glanced anxiously at Wilmot, but he was selecting slices of cold ham and mutton from the serving dish and arranging them neatly on a plate, which he then passed to her. 'Help yourself to bread and pickles, my dear. You look as though you could do with a good meal. I'm sure that miser Dawkins is as mean with his food as he is in nature.' He glanced at his nephew who was about to take his place at table. 'Pour the wine, Dan, there's a good chap. I enjoy a good claret with my meal, Charity.'

Charity was about to refuse when Daniel handed her a glass of wine, but Wilmot insisted that she take a sip. She did, and not wishing to insult him she smiled and nodded, but she would have preferred a glass of lemonade or a nice hot cup of tea. The wine, however, did not taste so bad after a mouthful or two, and it went straight to her head, loosening her tongue and making her relax in their company.

When the meal was finished Wilmot made himself comfortable in a chair by the fireplace and lit a pipe. Daniel sat beside Charity on the sofa and they slid closer together as the middle sagged beneath their combined weight. She edged away, conscious of his presence and feeling suddenly shy. Her head was spinning from the wine and she felt slightly sick after eating too much of the comparatively rich food. 'I really ought to be going,' she said, trying not to cough as tobacco smoke wafted her way. 'It was a lovely meal, thank you, sir.'

Wilmot puffed on his pipe, allowing smoke to trickle out of the corners of his mouth. 'But we haven't even begun our talk. Let's start with your earliest memories. How far back can you remember, Charity, and where were you living then?'

It seemed churlish to insist on leaving when she had taken advantage of his hospitality. Charity thought hard. 'I dunno where to start, sir.'

'Where were you born? Can you remember the house where you lived, and what your father did for a living? You didn't start out begging on the streets; you told me that the first day we met, and I realised that you had come down in the world. When did your parents die? All these things are valuable social comment on our times. I have a huge respect for Henry Mayhew and his research into London's underprivileged classes, but his works were written more than forty years ago, and while they are of enormous importance, things have changed since the middle of the century. Start at the beginning, Charity. I'm eager to hear your thoughts.'

Once she had begun it was surprisingly easy to talk about her early years, and memories of her childhood in Chelsea came flooding back. Wilmot listened attentively, making notes and offering encouragement when she faltered. At one point he reached out and laid his hand on her knee, and although he removed it quickly she had been conscious of the warmth of his touch and the disturbing gleam in his eyes when he smiled. She was caught off guard and had begun to tire; a quick glance at the brass clock on the mantelshelf revealed that it was past midnight, and she leapt to her feet. 'I've stayed too long, Mr Wilmot. I really must go.'

Daniel stood up and yawned. 'Is that really the time? I was so interested in what you had to say that I didn't notice the minutes flying by.'

Wilmot turned away and knocked the ash from his pipe into the empty grate. 'That was a very good start, Charity,' he said casually. 'When will you be free to come again? I would like to keep going now we've begun.'

'I dunno, sir. I just hope I haven't been missed.'

'I'll see you home,' Daniel said, opening the door. 'I'll make sure you don't get into trouble with Mr Dawkins.'

Charity put on her bonnet and wrapped her shawl around her shoulders. 'You and whose army, Daniel Barton?' she said, laughing.

It might be late but Gray's Inn Road was almost as busy as it was in daytime, and the night people had emerged to drink in the pubs or take refuge from life in the opium dens to be found in the narrow alleys and courts. Prostitutes hung about beneath street lamps, smoking and chatting to each other in a desultory fashion as they waited for a likely client. Feral cats roamed the streets, vying for food with rats which were even bolder, seeing off any unfortunate mongrel cur that happened to challenge their supremacy.

With a firm grip on her arm, Daniel escorted Charity to the service alley at the rear of Liquorpond Street, only to find that someone had locked the gate from the inside. 'I'd forgotten what Violet said about climbing the wall.' She eyed it doubtfully. 'I'm not sure if I can manage it without some help.'

Daniel took off his bowler hat and jacket and handed them to her. 'I spent half my childhood climbing trees at home. Give me the key and let's see if I've still got the knack.' He took a few steps back and did a running jump at the wall. He failed at the first attempt but he tried again and this time he managed to get a grip and heaved himself onto the top. With a cheery wave he let himself down, landing on the other side with a dull thud.

The gate whined on its hinges as he opened it and let her in. 'Thanks, Daniel,' she whispered. 'I dunno what I'd have done if you hadn't come with me.'

He took his jacket from her and shrugged it on, placing his hat on his head at a jaunty angle. 'To tell the truth I enjoyed the challenge. I'm not a city type, Charity. The first opportunity I get I'll go on a dig, preferably somewhere warm and sunny.'

'You are so lucky being a man.' Charity stood on tiptoe and brushed his cheek with a kiss. 'Goodnight, Daniel, and thanks again.'

He tipped his hat. 'Always glad to help a lady. Goodnight, Charity. See you again very soon.' He left the yard and she closed the gate, locking it before making her way towards the back door. The whole house seemed to be asleep and for once there was not a sound emanating from the building or its neighbours, but as she entered the scullery she could hear dismal howls and banging, which grew louder as she entered the kitchen.

Chapter Six

'Where the hell have you been, you little trollop?' Jethro lay on the flagstone floor close to his bed. His right leg was twisted at an ugly angle and his face, caught in a shaft of moonlight, was deathly pale. 'Where were you when I needed you?'

Charity rushed to his side and knelt down. 'What happened?'

'Are you blind as well as stupid and immoral? You've been with a man. I can smell him on you.'

'That's not true,' Charity said angrily. 'How dare you say such a thing?'

'You stink of tobacco smoke and Macassar oil. You're a worthless slut and I should have known better than to take you on.'

'We should get you back to bed.' Charity made an effort to sound calm when really she felt close to panic. It was obvious that he had injured himself badly, but she was at a loss as to how to handle him.

'Are you mad? I've broken my hip. I need a doctor. Give me laudanum and go for help.'

Charity reached onto his bed and picked up a pillow, placing it carefully beneath his head. 'All right. I'll do as you ask, but please try not to move. You're only making matters worse.'

He bared his broken teeth in a scowl. 'Don't tell me what to do.'

She rose to her feet. 'I'll fetch your medicine, but you need to go to hospital.'

'No hospital for me.' His voice rose to a high-pitched scream. 'I won't go to one of those places. Never again.'

Having sedated him with a hefty dose of laudanum, and not knowing who else to call upon, Charity sought help from Bert Chapman who was the only man in the building strong enough to lift Jethro. She had to rouse him from his bed and he was sleepy, but comparatively sober. At first he was reluctant to lift a finger to aid a man he obviously loathed, but with a mixture of flattery, persuasion and a bribe of five shillings, Charity managed to persuade him and he lumbered downstairs after her. By this time Jethro was in a drugged state and barely conscious.

'He says his hip is broken,' Charity whispered. 'I think he must have fallen out of bed.'

'It's a pity it wasn't his neck what broke,' Bert said unsympathetically. He bent down and hoisted Jethro into his arms as if he were a sack of feathers instead of a solidly built adult. 'It's not far to the Royal Free Hospital. I'll carry the brute, but I'm not moving a step until you give me what you promised.'

Charity felt under Jethro's mattress for his bunch of keys and unlocked the cash box he kept hidden beneath his bed. She took out two silver crowns and placed them in Bert's hand. 'There you are.'

'Put them in me pocket, dearie.'

She did as he asked. 'Now will you take him to the hospital?'

'Give us a kiss first.'

'What?'

'I said give us a kiss, or I'll dump the old bugger on the floor and break his other hip.'

'That wasn't in the bargain.'

'It is now.' He leaned forward and Jethro's arms dangled limply like a puppet whose strings had been cut.

Charity held her breath, closed her eyes and gave him a peck on the cheek. He threw his head back and roared with laughter. 'That'll do for now, but I want a proper one when we get back. I fancy you, young Charity. You could have all the free beer you can drink if you'd be nice to me.'

A wave of nausea threatened to overcome her but she swallowed hard and backed away. 'We'll talk about that later, Mr Chapman. You've got what you wanted so please let's get Mr Dawkins to hospital before the laudanum starts to wear off.'

Bert followed her through the shop and out into the street. 'With a bit of luck the misshapen monster will die and go to hell. That's where his sort belongs.'

Charity said nothing and she quickened her pace, heading towards Gray's Inn Road.

Jethro was kept in hospital for six weeks. As its name implied, the treatment was free for the poor and destitute, but being a man of significant means Jethro had to pay in part for the care he received and Charity had to find the money. She would have been hard pressed to raise such a sum from the shop takings, but, quite by accident, she had found a secret stash concealed behind a false back in one of the kitchen cupboards. She had discovered it when cleaning up spilt sugar, a small luxury she allowed herself now that she was in charge of the housekeeping money. The wooden plank had fallen down to reveal a cocoa tin, which on further inspection was found to be crammed with five-pound notes. It must, she thought, be Jethro's life savings, and although she would not take a penny for herself she used some of it to pay for his stay in hospital.

It was a relief to be on her own, and she took full advantage of the unexpected freedom to do as she pleased, but she did not neglect her duty as far as the shop was concerned. She opened each day on time and closed at six o'clock in the evening. It was dark by then and winter was on its way, but she resisted the temptation to close at dusk and placed an oil lamp in the window to make sure that passers-by realised that they could still call in and browse or purchase a book on their way home from work. With Jethro safely ensconced in his hospital bed she was able to visit Doughty Street twice a week to have supper with Wilmot and Daniel, who had now resumed his studies. He would sit at the desk, supposedly working on his latest thesis, while Wilmot listened to Charity's account of what it was like to live on the streets and beg for money. When she had exhausted her own experiences she had many stories to recount of the dispossessed forced to live rough and dependent on the charity of others, or eking out a living by selling bootlaces or matches. Even worse off were the toshers who risked their lives searching the sewers for anything of value that might have been swept into the drains, and the pure finders who collected buckets of dog faeces which they sold to the tanneries.

Wilmot made copious notes and encouraged her to talk, and for her part Charity felt that she was the one who benefited most from these quiet evenings. The strange thing was that she had begun to speak in the well-modulated tones that came so easily to Wilmot and Daniel. She had gradually dropped the strident cockney tones she had adopted at a young age in order to melt into the background of her new surroundings. She had learned early on that to use a style of speech and an accent foreign to the denizens of the back streets led to trouble, and she had become one of them. Now, with the benefit of Wilmot's coaching, she had put the recent past behind her and had reverted to the ways of her childhood. Memories of her grandmother's strict edicts on table manners and etiquette came flooding back, and she wondered how she could have forgotten so much in so short a time. She felt as though she had been masked and wearing a cloak of invisibility, and now she had cast it aside and remembered who she was, but this also brought problems. She might be able to converse on almost equal terms with Wilmot and Daniel, but Violet accused her of turning into a stuck-up snob, and Bert was even more vocal.

Since the night she had asked for his help Bert Chapman had not allowed her to forget that she was in his debt. She had managed so far to avoid his clumsy advances, but at night she dared not venture outside to the privy in case he was lurking in the shadows. He had come into the shop on several occasions but, as luck would have it, there had been customers browsing the shelves and Charity had threatened to scream if he laid a finger on her. He had left with the promise that it was not over. He would catch her on her own sooner or later and then she would see what a real man was made of. It was something she hoped she would never discover, at least not from a brute like him.

Jethro's return in the middle of November thwarted Bert's attempts to make free with Charity, and for that she was grateful, but Jethro Dawkins was a bad patient and even more demanding now that he was more or less confined to his bed. He could stagger a few paces with the aid of a crutch, but it was plain that he would never walk unaided, and the doctors had discharged him with the warning that his bones were brittle and would break easily. The only way he could escape from the pain and misery of losing even more of his independence was with laudanum in ever increasing doses. Charity was now his nurse as well as his housekeeper and she worked in the shop, but was no longer in charge. Every evening she had to give the ledger and the takings to Jethro, and he would sit in his chair by the range checking every last penny, and making lists of the replacements they needed. Eventually, and with great reluctance, he allowed Charity to visit the warehouse in his stead.

On these occasions it was necessary to have someone in the shop and Charity immediately thought of Violet, who had learned to read and write and do simple arithmetic at a board school and would be pleased to have the opportunity to earn a few pennies. Violet said she would be happy to leave her younger brothers and sister in the charge of ten-year-old Emmie for a while, but Emmie was not the sharpest knife in the box and she might have to dash upstairs if anything went wrong. It was a solution that was reasonably satisfactory to everyone except for Jethro, who disliked change almost as much as he disliked Violet. 'She's a common little tart,' he said bitterly when Charity put the idea forward. 'I don't want her fingering my books and making eyes at my customers.'

'But I have to go to the warehouse,' Charity said reasonably. 'You can't manage the shop on your own, and it's only for a few hours.'

'I want the door left open so that I can keep an eye on her. I won't have my business turned into a place of assignation for that cheap trollop.'

'Violet is a good girl,' Charity said, biting back a sharp retort. 'She's very willing and she knows exactly what she has to do. If she needs help she'll come and ask you.'

'I don't suppose she's read a book in her life.' Jethro reached for the glass of water laced with laudanum. 'My heart is racing. I think I'm going to die.'

Charity picked up the glass and placed it in his hand. 'You're just working yourself up, Mr Dawkins. Take a sip of this and it will calm you.'

He gulped the mixture and closed his eyes. 'If I find there's a penny short in the day's takings it'll come out of your wages, miss.'

Charity sighed and rescued the glass from his limp hand before it crashed to the floor and smashed. She left him to sleep off the excess of the drug and went outside to call for Violet. If luck was on their side she would return from the warehouse before Jethro became fully conscious and could make things difficult. It was raining and bitterly cold. The raw east wind had carried the chill from Siberia over the flatlands of Essex and it slapped her cheeks and nipped at her ankles. The wooden steps were wet and slippery and she made her way carefully, holding up her skirts so that she did not catch the toe of her boot in the hem.

She had reached the first floor and was about to climb the next flight when the door opened and a hand shot out. She was dragged bodily into the narrow passage and her arms were clamped to her sides. Bert Chapman sought her lips in a rough embrace. She opened her mouth to scream but he was too quick for her and he thrust his tongue into her mouth, pressing her against the wall as he tore at her blouse, sending the buttons flying in all directions. She struggled and kicked out but he was a strong man, used to hefting barrels of beer onto the dray, and he rubbed himself against her in a frenzy of desire. A satisfied grunt escaped his lips and Charity seized the opportunity, nipping his bottom lip and causing the blood to run. He released her with a yelp of pain and she kicked him hard on the shin. She could hear a woman screaming and she realised that the sound came from her own throat as she staggered outside. She retched and gasped for breath but he was close behind her and had her round the waist before she had a chance to escape.

'Leave her alone.' Violet's shout from above gave Charity the opportunity to break free and she hurtled down the steps, sliding down the last of them to land in a heap on the wet ground.

Violet was close behind her. 'Are you hurt?'

Above them Bert was shouting and swearing. 'You'll suffer for this, you stuck-up cow.' He turned on his wife, who had appeared in the doorway, and thrust her inside slamming the door.

'I'm all right,' Charity said, clutching her torn blouse over her bare breast. 'Thank goodness you distracted him, Violet. He almost had me.'

Violet helped her to her feet. 'He's got his eye on you. He may be my dad but he's a wrong 'un.'

'I'll have to change my blouse,' Charity said through chattering teeth. 'I can't go to the warehouse looking like this.'

'You nearly got raped and all you can think about is buying bloody books. What am I going to do with you, Charity Crosse?'

'He won't catch me out again. I'll be extra careful from now on.'

They hurried inside and Violet took up her position in the shop while Charity changed her blouse. She was still shaken, and now that the shock was wearing off she was angry. Bert Chapman was the sort of man who ought to be locked up and punished for his treatment of women, but she knew very well that the law would do nothing. He would have to kill someone before the police would take allegations about him seriously. It was a man's world and women had to deal with it as best they could. She put on her bonnet and a jacket she had purchased at a good price in the dolly shop, and checked that Jethro was still sleeping. She pulled the coverlet up to his chin, thinking how defenceless he seemed as he slept, and she felt a surge of pity for him, despite the harsh treatment she had received at his hands. The world had not been kind to Jethro Dawkins, and he had fought back the only way he knew how. She was about to join Violet when she heard a familiar male voice, and she hurried into the shop. 'Mr Barton, I thought it was you. Have you come to browse or to buy?'

He came towards her smiling. 'I came to see you, but you are obviously on your way out.'

'I've been entrusted with the task of visiting the warehouse in Cheapside to order more books,' she murmured, feeling suddenly shy.

'As it happens, I'm going that way too and there's something very important I have to say to you. Perhaps we could share a cab?'

She was going to refuse, but the thought of walking such a long way overrode her reluctance. 'That's kind of you, sir.' Charity gave Violet an encouraging smile. 'I'll be as quick as I can. Mr Dawkins should sleep until I return.'

It did not take long to find a cab and Charity settled

down beside Wilmot. 'You said you wanted to speak to me, Mr Barton.'

'I've been thinking, and it seems to me that you're wasted working in the shop with Dawkins as an employer. It's slave labour and you could do better. You're an intelligent girl, Charity.'

'Thank you, sir. But I'm happy with matters as they stand at the moment.'

He turned his head to give her a searching look. 'Are you really? You're Dawkins' nurse and housekeeper and you run his business for him, but you sleep under the counter in the shop and you're paid a pittance. He rules your life and keeps you from bettering yourself.'

She frowned. 'I hadn't thought about it like that. I still remember the days when I had nothing and was forced to beg on the streets. I wouldn't want to go back to that.'

'And you won't. I wouldn't allow that to happen, my dear girl. You've been a great help to me in my work, and I think you ought to further your education. I'm offering you the chance to attend some of my lectures and I will give you private tuition.'

'Me?' Charity stared at him in amazement. 'But I can't afford to pay for lessons, and Mr Dawkins wouldn't let me have time off to attend classes.'

'The cost is the least of your concerns, Charity. I'm prepared to cover any expenses in order to give you the education that your late father would have wished for his daughter. You would, of course, have to leave Dawkins to fend for himself and it would be beneficial to both of us if you took a room in my lodging house so that I can supervise your studies. You owe him nothing.'

'But I couldn't just walk out and leave him to cope on his own. He's a sick man.'

'And he's not your responsibility. I'm sure we could find someone to take your place. There are plenty of people who would be glad of a roof over their head in return for a small wage.'

'People like me,' Charity said, turning her head away. 'I was aptly named Charity.' She shot him a sideways glance. 'Why would you do this for me? And how would I live if I wasn't earning anything?'

'I would give you an allowance.' He held up his hand as she was about to protest. 'I'm a confirmed bachelor. I have neither wife nor children to care for, but suddenly I have an opportunity to do something good and I see in you a love of learning that should be nurtured.'

'You have Daniel.'

A wry smile curved his lips. 'I love the boy as if he were my own son, but he has parents who also love him. Daniel doesn't need me.'

'He's very fond of you, sir. That's quite obvious.'

'I'm useful to Dan, and we get on very well together, but he'll make his own way in the world without my assistance.'

Charity was silent for a moment, staring between the horse's ears as it trotted along the busy streets, weaving in and out between costermongers' barrows and horse-drawn vehicles of every shape and size from hackney cabs and brewery drays to private carriages and delivery carts. Wilmot's suggestion was tempting, but impossible. She shook her head. 'It's very kind of you, sir. I'm touched that you should want to help me, but you must see that I couldn't accept money from you, and I have nothing other than my wage at the shop. I wouldn't be able to support myself, let alone buy books and all the things I would need as a student.'

'I was serious when I said I could make you an allowance. I'm not a rich man but I have a small private income as well as my salary from the university, and with no dependants I could well afford to support you while you were studying.'

'I couldn't impose on you like that, sir. I really couldn't.

'You needn't be afraid that I would want anything very much in return,' he said hastily. 'I would be doing it to make myself feel that I was doing some good in the world, which is quite a selfish aim. You would be doing me a favour by accepting.' He laid his hand on her knee. 'And who knows? Maybe you could find a way to be a comfort to a lonely bachelor?'

To her intense relief the cab had pulled into a narrow street lined with warehouses. Charity called out to the cabby to stop. 'I don't think that would suit me at all, Mr Wilmot,' she said, opening the low doors that protected them from the worst of the weather. 'You've chosen the wrong person to proposition.' She opened her purse and was about to give him the fare but he shook his head.

'Don't worry about that. I'm returning to Doughty Street.'

'You didn't need to take a cab at all, did you?'

'It seemed like the only way I could speak to you in private, my dear.' Wilmot climbed down to the pavement and helped her alight. 'Doughty Street, please, cabby.' He leapt back into the cab. 'Think about it, Charity. The offer still stands.'

The cabby flicked his whip and the cab pulled away, leaving Charity standing in the rain. She hurried into the warehouse, putting Wilmot's offer out of her mind as she concentrated on business matters.

It was not until she was on the return journey that she had time to mull over Wilmot's suggestion. Even so, by the time she reached the shop she had come to the same conclusion. It was an impossible dream, and she could not abandon a sick man any more than she could allow Wilmot to support her while she pursued her studies. Vague doubts as to his intentions had haunted her since that first night in his lodgings, despite her efforts to think the best of him. She paid the cabby and carried a box filled with books into the shop.

Violet leapt down from her perch behind the counter. 'I'm so glad to see you. He woke up soon after you left and he was calling for you. I didn't know what to do, so I left him. He's gone quiet now, but I daren't go into the back room in case he starts shouting again.'

Charity dumped the box on the floor. 'Don't worry, Vi. I'll see to him. I expect he just wants another dose of his medicine.' She hurried through to the kitchen, shedding her bonnet and shawl as she went.

At first she couldn't see him. Jethro was not in his bed, or his chair. Then she spotted his crumpled body lying on the floor behind the table.

'Gawd love us, he's dead,' Violet gasped, clamping her hand to her mouth.

Charity threw herself down on her knees at his side. She laid her head on his chest but she could not hear a heartbeat, nor could she feel a breath when she held her hand over his mouth and nose. She sat back on her haunches, staring at him in disbelief. 'Mr Dawkins.' She shook him gently but he did not stir. 'Mr Dawkins, please wake up.'

Violet uttered a loud shriek. 'He'd dead and gone and it's my fault. I should have answered his cries, but I was scared.'

'He can't be dead. I thought he was getting better.' Charity scrambled to her feet, dazed with disbelief.

'What's that?' Violet swooped on a medicine bottle that lay a few inches from Jethro's right hand. 'It's empty.'

Charity took it from her. 'It was almost full of laudanum. He must have crawled over to the table and helped himself to all of it.' She sat down suddenly as her knees buckled beneath her. 'I shouldn't have left him, but I had to visit the wholesaler.'

'I might have stopped him if I'd come when he called.' Violet burst into tears. 'What shall us do?'

'I suppose I should fetch the doctor,' Charity said slowly. 'Yes, that's what I must do. I'll get Dr Marchant, he was his friend.' She rose unsteadily to her feet. 'Will you watch the shop while I go to Old Fish Street?'

Violet backed away, dashing her hand across her eyes. 'Not me. I'm not staying here with a dead body.'

'Then will you go, Vi?'

She shook her head. 'I'd better get back to the nippers. Write a note and I'll give it to Emmie. She'll run all the way.'

Charity put her hand in her pocket and took out her purse. 'No, better than that. Send her to me and I'll get a cab to take her there and bring the doctor back. It's Mr Dawkins' money, but he doesn't need it now.'

Dr Marchant examined the body. 'It was definitely an overdose of laudanum,' he said, shaking his head.

'If I'd been here I would have given him the right amount,' Charity said sadly. 'It was too much to expect Violet to look after him and the shop.'

'It wasn't your fault, my dear. I think Jethro wanted to end it all, and who could blame him? He knew that he wasn't going to get better and he couldn't stand the pain or the humiliation of being dependent on you.'

'But I never complained, doctor. I tried to look after him the best I could.'

'I'm sure you did, and he knew that too.' Dr Marchant handed her a crumpled envelope. 'I found this under his body. I think he had it in his hand when he collapsed.'

'What is it?'

'It appears to be Jethro's last will and testament. It confirms my belief that he intended to end his life.'

Charity stared at the creased paper, but the words danced about like tiny black tadpoles as she tried to make sense of what had happened. 'What will I do now, sir?'

Dr Marchant laid a sympathetic hand on her shoulder. 'I'll contact Wiggins and he'll do the rest.'

'But what will happen to the shop? Who will look after it now?'

'You have the answer in your hand, my dear. Jethro's will must go to probate, but we need to know what his last wishes were. I suggest you open it now.'

Charity dropped the envelope on the table as if it had burned her fingers. 'I'm not related to him. There must be someone.'

'As far as I know he was alone in the world. His mother abandoned him as a baby and he grew up in an orphanage. He was fortunate enough to find work in this shop and was taken in by the previous owner, rather like you. I think that's why he took you on.'

'I can't touch it, sir,' Charity said, taking a step away from the table. 'Will you read it for me, please?'

Dr Marchant took his spectacles from his inside pocket and put them on. He picked up the envelope and opened it, taking out the single sheet of paper. He studied it for a moment. 'I suspected as much, Charity. Here, read it for yourself.'

Chapter Seven

The single sheet of paper fell from Charity's nerveless fingers. 'But he can't have left the shop to me. It's not possible.'

Dr Marchant stooped and picked it up, studying the spidery writing with a puckered brow. 'It's here in black and white, but it seems that the lease has only another year to run and then it must be renewed. The stock was owned by Jethro and that is yours.' He laid the will on the table where it shifted in the draught from the window as if twitched by unseen fingers.

'It's a sign,' Charity breathed, clasping her hands to her chest in an attempt to steady her erratic heartbeats. 'Jethro's trying to tell us something.' She raised her eyes to give Dr Marchant a searching look. 'Has he really left me all those books?'

A tired smile curved his lips. 'It seems so, Charity.'

'They must be worth a fortune.'

'Perhaps they are, but that depends on whether or not you can sell them.'

'I've been managing the shop since his accident,' Charity said thoughtfully, 'but I haven't paid much attention to the business side. I'm afraid I got carried away with my attempts to better myself, Dr Marchant.

I've been spending too much time with Daniel and Mr Barton when I should have been thinking about how I could make the shop do better. Even worse, I've had my head stuck in a book more often than not when I should have been trying to persuade customers to make a purchase.'

He laid his hand on her shoulder. 'Come now, my dear. You're little more than a child. Jethro's business was his own affair and you were an underpaid shop assistant. If trade was poor it wasn't up to you to make improvements.'

'But it is now. The landlord will send the bailiffs in if I can't pay the rent at the end of each month.'

'You've managed so far.'

'Yes,' she said slowly. 'I have, but now I'm on my own.'

Dr Marchant pulled up the one and only chair and sat down. 'I should be on my way, but I have a feeling that there's something else bothering you. I know that Jethro's death has been a shock, and that you felt responsible for him in some way, but that's not all, is it?'

'No, sir.' Charity hesitated as she recalled her conversation with Wilmot. His offer had been startling and it had opened up a whole new world to her. Now she could see it slipping away and with it her chance of making a new life for herself.

'Do you feel you can tell me about it?' Dr Marchant's tone was gentle.

'Mr Barton offered to take me on as one of his students.' The words tumbled from her lips. 'He wants me to go and live in Doughty Street. I could learn to be a lady, Dr Marchant. I could better myself.'

'It sounds like a very generous offer, but are you sure you want to put yourself so heavily in debt to someone you hardly know? Have you considered that there might be strings attached to such a proposition?'

Charity turned away to hide her blushes. 'It had occurred to me, doctor. I'm not sure that Mr Barton's intentions are honourable.'

'I'm an old man, my dear. I've seen much in human nature that is good and a great deal that is bad. I don't know Barton, but I would advise you to think carefully before committing yourself to such a dependent relationship. Jethro's life was blighted by his suffering, but I think he saw more than you imagine. His will gives you a modicum of independence and a chance to succeed without relying on the charity of others. Do you understand what I'm saying?'

'Yes, I think so, doctor.'

He rose from his seat and patted her on the shoulder. 'The decision is yours. And now I must go and pay a call on Mr Wiggins and he'll make all the necessary arrangements. I take it that Jethro will receive a pauper's burial?'

Charity shook her head. 'No, sir. He deserves better than that. He had some money tucked away and I can afford to give him a proper send off. It's the least I can do.'

'I'm proud of you, my dear.' Dr Marchant wrapped his muffler round his neck and picked up his medical bag. 'I'll see you at the funeral. I doubt if there will be anyone else there but us.'

As Dr Marchant had predicted they were the only mourners accompanying Jethro's coffin on the necropolis train to Brookwood cemetery. None of his regular customers had shown the slightest bit of interest in his demise, and even though she had draped the shop window in black crêpe, very few people had offered any words of condolence. Charity had been well aware that her employer was generally disliked, but it saddened her to think that his life had meant so little. He had been unwanted at birth and unloved in death. His legacy was bound in leather and cardboard, crammed together on the shelves in the dingy little shop. She felt responsible for each and every volume.

Charity and the doctor alighted at the north station, which served the nonconformist section in the vast Brookwood cemetery. It seemed appropriate for a man who had long ago abandoned any form of religion, and professed to hate the God that had created him in such a misshapen form. In a brief ceremony Jethro's remains were interred and Charity said a final farewell to the man who had taken her in from the streets. She chose to forget his acts of violence against her person and his meanness, and she shed genuine tears of grief as she threw a handful of soil onto the coffin.

Dr Marchant placed a comforting arm around her shoulders as they battled against a bitter wind on their way back to the station. 'He is free from his crippled body now,' he said gently. 'Jethro Dawkins was a troubled soul and he suffered much.'

'People were cruel to him,' Charity said breathlessly as the wind whipped her veil around her face. 'He had a sad life, but he loved his books. I'll do my best to carry on where he left off.'

'So you've decided to turn down Barton's offer?'

'I told him so last evening. He tried to persuade me otherwise, but I had made up my mind.'

'And what of your friend Daniel?'

'He was sorry, but he said he understood, and he teased me about becoming a shopkeeper.' She tried to avoid a puddle left by a recent downpour but icy water seeped through a gap between the sole and the worn uppers of her boots. She was in desperate need of a new pair, but she had chosen to spend the money on Jethro's funeral. 'I'm going to do my best to make a go of it, doctor. I have a little of Jethro's money left, and that will keep the rent collector off my back for this month at least.'

'There's a return train due any minute now.' Dr Marchant quickened his pace. 'We'll catch it if we hurry.'

'I closed the shop for the morning,' Charity said, lengthening her strides in an attempt to keep up with him. 'But I'll open up when I get back.'

'Really?' He turned his head to give her a worried look. 'You ought to rest, my dear. This has been a very trying time for you.'

'I need to keep occupied and I can't afford to lose even more trade.' She did not add that she had spent half the night studying the ledgers and Jethro's attempts at book-keeping. The shop had been running at a loss, and she must reverse that if she was to stay in business.

Daniel breezed into the shop next morning. 'I've just had some amazing news,' he said cheerfully. 'You'll never guess what it is.'

Charity stopped dusting the shelves, turning to face him with a suppressed sigh. He had obviously forgotten that Jethro was barely cold in his grave, or he simply did not care. 'What news?'

He moved closer, his smile fading. 'Are you all right, Charity? You look a bit peaky.'

'I'm fine, thank you. Just a bit tired.'

'Oh, yes. Sorry, I forgot that the old devil was buried yesterday. At least it's over now and you're a business-woman in your own right. I'd say that was a step up, wouldn't you?'

'Yes, of course. Now tell me what's happened to make you so happy?'

'I've been offered the chance to join an archaeological dig on my uncle's estate in Dorset. One of my professors is in charge and I'll be a very junior assistant, but I'll learn such a lot. It really is the opportunity of a lifetime. Not only will it work towards my degree but I'll be gaining valuable experience, and James Carruthers is the best in the business.'

For a moment she could not speak. Her lips were numb with shock and she could only stand and stare. He was joking, she thought dazedly. It was a ploy to make her laugh and cheer her up, but then she realised that he was in deadly earnest. 'Wh-when did all this happen?'

He gave her a searching look. 'What's the matter? I thought you'd be pleased for me.'

'Of course I am, Daniel. It's just a bit sudden, that's all.'

'The offer came out of the blue. I did rather well last term and apparently it was my tutor who recommended me, which was odd because we've never exactly hit it off. He gave me the news yesterday. I would have told you last evening, but I thought you might be a bit tired after all that business at Brookwood.'

'If you mean Jethro's funeral, then yes, I was tired and upset for his sake. Dr Marchant and I were the only ones who cared enough to attend.'

Daniel looked away, avoiding her angry gaze. 'It's not as if he would know who was there and who wasn't.'

'That's not the point. It's a matter of respect. The man is dead.'

'I'm not going to apologise, Charity. I'd be a hypocrite if I said I was sorry the old devil has met his maker. He was a mean man and he treated you like a slave. You don't owe him anything.'

'That's where you're wrong. Jethro left me all he had in his will. The shop is mine for as long as the lease lasts, and longer if I can make enough money to renew it.'

Daniel's eyes opened wide. 'Well I'm blowed. Who'd have thought it?'

'I know. I'm still a bit shocked, but then he had no one else.'

'Then we've both had a stroke of good fortune.' Daniel threw his arms around her and gave her a brotherly hug. 'You'll be all right and I don't have to worry about you while I'm away.'

She drew back, forcing a smile. 'When are you going?'

'I'll be leaving on Monday.'

'Will you be away for long?'

'Months, I should think. I'll have to return for the spring term at university, but the site might be active for a year or more. It all depends on how well we do and I suppose on the funding. I won't earn very much, but I don't care about money.'

'I'm really glad for you, Daniel.' Charity managed a smile but inwardly she was crying. He had been her one true friend and now he was going away. He would become immersed in his new life and forget all about her. She would have no excuse to visit Doughty Street, and Wilmot would have no need for her now that her contribution to his studies was complete. She felt more alone than she had since her grandfather's sudden death.

'Are you all right, Charity?' Daniel grasped her by the hand. 'You're shivering. I hope you didn't take a chill at the cemetery. The weather was foul yesterday.'

'I'm all right.' She squeezed his fingers gently. 'Don't worry about me. I'm much tougher than I look.'

'I should hope so. A puff of wind would blow you away. You must take better care of yourself.' He took his watch from his waistcoat pocket. 'Just look at the time. I have an appointment with my tailor. He'll have to work fast if he's to make me a hacking jacket and a new pair of jodhpurs before I leave. I've no idea what one wears for such work.' He headed for the doorway. 'I'll see you before I go, of course. You must come to dinner in Doughty Street. I'll ask Mrs Bragg to make something special.' He opened the door and stepped outside. A gust of ice-cold wind rushed in like a customer who had arrived at closing time desperate to make a purchase. It rustled the leaves of books and lifted a pile of leaflets off the counter, scattering them on the floor. The door closed again leaving a chill in the air and silence.

Charity stooped to pick up the papers but as she stacked them tidily on the counter the full realisation of her situation hit her. The book-filled shelves seemed to close in on her, each edition thrusting itself forward and demanding to be sold. The shop and all the stock were now her responsibility, and its success or failure depended upon her efforts and hers alone. She picked up a cloth and dusted the books one at a time, wiping the spines and the covers, giving them a gentle shake to dislodge the city smuts and grit that blew in from the street. She worked patiently and lovingly, treating each volume with the same amount of care. They were precious objects and their pages were filled with knowledge. She loved each and every one of them and the simple repetition of a mundane task was comforting, and brought with it a sense of normality even though events seemed to have been spiralling out of her control.

Business was slack that morning. Perhaps it was the weather that was putting people off venturing out, or maybe it was the fact that Christmas was only a few short weeks away and people were saving their money in order to buy gifts and food for the feast day. Outside the rain had turned to sleet and when Charity looked out of the window she could see ominous fat-bellied clouds hovering above the workhouse, heavy with the promise of snow. Her stomach rumbled and she realised that she had not eaten that day.

She had so far avoided spending much time in the kitchen where the memory of finding Jethro's inert body was still fresh in her mind. She had slept under the counter that night and would probably continue to do so as the thought of lying on Jethro's bed made her feel sick. She had had to brace herself to enter the room that morning in order to make up the fire and boil a kettle, and at midday she made her way outside not daring to look to her right. She had seen Jethro laid to rest in the cold dark earth, but some primitive instinct made the hairs on the back of her neck stand up as she scuttled past the bed where he had endured so much pain and suffering. She covered her head with her shawl and made her way to the privy, treading carefully to avoid the puddles that were skimmed with a thin layer of ice. When she stepped outside again it had started sleeting and she hurried across the yard with her head down, and almost collided with Violet who had just emptied a bucket of rubbish into the communal dustbin.

'What on earth is the matter with you?' Violet demanded, shielding her eyes against the sleety rain. 'You look as though you've seen a ghost.'

'It's Jethro,' Charity murmured, glancing nervously over her shoulder. 'It's as if he's still there. I can't get him out of my head.'

Violet clutched her ragged shawl around her, shivering. 'Have you had anything to eat today?'

'I've been in the shop all morning, and all last night for that matter.'

'You got to eat, even if it's just a crust of bread. Anyway, you're in charge now. You've got the old geezer's money. You can do what you like.' She took Charity by the arm. 'Come inside. I ain't afraid of ghosts and you shouldn't be either. You did what you could for him and he might have been a mean old miser but he was no fool. He knew when he was well off.'

Somewhat reluctantly Charity allowed Violet to have her way. 'There,' Violet said triumphantly as they stood in the kitchen. 'It's just the same as it ever was.'

'But I can still see him in his bed, Vi. I can't bear to look at it, let alone sleep in it.'

Standing arms akimbo, Violet stared at her aghast. 'Do you mean to tell me that you're still sleeping under that blooming counter in a freezing cold shop?'

'I can't face the thought of sleeping in his bed.'

Violet strode across the floor and began ripping the bedding off and tossing it onto the floor. 'This will fetch a couple of bob in the pawnshop, and it's a perfectly good bed. I wish I had such a one. I sleep on the floor top to toe with Emmie, Gertie and Flossie.'

'You can have it,' Charity said recklessly. 'Get someone to take it upstairs and it's yours. I can't bear to look at it.'

Violet pummelled the mattress. 'Lucky I ain't as squeamish as you, love. This is luxury compared to a couple of bags of straw nicked from the brewery stables. I'll get me dad to heft it upstairs.'

'Must you?' Charity struggled to find a way to refuse without hurting Violet's feelings. 'I mean, you know how he is, Vi. Is there someone else who could do it?'

Violet stared at the bed, frowning. 'Maybe it wouldn't be such a good idea.' She thought for a moment. 'I know. I'll get Maisie and her ma to help me with the mattress. Mrs Spinks spends all day lifting heavy pans in the workhouse kitchen and she's got muscles like a bare knuckle fighter; she'll do anything if the price is right.' She tapped the side of her nose. 'She drinks. She thinks no one knows but I seen all the empty gin bottles left out for the dustcart. Anyway, you've got an excuse to visit the second-hand furniture shop in Leather Lane and buy yourself a new bed.'

Charity blinked hard, staring at Violet and seeing a different person from the scatterbrain who crept out at night to meet her latest beau. 'I haven't slept in a proper bed since I was a nipper,' she said slowly. 'Grandpa and I dossed down anywhere we could lay our heads, and I've slept under the counter for so long it seems natural.'

'You're a shopkeeper now, Miss Crosse. I suggest you put the kettle on and we'll have a cup of tea.' Violet gazed round at the empty shelves. 'You wouldn't happen to have any food in, would you? I gave the last slice of bread to young Flossie, and we're broke until Pa brings his wages home tonight. That's if there's any left after he's been to the pub.'

'I don't think so. I wasn't hungry yesterday, but I can make a pot of tea. Jethro always had to have his tea, strong and sweet with a dash of milk.' Suddenly she was crying and she could not stop.

Violet took her by the shoulders and propelled her to the chair, pressing her down on the seat. 'I'll put the kettle on and if you'll give me a few coppers I'll go out and get us something to eat. You'll feel better with a full belly.'

Half an hour later, having eaten a hot meat pie and drunk several cups of sweet tea, Charity was beginning to feel better and Violet was triumphant. 'You've got a bit of colour in your cheeks now, girl. You've got to look after yourself or you'll fall sick.' She licked each finger in turn. 'That was a bloody good pie and it was a treat. I'd have had to share mine with the kids if I'd been at home.' She rose from the bed where she had perched while they shared the meal. 'I should feel guilty for eating like a queen and leaving them upstairs with bread and scrape, but I don't. I go without often enough so that the little 'uns can eat.' She bent down to pick up the soiled sheets. 'Can I have these too? I'll take them to the laundry when Ma does her monthly wash and they'll come up like new.'

'Take them,' Charity said with a wave of her hand. 'And the rest of the bedding. I'll sort something out for myself, but I'll have to wait until I can close the shop before I go out.'

'No, you don't,' Violet said firmly. 'I know you,

Charity. If I leave now you'll get your head stuck in a book and end up sleeping under the counter again. I'll watch the store for an hour or so. I left Emmie in charge and she'll come and get me if the kids play up or do something stupid. Go and get what you need, afore I change my mind.'

The bed was delivered by two strong youths who carried it through the shop leaving a trail of melting snow in their wake. Charity took the opportunity to offer them an extra large tip if they took Jethro's bed and mattress up to the second floor, and they obliged willingly enough when she handed over the money. She suspected that she had been overgenerous but at least it saved her from having nosey Mrs Spinks poking around the kitchen, or even worse having Bert Chapman using it as an excuse to leer at her and make suggestive remarks. He seemed to have forgotten their previous encounter but she had not, and she did her best to keep out of his way.

The brass bedstead, bought in the second-hand furniture shop together with a flock-filled mattress and feather pillow, looked strangely out of place in its new surroundings. Charity had thought long and hard before spending money on sheets and a pillowcase in the pawnshop, but she had eased her conscience by resisting the temptation to purchase a colourful patchwork coverlet. She made up the bed and fetched the old horse blanket from beneath the counter. The smell of the stables still lingered in the coarse fabric, but that was preferable to the stench of the sickroom.

That night she settled down in unaccustomed luxury. Outside the snow was falling steadily and a pale grey light filtered through the window, but the fire in the range radiated heat and, for the first time since she had moved into the shop, Charity was warm and comfortable. She had eaten the scrap of meat pie she had saved from her midday meal, washed down with a cup of cocoa. Her belly was full and she was able to stretch out her limbs without cracking her shins on the wooden counter. She slipped into a deep and dreamless sleep.

She awoke early next morning filled with energy and the determination to make the most of her unexpected inheritance, but even as she entered the shop she realised that she must do something to attract custom. It was dark and dingy and the brightness of the snow-covered street made even more of a contrast. It was hardly welcoming and they were not in a prime selling position. The Holborn Union Workhouse opposite and Reid's Brewery next door did nothing to encourage passing trade, and it was possible to walk past Dawkins' bookshop without noticing it was there. She went to the window and took down the black drapes. Jethro was gone and he wanted her to carry on his work. If she was to attract business she must make the premises look more inviting.

It was still early and she put on her bonnet and shawl, picked up a rush basket and braved the cold. The snow was crisp beneath her feet but the pristine covering on the road surface had been churned up by cart wheels and horses' hooves. Soon the pavements would be a slushy mess, but for the moment the world looked clean and beautiful. She made her way to the nearest street market and filled her basket with rosy-cheeked apples, a handful of wrinkly walnuts and two bunches of holly. The stallholder tried to sell her some mistletoe, holding a sprig over her head and planting a kiss on her cheek, but although it made her laugh she declined his offer.

The heady aroma of hot coffee led her to a stall close to the entrance and she treated herself to a drink and a currant bun, which she ate hungrily. The cold air and exercise had given her an appetite and the hot coffee was just what she needed. On the way home she bought a loaf of bread, a pat of butter and a thick wedge of cheese, but she had spent far more than she intended and she knew that she would have to be extra careful from now on. The rent man called on the last Friday of the month and that was in two days' time. She hurried back to the shop with her purchases, and before she had even taken off her bonnet and shawl she sat down to count her money. She was shocked to realise just how much she had spent, but she had just enough left to keep the rent collector happy. There was little enough for necessities, but she was used to being frugal, and she hoped that her idea of a cheerful window display would entice new customers into the shop.

She opened up on time and spent the morning decorating the window with bunches of holly interspersed with small pyramids of fruit and nuts. She decided to put children's books in the most prominent position, starting with *Alice's Adventures in Wonderland* and *Through the Looking-Glass*. She added the *Adventures of*

Tom Sawyer and a copy of the *Adventures of Huckleberry Finn*. She had found several volumes of Grimms' Fairy Tales on one of the back shelves and slipped these in behind a leather-bound edition of *Treasure Island*. That, she thought, as she stood on the snowy pavement surveying her work, should give well-off parents something to think about when they chose a Christmas present for their sons and daughters.

But sadly the well-off parents did not seem to frequent Liquorpond Street, and if they did travel that way it was probably in a hansom cab or a hackney carriage. Charity sold two children's books that week. The first was to the workhouse master, who bought a copy of *Treasure Island* for his son, and the second was to the brewmaster at Reid's Brewery who purchased *Alice's Adventures in Wonderland* for his youngest daughter. By the time Friday came Charity had been forced to eat the fruit and nuts or starve. The holly berries had shrivelled and fallen off leaving the window display sadly denuded, but she had just enough money to pay the rent.

She sat shivering behind the counter with the exact sum in the cash box, and she was not in the happiest of moods. Daniel had rushed in to say goodbye, apologising profusely for having neglected her all week and the fact that he had not arranged the celebration dinner. He had been busy getting things together and had had to finish his thesis in record time or he would have been in trouble with his tutor. Wilmot had sent his regards, which Charity took as meaning that she had served her purpose, and since she had refused his offer to take her under his wing he had lost interest, and she was of no further use to him.

Daniel had hugged her, promising to write and to return as soon as he had some spare time. When she had asked him if he would be in London for Christmas he had admitted that he would be spending it with his family in Devon. 'I'd ask you to join us, Charity, but my parents are a bit old-fashioned. They wouldn't approve of me inviting a young, attractive, unattached female to stay. You do understand, don't you?'

Charity had understood only too well. She was not the sort of girl that Daniel's mother and father would wish their only son to associate with. She had tried to appear unconcerned and cheerful, but she had wept a few tears after he left, and now she was waiting for Seth Woods, the rent collector. She had disliked him at their first meeting and liked him even less now. Jethro had always dealt with him in the past, but now it was her responsibility. She looked up with a start as the door opened and Woods strolled in. He looks as though he owns the place, Charity thought dismally. He thinks I won't be able to pay, but I can. She forced her lips into a smile. 'Good morning, Mr Woods. I have the rent ready for you.'

He marched up to the counter, his boots leaving wet footprints on the scrubbed floorboards. He glanced round at the full shelves with raised eyebrows. 'Trade is good, is it, miss?'

'Good enough to pay the bills, Mr Woods.' She opened the cash box and counted out the coins. 'The exact amount, I think.'

He took them one by one, counting them as they dropped into a leather pouch. 'That's correct for this month, but it's going up by five shillings at the end of December.'

'Five shillings?' Charity stared at him aghast. 'That's a huge jump, Mr Woods.'

'It's in line with all the other properties round here, miss. Ask anyone and they'll tell you so. If you can't pay, my employer will have to send the bailiffs in and seize goods to that value, as I'm sure you are aware.'

'But it's the middle of winter, sir. Trade will be slack after Christmas. Surely the landlord will allow me a month's grace if I can't raise the exact amount?'

He smiled, revealing two missing front teeth and two rows of rotting stumps. 'Not a chance, girl. Pay up on the dot or face the bailiffs.' He leaned closer and she recoiled at the smell of his breath. 'You might have thought you was well off when Jethro left the shop to you. Well, I'm telling you that he was having a laugh at your expense. The old codger knew that you wouldn't be able to make a go of it. You'll be out on your ear before you know it, and even if you do scrape up the money, you won't be able to afford to renew the lease.' He tightened the strings on the pouch and headed for the doorway. He paused, looking over his shoulder. 'The landlord has had an offer for all the buildings in the block. This time next year you'll all be out on the streets anyway.'

Chapter Eight

Charity could have gone to Wilmot for help, but her pride would not allow her to beg for money from a man she had once thought of as a friend. She had not heard from him since Daniel's departure, and now it seemed obvious that Wilmot had only wanted her while she was of some use to him. Dr Marchant's warning words had made her suspect the motive behind Wilmot's seemingly generous offer to pay for her university education, and had she accepted she would have been forever in his debt. Business might be slow, but at least she had her pride. Not that it was much comfort when she went to bed hungry every night and could not afford to buy coal or candles. Trade had not picked up as she had hoped, and the students on whom they depended so much would not return until the start of the spring term.

At closing time on Christmas Eve Charity knew for certain that she would be unable to find the rent at the end of the month. It was Saturday and the prospect of a lonely Christmas Day filled her with horror. Violet had told her she was welcome to join them for their festive meal of boiled bullock's head and carrots, but Charity had improvised wildly and said that Dr Marchant had invited her to Old Fish

Street for the day. It was untrue, but Bert Chapman was still a menace and she was finding it more and more difficult to avoid him. He worked odd hours at the brewery and she never knew when she was going to find him lurking in the back yard. His poor downtrodden wife was thin and shrewish and spent much of her time scolding her numerous offspring. When she could cope no more she would have one of her funny turns and take to her bed, leaving Violet to manage on her own. It would be better to spend the day alone than to become involved in the family's interminable squabbles.

Next morning the bells of Trinity Church rang out over the silent streets, their chimes like molten silver in the cold crisp air. Charity had not been able to sleep and had risen early. She stood in the back yard, listening to the joyful sound, but to her ears it was a death knell to all her hopes and dreams. When Woods arrived on Friday she would have less than half the rent money, even without the extra cash he had demanded. In a desperate effort to boost sales she had marked down the price of all the stock, but it had not helped.

She stepped over the detritus that littered the narrow pathway through the banked snow and hurried back to the comparative warmth of the kitchen. Her small stock of coal had run out days ago, and she had been existing on bread and water. She had been profligate with Jethro's money, she realised that now, albeit too late. A pauper's funeral would have left her with enough cash to keep the shop going until trade picked up, but even if she starved on the street she knew that she had done the right thing. When all was said and done he had taken her in, given her bed and board, and had named her in his will. She had done her best to make the shop pay, but the purchase of a second-hand bed had been a wild extravagance. She knew now that she had been over-confident in her own ability, and had discovered to her cost that there was more to running a small business than mere enthusiasm. Her youth and inexperience had been her downfall.

Hunger gnawed at her belly like a wild beast that was slowly consuming her. She spent the morning in the shop, dusting the books one by one, and making sure that they had been put back in the correct section and in strict alphabetical order. It was a routine she went through every day, and each volume was like an old friend. She could not neglect them even though she felt sick and light-headed, and she knew she must eat soon or she would not have the strength to go on. The Chapmans' chaotic, ill-tempered household seemed a better prospect than dying alone of cold and starvation, but she could not bring herself to climb the steps and knock on their door. To accept their charity would leave her open to Bert's advances and there would be no turning back, but if the landlord sent the bailiffs to take her stock she would lose everything. If she could not find work she would be reduced once again to begging on the streets. There was only one place where she was assured of a warm welcome, and perhaps Dr

Marchant could advise her on what to do for the best.

'You turn up like a bad penny,' Mrs Rose held the door open. 'Come in, Charity.'

The aroma of roasting goose and simmering plum pudding made Charity's stomach clench with anticipation and her mouth watered. Her hands were shaking as she took off her bonnet and shawl and hung them on the hallstand, and her knees were trembling as she followed Mrs Rose through to the kitchen.

'Charity.' Dorrie rushed towards her, arms outstretched. 'I hoped you come today. Merry Christmas.'

'I – I haven't come to stay,' Charity stammered. 'I mean, I only came to wish you the compliments of the season. I wasn't inviting myself to dinner.'

Mrs Rose gave her a pitying smile. 'Pride goes before destruction and a haughty spirit before a fall, Charity. I'm afraid that's a lesson you haven't yet learned.'

Charity hung her head, unable to look Mrs Rose in the eye. 'I'm sorry.'

'You're all skin and bone, girl. You look like the wretched little starveling the doctor brought home less than a year ago. What happened?'

'I've been foolish, Mrs Rose. I thought I knew everything about keeping a shop and found I knew nothing.'

Dorrie wrapped her arms around Charity's waist, clinging to her as if she would never let go. 'You're not foolish. You're lovely.'

'I'm afraid I made a dreadful mess of things.' Charity stroked Dorrie's wispy hair back from the child's flushed face. 'I was hoping that Dr Marchant could give me some advice.'

'He's out on a call,' Mrs Rose said, sighing. 'The poor man never gets a moment's rest.'

'Will he be long, do you think?' Charity extricated herself gently from Dorrie's grip. 'If you don't mind I could sit and wait.' Her knees buckled and she sank down onto the nearest chair.

'When did you last eat?' Mrs Rose eyed her sternly. 'Dorrie, fetch a cup of milk from the larder and butter a slice of bread.'

'Perhaps I'd better leave now if he's going to be away for a long time.' Charity half rose from the chair but once again her legs gave way beneath her.

'He's gone to help a destitute woman in labour. That man is a saint, if you ask me. He was out half the night and again first thing this morning with no thought for himself.' Mrs Rose took the cup from Dorrie and pressed it into Charity's hand. 'Drink slowly if you want to keep it down. I'd say by the looks of you that you haven't eaten much for days. Hurry up with the bread and butter, Dorrie.'

The milk was rich and creamy and sweet to the taste, but Charity could only manage a few sips. Mrs Rose took the cup and thrust a slice of buttered bread into her hand. 'Eat this and sit quietly. Dr Marchant would never forgive me if I let you go without seeing him.'

'Thank you, ma'am,' Charity murmured through a mouthful of food.

'Get on with your work, Dorrie,' Mrs Rose said

sharply. 'The doctor will want his dinner when he returns and we must have it ready.'

It was early evening when Dr Marchant eventually arrived home. He did not seem surprised to see Charity when he entered the kitchen, but she was shocked by his appearance. Dark circles underlined his red-rimmed eyes and his skin was the colour of aged parchment. 'Are you all right, sir?' she said anxiously.

He gave her a tired smile. 'Just a little fatigued, my dear. But it's good to see you, even though I suspect you have a sorry tale to tell.'

Mrs Rose took his overcoat and hat from him with a disapproving sniff. 'You should take better care of yourself, doctor. You'll be no use to your patients if you take to your bed.'

'Don't worry about me, Enid. I'm perfectly all right and looking forward to my festive meal.'

Mrs Rose held out her hands for his scarf and gloves. 'Dinner will be on the table in fifteen minutes, sir. There's a fire lit in the dining room as it's Christmas Day, and there's a glass of sherry wine waiting for you.'

'What would I do without you, Enid?' Dr Marchant held his hand out to Charity. 'We'll get out of Mrs Rose's way.'

Charity followed him out of the kitchen and along the narrow hallway to the oak-panelled dining room at the back of the house. A fire blazed in the grate and the gas mantles had been lit although it was not yet dark. The wine-red wallpaper and thick Turkey carpet added to the warmth and homely comfort of the room. Dr Marchant pulled up a chair. 'Take a seat, my dear. You look done in.'

'I should be taking care of you, sir. Mrs Rose told me that you'd been called out in the night as well as this morning.'

'Babies come in their own good time. They don't keep surgery hours,' he said with a wry smile as he took his seat at the head of the table. 'Now tell me what brought you here today.'

Charity had not meant to blurt it all out, but once started she had to tell him everything and confess that she had failed. Jethro had put his trust in her and she had let him down. She was about to lose everything.

Dr Marchant listened intently, leaning his elbows on the table and steepling his fingers. 'You mustn't blame yourself, Charity,' he said slowly. 'Jethro must have known that you weren't ready for such responsibility, or else he was not thinking straight at the last.'

'Perhaps I should have accepted Mr Barton's offer,' Charity said miserably. 'With a better education I could find work as a governess or even a schoolteacher, but as it is I'll probably end up begging on the streets.'

'Nonsense. It won't come to that, but it sounds to me that your landlord has planned all along to raise the rents so that he can evict the tenants. It would have been the same had Jethro lived.'

'I just feel that I've failed and I don't know what to do next.'

Dr Marchant looked up as the door opened and

Mrs Rose brought the roast goose to the table, placing it in front of the doctor for him to carve. Dorrie had followed her into the room carrying a tureen of spiced red cabbage and a jug of apple sauce. The appetising smell made Charity feel faint with anticipation. Dorrie placed the dish and jug on the table and sat down next to her. 'I'm allowed,' she whispered. 'It's the one day of the year when I sit with the master and Mrs Rose.'

Dr Marchant picked up the carving knife and fork. 'We are a small family, but today I want to invite Charity to join us.' He cut a thick slice of meat and passed the plate to her. 'It seems that you will be forced out of the shop, but you will always have a home here with us. Isn't that so, Enid?'

Mrs Rose recoiled and her eyes widened, but she recovered quickly and managed to smile. 'Of course, sir. If that's what you wish.'

'I couldn't impose,' Charity said quickly. 'I mean it's very good of you and I'm very touched, but I'm not your responsibility, Dr Marchant. I can take care of myself.'

He continued carving the bird. 'You came here today for my advice, and it seems to me that the answer is obvious. We have plenty of room and I'm sure that Mrs Rose could do with someone to relieve her of some of her household duties.'

'I manage very well, sir.' Mrs Rose pursed her lips, frowning.

'It would only be until Charity has found herself a more permanent position. Her grandfather and I were friends in the old days, before he became addicted to alcohol. I would be letting him down if I did nothing to help his granddaughter.'

'You'll come and live here,' Dorrie said, nudging Charity in the ribs. 'That's the best Christmas present I ever had.'

'Where's the gravy, you stupid child?' Mrs Rose pointed her knife at Dorrie. 'Fetch it at once before the food gets cold.'

Dorrie slid off the chair and raced from the room.

'Walk, don't run,' Mrs Rose called after her. She sighed. 'I hope you're not going to be a bad influence on the child, Charity. She needs a firm hand or she'll never learn how to tie her own bootlaces.'

'Come now, Enid,' Dr Marchant said before Charity had a chance to speak. 'Don't be hard on the girl. It's Christmas Day, after all, and she obviously has a fondness for Charity.'

'Yes, doctor.' Mrs Rose folded her lips together in a thin line of disapproval, but she refrained from making further comment when Dorrie returned with the gravy boat, slopping some on the tablecloth in her haste.

Charity had been about to stand up for Dorrie but she thought better of it. She was grateful to the doctor for his suggestion, but she doubted whether Mrs Rose would be as welcoming.

Dr Marchant said grace and the room was silent except for the clatter of the cutlery on the best china dinner service. If the goose was delicious, the plum pudding was a triumph. The blue flames of heated brandy licked about its glossy surface, filling the room with a heady aroma. Dorrie managed to get the custard sauce to the table without spilling it and Mrs Rose served the doctor first, waiting eagerly for his verdict.

'Wonderful,' he said, wiping his lips on his napkin. 'Another of your culinary masterpieces, my dear Enid. Truly delicious.'

Mrs Rose glowed with pleasure as she passed heaped plates to Charity and Dorrie. 'Thank you, doctor.'

'I remember my granny's puddings,' Charity said, licking her lips. 'But they weren't anything like this, ma'am. It is truly delicious.'

Dorrie had taken such a large mouthful that she was unable to speak. Her thin cheeks were puffed out and a dribble of custard ran down her chin. Charity distracted Mrs Rose's attention by raising her glass of water as she had seen Wilmot do on several occasions when there was something to celebrate, only then it had been a wine glass filled with expensive claret. 'A toast,' she said grandly. 'To Mrs Rose and her unforgettable Christmas dinner.'

Dr Marchant rose to his feet, holding up his glass of sherry. 'Mrs Rose.'

Dorrie choked down the last of her pudding and in her haste to join in somehow managed to knock her glass over. Mrs Rose leapt to her feet and began clearing the table. 'You stupid clumsy little girl,' she hissed. 'We must get the cloth off before the water ruins the French polish. I knew it was a mistake to let you eat with us.'

Dorrie burst into tears and fled from the room.

'It was an accident, Enid.' Dr Marchant rose slowly. 'If the table is marked we can call in the French polisher. It's not the end of the world.'

Charity was already on her feet and had begun piling up the plates. She waited until Mrs Rose had marched out of the dining room with the remains of the Christmas pudding. 'I'll help, sir. Why don't you sit by the fire and rest?'

'I think I might. I'm not as young as I was, Charity.' Moving slowly, as if each step was an effort, he went to sit by the fire. He leaned back in the armchair, resting his feet on the brass fender with a contented sigh.

'I'll help Mrs Rose with the washing up and then I'll be on my way.' She glanced at the window but darkness had fallen and lacy flakes of snow clung to the windowpanes.

Dr Marchant followed her gaze. 'You must stay here tonight, my dear. I won't take no for an answer. It will give you time to think about my suggestion that you reside here on a more permanent basis, or at least until I can find you a more suitable position.'

Charity folded back the tablecloth and mopped up the water. 'No harm done,' she said. 'A little wax polish and a lot of elbow grease will soon set that to rights.'

'Tell Mrs Rose to make up a bed for you,' Dr Marchant said firmly. 'We'll talk more in the morning, but now I'm a bit tired.' He lay back against the cushions and closed his eyes.

Charity picked up a pile of dessert plates and carried them to the kitchen. She could hear Dorrie clattering about in the scullery, and the swish of water as she washed the dishes. Mrs Rose was about to put the remains of the goose in the larder but she stopped in the doorway, giving Charity a questioning glance. 'Well? Has he persuaded you to move in with us?'

'Dr Marchant insists that I stay tonight, but I'll go home first thing in the morning.'

'What will you do when you lose the shop? He found you on the street and that's where you'll end up, I've no doubt.'

'Don't worry, Mrs Rose. I won't accept the doctor's offer to come and live here. It was more than kind of him to suggest it, but I have to make my own way in the world. I'll find work somehow and a place to live.'

Mrs Rose's taut features relaxed just a little. 'It's not that I have anything against you personally, but we have our own ways here, and another person in the house would make life difficult.'

'I ought to help Dorrie with the washing up.' Charity made a move towards the scullery but Mrs Rose held up her hand. 'No need. The girl has to earn her living. It's what she's paid to do and I don't want her to get it into her head that you'll be here on a permanent basis.'

'I think you're very hard on her, ma'am. She's just a child.'

'And children have to learn their place. What use will she be in service if she can't obey orders? I can't have her talking back when I tell her what to do, and if you're here she thinks she can get away with anything.' Mrs Rose put the plate on the marble shelf and closed the larder door. 'Come with me. I'll give you clean linen and you can make up your own bed. I'll send Dorrie up with coal and kindling and you'll be able to make yourself comfortable in the spare room, but it is just for one night.'

'One night,' Charity said tiredly. 'I'll be gone in the morning. You need not worry about me, Mrs Rose.'

'Good. We understand each other.' Mrs Rose sailed out of the room, a bunch of keys jangling on the chatelaine hanging from her belt. Charity had a sudden vision of Enid Rose as a jailer, escorting her to a cell, and it made her even more certain that they would never be compatible. The doctor's house was Mrs Rose's domain and she would bitterly resent intrusion by another female whatever her age or circumstances. Poor little Dorrie was only tolerated because she was a slavey and too young to make a stand.

When she was comfortably ensconced in the double bed with its starched cotton sheets that felt like glass as she slid between them, and a fire burning merrily in the grate, Charity came close to having second thoughts. The wallpaper was patterned with bunches of violets tied with pink ribbons, which matched the cretonne curtains that shut out the cold winter night. Mrs Rose might have her faults but she was an excellent housekeeper, and the rich mahogany dressing table and wardrobe gleamed with polish. The scent of lavender emanated from the clean bedding and was echoed in a faint scent of beeswax polish. Charity lay back against the feather pillows, watching the shadows created by the firelight, and once again her thoughts travelled back to her early childhood and her tiny bedroom in her grandparents' house. That, she thought dreamily, was the last time she had enjoyed the luxury of her own bedroom. She closed her eyes and tried not to think about the future, but in five days' time she might find herself reduced to begging on the streets.

On Boxing Day morning, despite the fact that it was now officially a bank holiday, Charity insisted on returning to the shop. Dr Marchant sent Dorrie out to hail a cab and Charity travelled home in style. He had pressed money into her hand as she was leaving, with strict instructions to spend it on necessities such as food, coal and candles. 'Don't forget, my dear. You will always have a home here should the worst happen.'

His words rang in her ears as she alighted from the cab outside the shop. She paid the cabby and made her way carefully across the frozen snow to unlock the door. She let herself in and the familiar musty smell of books enveloped her as she walked between the stands to the back of the shop. The kitchen was cold and dark and she could feel Jethro's presence as if he were still huddled up on his bed giving her a reproachful stare. She placed the rush basket that Mrs Rose had given her on the table. It had been a parting gift, given, no doubt, in the hope that it would be the last she would see of her master's protégée. A quick glance beneath the spotless white napkin revealed a bundle of candles, a loaf of bread and a pat of butter wrapped in a cabbage leaf. There was also a slab of cheddar cheese and two slices of ham, an apple and an orange.

Charity picked up the fruit and held it close to her face, breathing in its zesty aroma. She had not tasted an orange since her last meal in Doughty Street. Wilmot had peeled one for her and divided it into segments so that it was easy to eat. She felt her throat constrict at the memory. They had been a happy threesome that particular evening. She had felt at ease with Wilmot and Daniel then, and had not foreseen the sudden end to their friendship, but it had happened all the same. Daniel's departure to the wilds of Dorset had left a gap in her life, and it was unlikely that she would have any further contact with Wilmot. She must look to the future now, and her most pressing need was for warmth, but first she would have to brave the cold and go in search of somewhere that was open on Boxing Day. She walked back through the shop and was about to open the door when a hackney carriage pulled up at the kerb. She raised her mittened hand and scraped a circle in the ice on one of the small panes in the half-glassed door. To her astonishment it was Wilmot who alighted first, followed by a younger man. She took a step backward as Wilmot approached the shop. The *Closed* sign was on the door but he rattled the handle and tugged at the chain. The bell clanged noisily above her head and, driven by curiosity, she unlocked the door. Wilmot and his companion entered, stamping the snow off their shoes on the doormat.

Wilmot embraced Charity as if she were a long lost friend, holding her a little too long for comfort.

'Compliments of the season, my dear. I'm afraid it's a bit late, but I've been up to my eyes in preparing lectures for next term and time has flown by. How are you?' He held her at arm's length. 'You look pale, but the light in this emporium is appalling.'

'I'm quite well, thank you, sir.' Charity shot a curious glance at the young man, who was looking round the shop with a disdainful expression on his handsome features.

Wilmot released her with an apologetic smile. 'You'll never guess who this is, Charity.'

Chapter Nine

'Allow me to introduce my step-nephew, if there is such a relationship.' Wilmot turned to the young man who was standing behind him. 'This, my dear, is Daniel's elder brother, Harry.'

'Half-brother, to be exact – Harry Elliott. How do you do, Miss Crosse?' Harry doffed his top hat, and there was a teasing, mischievous gleam in his dark eyes as he took her hand and raised it to his lips.

'How do you do?' Charity met his steady gaze without blinking. She had come across mashers like him in theatre crowds and outside expensive restaurants. They were men who could not resist a pretty face even if the girl was dressed in rags, and she had got Harry Elliott's measure. Even though questions about Daniel buzzed in her brain like a hive of angry bees, she could not bring herself to mention his name. He had obviously forgotten her and she did not want his brother to see how much that hurt. 'I'm afraid the shop is closed today,' she added in an icy tone. 'I was going out.'

'Come now, Charity, that's no way to treat friends.' Wilmot was smiling but there was a warning look in his grey eyes.

'It's my fault entirely, Miss Crosse,' Harry said with

a disarming smile. 'Daniel sent me a note asking me to get a book for him that he could not find locally. He thought you might have it in stock.'

'Then why didn't he write and ask me? We were good friends, or so I thought.'

'You know Daniel,' Harry said casually. 'He's not the most thoughtful chap in the world, and anyway he knew that I was duty bound to visit our mother at some time during the twelve days of Christmas.'

'I don't see that it matters who he asked to find the wretched book. I'll look for it myself.' Wilmot moved away and began browsing, and there was an awkward silence.

'I seem to have put my foot in it,' Harry said, grinning. 'Tact and diplomacy were never my strong point. Have I offended you, Miss Crosse?'

'No, of course not.' She met his amused gaze with a steady look. 'Are you an archaeologist, Mr Elliott?' He was as unlike Daniel as it was possible to be when they were so closely related. Whereas Daniel was not much above medium height, his half brother was a good head taller, and his hair was much darker and waved back from a high forehead. Daniel had boyish good looks, but his brother had a cynical, world-weary look. His hand, when he touched her fingers, was satin smooth, as if he had never done a hard day's work in his life, and she suspected that he was more at home at the gaming tables or at the races than he was in the country.

'Good Lord, no. I'm what you might call a gentleman of fortune.'

'You're a gambler?' Her first impression of him had been correct, and she could not keep a note of triumph from her voice.

'I've been known to play the tables occasionally, and you are a shopkeeper. Aren't you rather young to be bound in leather and condemned to spend all day in this dreary emporium with only books for company?'

'I love books,' Charity said with a break in her voice. 'And I'm seventeen today, as it happens.' Until that moment she had all but forgotten her birthday. Since Jethro's untimely death her mind had been focused on survival, and in the past such anniversaries had meant little. Life had been a struggle when she was trying to prevent her grandfather from ending up in the gutter, and it was not much easier now.

'Wilmot, did you hear that? This young lady is seventeen today. I think that calls for a celebration, don't you?'

Wilmot appeared from behind one of the stands clutching a heavy tome. 'Most certainly, Harry. What do you suggest?'

'How about the Café Royal?'

'Excellent notion,' Wilmot said, slamming the book down on the counter. 'Allow me to pay for this, Harry. Consider it my Christmas gift to Daniel. I've missed the boy.'

'He's only happy when he's up to his armpits in mud and shards of ancient pottery. I expect he'll be bored to death with my mother and stepfather in Devon, which is why I seldom visit the family home.'

'So you're not exactly a dutiful son.' Wilmot took a leather wallet from his pocket. 'Have you change for a five pound note, Charity?'

She shook her head. 'You must know that I can't, sir.'

He delved in his pocket and took out a golden guinea. 'Will that suffice?'

'The book is twelve and six, Mr Barton, as you will see if you look inside the cover.' She moved swiftly round the counter and unlocked the cash box, taking out four florins and a sixpenny bit, which she handed to Wilmot in exchange for the guinea. The sale of an expensive volume meant that she had almost enough money for the rent at the old rate. Perhaps Woods might allow her time to find the extra, or give her a month to make up the shortfall. Maybe this was the turning point and she had Daniel to thank for a second chance.

Wilmot put the change in his pocket, staring at her expectantly. 'Are you ready?'

'Ready for what, Mr Barton?'

'To come with us to the Café Royal, of course.'

'Look at me, sir,' she said in a low voice. 'Do I look like someone who would be welcome at a place like that?' She was uncomfortably aware of the soaked hem of her skirt where it had trailed in the snow, and the patch she had inexpertly sewn on to cover a tear in the material where it had snagged on a protruding nail in the back yard. The only other clothes she possessed were a faded cotton frock, or an even shabbier serge skirt and a blouse with frayed cuffs.

Wilmot shrugged his shoulders. 'You look all right to me. A bit shabby, maybe, but who's going to look at you?' He threw back his head and laughed. 'Harry and I will be the peacocks today. We had best enjoy the moment.'

'I suggest we get a cab to Fleet Street,' Harry said, ignoring Wilmot's crass remark. 'We could try one of the chop houses there, and maybe a visit to the Gaiety Theatre would be in order. A new play opened on Christmas Eve with Nellie Farren and Fred Leslie in the lead roles.'

'A play?' Charity could hardly believe her ears. She had often stood outside theatres begging from the wealthy patrons, but to go inside one would be a new and exciting experience. She forgot everything else in her enthusiasm. 'I'd love to go to the theatre. What play is it?'

'*Frankenstein, or The Vampire's Victim*. It sounds suitably chilling, don't you think?'

Replete after an excellent meal in the Old Cheshire Cheese, Charity sat in the stalls between Wilmot and Harry. The musical burlesque did not seem to be going down well with the rest of the audience, but she loved every moment of the bizarre drama. It was both shocking and fascinating to see the famous Nellie Farren, darling of the London stage, in the role of Dr Frankenstein with Fred Leslie as a somewhat effeminate monster. When the final curtain fell Charity clapped until her hands were sore, but Wilmot rose from his seat and hustled them out of the theatre.

'Absolute rubbish,' he said angrily. 'That was a waste of money.'

'It wasn't that bad,' Harry said, grinning. 'I've seen worse.'

'Hail a cab, there's a good fellow. I can't wait to get home and have a hot toddy before turning in.'

Charity stood ankle deep in snow, shivering. She had thoroughly enjoyed the experience, but Wilmot's angry words had made her feel that she was to blame for ruining his evening. Harry took off his overcoat and wrapped it around her shoulders. 'There's no need to labour the point, Wilmot. This was Charity's treat and I think she had a good time.'

She felt the warmth of his body in the thick cashmere coat and the faint aroma of bay rum and Macassar oil clung to the garment. She managed a tired smile. 'Thank you, yes. I loved every minute of it.'

'Which just goes to prove that education would have been wasted on you, Charity.' Wilmot stepped off the pavement to flag down a hackney carriage.

'That was uncalled for,' Harry said angrily. 'I don't know what's been going on between you, but you have no right to speak to her like that, Wilmot.'

Charity tugged at his sleeve. 'It doesn't matter.'

'Yes, it does. I'm no saint, but I wouldn't talk to anyone in that manner.'

Wilmot turned on him. 'It's a private matter and one which is no longer relevant.' He wrenched the cab door open as it drew to a halt and climbed inside. 'Get in, Charity. We'll drop you off first.'

Harry handed her into the cab and she sat opposite

Wilmot, huddling down inside Harry's coat. 'Thank you for taking me out,' she said in a low voice. 'But there was no need to insult me in front of a stranger.'

'I'm hardly a stranger,' Harry said, making himself comfortable beside her. 'We've had a very pleasant evening together and that makes us friends.' He leaned towards Wilmot. 'I'd say an apology was in order, wouldn't you?'

'Go to hell, Harry. I'm not apologising for speaking the truth. Charity was paid to tell me about the sordid life she'd led begging on the streets. I treated her extremely well considering the fact that I'd plucked her from the gutter. She's done well for herself since then.'

'No thanks to you,' Charity said angrily. 'It was Dr Marchant who found me a place with Jethro.'

'The old freak couldn't get anyone else to put up with his weird ways. I taught you how to behave in company and how to speak properly.' He leaned back against the squabs, closing his eyes. 'Wake me when we get to Doughty Street, Harry.' He opened one eye. 'You've had all you're going to get from me, Charity, so don't come begging at my door when you're thrown out onto the streets.'

Harry banged on the roof of the cab. 'Stop here, cabby.'

'What's the matter?' Wilmot opened his eyes. 'We can't be there yet.'

'I'm going to see Charity home, but I'd prefer not to travel with a jumped-up schoolmaster who thinks he's a cut above everyone else simply because he's got a university degree. You're a boor and prig, Wilmot.'

He thrust the door open and leapt to the snowy ground. He held his hand out to Charity. 'We'll get another cab.'

'I used to think the world of you, Mr Barton,' Charity said as she slid towards the open door. 'But now I see that I was mistaken.' She alighted from the vehicle with Harry's help and he slammed the door.

'Take the gentleman to Doughty Street, cabby.'

Charity's boots had leaked and despite the cashmere coat she was chilled to the bone. 'Thank you for standing up for me,' she said through chattering teeth.

'I hate bullies.' Harry placed his arm around her shoulders. 'Let's get you home before you catch pneumonia.' He raised his arm to hail a hansom cab but it drove past them. 'I'm sorry your birthday ended on a sour note.'

'It doesn't matter. I had a lovely time at the theatre and I enjoyed my dinner. I'm just glad now that I didn't accept Mr Barton's offer to take me in and further my education.'

'So that's what he called it. I think you had a lucky escape. Anyway, let's walk on. There'll be another cab along soon, but we need to keep moving.'

'You should have your coat. You'll be the one to fall sick.'

'Not I. I'm tough as an old boot, and there's enough alcohol in my veins to keep me warm for hours, if not days.'

She frowned, casting him a sideways glance. 'You shouldn't drink. It killed my grandpa.'

'And it will probably do for me in the end, that's if I don't get shot by a jealous husband or murdered by one of the London street gangs who run the gaming houses.'

'Is that really how you live?'

'I'm not the sort of chap you should associate with, young Charity. If your grandpa was alive now he'd tell you to avoid gamblers like the plague, and he'd be quite right.' He hailed another hansom cab and this time it pulled in and stopped.

By the time they reached Liquorpond Street Charity had told him all about herself, sparing no detail about life on the streets or the occasions when she had been desperate enough to steal food for herself and her grandfather. She confessed to being profligate with Jethro's money with a break in her voice.

'You mustn't blame yourself,' he said sternly. 'Giving the old man a proper burial was the decent thing to do. I don't think I would have been as forgiving or as generous, but you did what you thought was right. As for me, I always know what is right but more often than not I do the exact opposite. I admire your courage, Charity Crosse.'

'We're here already,' Charity said as the cabby reined his horse in. 'Thank you for everything.'

'Don't mention it. I enjoyed myself. It was a refreshing change from smoky gaming halls or spending the evening humouring Wilmot. He's not an easy man to get on with.' Harry alighted first and helped her to the ground. 'Wait for me, cabby. I'll only be a minute or so.' He took Charity by the arm, and although she was perfectly capable of navigating the slippery pavement on her own, she did not protest. He stood by while she fumbled in her pocket for the door key and followed her into the shop. She made her way to the counter and lit a candle.

'Will you be all right?'

She took off Harry's overcoat and handed it to him. 'I'm used to being on my own. Thank you for the loan of your coat, and for the evening out. It was all lovely.'

'I'm glad you had a good time. It's not every day you turn seventeen. Goodnight, Charity.'

It was only when she locked the door after him that she realised he had not picked up the book for Daniel. 'I don't know where to send it,' she said out loud as she made her way through the shop to the kitchen. The air was dank and her breath steamed around her head. She could feel the coldness rising from the flagstones and the windows were filmed with ice. A cup of hot cocoa would have been more than welcome but she had forgotten to buy coal and kindling and the range seemed to glare sullenly at her, baring its bars like blackened teeth in a rictus grin. She climbed into bed fully dressed, only stopping to take off her sodden boots and stockings. She pulled the coverlet over her head and curled up in a ball.

She lay shivering with Wilmot's spiteful words echoing in her ears as sleep evaded her. There had been an element of truth in them, which made it even worse. Wilmot had said that she might end up on the streets, but she would not allow that to happen. One way or another she would make something of her life. She would become a person who counted for something and no one, not even an important and well educated man like Wilmot, could take away her spirit or her ambition. She grew calmer as warmth seeped into her chilled bones and gradually drowsiness overtook her and she drifted off to sleep.

First thing in the morning she went out to buy the necessities needed to get through the next couple of days. She had until Friday to scrape up the rent money, and selling the book to Wilmot had helped, but she did not have quite enough. She staggered home carrying a bag of coal and a bundle of kindling, and after a few abortive attempts she managed to get the fire going. Within minutes the flames were licking around the coal with tongues of orange and blue. The kettle began to simmer on the hob and the aroma of toast filled the kitchen; the ghosts that haunted the night vanished as a feeble ray of sunlight filtered through the window. She speared a second slice of bread with the brass toasting fork and held it close to the fire.

She was just finishing her breakfast when the shop bell jangled noisily on its spring. She leapt to her feet and went to investigate. A customer this early in the morning was a good start to the day.

'Good morning, Charity. I've come to collect Dan's book.' Harry stepped over the threshold, taking off his top hat with a flourish. 'How are you today?'

'You're up early. I thought you were a night person who didn't rise until midday.'

'I plan to catch the eight thirty train from Paddington. My mother will never let me hear the last of it if I don't visit her before New Year.'

Meeting his smiling gaze she remembered blurting out her entire life story during the carriage ride home and her cheeks flamed with embarrassment. She took refuge behind the counter, searching for the book, although she knew very well that it lay where she had left it the previous evening. She wished that she had held her tongue. Only a child or a simpleton would have admitted to petty crimes and recounted the sordid details of life on the streets. She snatched up the book. 'Shall I wrap it for you? It might get damaged during the train journey.'

'I'll put it in my valise amongst my unmentionables.' He moved closer, studying her flushed face with an amused grin. 'I do believe you're blushing, and I thought you were a woman of the world.'

'You're teasing me and it's not fair.'

'You're a sweet girl, Charity, and very pretty into the bargain. Take my advice and keep away from men like Wilmot and me.' He leaned over to take the book and kissed her on the cheek.

She watched him walk out of the shop and out of her life. He had treated her like an equal, and now he was gone. Like Daniel he had come into her world briefly and now he had returned to his life, which might as well have been on a distant star, and she was left with only her books as companions. She picked up her duster and began her morning routine, but she had barely finished the first stand when Violet burst through the kitchen door as if the devil himself were on her heels.

'What's the matter?' Charity demanded anxiously. 'Is there a fire?'

Violet collapsed in a heap on the floor. 'Worse, much worse.'

Charity dropped the duster and rushed over to lift her to her feet. 'What's wrong? Has your father beaten you or your poor mother? Are the little ones ill?' She helped Violet to the chair behind the counter.

'My pa will kill me when he finds out.' Violet buried her head in her hands, babbling incoherently, and tears spurted out between her fingers.

Charity took her by the shoulders and shook her. 'Calm down. Take a deep breath and speak slowly. I can't understand a word you're saying.'

'It's me. I'm the one who's made a dreadful mistake.' Fresh tears ran unchecked down Violet's cheeks. 'I – I'm in the family way and I dunno what to do.'

'You're going to have a baby?'

Violet glared at her. 'My, aren't you the bright one? That's what I said, didn't I.'

'But are you sure? It could be a false alarm.'

'I've seen Ma go through it more times than I care to remember. I've been sick in the mornings and I haven't started yet. It's been three months and nothing.'

'I'm so sorry, but have you . . .' She hesitated. 'I mean did you? You know what I mean.'

'Only standing up in the alley. He said it was safe that way.'

'Who is he?'

'It could have been Arthur or maybe it was Sid. They both promised me that I'd be all right.'

'They were both wrong then. I don't know much about it, but I've seen a lot of girls get into trouble because they listened to blokes' sweet talk.' Charity gave her a hug and then released her with a sigh. 'I thought you had more sense, Vi. But what's done is done.'

'If that's all the sympathy I get from you I might as well throw meself in the Thames and be done with it.' Violet paced the floor, wringing her hands.

'Come into the kitchen. I'll make you a cup of tea and we'll think what to do next.'

'A cup of tea isn't going fix me up. I need to find someone who can get rid of it for me.'

'No.' Charity raised her voice in alarm. 'No, you mustn't even think of going to one of those old crones. They'll do more harm than good.' She glanced over her shoulder as someone rattled the door handle. 'Go into the kitchen. I'll serve the customer and I'll be back in two ticks. Put the kettle on, it'll give you something to do.' She hurried to greet the man who had strolled in and was looking around with a baffled expression. 'Can I help you, sir?'

'I need a railway timetable. Do you keep them here, miss?'

'You'll need to go to the station, I'm afraid, sir. I only sell books.'

'You're no bloody good then, are you?' He marched out, slamming the door behind him.

'Some people have no manners,' Charity muttered as she hurried into the kitchen. She found Violet slumped on the bed, sobbing. 'Oh, Vi. This won't do. You have to face up to things.' She put the kettle on the hob. 'You've got to tell the one you think might be the father. Perhaps he'll do the right thing by you.'

Violet raised her head to give Charity a scornful look. 'They'd only deny it or blame each other. I'm done for. Ma will throw me out, if Pa don't kill me first.'

'What do you want?' Charity said gently. 'It's your baby and no one should tell you what to do.'

'It's all right for you to talk,' Violet said bitterly. 'You aren't three months gone.'

Charity busied herself making a pot of tea. 'I'm trying to be practical, Vi. I'm only thinking of you.'

'I know. I'm sorry, but I'm scared. I dunno what to do.'

'There's one person who might be able to help you. We'll go and see Dr Marchant this evening after the shop closes. Can you get away without them suspecting anything?'

'D'you really think he'd help a girl like me?'

'He's a wonderful man. I don't know where I'd be without him.'

Violet managed a watery smile. 'I'll come down as soon as I've given the nippers their supper. Ma's doing a shift in the workhouse kitchen tonight, and Pa will be in the pub, as usual.'

* * *

Charity closed the shop early. She had only had two customers all day, and the second one had been a student who was looking for cheap second-hand books. In the end she had taken pity on him and let him have the volume he needed at less than half price. She tried not to think of what Jethro would have said in the circumstances, but a few pennies here or there was not going to make much difference when Seth Woods came to call.

She went to the kitchen and snatched a hasty meal of bread and cheese while she waited for Violet to put in an appearance, but an hour went by and then another and there was no sign of her. Charity had almost given up hope when someone tapped on the back door. She hurried through the scullery and opened it to find Violet shivering on the step. 'Come inside.'

'I can't,' Violet said, clutching her shawl around her skinny shoulders. 'I said I was going to the privy. Me dad came home early, and he was drunk but not the sort of drunk that makes him pass out. I've got to get back before he gets suspicious.'

'Don't worry. We'll go tomorrow or whenever you can get away. I don't suppose another day or two will make much difference.'

'I'm counting on him, Charity. It'll be the river for me if he can't do anything about my problem.' She backed away and was swallowed up by the darkness.

It was not until Thursday that Violet had a chance to get away. The weather had taken a turn for the worse and sleety rain had turned the snow into slush. Charity insisted on taking a cab to Old Fish Street, despite Violet's protests. 'We'll both die of pneumonia if we walk there,' she said, hoping that Seth Woods would be sympathetic when he came to collect the rent next day. Somehow her own problems seemed small in comparison to what had happened to Violet. The world was cruel and unforgiving to unmarried mothers and their babies. At best it would be the workhouse for Violet and at worst she might carry out her threat to end it all.

'You're too good to me. I don't deserve a friend like you.' Violet's bottom lip trembled ominously as she stood beside Charity on the pavement outside the shop.

'Don't cry,' Charity pleaded. 'There's a cab. We'll soon be there.' She stepped off the kerb and waved, heaving a sigh of relief when the cabby reined his horse in and it stopped. 'Old Fish Street, please, cabby.'

'I ain't never took a cab in me life,' Violet said breathlessly as she climbed in beside Charity. She glanced round furtively and wrapped her shawl around her head, covering her face. 'I'll be a dead duck if anyone sees me.' She huddled down and refused to budge until the cab drew to a halt outside the doctor's house.

'We're here,' Charity said, nudging her in the ribs.

Violet almost fell in her haste to alight from the cab. 'I'm scared,' she said in a hoarse whisper. 'Maybe we should just go home.'

Charity paid the cabby and he drove off. She gave Violet an encouraging smile. 'Be brave. We've come this far . . .' She broke off suddenly as she turned towards the house and realised that the curtains were drawn, and there was a wreath on the front door, tied with a black ribbon. It could only mean one thing and her heart was hammering against her stays as she raised the knocker and let it fall.

Dorrie opened the door and Charity knew by her red eyes and stricken expression that the worst had happened.

Chapter Ten

Dorrie threw herself into Charity's arms. 'He's gone. The doctor died yesterday morning. It were so sudden.'

Mrs Rose appeared in the hallway, dressed in deep mourning. 'I was going to send word to you, Charity, but I haven't had time to think since . . .' Her voice trailed off and she dabbed her eyes with a handkerchief.

Charity disentangled herself from Dorrie's frantic grip. 'What happened? Was it an accident?'

Recovering her composure, Mrs Rose grabbed Dorrie by the arm. 'Come inside, you silly girl.' She gave her a shake and pointed her in the general direction of the kitchen. 'Get back to work. Mr Marchant wants his supper and you can take it to him. I'm leaving.'

Violet had started to sob hysterically and Charity had to drag her bodily over the threshold.

'What's the matter with the girl?' Mrs Rose demanded impatiently. 'If she's ill she'll have to find another physician.'

'She's not sick, ma'am. We came to see Dr Marchant for advice.'

'Well you won't be getting any of that here. The doctor took sick with cholera. He must have caught it on Christmas Day when he attended the homeless woman.

I told him not to go but he wouldn't listen. Those people are little better than sewer rats. I don't doubt that he caught the infection there, breathing in the miasma from the filth and mud. Two days, that's all it took.'

'I'm so sorry, Mrs Rose. I know you were devoted to him and I loved him too.' Charity struggled to support Violet's weight.

'It's a pity his own flesh and blood didn't show him as much respect.' Mrs Rose pursed her lips as if she had been sucking a lemon, and her eyes flashed angrily. 'His son never visited unless he wanted something. He didn't care for his father like I did, but he was quick enough to put in an appearance the moment he heard his pa had died. He's here now, going through the doctor's things.'

Violet made a choking sound and collapsed against Charity in a dead faint.

'You say she's not sick, but she doesn't look too good to me, and you won't get any help from the doctor's son,' Mrs Rose said, curling her lip. 'He works in a bank, and he intends to sell up and keep the money for himself. I'm no longer needed here, and I walk away without a penny. That's all the thanks I get for twenty years' faithful service.'

Charity's knees almost buckled beneath Violet's weight. 'Would you be kind enough to pull up a chair, Mrs Rose? I can't support her much longer.'

Mrs Rose obliged with a disapproving sniff, and Charity settled Violet on the seat, fanning her vigorously with her hands. 'She's in the family way, Mrs Rose. It's not catching.'

'The silly girl's plight has nothing to do with me. I need to get to the station and catch a train for Brighton. I sent my sister a telegram this morning informing her of my impending arrival, but we were never close.' Mrs Rose picked up a suitcase and a carpet bag. 'I don't know how she'll receive me.' She headed for the door, but Charity barred her way.

'What about Dorrie? Will Mr Marchant look after her?'

'He said she can stay on until morning and then she has to find another position.'

'But she's just a child, Mrs Rose. How will she manage on her own in the middle of winter? Can't you take her with you?'

'I'm not responsible for the girl. She'll have to take her chances like the rest of us. Now let me pass. I have to find a cab and it's getting late. I'd have left hours ago but Mr Marchant insisted that I cook his supper and made his bed up for the night. He's dining on lamb chops and cabbage as we speak, and his father's lying in the funeral parlour with no one to keep vigil during the night. I wouldn't work for that man if he paid me a king's ransom.' Mrs Rose put her cases down briefly while she opened the front door. It swung shut after her, as if the house itself were casting her out.

A moan from Violet made Charity turn her head. 'Sit quiet for a moment, Vi. I'll fetch you a glass of water.' She tried to move, but her limbs felt leaden and she was unable to put one foot in front of the other. The shock of Dr Marchant's death was just beginning to sink in and had robbed her of the ability to move. She had lost the one person left in the world who cared about her and that doubled her grief, but she could not cry. She stood like a marble statue, hardly able to breathe.

'Who the hell are you?'

The sound of a man's deep voice made Charity turn with a start. She knew it must be Dr Marchant's son, but somehow logic had deserted her along with the power of speech and she stared dumbly at him. He erupted from the dining room, repeating the question. 'Who are you? Don't you know that my father is dead? The doctor is not here.'

'H-he was my f-friend.' The words tumbled from her lips but her voice sounded strange even to her own ears. It was as if a stranger was speaking for her. 'He was my dear friend, and now I'll never see him again.' She struggled to hold back a sudden rush of tears.

'My late father was everyone's friend, except mine.' Mr Marchant glared at Violet. 'What's the matter with her? If she's ill you've come to the wrong place. You must leave immediately.'

His harsh tone cut through the silken ties that had tethered Charity's emotions and she burst into tears. 'Dr Marchant was a saint. You are a bad son.'

'Get out.' He strode to the front door and opened it. 'Get out now or I'll call a constable.'

Charity dashed her hand across her eyes, choking on a sob. 'I – I'm going.' Fuelled by anger she dragged Violet to her feet. 'Come on, Vi.'

Violet's eyes rolled back in her head and she slid to the floor in a dead faint.

'For God's sake, what sort of play-acting is this?'

Marchant's strident tones echoed throughout the house. 'Dorrie! Fetch a bucket of cold water. That will bring the trollop round.'

Dorrie stepped out of the shadows, her face a pale oval in the half light. 'You are a wicked man,' she cried, her voice breaking on a sob. 'The doctor loved Charity like his own daughter. I heard him say so.'

'Get out, all of you.' Marchant crossed the floor and hefted the unconscious Violet over his shoulder, ignoring Charity's protests. 'I'm throwing you all out, and that goes for you, Dorrie, you useless child. I don't want you in my house a moment longer.'

He reached out with his free hand and grabbed her by the ear, dragging her after him as he headed for the front door. Charity tried to intervene but he elbowed her out of the way as he dumped Violet unceremoniously on the top step. He released Dorrie so suddenly that she stumbled and fell, landing in a heap on the pavement.

Charity hesitated in the doorway, drawing herself up to her full height, although she was still a head and shoulders smaller than her aggressor. 'Your father would be ashamed of you,' she said icily.

He went inside and slammed the door in her face. She bent down to help Violet up. 'Come on, Vi. Let's get you home.' She hooked her arm around her shoulders. 'Are you hurt, Dorrie?'

Dorrie scrambled to her feet. 'No, miss.' She brushed her fair hair back from her forehead, leaving a streak of mud on her face. 'What'll I do, miss? I got nowhere to go. I'm frightened.'

'You'll come home with us,' Charity said firmly. She looked up and down the street but there were no cabs in sight. 'Take Vi's hand, Dorrie. We'll go and find a cab. You mustn't be afraid – I'll look after you.'

Outside the shop in Liquorpond Street Charity paid the cabby. She was uncomfortably aware that she would not be able to give Seth Woods the full amount of rent, let alone the extra five shillings he had demanded, and even worse, she had failed to get help for Violet, who had sunk into a deep depression. She had barely said a word during the journey home from Old Fish Street, although Dorrie had made up for her silence by chattering volubly. With a child's optimism she seemed to have taken it for granted that Charity would make everything turn out well. Charity herself was not so certain. Unless she could persuade Woods to give her more time to make up the difference the bailiffs would be sent in, and then she would have little or nothing to sell. She would spiral into bankruptcy and lose everything. She turned to Violet with an attempt at a smile. 'Try not to worry, Vi. We'll think of something.' She took the key from her reticule and let them into the shop, locking the door behind her.

'Is this where you live, miss?' Dorrie looked round, wide-eyed. 'Are these books yours?'

Despite the seriousness of their position, Charity had to smile. 'Yes, in a manner of speaking, I suppose they are.'

'You must be very rich, and very clever if you've read all them words.'

Violet leaned against the counter. 'I can't face the family,' she murmured. 'I'm done for, Charity.'

'Don't say things like that, Vi. We'll find a way.'

'There's no escaping from this.'

'What's up with her, miss?' Dorrie peered up at Violet, her small face creased in a puzzled frown. 'Are you sick, lady?'

Violet uttered a derisive snort. 'She called me lady. That's the last thing I am.'

'There's nothing wrong with Violet. She's just a bit tired.'

'You should tell her the truth,' Violet said angrily. 'It'll be obvious to everyone soon enough.'

'You'd best go home, Vi. We'll sort this out, I promise.' Charity lit a candle and the shop was suddenly filled with shifting shadows. She took Dorrie by the hand. 'Come through to the kitchen. We'll both feel better with a hot drink inside us and a bite to eat.'

Violet followed them, dragging her feet. 'If Pa don't kill me he'll throw me out, and I'll end up on the streets.'

'I won't let that happen,' Charity said firmly. 'Us girls will stick together, won't we, Dorrie?'

'I hope so, miss.'

Charity barely slept that night. Grief for the doctor's untimely demise was compounded by worries about her inability to pay Woods the amount he had demanded. Violet's problems also weighed heavily upon her, and without the doctor's wisdom and advice she was at a loss to know how best to help her hapless friend. Then there was Dorrie. The child slept soundly on the floor beside Charity's bed, curled up on a pile of sacks with the old horse blanket wrapped around her. Her wispy hair stuck up around her head like a dandelion clock, and she looked so peaceful that Charity had not the heart to wake her when she rose from her bed next morning. It was still dark and the fire had burned down so that there was barely a glimmer amongst the embers, but with the aid of a pair of bellows and a few sticks of kindling she soon had a blaze roaring up the chimney. She made a pot of tea and took her cup into the shop, sipping it while she counted the money in the cash box.

She sighed. Taking a cab to the doctor's house had been an extravagance, but a necessary one, and now she had Dorrie to feed as well as herself, and the poor child had only the clothes she had been wearing when Marchant threw her out. Charity suspected that Mrs Rose had dressed Dorrie from the missionary barrel, and then only when she had outgrown the garments she was wearing. Young slaveys were rarely treated generously, and were considered to be at the very bottom of the pile in the hierarchy of servants' halls. Charity had often spoken to girls who had run away from intolerable conditions in service, only to find themselves worse off and close to starvation in the gutter. She had seen dead bodies pulled out of the Thames or huddled in doorways having died of cold and hunger during a winter's night. Whatever happened, she was determined that neither she, Violet nor Dorrie would share that fate.

She looked up with a start at the sound of a childish

voice calling her name. Dorrie presented an odd figure, standing in the doorway, wrapped in the horse blanket with just her head showing above the coarse folds. 'I thought you'd gone and left me,' she sobbed. 'I didn't know where I was when I opened me eyes, and then I remembered.'

Charity abandoned the cash box and went to comfort her. 'This is your home now, Dorrie. I'll look after you. That's what the doctor would have wanted.'

'I'm hungry, miss.'

'Of course you are, and so am I.' Charity gave her a quick hug. 'There's some tea left in the pot and bread in the crock. It's stale but I'm sure you know how to make toast.'

Dorrie brightened visibly. 'I makes the best toast in London. Dr Marchant always said so.' Her blue eyes filled with tears. 'He was a good 'un.'

'And we'll always remember that.' Charity swallowed a lump in her throat. She must not cry in front of the child. She had to be strong. 'When you've had breakfast we'll go out and get some food. I'll show you where the shops are so that you can run errands. It will be lovely to have someone to help me.'

'I'll work hard for you, miss. I'm good at scrubbing floors and polishing furniture.'

'We'll do very nicely together, and you must stop calling me miss. My name is Charity.'

'I dunno, it don't seem proper.' Dorrie plugged her thumb in her mouth, looking suddenly much younger and more vulnerable than ever.

Charity's heart swelled with sympathy for the

unwanted orphan. She dropped a kiss on her forehead. 'It's what I want, so you'll just have to get used to it.' She tempered her words with a smile. 'Now, have your breakfast and we'll go out before I open the shop.'

Despite having qualms about spending yet more of the rent money on food, there was no alternative unless they were to go hungry. Charity took Dorrie to the dairy and the bakery, and on the way back they were about to walk past the second-hand clothes shop when she came to a sudden decision. Dorrie's needs were uppermost in her mind. The thin woollen dress the child wore beneath a cotton pinafore was no protection against the bitter winter weather, and Charity hurried her into the shop. The smell of stale sweat and mothballs made her wrinkle her nose as she sorted through a pile of grubby garments, but she forced herself to sound positive. 'What you need is a warm jacket and some mittens. You can't run errands for me if you're not properly dressed.'

They emerged from the fusty interior of the shop with Dorrie warmly clad in a red woollen coat, albeit a size too large and threadbare at the elbows and cuffs, and a knitted woollen hat, which was slightly moth-eaten, but the holes were barely noticeable if it was put on with care. A pair of purple mittens completed the outfit and Dorrie beamed with pride. 'I never been so warm,' she declared, jumping over an icy puddle. 'I could walk miles in the snow and not feel the cold. Thank you, miss – I mean thank you, Charity. It's all lovely.'

'You look very smart, Dorrie.' Charity's smile faded as they approached the bookshop. Someone was hammering on the shop door. 'Oh, dear Lord. It's Woods. He's early.' She took Dorrie by the hand. 'For heaven's sake don't tell him that we've been shopping for clothes.' She quickened her pace. 'Good morning, Mr Woods. You're up bright and early.'

He turned to her, scowling ominously. 'The shop should have been open by now. How do you expect to pay the rent if you don't open up?'

'I'm here now,' Charity said, unlocking the door. 'We had to go out to buy food. I can't work on an empty stomach.'

He grabbed the handle of the shopping basket and peered in. 'Bread, milk, butter and jam. If I find out that you've squandered the rent money on jam I'll be forced to tell the landlord.'

Charity might have laughed at the ridiculousness of his accusation had it not been serious, and too close to the truth for comfort. 'A small pot of jam is hardly an extravagance, Mr Woods. It's all we'll have to eat today.'

He followed them into the shop, glowering at Dorrie, who took refuge behind Charity. 'Who is that?' he demanded. 'Are you taking in waifs and strays and feeding them on jam?'

'This is my little sister.' The lie tripped off her tongue so easily that Charity almost believed it herself. 'She's come to stay for a couple of days.'

He shrugged his shoulders, leaning over her so that his face was close to hers. His breath stank of stale beer, onions and tobacco smoke. 'Where's the rent money? Give it here now.'

She hurried round the counter and picked up the cash box. She knew exactly how much there was in it, but she made a show of counting out the coins and feigned surprise when she found it was not enough. 'I must have miscalculated,' she said airily. 'No matter. I'm sure I can make up the difference in a day or two.'

He slammed his hand down on the counter top. 'You're a liar, Miss Crosse. You knew damned well that you hadn't got the rent. You've been stringing me along, you little bitch.'

Dorrie emerged from behind Charity, fisting her small hands. 'Don't you talk to her like that, mister.'

Woods raised his hand to her. 'Come near me and I'll knock your block off, kid.'

'There's no need to speak to her like that.' Charity moved swiftly, placing herself in between them. 'If the rent is a bit short I just need a little more time. Trade is good and will get better when the new term begins at the university.'

Woods straightened up, pocketing the money. 'No one can say I'm not a reasonable man. Sunday is New Year's Day and so I'll give you a few days' grace before I send in the bailiffs. You have until Monday to find the full rent, plus ten per cent interest to cover the extra paperwork and inconvenience.'

'But that's outrageous,' Charity said angrily. 'You know it's impossible.'

His thin lips curved into a lupine snarl. 'I'll be back on Monday morning with the bailiffs, so you'd better be ready to move out.'

'That's impossible,' Charity protested. 'You know

very well that I can't hope to raise that sort of money in two days.'

'My heart bleeds for you, Miss Crosse.' Woods uttered a mirthless bark of laughter. 'I hear the railway arches are very cosy at this time of year.' He marched out of the shop, leaving a trail of body odour in his wake.

Charity stared after him, speechless and too shocked to move. She had been prepared for his wrath, and had expected the bailiffs to come in and seize goods to the value of what she owed, but she had thought they would leave her with enough stock to continue trading. She had paid scant attention to his declaration that the landlord planned to evict all the tenants so that the site could be redeveloped, but she realised now that it might not just have been an idle threat. The prospect of losing her home was terrifying.

Dorrie tugged at her sleeve. 'I'm hungry, miss.'

Charity came back to earth with a start. The sight of Dorrie's pale face looking up at her with pleading blue eyes was enough to bring her to her senses. 'We'll show him,' she said, snatching the basket by its handle. 'We're not going to allow Mr Woods to wreck our lives, are we, Dorrie?'

'No, miss. I mean, no, Charity.' Dorrie brightened visibly. 'Can I have some bread and jam now, please? I promise I'll scrub every inch of the floor afterwards, and clean the windows, and . . .'

Her desire to please brought a smile to Charity's lips, and she thrust the basket into Dorrie's eager hands. 'Take this into the kitchen and help yourself. I'll settle for a cup of tea for the moment.'

Dorrie bounded off like an eager puppy and Charity's smile faded into a frown. She had been a fool to imagine she could persuade Seth Woods to grant her time to pay, or that she could sell enough books to raise that amount of rent each month. She walked slowly round the shop floor, trailing her fingers on the leather book bindings. The embossed gold leaf was smooth and tactile, absorbing a little of the heat from her fingertips. She could not abandon these works of art and literature to the unfeeling hands of the bailiffs. They had been left to her care by Jethro and they were her responsibility. The characters in many of them had been her companions during lonely nights curled up beneath the shop counter when it was too cold or too hot to sleep. It was up to her to see that they went to purchasers who would love them and care for them as she did.

'I made you some bread and jam.' Dorrie appeared at her elbow, holding up a chipped china plate with jam dripping off a thick doorstep of bread. 'You must be hungry too.'

One look at Dorrie's eager expression was enough to make Charity bite back any criticism of her liberal use of their meagre food supply. 'Thank you. That was a kind thought.' She accepted the plate with a smile, saving the lecture on economy for later. The main thing now was to make Dorrie feel wanted and that this was her home; she was too young and insecure to know how close they were to losing everything. Charity bit into the sticky treat, chewed and swallowed. 'Delicious,' she said appreciatively. 'We'll save the rest for later.'

'I can go to the shops whenever you want me to,' Dorrie said proudly. 'I can go out in the cold now I got a new coat and hat and mittens too. I could deliver books to your customers and help you in the shop. I can do anything you need.'

'That's splendid.' Charity finished the slice of bread and jam, knowing that Dorrie would not be satisfied until she had eaten the last crumb. She handed her the empty plate. 'Perhaps you could start by washing up and making things tidy in the kitchen.'

Dorrie beamed at her. 'Don't worry. It'll be like a new pin by the time I've finished.' She raced back to the kitchen, leaving Charity to worry about their future. There had been no customers so far that morning and the people who passed by barely stopped to glance in the shop window. It would take a miracle to save them.

A few people seemingly intent on browsing the shelves trickled in that morning, but Charity suspected that they were merely sheltering from the intermittent storms when hailstones the size of pigeon's eggs pelted pedestrians and lay in glittering heaps on the pavements. She made one sale when a young nursemaid sheltering from a downpour bought a second-hand copy of *North and South* by Mrs Gaskell. It cost very little when compared with the amount owing on the rent, but the young woman had gone off with a smile on her face at the prospect of escaping into the world of romantic fiction. Others walked out without making a purchase. By mid-afternoon Charity was beginning to feel desperate, and when Violet rushed into the shop her expression was not encouraging.

'What is it, Vi? Are you all right?'

'Ma knows.' Violet lowered her voice when she saw Dorrie, who was supposed to be dusting the book stands but was looking at the illustrations in a volume of *Alice's Adventures in Wonderland*.

'How did she find out?' Charity asked in a whisper.

'She heard me being sick in the privy this morning. She said she'd suspected for some time and she clouted me round the lughole.' Violet nursed her reddened ear, and her eyes filled with tears. 'I begged her not to tell Pa, but it's only a matter of time before he finds out. What am I going to do?'

'You could try telling the young men you think might be the father,' Charity suggested hopefully. 'Maybe one of them might have a streak of decency in him.'

Violet uttered a hollow laugh and began to sob uncontrollably. 'You know that won't happen. I'm done for, Charity. It's the river for me.'

Chapter Eleven

Charity stood in the shop, gazing out of the window at the deserted street. It was Sunday and it was the first day of a new year, but the future was an unfriendly place and she could see nothing ahead but destitution. She had done reasonably well as far as trading went on Saturday, but had not taken nearly enough to satisfy Seth Wood's greed. She suspected that the extra ten per cent he had demanded would have gone into his own pocket had she been able to raise that amount, but as she had nothing like it she knew she would receive little sympathy from him or the bailiffs. With the huge rise in the rent each month it would happen again and again until there was nothing left for them to take. This was the last day she would spend in the place she had come to think of as her own. Students would have to find somewhere else to purchase the books they needed for their studies and the shop would be closed. The building would ultimately be torn down and several centuries of history would be razed to the ground.

She had racked her brains to think of a solution, but the only one that came to mind was to pack up her belongings and move out before she had to suffer the humiliation of being evicted. She would take Dorrie and go in search of cheap accommodation in the part of the city she knew best, but that would mean leaving Violet to face her future alone. Charity knew she was not responsible for her friend, but Violet's plight was grim indeed and Bert Chapman was not a forgiving man. He was mean when sober and brutish when drunk.

Charity was about to return to the kitchen, where she had left Dorrie sleeping peacefully, when she heard the rumble of carriage wheels and the clip-clop of a horse's hooves. It was unusually early for anyone to be out and about particularly if they had been revelling on New Year's Eve. She was even more surprised when the hansom cab drew up outside and a familiar figure dressed in a caped overcoat and top hat leapt to the ground. She hurried to open the door. 'You're the last person I expected to see today,' she said as Harry Elliott breezed into the shop.

'Good morning, Miss Crosse. You're up bright and early.'

'I thought you were in Devon, visiting your mother and stepfather.'

He took off his hat and tossed it onto the counter. 'I was and I did my duty, but the countryside bores me, and I couldn't wait to get back to London.'

'And the lure of the gaming clubs, I suppose.'

'You have my measure, but I came hotfoot to give you a message from Daniel. He asked me to thank you for the book.'

'And you came all the way here to tell me?' She stared at him in amazement. 'It was his uncle who paid for it.'

'Well, you have me there. As a matter of fact Daniel asked me to make sure you were all right. I told him that Wilmot had behaved badly towards you and he was concerned. My brother is a kindly fellow and a solid citizen, unlike me.'

'I think you like to make yourself out to be a villain.'

He gave her a searching look. 'You look tired. Is everything all right? Wilmot hasn't been pestering you, has he?'

She dropped her gaze, clutching her hands together in an attempt to stop them from trembling. 'The bailiffs are coming tomorrow. They'll take part of my stock and we'll be evicted.'

'We? Is there someone else?'

'Dorrie. She's just a child – it's a long story.'

He took her by the shoulders and pressed her down on the chair reserved for elderly or infirm customers. 'Never mind her for now. Why are you being evicted?'

'The landlord raised the rent so high that I'll never make enough to cover it.'

'Have you tried reasoning with the rent collector? Maybe you could come to a mutually agreeable solution?'

'He won't listen, and trade is bad.' She raised her head to look him in the eye. 'I can't let them take my books. They're mine – Jethro left all the stock to me.'

Harry was silent for a moment. 'In that case, I'd suggest a moonlight flit. I've taken that course many times in the past when I was being dunned by debt collectors.'

'You have? But you're rich.'

'Far from it,' he said, chuckling. 'I live by my wits, and sometimes fate is capricious and I find myself financially embarrassed.' His smile faded. 'But I do understand your predicament, and it's fortunate that I returned to London at this particular time.'

'Can you help me?'

'I'm a bit short of funds at the moment or I'd gladly stump up for the rent, but as it is I can only see one way out.'

'I couldn't take your money,' Charity said firmly. 'I'm sure I can find a cheap lodging house in the city, but I don't want to leave my books.'

He frowned thoughtfully. 'I suppose they are a saleable commodity, but they won't make your fortune, as you've already discovered. It might be better to cut your losses and beat a hasty retreat.'

'I just need a barrow,' Charity said, warming to the subject. 'A handcart would do. I could take at least some of them and sell them in one of the street markets. It will keep Dorrie and me until I can find work.'

'I can see that you're determined, but finding something suitable will be difficult on a Sunday, especially at this time of the year.'

'Does that mean you'll help me?'

'I returned to London thinking I would be almost as bored here on a Sunday as I was in the country, and now you've issued me with a challenge.'

'I can be ready in no time at all.'

He laid his hand on her shoulder. 'Take the advice of someone who has vast experience in such things and wait until after dark. Pack your books in bundles while you wait, but keep them out of sight. If the landlord gets wind of your intentions he'll try to stop you.' He snatched up his hat and put it on at an angle. 'I'll see what I can do, but don't expect me back until this evening.'

She leapt to her feet. 'I don't know how to thank you.'

'Don't expect miracles, but I'll do all I can to help you. It's not often I get the chance to be a knight in shining armour. I'm usually cast as a libertine.' He doffed his hat and let himself out into the street.

Charity watched his tall figure striding down the street towards Leather Lane. She turned and walked slowly amongst the stands, working out which books she would take and which she would have to abandon. It was not going to be an easy decision to make, but she had to be practical.

Later that morning, having enlisted Dorrie's help, she began sorting and making bundles of the volumes she intended to save from the grasping hands of the bailiffs. Dorrie had been upset when she discovered the reason for all this activity and Charity had tried to make their impending departure sound like a great adventure, although deep down she was just as scared as Dorrie. She had put her trust in Harry and all she could do now was wait and hope that he would bring transport, but what she would do then and where they would go remained a problem to which there seemed no easy solution.

It was dark outside, but the night air sparkled with frost and Charity's feet crunched on the frozen slush in the back yard as she made her way to the privy. The door was shut and she waited for a moment or two before knocking on the slatted wood. 'Is anyone in there?'

A low moan answered her question and Charity lifted the latch, but the door only opened a crack before it came up against an obstacle. 'Are you all right?' Her stomach clenched with anxiety. She had a horrible feeling that she knew who was slumped on the dirt floor. 'Vi, is that you?' She put her shoulder to the wood, pushing gently. A groan confirmed her suspicions, and after a great deal of manoeuvring she managed to get into the privy. She helped Violet to her feet. 'What happened? Are you hurt?' It was too dark to see but as she brushed a lock of hair from Violet's face she felt something warm and sticky. 'You're bleeding.'

Violet leaned against her. 'Me dad knows,' she gasped. 'He done this to me.'

'Let's get you indoors.' Charity looped Violet's arm around her shoulders. 'Slowly does it.'

'I can't do it no other way,' Violet murmured with a hint of wry humour. 'I thought he was going to kill me.'

They made their way across the yard and as soon as they were safely inside the scullery Charity locked and bolted the door. 'You're safe now, Vi. Come into the kitchen and let's have a look at you.'

Dorrie had been sitting at the table but she jumped to her feet at they entered the room. 'What happened? Has she had another fall?'

'She slipped on the ice,' Charity said hastily. 'Why don't you make her a nice hot cup of tea? I'm sure that would make her feel better.'

Dorrie rushed over to the range and placed the kettle on the hob. 'Will she be all right?'

'Don't worry about me, young 'un,' Vi said stoutly.

Charity filled a bowl with warm water from the kettle and replaced it on the heat. 'We'll soon have you fixed up,' she said, making an attempt to sound cheerful for Dorrie's sake.

The head wound appeared to be superficial, although Charity suspected that Violet would have a nasty scar on her forehead when it healed. She was badly bruised and had obviously endured a severe beating. Her lip was split and she had lost a front tooth. 'You'll have a real shiner tomorrow morning,' Charity murmured as she bathed Violet's face and applied arnica to the bruises. 'Have you pain anywhere else?' She lowered her voice. 'You know what I mean.'

'I don't think so. I dunno really because I ache all over. Maybe I could sleep here tonight?' She cast a wary look at Dorrie, who was taking it all in. 'I don't think I could make it up them steps, Charity.'

'We're leaving soon,' Dorrie said eagerly. 'We're going on a big adventure. Charity said so.'

'What?' Violet caught Charity by the hand. 'Leaving? Why? What's happened?'

'Don't get upset, Vi. We've got to go or the bailiffs will take everything. Woods is threatening to evict us tomorrow anyway.'

Violet released her with a cry of disgust. 'You were

going to leave without telling me. I can't believe you'd do that.'

'I was going to come upstairs when I thought your pa would be sleeping off the booze.'

'You could have told me sooner.'

'I only decided today and then Harry turned up and . . .'

'You're running away with that chap you told me about?'

'No, of course not. I hardly know him.'

Violet held her hand to her head. 'I don't understand all this. I thought you had the rent money.'

'I didn't have quite enough.'

'It was because you took me to the doctor's, wasn't it?' Violet's swollen lips trembled and her eyes brimmed with tears. 'This is all my fault, and now you're leaving me.'

'You can come too,' Dorrie said excitedly. 'Me and Charity will take care of you and make you better.'

'Ta, Dorrie, but you don't know the whole of it.' Violet raised her head to give Charity a beseeching look. 'I c-can't stay here, and I don't think I've got the courage to throw myself in the river. It'll be the workhouse for me. I've no choice now.'

Charity knew she was beaten. With Dorrie gazing at her expectantly and Violet having lost the will to live, she had no choice. 'Of course you must come with us, Vi. I'm not sure where we're going but Harry should be here soon with some sort of transport. We just have to wait for him to arrive.' She turned to Dorrie. 'Where's that tea? I'm sure we could all benefit from something warm in our stomachs before we set off on our big adventure.'

It was close to midnight before the shop bell rang announcing Harry's arrival. Charity had been keeping watch in the shop for an hour or more, while the others snatched some sleep in the kitchen. As the minutes ticked by she was on the point of giving up, thinking that he had either been lured away by a game of cards or had been unable to find a suitable vehicle, but he had proved her wrong. She rushed to unlock the door. 'I thought you weren't coming,' she said breathlessly.

He entered on a blast of cold air. 'I always keep my promises, but it wasn't an easy task. Anyway, I'm here now.'

She glanced out into the street. 'That's a private carriage. Is it yours?'

'You might say that someone is returning a favour.' He beckoned to the coachman who climbed down from his box and came to join them. 'Yes, sir?'

'These are Sir Hedley's books.' Harry indicated the bundles with a casual wave of his hand. 'Load as many of them into the growler as possible, Jackson.'

'At once, sir.' The coachman picked up several bundles and took them out to the waiting carriage.

'Who is Sir Hedley?' Charity asked anxiously. 'You haven't sold my books, have you?'

'I found them and you a temporary home.'

'But the carriage and the titled gentleman – I don't understand.'

'A little gentle persuasion secured a place of safety for you and the child, and your wretched books.'

'There are three of us now,' Charity said, lowering her voice so that the coachman could not hear. 'Violet's father discovered that she's in the family way and beat her senseless. She can't stay here.'

Harry shrugged his shoulders. 'Why am I not surprised? You seem to go round collecting waifs and strays as well as leather-bound volumes that no one wants.'

'Violet is a friend and she's in trouble.'

'I hope you know what you're doing.'

Charity could see that it would be futile to enter an argument about the rights and wrongs of her decision. She watched the coachman as he filled the floor of the carriage with piles of books. 'Will there be room for all of us?'

'I'll ride with Jackson and you ladies will have to sit with your feet resting on the books until you get to Sir Hedley Bligh's house in Nevill's Court.'

'Who is this man, Harry? And why has he agreed to take complete strangers into his house?'

'He's my father.'

Charity put her head on one side. 'But why is your name Elliot when your father's name is Bligh?'

'Let's just say that we don't exactly see eye to eye. I left home several years ago and chose to use my mother's maiden name.'

'Will he mind having us to stay, even temporarily?'

'Nevill's Court is a huge house. I doubt if he'll even realise that you're there.'

'I'm not sure about this, Harry. What about my books?'

'Ah now, that's the best part. My father has an extensive library, although I doubt if he's ever read any of them. He's a well-known collector of antiquarian books. You may find you have something in common with him.'

'Am I going into service in his household? What will I have to do there?'

Harry threw back his head and laughed. 'Let's worry about that later. As I said, the house is big and run down, and your main difficulty will be in finding your way around.'

'Are you sure this is a good idea, Harry?' Charity watched the last of her precious books being loaded into the carriage with a feeling of misgiving. 'It all sounds a bit odd.'

He patted her on the shoulder. 'Go and gather up your flock, shepherdess. It's time to go.'

She hesitated. 'I'm not sure . . .'

'Do you want to lose everything?'

'I'll go and get Vi and Dorrie.'

The carriage drew up in Fetter Lane outside the entrance of Nevill's Court, a narrow alley sandwiched between the Moravian chapel and a terrace of tall buildings. Charity's heart sank as she peered into the dark maw of the passage that smelled strongly of cat urine and worse. It was not what she had been led to expect and she could not imagine that a wealthy man would make his home in such a place. She helped Dorrie from the carriage and Harry leapt from the box to assist Violet.

'Do you want me to unload the books now, sir?' Jackson did not sound very enthusiastic.

'Best leave it until morning,' Harry said, without stopping to consult Charity. 'I take it that we still own the coach house and stables?'

'Yes, sir.'

'Then the morning will do nicely. Wait here and you can take me back to my lodgings.'

Jackson tipped his hat. 'Right you are, sir.'

'What sort of place is this?' Charity demanded as Harry led them into the darkness. She covered her mouth and nose with her hand in an attempt to escape from the noxious smell.

'You'll see.' He quickened his pace.

Dorrie clutched Charity's arm. 'I'm scared.'

'We'll be fine,' Charity said with more conviction than she was feeling. 'Are you all right, Vi?'

Leaning heavily on Harry's arm, Violet turned her head. 'I think so.'

A shaft of moonlight dazzled Charity's eyes as they emerged into a hidden part of London that had been saved from the Great Fire by an act of God or pure chance. Four-storey seventeenth-century houses with small cottage gardens formed three sides of a square, abutting a magnificent but slightly dilapidated town house of the same era. Beneath a portico supported by two Doric columns was an eight-panelled front door boasting a brass lion's head knocker, which even by moonlight Charity could see was sadly in need of polishing. The house was in darkness but the small-paned windows glittered in the moonlight, creating an eerie impression of invisible hands holding dozens of candles as ghostly entities moved from room to room. A shiver ran down Charity's spine and she longed for the comfort of her own bed in the place that had become home.

Harry seemed to have no qualms as he marched up to the door and knocked. The sound echoed as if the house was an empty shell, and they waited in breathless silence. Then slow, measured footsteps came closer and closer. Charity was ready to run, expecting to see a hideous ghoulish figure like the monster created by Dr Frankenstein in Mary Shelley's novel. The door screamed on unoiled hinges and Charity stifled a gasp of fear, but the person who stood on the threshold was no monster. They were ushered inside by a small, plump woman with a kindly face like a wizened crab apple. 'I haven't had much time to prepare for the young ladies, Master Harry, but I've done my best.'

'Thank you, Mrs Diment. Whatever you've done will be excellent. I'll leave them in your capable hands.' Harry helped Violet to a carved oak chair before turning to Charity with an encouraging smile. 'You'll be safe in this haven between the Inns of Court and the bustle of Fleet Street. This place is a secret hidden from all but the most discerning eyes.'

'What happens now?' Charity followed him to the door. 'Are you going to abandon us in this creepy old house? What am I supposed to say to Sir Hedley in the morning?'

'I doubt if you'll see very much of the man himself.

He's mostly nocturnal and sleeps all day until it's time to visit his club or the gaming houses.'

She lowered her voice, not wanting to upset Dorrie or Violet any more than was necessary. 'But surely he won't allow us to live here rent free? Why would he do that for complete strangers?'

Harry laid his finger on her lips. 'Stop worrying. When you see him you have only to mention that you've brought a fresh supply of books and he'll welcome you with open arms.'

'I wish I could believe that,' she said doubtfully.

'You'll be fine, Charity Crosse.' He leaned over to brush her cheek with a kiss. 'Goodbye, my dear. I'll let Daniel know where you are when I next see him.' He opened the door and stepped outside.

'Come with me, ladies.' Mrs Diment walked slowly towards a wide staircase with ornately carved newel posts and banisters. She held an oil lamp high above her head and they followed her up to the second floor. Charity supported Violet on one side and Dorrie did her best to help by taking her free arm, but it was slow and painful progress.

The room that Mrs Diment showed them into was large and smelled of soot and damp. The beamed ceiling was festooned with lacy cobwebs and the four-poster bed was hung with threadbare damask curtains on which moths must have been feasting for a century or more. She lit a candle and placed it on a dressing table set between two windows. She drew the curtains and clouds of dust filled the air, making them all cough. 'This will have to do for tonight. There are other bedchambers, but I wouldn't advise you to go wandering about in the dark as some of the floorboards are in a sorry state of repair and might give way.' With a nod and a smile she left them with only the one candle to light the large room.

Charity helped Violet to a low boudoir chair and made her sit while she and Dorrie made up the bed. The sheets and blankets felt damp to the touch and eventually they huddled together, still fully clothed, beneath the covers. Despite her reservations about the house and its owner and her fears that Violet's injuries might bring on a miscarriage, Charity fell asleep with Dorrie curled up at her side.

She could not think where she was when she opened her eyes next morning, but when Dorrie turned over in her sleep, digging her in the ribs with her elbow, Charity realised that she was not dreaming. She sat up, swinging her legs over the side of the bed and slithered to the floor, taking care not to wake the others. At least there had been no emergency during the night, and it looked as though the baby had survived the vicious beating that Violet had suffered at the hands of her father.

The bedroom was in semi-darkness with a sliver of daylight forcing its way through a tear in the damask curtains, and she padded across the floor in bare feet to draw them and allow daylight to filter in through the grimy windowpanes. She felt as though she had stepped back into the past as she gazed out at the ancient houses with their tiny gardens blanketed in snow. She would barely have been surprised if she had seen people emerge from their doors dressed like cavaliers or roundheads, but she knew that this was no dream and she needed to face reality. They were here under sufferance, although Harry had been vague as to the terms under which she was to be employed in the home of Sir Hedley Bligh. She took a clean pair of woollen stockings from her valise and put them on before slipping her feet into her boots. They were still damp, but she had no choice as they were the only footwear she possessed. She brushed the tangles from her hair and tied it back with a ribbon, checking her appearance in the fly-spotted mirror on the dressing table. She would have liked to wash her hands and face before meeting her new employer, but at least she looked reasonably presentable, even if her plain grey gown was slightly crumpled.

She left Violet and Dorrie to sleep and made her way downstairs to the oak-panelled entrance hall. The portraits of sober-looking ancestors looked down at her with disapproving stares, but there was no sign of life apart from the scurrying of mice behind the wainscoting. She made her way towards the back of the house, hoping to find Mrs Diment, who had seemed to be a sensible sort of woman. She had to negotiate a maze of corridors, and she kept stopping to peer into rooms where everything was shrouded in dust sheets, and the air was heavy with silence. Eventually she came to a door that led into a huge kitchen that must have changed little since the builders laid the last flagstone.

An open fireplace occupied half the wall at one end of the kitchen, complete with an ancient spit and a weight-driven jack. A pine table, such as monks might have sat round in a refectory, ran almost the length of the room, and beneath a window overlooking a small courtyard was a stone sink and a pump. A desultory fire burned in the grate and a kettle hung on a trivet over the flames. Charity had seen pictures of old-fashioned kitchens in books, but this was archaic even by the standards in Liquorpond Street. She turned with a start as a shabbily dressed man emerged from the larder with a large Irish wolfhound at his heels. He clutched a leg of roast chicken in his hand and was gnawing on it like a hungry lion. Judging by his stained leather waistcoat, knee breeches and gaiters, she assumed he must work outdoors or in the stables. 'Good morning,' she said politely. 'I was hoping to find Mrs Diment.'

He continued chewing for some time before answering. 'I can't help you.' He took another bite. 'Who are you?'

'I'm Miss Crosse and I'm here by invitation. Sir Hedley knows all about it.'

'You're a liar.'

She stared at him, stunned by his rudeness. 'I beg your pardon?'

'Sir Hedley knows nothing about it.'

'I can assure you that he does. Anyway, who are you?'

'I'm Sir Hedley Bligh.' He tossed the bone onto the floor and the hound leapt upon it.

Charity was at a loss for words. At first she thought he was joking, but there was not a glimmer of humour in his flinty grey eyes. She took a deep breath and bobbed a curtsey. 'How do you do, sir?'

'Bah!' He strode towards the door. 'Bosun, come.' With the bone sticking out of his mouth the dog followed him from the room, leaving Charity staring after them.

Chapter Twelve

'If a proposition seems too good to be true, you should make further enquiries, Charity my love.' Her grandfather's words came back to her with such force that she began to tremble convulsively. She had taken Harry at his word, but he had literally dumped them in his father's house without gaining his parent's consent. Fear and anger roiled in her stomach. Sir Hedley was more than an eccentric, he was probably quite mad, and he was rude into the bargain. She would have to break the news gently to Violet in order not to cause her even more distress, and Dorrie would be heartbroken, but it was clear that they could not remain in a place where they were unwelcome.

She controlled her ragged breathing with difficulty as she paced the floor, wringing her hands. It was an impossible situation, but it was too late to return to Liquorpond Street – the bailiffs would be there by now and her sudden flight would have been discovered. Seth Woods might report her to the police and she would be labelled as a debtor and a thief for taking the books, even though they were rightfully hers. She was in a state of panic and did not realise that she was no longer alone in the kitchen until someone tapped her on the shoulder. She spun round with a cry of fright and found herself looking into Mrs Diment's smiling face. 'What's the matter, dearie? You look troubled.'

'I've just met Sir Hedley. He knows nothing about us.'

Mrs Diment smiled and patted her on the shoulder. 'He's probably forgotten all about it. I did tell him yesterday, but likely as not it went out of his head.'

'He didn't seem too pleased,' Charity said warily. 'I don't think we should have come here.'

'You don't want to worry about the master. He's probably forgotten your existence by now and retired to bed.'

'I'm confused. Are we to stay here, or not? Am I to work for Sir Hedley? Harry seemed to think it would be all right.'

'Master Harry said something about the library. You're to sort out the books, or some such thing.'

'Sir Hedley really didn't seem to know anything about it.'

'He's a bit vague these days, my dear. Too many late nights and too much brandy have made him a bit forgetful, but you need not worry about that.'

Charity digested this in silence. She glanced round the room, wondering where the rest of the servants were hiding. 'This is a big house,' she said lamely. 'Are you the only one who works here, ma'am?'

'We used to have a large staff both here and at Bligh Park, but now there's only myself and Jackson.' Mrs Diment puffed out her chest. 'I'm Sir Hedley's cook/housekeeper and this is my kitchen.' She indicated her domain with a wave of her hand and a proud smile.

'Isn't it fine? I have running water at the sink and a clockwork jack to work the spit. I doubt if many London houses can boast such luxuries.'

Charity eyed her warily. She had no experience of the domestic arrangements in well-to-do establishments, but the modest range in Liquorpond Street was far more modern than the facilities in Sir Hedley's establishment, which were positively medieval. Mrs Diment was pleasant enough, but she seemed to be almost as eccentric as her employer, or maybe she had lived in this house for so long that she was unaware of the outside world. 'It's a fine kitchen,' she said, not wanting to give offence.

Mrs Diment beamed at her. 'I started as a scullery maid in Sir Hedley's country house in Dorset when I was just eight years old. I knew him as a boy and as a young man; he was handsome then, and charming too. He inherited the baronetcy and a fortune from his father and he was a great catch. It's just a pity she got her claws into him, the minx. She married him for his money and title and then left him broken-hearted.'

Dazed by this unasked-for information, Charity could only nod her head and make sympathetic noises.

'But you must be hungry, my dear. And what about the other young lady and the child? Is she still asleep, poor mite. Harry told me that she can't be much older than eight or nine, just the same age as I was when I went into service.'

'Dorrie is nearly nine.' Charity wondered whether to mention Violet's condition now or leave it until later.

'I'll make a pot of tea and put some bacon in the

frying pan. We keep hens in the back yard and they provide us with plenty of eggs, even in winter, because I feed them well and keep them safe. Go upstairs and wake the child while I make breakfast.'

'Mrs Diment, there's something I have to tell you.'

'Yes, my dear?' Mrs Diment disappeared into the larder, reappearing almost immediately with a side of bacon which she heaved onto the table. 'Sir Hedley is very fond of bacon and has a flitch sent up from his country estate, smoked in his own smokehouse.'

'Mrs Diment I think I ought to tell you about Violet. She's had some bad luck recently. Her father threw her out and . . .'

Mrs Diment's beady, bird-bright eyes sparkled with curiosity. 'In the family way, is she?'

'I'm afraid so. I couldn't just walk away when she needed help, and Harry said . . .'

'I know, he said it would be all right to bring her here too. That's typical of Master Harry.'

'But he doesn't live here any more. And he doesn't get on well with his father.'

Mrs Diment shrugged her plump shoulders. 'His mother was no better than she should be, in my humble opinion. She left Sir Hedley when Master Harry was just three and went to live with Sir Philip Barton. She returned some months later, crying and carrying on, begging Sir Hedley to divorce her so that she could marry the father of the child she was expecting. He agreed, even though it broke his heart.'

'I'm sorry,' Charity said softly. She could see that the memory had upset Mrs Diment, who was obviously devoted to her master. 'But I don't understand why Harry uses his mother's maiden name when she deserted him.'

'He blamed his father for his mother's departure, although it wasn't strictly true. Myrtle Elliott had her eye to the main chance and she didn't care who she hurt in order to get her own way, but Master Harry was just a child and you wouldn't expect him to understand. He never got on well with his father and he ran away from home when he was fourteen.'

'Are they reconciled now?'

'Not exactly, my dear. They have an uneasy truce, but I think Master Harry still bears a grudge against Sir Hedley.' Mrs Diment began slicing the bacon with grim determination.

'I'll fetch the girls,' Charity said hastily. 'But I really should speak to Sir Hedley about Violet. I'm afraid he might decide to throw us out when he learns more about us and how we came to be here.'

'He remembers what he chooses to remember,' Mrs Diment said, tossing bacon into the frying pan. She placed it on a trivet over the fire. 'Leave him to me.'

'We'll earn our keep, ma'am. We're all used to hard work.'

'As I said, Master Harry suggested that you might sort out the library. It's in a terrible state and you'll have your hands full. Violet can help with the chores. We haven't had a housemaid for years, and the child can work too. You'll earn your keep a hundred times over, I promise you that.'

Charity hurried upstairs to the bedroom, where

she found Violet sitting up in bed with her arm around Dorrie. They both jumped when she entered the room, clinging to each other like survivors in a shipwreck.

'Oh, it's you,' Violet said, heaving a sigh of relief. 'We was scared, Charity. We didn't know where you'd gone.'

'It's all right, you needn't worry,' Charity said, smiling. 'I've spoken to Mrs Diment, the cook, and she's making breakfast for us all, so we mustn't keep her waiting.'

'Breakfast.' Dorrie threw back the covers and slithered onto the floor, landing in a giggling heap on the threadbare mat. 'I'm starving.'

Violet rose more slowly, easing her bruised body off the mattress with a groan. 'I feel a bit sick.'

'You have to eat.' Charity picked up her hairbrush and handed it to her. 'Make yourself presentable, Vi. I've told Mrs Diment why you came with me and she's taken it really well. It's a crazy household, but at least we've got a roof over our heads, and the owner, Sir Hedley Bligh is Harry's father.'

Dorrie looked up from lacing her boots. 'Is he really?'

Violet frowned into the mirror as she attempted to untangle her long, chestnut tresses. 'Why didn't you tell us that last night?'

'We were all so tired, and I didn't know what we were letting ourselves in for. Anyway, I've found out more from Mrs Diment and I'll explain later. We'd best get downstairs, and I should warn you that there are strings attached to us being here.'

'I thought as much,' Violet said with a sigh.

'We're to help in the house, but it's not as if we're strangers to hard work, is it?'

Mrs Diment fed them well and after breakfast they were each assigned tasks. Charity was shown to the library, which was situated on the ground floor. Shelves from floor to ceiling were crammed haphazardly with tomes of all sizes, and Charity's books were piled on the floor beneath one of the three tall windows overlooking the square. 'This is where you'll work,' Mrs Diment said in a hushed tone, as if they were in a sacred place. 'These books are the master's pride and joy. Some of them are very valuable, or so I've been led to believe.'

'What exactly am I to do?' Charity asked, gazing in awe at the collection.

'It's not up to me to say. You'll have to ask the master when he's in a good mood.' Mrs Diment moved to the door and held it open. 'Anyway, I've got work to do, so I'll leave you to get on as best you can.' The door closed behind her and Charity was left to deal with the chaotic jumble of literary works.

She decided to find a place for the books she had rescued from the bailiffs' clutches before trying to make sense of Sir Hedley's attempts at building a library. She was soon deep in concentration, forgetting all her worries as she untied the bundles of books and sorted them into some kind of order. She was so engrossed in her task that she lost all sense of time, and she turned with a start at the sound of the door opening and Bosun's paws padding across the floorboards. She straightened up and came face to face with Sir Hedley. She bobbed a curtsey. 'I've made a start, sir.'

He bent down and picked up one of the bundles of books she had brought with her. 'Where did these come from?'

'They're mine, Sir Hedley. I used to have a bookshop in Liquorpond Street . . .'

He studied the spines, frowning. 'I know it well.' He looked up, giving nothing away by his expression. 'What happened to the strange chap who owned it?'

'He died and left the contents of the shop to me.'

'I thought he had more sense. It's obvious that you haven't made a go of things or you wouldn't be here now.'

'Harry said he explained everything, sir.'

'He only visits me when he needs money or a favour. I don't recall agreeing to all this.' He replaced one bundle and picked up another. 'I'll say one thing for you though; you have good taste in literature. But are these stolen property?'

'Certainly not, sir. I told you that Jethro left them to me. I did my best to keep the shop open but the landlord raised the rent and I couldn't pay.'

'So the bailiffs were sent in.' He put the books down. 'And you are homeless. My gallant son rescued you and then abandoned you to my care.'

'I'll earn my keep, Sir Hedley. It's just a temporary measure until I can find paid employment, or a small shop where I can start again with the books I managed to save.'

'But these are my books now. They will be a nice little addition to my collection.'

'They're mine, sir. I just needed somewhere safe to store them.'

'You expect a lot and give little. While the books are under my roof they belong to me. You may leave now and take them with you, or you can remain here on my terms. Which is it to be?'

Charity thought quickly. If it had just been for herself she might have taken her books and left, but she had to think of Violet and Dorrie. They were depending on her and she could not let them down. 'What exactly do you expect of me, Sir Hedley?'

He curled his lip in a wry smile. 'Not that, anyway. I'm not interested in your body, child. My books are my one and only love and they need care and attention. You will divide them into categories and place them in alphabetical order. Then you will catalogue them, including the ones you stole from the bailiffs. They will be safe here.'

'And what am I to expect in return?'

'I'll reward you with bed and board.'

'What about Dorrie?' she asked anxiously. 'She's only a child.'

'Mrs Diment informs me that she's already put her to work as well as the young woman you foisted upon us, who is apparently in an interesting condition.' He glowered at her beneath his bushy grey eyebrows. 'I am not a charitable institution, Miss Crosse, and I am not a rich man. You and your friends will stay only as long as you earn your keep. There is no question of remuneration.'

'Servants are paid a wage, Sir Hedley. Mr Wilberforce fought to abolish slavery.'

'The workhouse is filled with people who don't wish to work for their daily crust. Leave or stay, it's your choice. Come, Bosun.' He clicked his fingers and the dog leapt up and followed him out of the room, leaving Charity staring after them.

Trapped, she thought sadly. We're stuck in this awful mausoleum with a mad miser and there seems no way to escape, at least not until Violet has given birth and that is months away.

That night, when they had finished their work for the day, Charity, Violet and Dorrie huddled around the fire in their bedroom. Violet and Dorrie had dusted and polished the furniture and swept the floor. Mrs Diment had told them they could each have a room to themselves, but they had been too nervous to accept her offer. Dorrie was certain that ghosts walked at night and that the spirits of the dead lurked in the shrouded rooms. Violet made an effort to appear unconcerned, but Charity could see that she was influenced by Dorrie's vivid imagination. Mrs Diment had accepted their decision without comment and had gone as far as to search the linen cupboard for a pair of curtains to replace the ones which were in threads.

Dorrie had carried coal and kindling up from the cellar and Violet had found a supply of tallow candles in a long-forgotten cupboard. The room still smelled strongly of damp, mothballs and mutton fat as the cheap tallow candles flickered and melted, but it was warmer and more welcoming than it had been when they arrived.

Charity explained their circumstances in detail. 'So you see,' she concluded, 'Sir Hedley has the upper hand. He will allow us to stay but only if we work for nothing more than our keep.'

Dorrie huddled against Charity. 'I never got paid at the doctor's house,' she said in a whisper. 'I got fed, and clothed out of the missionary barrel, and Mrs Rose told me I should be grateful for that.'

'And I never got nothing from me dad for keeping house.' Violet covered her mouth to stifle a yawn. 'At least we're well fed here, and Mrs Diment is a diamond.' She chuckled at her own wit. 'That's a good 'un. She's a true diamond, and I ain't seen the master yet, so I can't give an opinion on him.'

'He's not as crazy as he makes out,' Charity said, recalling their conversation that morning. 'He's obsessed with his books, and he wants to add mine to his collection, but I don't see we've got much choice, at least until the baby comes, Vi. You'll be well looked after here.'

Violet hung her head and bright spots of colour appeared on her pale cheeks. 'I've brought this on you, Charity. You would have done better without me. I'm a wicked girl.'

Charity moved closer and slipped her arm around Violet's shoulders. 'No, you're not wicked. I won't have that. You made a mistake, but what's done is done.

Dorrie and I are your family now, and in the summer you'll have a baby to love and care for.'

'I like babies,' Dorrie said stoutly. 'I'll help you look after it.'

'We both will.' Charity placed her free arm around Dorrie and hugged them both. 'So we're agreed, are we? We stay here and slave away for Sir Hedley, for the time being anyway.'

'Agreed,' Violet said, wiping tears from her cheeks.

Dorrie nodded her head. 'That goes for me too.'

Charity felt the atmosphere in the room shift as if the lonely spirits in the house approved of their plan.

It was not easy at first to settle into an entirely new way of life. Charity was surprised to find that she missed the shop and its customers. She had grown independent and used to doing things her own way, but now she had to bow to Sir Hedley's dictates and comply with Mrs Diment's wishes. Not that the latter was too much trouble as the good lady seemed delighted to have their company, and did not make many demands on Charity's time. She was patient with Dorrie and took care not to overtax Violet, and despite Sir Hedley's penny-pinching ways they were warm and well fed during the worst of the winter weather.

Sir Hedley himself rarely put in an appearance, and Charity began to realise that her first meeting with him had happened by chance. She had thought he had risen early that morning, when in reality he had only just returned after one of his card-playing marathons, and had been preparing to retire to his bedchamber. He slept by day and rose in time for dinner, after which he would go out and not be seen again until next morning when he arrived home bleary-eyed and smelling of drink and stale tobacco smoke. She soon found that this worked to her advantage as, having given her instructions as to how he wanted his collection sorted and catalogued, he left her to her own devices. She made certain that the books she had brought from Liquorpond Street were kept apart from his, so that when the time came for her to move on it would be easy to separate them.

She worked diligently, rarely allowing herself the time to think about anything other than the matter in hand, but sometimes when she stopped to eat the food that Dorrie brought to her at midday, she allowed her thoughts to turn to Daniel. She missed his company and she wished that she had had the forethought to ask Harry for his half-brother's address. She wondered how the dig was progressing or if they had been forced to abandon it when winter came. For all she knew Daniel might be in London, living in Doughty Street, but if she went there she might come face to face with Wilmot Barton and that was the last thing she wanted. She would have liked to see Harry to thank him for finding them a place to live, albeit temporary, but he had kept well away from Nevill's Court and had apparently forgotten her existence. Mrs Diment did not know where to find him and Charity had not the courage to question Sir Hedley as the mere mention of Harry's name seemed to irritate him.

She had all but resigned herself to spending the rest

of her life working in the library when, one morning in March, Sir Hedley strode into the kitchen where they were just finishing breakfast. They rose to their feet but he motioned them to sit with an impatient wave of his hand. 'Finish your food. I don't pay for good vittles to see them wasted. There are plenty of starving people out there who would be grateful for a crust of bread, let alone a bowl of porridge and a goodly helping of toast and butter.' He leaned over to peer at the spread. 'Marmalade? Do you treat them to marmalade, Mrs Diment?'

She half rose from her seat. 'It's not every day, sir. I paid for it myself from the sale of eggs. The hens have been laying particularly well recently and our neighbour at number fourteen . . .'

He held up his hand. 'I don't want to hear any more, but I think you're forgetting that the chickens, like everything else in this establishment, belong to me. I am not paying for feed so that the neighbours can enjoy eggs for their breakfasts, nor for you women to gorge on marmalade when you should be at work.'

Charity pushed back her chair and stood up. 'Mrs Diment is a good, kind woman who has only your best interests at heart, Sir Hedley. You shouldn't speak to her like that.'

Mrs Diment clasped her hand to her mouth in an attempt to stifle a sharp intake of breath, and Violet clutched her belly as if her baby had made a sudden movement. Dorrie sat there open-mouthed and wide-eyed with a slice of toast clutched in one sticky hand. They waited in silence for the storm to break.

Sir Hedley stared at Charity with narrowed eyes and then, to her surprise, he chuckled. 'By God, woman, you've got a damned cheek.'

'I'm sorry, sir. But I only spoke the truth.'

'Yes, yes, well maybe I was a bit hasty.' He jerked his head in Mrs Diment's direction but he did not look her in the eye. 'She knows me well enough not to take umbrage. Isn't that so, Mrs Diment?'

'I should think so, sir. After all these years I should be used to your ways.' She reached for the teapot. 'May I get you something, Sir Hedley? A nice cup of tea?'

'Or a slice of toast and marmalade?' Dorrie added innocently. She turned her head to stare at Violet, who had nudged her in the ribs. 'What's wrong? What did I say?'

'Eat up and we'll go and make a start on the bedrooms,' Violet said in a low voice.

Sir Hedley slammed his hand down on the table. 'Enough of this idiotic prattle – it's like living in a house filled with chattering starlings.' He turned to Mrs Diment. 'Send a tray of tea and toast to my study, but I'll say what I came for in the first place before you silly women started jabbering.'

Mrs Diment opened her mouth and closed it again without uttering a word. Charity sank down on her chair, wondering what was so important that it brought him into the servants' quarters.

'Urgent business makes it imperative that I leave today for Dorset.' He pointed his finger at Charity. 'You will travel with me. We leave within the hour.'

He marched out of the kitchen and there was a moment of stunned silence.

'Why you?' Violet demanded anxiously. 'Why would Sir Hedley make you go with him to Dorset? I dunno where that is.'

Mrs Diment jumped up from the table. 'Dorrie. Make yourself useful and toast some bread for the master. Violet, make a fresh pot of tea.' She grabbed Charity by the arm and raised her to her feet. 'Go and pack a few things. You'll no doubt be gone for several days.'

'I don't understand,' Charity murmured. 'Why me? And why are we going to Dorset?'

'It's not for you to question the master,' Mrs Diment said primly. 'At a guess I'd say that he has some urgent business to attend to at Bligh Park.'

'That doesn't explain why he wants me to go with him. I can't leave my work here.'

'Try telling that to Sir Hedley when you take him his breakfast.' Mrs Diment thrust the toasting fork into Dorrie's hand. 'Have you put the kettle on to boil, Violet? Hurry up, do.'

'You will look after them, won't you, Mrs Diment?' Charity whispered, indicating Dorrie and Violet with a nod of her head. 'I mean, I feel responsible for them, and Dorrie's just a little kid, and with Violet and her baby . . .'

Mrs Diment laid her hand on Charity's shoulder. 'Stop worrying, girl. You won't be gone for long, if I know Sir Hedley. He hates the country and he won't stay there a moment longer than necessary.'

Charity was not convinced. She knew they were safe

in the confines of Nevill's Court, but she lived with the fear that Bert Chapman might discover their whereabouts and would come looking for his daughter. She did not doubt that he saw Violet as a future wage-earner who would go out to work as soon as Emily was old enough to look after the younger children.

'Hurry up with the tea and toast,' Mrs Diment said cheerfully. 'We haven't got all day.'

Within minutes they had a tray ready and Charity took it to the study on the ground floor. She knocked and entered. Sir Hedley was at his desk going through a pile of documents. He gave her a cursory glance. 'Put it down, girl. Don't stand there like a ninny.'

She looked in vain for a space on the tooled leather, but she dared not move anything and she placed the tray on a pile of papers, taking care not to dislodge anything. 'May I ask why you want me to accompany you, Sir Hedley? I still have much to do here.'

'It's not up to you to question me, miss. I'm your employer and you do what I tell you.'

'I'm not exactly a paid employee, sir. I work for nothing other than my keep.'

'And you're lucky to have that.' He glanced at her, frowning. 'I did you a favour by taking you in, not to mention the trollop and the child. Don't look daggers at me, girl. I'm impervious to your moods as well as to your maidenly charms, which undoubtedly attracted my errant son to you in the first place.'

'If you're talking about Harry . . .'

'Don't mention that libertine's name in my hearing. He's partly to blame for my present difficulties. I have to raise some money urgently and I believe I can do so by parting with some rare editions housed in the library at Bligh Park. I want you to go through them for me.'

'But surely you know more about them than I do, sir? I know almost nothing about rare books.'

'I have other business to attend to or I would do it myself. I'm not asking you to do the impossible, but you have a smattering of valuable knowledge and I'm trusting you to go through the collection and give me a selection. I, of course, will have the final say. Now go and get ready. It's a long journey.'

She hesitated in the doorway. 'Will Harry be there, sir?'

He looked up from his papers, scowling. 'What's that got to do with you?'

'Nothing, sir. I was just asking.'

'If you know what's good for you you'll mind your own business. I stand to lose everything if this fails, so don't delay.'

Sir Hedley said little on the long journey to Dorset. Charity dare not ask questions but leaned back against the leather squabs, which were stained and had split in places to reveal the padding, and held her peace. The carriage smelled of stale tobacco and wet dog, and there were cracks in the windows. The body swayed from side to side on leather straps as the wooden wheels lurched over cobblestones and rutted tracks, shaking its occupants until their teeth rattled.

They changed horses several times and put up at an inn that evening. Charity was saved from the embarrassment of sharing her employer's dinner table by the fact that he refused to allow her to sit with him. She took her supper in the taproom and retired to the small attic room which had been assigned to her as soon as she had finished eating. She slept beneath the eaves, listening to the pitter-patter of rodents' feet and the unearthly screech of hunting barn owls, with the odd bark of a dog fox thrown in for good measure. She could hear male voices raised in song emanating from the taproom two storeys below, and the snores of a maidservant who slept in the adjoining room, but even with this cacophony she soon fell asleep, exhausted by the events of the day.

Chapter Thirteen

March winds whipped through the trees, shaking branches that were misted with a green haze of leaf buds, and bending the stately trumpets of daffodils so that they made obeisance like courtiers bowing before royalty. Charity had never seen fields and farms, much less pretty villages with thatched cottages and ancient flint churches. She had been born and bred in London and this was her first trip west of Chelsea. She might have enjoyed their second day on the road had it not been for Sir Hedley's moody expression. He had obviously drunk too much wine and brandy the previous evening and the smell of stale alcohol and tobacco filled the carriage, despite the draughts that whistled through the cracked windows.

Charity sat huddled in the corner, wrapped in an old boat cloak that Mrs Diment had unearthed from a sea chest in the attic. Its coarse folds still smelled of tar with a hint of salt fish, but it was warm and its odour preferable to the one emanating from her employer. She took comfort in knowing why she had been spirited away from London and what would be expected of her at Bligh Park. She stared out of the window, preferring the view of hedgerows to the sight of Sir Hedley's grim countenance, and suddenly her attention was caught by what looked like an army bivouac in the middle of a ploughed field. She leaned forward in an attempt to see more.

'What's the matter, girl? Can't you sit still for a moment?' Sir Hedley's irritable tones made her turn her head.

'There seems to be some activity in that field. It looks like an army encampment. I don't think it's gypsies because there are no caravans.'

He peered over her shoulder. 'It's just possible that boggy morass might hold the answer to all my problems.'

'Really, sir? How is that?' For a moment she thought she had gone too far by asking a direct question and she fully expected a swift reprimand, but Sir Hedley seemed to relax and his thin lips curved in a smile.

'Buried treasure. That's what they're digging for.'

'Do you mean like pirate gold, sir?'

His sudden bark of laughter made her jump. 'Don't be silly, girl. Your head is so stuffed with fairytales that you don't live in the real world. I'm talking about ancient artefacts made of pure gold – coins and jewellery buried and lost for centuries – and it's on my land.'

'If it's yours, why do you need to sell your precious books, Sir Hedley?'

His expression darkened. 'Because I've been betrayed by my own flesh and blood and I need funds urgently. I've only just discovered that my former wife's brother-in-law put up the money for the archaeological dig and that her son, Harry's half-brother, has been working on it for months.'

'Do you mean Daniel Barton?'

He shot her a scornful glance. 'Who else? Myrtle will have delighted in persuading her husband and his brother Wilmot to finance such a venture. She had heard rumours of treasure buried somewhere on the estate, and she couldn't wait to get her grasping hands on it.'

'But surely she's not entitled to any of it now, sir. And how do Daniel and Harry come into it?'

'They're both pawns in their mother's game. Daniel is young and he's weak and Harry has inherited the Bligh gambling streak. It wouldn't have been difficult to get him on their side. His mother always had a hold on young Harry.'

'But the land is yours, sir. Surely they can't take what belongs to you?'

'I'm on the verge of bankruptcy.' He sat for a moment, staring morosely out of the window. He sighed heavily. 'My solicitor told me yesterday that an application to have me declared incompetent to handle my own affairs has been lodged with the courts. He named no names but I've no doubt it was Harry – his mother will have put him up to it. Myrtle is a vindictive woman who would delight in my downfall, which is imminent unless I can do something to save myself from being declared bankrupt.'

Charity knew better than to question him further, but even with what little she knew of Harry she could not believe that he would treat his own father in such a cruel way. She sat in silence, looking out of the window as the fields gave way to parkland studded with grazing deer, and through an avenue of trees she had her first sight of the Blighs' ancestral home.

From a distance Bligh Park looked solid and welcoming. She had seen enough illustrations of architectural styles to recognise the E-shape of an Elizabethan house constructed in mellow red brick with a slate roof and mullioned windows. It was hard to believe that Sir Hedley was poor when he owned such a splendid country estate as well as the house in Nevill's Court. As far as she was concerned, being poor meant living in a hovel or sleeping beneath railway arches, and always being hungry. She shot a wary glance at him as the carriage drew up outside the house, but he seemed to have forgotten her existence. He opened the door and climbed to the ground without waiting for the coachman to assist him, and he strode off leaving Charity to alight on her own.

She followed him into the house, where he was greeted by an aged manservant. 'Welcome home, sir.'

'Thank you, Parkin. Is my son here?'

Parkin cupped his hand behind his right ear. 'I beg your pardon, sir. I'm a little hard of hearing.'

Sir Hedley repeated the question in a raised voice that shook the glass in the lantern hanging overhead.

Parkin's bottom lip trembled. 'The boy is in trouble again, sir. I believe he fled the country.'

'He was too cowardly to face me.' Sir Hedley uttered a derisive snort. 'Trust him to take the easy way out. He's his mother's son.' He turned to Charity. 'Don't just stand there. Go to the library and start sorting through the books. Look for anything that will raise the most cash.'

She could see that he was agitated and working himself up into a temper. 'I don't know where it is, sir,' she said mildly.

'Parkin will show you.'

'Is the young lady a guest, Sir Hedley?' Parkin peered at Charity with myopic, rheumy eyes. 'Shall I tell Cook to prepare dinner for two, sir?'

'Miss Crosse will eat in the kitchen with the rest of the servants.' Sir Hedley strode towards the wide oak staircase, leaving Charity standing in the middle of the wainscoted entrance hall, feeling very small and insignificant amidst the faded grandeur of the country house. Sunlight filtered through the leaded lights, creating diamond patterns on the floorboards, which were in need of a good polish, and dust motes danced in the sunbeams.

'I know what you're thinking, miss,' Parkin said gloomily. 'It wasn't like this in times gone by, but there's only myself and Mrs Trevett who live in these days. There is a girl from the village who comes in daily to clean, but there's only so much that one pair of hands can do. Come this way, miss. I'll show you to the library.'

She followed him through seemingly endless corridors to the library. It was not a large room but it was lined, floor to ceiling, with shelves containing books of all shapes and sizes. A rosewood table in the centre of the faded Persian carpet was also piled high with leather-bound tomes and others were stacked on the floor, but there was nothing to sit on, and the ornately carved Carrara marble mantelshelf was bare of ornament, not even a clock. Parkin cleared his throat. 'Most of the valuables have gone to auction, miss. I'll fetch you a chair from the kitchen if that would help.'

'Thank you, Mr Parkin. That would be very kind.'

A weary smile deepened the lines etched on his face. 'Just ring the bell if you need anything. I wouldn't advise you to wander off on your own. It's a big house and you could easily get lost. I'll come to fetch you when it's time for dinner.' He held his hands out to take her cloak and bonnet. 'I'll get the girl to light a fire in your room.'

Charity smiled and thanked him again as he ambled out of the room, leaving her to face what looked like an impossible task. She picked up one of the larger books on the table and opened it, turning the pages slowly and carefully. It was a beautifully illustrated book on ornithology, and she set it aside while she cleared the table. She would pick what she hoped were the most valuable items in this vast collection and set them out for Sir Hedley to inspect. She would have to work instinctively, but she could see now why her help was needed and she would do her best.

Parkin returned with a chair and an hour later he brought her a tray of food. 'Mrs Trevett sent you a slice of venison pie and a glass of cider,' he said, placing it on the table. 'She said you can't work on an empty stomach.'

Charity's belly rumbled in anticipation. 'Please thank

her for me, Mr Parkin. It looks delicious and we didn't stop to have breakfast this morning.'

'I'll pass the message on, miss.' Parkin shuffled out of the room, leaving her to perch on the chair and enjoy her meal. The pie filling was delicious and the pastry rich and crumbly. She drank the cider in thirsty gulps, only realising her mistake when her head began to spin. The sweet apple taste had masked the strength of the alcohol and she felt sleepy. 'Fresh air,' she said out loud. 'That's what you need, Charity Crosse.' She went to the window and opened it, taking deep breaths. The sun was shining and she had a sudden need to get away from the dust and musty smells in the library. She had found three volumes that might fetch a tidy sum, and she would work better if she took some exercise.

Having convinced herself that she would be justified in taking a short break, she left the room and retraced her steps heading towards the entrance hall, but all too soon she realised that Parkin had been right: it was very easy to get lost in the maze of passages. She began opening doors in an attempt to find Parkin or perhaps the girl who came in to clean, but she came across nothing but empty cupboards and rooms shrouded in dust covers. The house had a sorry air of neglect, like an unloved wife, and she wondered how many years it had lain like this, mourning the lack of attention in sorrowful silence. After a while she was beginning to get desperate and she had come to a dead end, but as she opened the last door she found herself in what must have once been a stately drawing room. The furniture was concealed beneath Holland covers but light filtered in through four tall windows, and double half-glassed doors led into a conservatory.

She pulled back the bolt and opened one of the doors. She stepped into the marble-tiled room, flooded with sunlight, but she came to a sudden halt when she realised that she was not alone. At the far end of the conservatory, seated at a table, were two men in their shirtsleeves. Their tweed jackets were flung over the backs of the rattan chairs and they were examining something that was covered in yellow clay. They turned their heads at the sound of the door opening and one of them leapt to his feet.

'Charity! What on earth are you doing here?' Daniel strode towards her, holding out his hands, his face wreathed in a genuine smile of pleasure. 'What an amazing coincidence.'

The shock of seeing him cleared her fuddled brain. 'I knew you were at the dig, but I didn't think to find you here.' She glanced over his shoulder and her heart sank as she recognised Wilmot. The memory of their last meeting was still fresh in her mind.

Daniel's smile wavered. 'What's the matter? It's only Wilmot. You look as though you've seen a ghost.'

She made a quick recovery as Wilmot stood up and walked over to them. 'I didn't think Sir Hedley would welcome either of you into his house.'

Wilmot's eyes held a warning even though his lips were smiling. 'What Hedley doesn't know won't upset him.'

'We came in to get warm and I persuaded Mrs

Trevett to feed us,' Daniel said, squeezing Charity's hand. 'I know it must seem odd, but I feel quite at home in Bligh Park. Harry and I used to spend our school holidays here when my parents were travelling abroad. Mrs Trevett used to spoil us rotten.'

Wilmot took a step closer, fixing Charity with a warning frown. 'I hope we can trust you to keep quiet about this.'

'I'd entrust Charity with my life, Wilmot.' Daniel's smile faded. 'But what are you doing here? Who's looking after the shop?'

'I thought that Mr Barton would have noticed that the shop was closed, or perhaps someone else has taken it over.' She faced Wilmot with a steady gaze. 'The landlord put up the rent and I couldn't pay.'

Wilmot shrugged his shoulders. 'I had no call to visit Liquorpond Street. You made it clear that you wanted nothing more to do with me, Miss Crosse.'

Daniel looked from one to the other, frowning. 'Harry did say that you two had fallen out, but I thought it would have been patched up by now. I haven't seen him since New Year so I'm a bit out of touch with events in London.'

'If it hadn't been for Harry I would have been homeless,' Charity said hastily. 'He took me to your father's house in Nevill's Court.'

Daniel stared at her in amazement. 'My God, you must have been in desperate straits to throw yourself on Sir Hedley's mercy.'

'Why are you here, Charity?' Wilmot's smooth tone belied the suspicious look in his eyes.

'Sir Hedley asked me to sort through his book collection. I believe he went looking for you.' Charity shot him a sideways glance. 'He seems to think that someone is cheating him.'

'If anyone is in the wrong it will be Harry,' Wilmot said carelessly. 'He had to leave the country in rather a hurry.'

'Why was that?' Charity turned to Daniel for an explanation.

'Don't worry about Harry,' he said cheerfully. 'He's always getting into trouble, but he usually manages to extricate himself if left to his own devices. He takes after his father in that respect.'

'There's your answer.' Wilmot strolled back to the table and resumed his seat. 'Hedley hopes to raise money by selling some of his precious books, and Harry set you up in his father's house with the intention of getting his hands on some of his inheritance. I'd hazard a guess that your instructions were to choose the most valuable books and set them aside for Harry to collect, but unfortunately he won't be in a position to return to this country for some time.'

The accusation was so unfair that it took her breath away. She spun round to face him. 'That is not how it was at all. Don't judge everyone by yourself, Mr Barton.' She glanced over his shoulder, staring pointedly at the muddy object on the table. 'Is that something you've just dug up on Sir Hedley's land?'

'You'd do better to mind your own business, Miss Charity Crosse. I know too much about your past.'

'Are you threatening me, sir? I can assure you that my past is no secret to those who know me.'

'What's all this?' Daniel demanded, frowning. 'What has been going on in my absence? When I left Doughty Street everything was going really well. You were going to take her on as one of your pupils, Wilmot.'

'There was more to it than that,' Charity said stiffly. 'Your uncle had other ideas for me, Dan. I'd rather not discuss it, if you don't mind. As to Harry, he took me to Nevill's Court, but he left me there to make my own way. I haven't seen or heard from him since that day.'

'I believe you,' Daniel said earnestly. He turned to Wilmot. 'That was uncalled for. We know Charity wouldn't do anything underhand and I don't believe that Harry would cheat his own father. You're quite wrong on all counts.'

Charity managed a weak smile. 'Thank you, Daniel. Now I have work to do, and you needn't worry that I'll say anything to Sir Hedley about this. I don't want to cause any trouble.' She turned her back on them, ignoring Daniel's plea that she stay a little longer, and she opened the door leading into the garden. She needed to breathe cool, clean air, uncontaminated by Wilmot's presence.

Her head was spinning as she struggled to understand the situation that was gradually unfolding. There were many questions buzzing around in her brain and she wondered why Sir Hedley had given permission for the excavation on his land when he suspected the motives of those involved. As to Harry, she could not believe that a mere gambling debt would be enough to make him leave the country. Wilmot's sly suggestion that he had deliberately installed her in his father's house for the purpose of stealing some of the precious book collection was as outrageous as it was insulting. She was hurt and she was angry. Wilmot was a liar, and worse than that he had convinced Daniel that he was genuine. Despite the beauty of the countryside, she had a sudden longing to return to London, leaving the haunting sadness of the dilapidated house far behind.

She decided to go in search of the servants' entrance so that she could find someone to guide her back to the library. She started off across what must once have been a well-kept parterre, but the flowerbeds and box hedges were now covered by brambles and the shaggy stems of old man's beard. She stumbled against the base of a statue, stubbing her toe, and she stopped for a moment, grimacing with pain. Perched on a pyramid of blackened brick-shaped objects, the marble mermaid gazed with sightless eyes into a mirror made of some kind of metal. Charity had come across many imposing statues in London, but this piece of sculpture was unlike anything she had ever seen. She supposed it was the whimsical creation of an artist sponsored by one of Sir Hedley's wealthy ancestors, and she wondered what other works of art were hidden in the wilderness that had reclaimed Bligh Park gardens.

The pain had eased and she hurried on, coming to a sudden halt when she saw Sir Hedley shambling towards her. She was tempted to tell him that Wilmot was in his house, plotting against him, but that would mean breaking her word to Daniel. She quickened her pace and called out to him.

He had seen her but his lowered brow and narrowed eyes were not exactly a friendly greeting. 'What are you doing out here? I told you to get to work in the library. This isn't a holiday, young lady.'

'I just wanted a breath of air, but I got lost and found myself in the garden. I was trying to find my way back.'

He grunted something beneath his breath and walked on.

She ran after him. 'It won't happen again, sir. I'll soon find my way around.'

'We won't be here that long.' Sir Hedley lengthened his stride. 'But I need to find Wilmot Barton before I return to London. If I'd known that he was involved in the archaeological dig I would never have sanctioned it in the first place.' He stopped and she almost cannoned into him. 'I don't suppose you've seen him or the boy, have you? They were seen coming this way about an hour ago.'

'I've seen no one in the grounds, sir,' Charity said truthfully.

'They've probably gone to the local hostelry. I'll try there.' He started off again. 'Follow me, girl. I'll get Parkin to take you back to the library.'

She had to bunch up her skirts and run in order to keep up with him, and she arrived in the kitchen breathless, her petticoat torn to shreds by thorns. Parkin had been turning the handle of the Kent mechanical knife cleaner but he stopped and rose unsteadily to his feet when his master entered the room.

'Take Miss Crosse back to the library, Parkin. I'm going to the village but I'll be back in time for dinner.' He left without waiting for a response.

Mrs Trevett shook her head. 'That man is always in a tearing hurry. Sit down, Mr Parkin, and drink your tea. I'm sure that another few minutes won't make any difference.'

Parkin sank back onto the hard wooden seat. 'If you say so, Mrs Trevett.'

Mrs Trevett beamed at Charity. 'You look hot and bothered, my dear. I'm sure a cup of tea would go down a treat, and I so seldom get the chance to have a chat with another female. Please sit down and I'll make a fresh brew.'

Charity pulled up a chair. For some reason her legs had turned to jelly, but it was not the effort of keeping up with Sir Hedley that had made her hands shake. The encounter with Wilmot had upset her more than she had thought possible and she felt she had betrayed Sir Hedley's trust by pretending ignorance of Wilmot's presence in the conservatory. 'Thank you, ma'am,' she murmured gratefully. 'That would be lovely.'

Mrs Trevett bustled about making the tea in a brown pot with a chipped spout. 'Mr Parkin tells me that you've come here from London. I've never been there myself, but my friend Fanny Diment writes to me at Christmas and tells me all the goings-on.'

'You know Mrs Diment?'

'Yes, my dear. We started here together as girls, but then Fanny was chosen to work for Sir Hedley in his

London house. I daresay it's much grander than Bligh Park.'

'I wouldn't exactly say that,' Charity said tactfully. 'You seem very comfortable here, ma'am.'

Mrs Trevett cast a critical eye around the kitchen. 'The range is very difficult to clean and blacklead. It takes the girl all day to do it and I have to help her. We have to survive on bread and cheese that day and water from the well, or small ale. Not that Parkin minds, do you, Mr Parkin?' She left the pot to brew and bustled over to the dresser to fetch two cups, and although the saucers did not match Charity could see that it was fine bone china, no doubt the remains of an expensive set that had once graced an elegant tea table. It was obvious that Bligh Park had seen better days, just like Nevill's Court, and it was sad to see such fine houses in a state of decline.

Mrs Trevett poured the tea and passed a cup to Charity. 'In the old days I would have had a seed cake in the larder and some biscuits in the tin, but we have to be frugal with the housekeeping, and sometimes we have to rely entirely on produce from the home farm.'

'We do well enough, Mrs Trevett,' Parkin said severely. 'We are luckier than most, even if we haven't been paid for the last two quarters.'

'It's more like a year now, Mr Parkin.' Mrs Trevett sipped her tea. 'I told Master Harry so and he promised to set things to rights, but then he had a bit of bother with the police.'

'That's idle gossip, Mrs Trevett.' Parkin stopped turning the handle of the knife cleaner and began taking the knives out one at a time. 'Master Harry has gone abroad for his health. We don't know any more than that.'

Mrs Trevett tossed her head and her mobcap tipped over one eye. She righted it with an impatient flick of her fingers. 'Someone lied,' she said, pursing her lips. 'Someone had it in for him, if you want my opinion. Master Harry may be a bit too fond of the horses and the gaming tables but he's not dishonest. I'll never believe bad of him. He was a lovely little boy, and I've always said that nice boys grow up into nice men.'

'Even nice men can fall foul of the law, Mrs Trevett.' Parkin placed the knives carefully in a velvet-lined box. 'But, having said that, I don't believe that he did wrong. There are some people who would like to see him discredited and disowned so that they can get their hands on the estate and the treasure of Bligh Park.'

Charity almost choked on her tea. 'Is there really a treasure?'

'It's just a silly old legend,' Mrs Trevett said, sniffing. 'I'm sure it would have been found years ago if there had been anything. They say that wreckers worked the coast round here, and that they sunk many a ship and buried their hoards in the grounds of Bligh Park.'

'Well, they're digging away in the ten-acre field.' Parkin rose to his feet and took the box to the dresser, stowing it away in one of the drawers. 'They're said to be looking for the remains of a Roman villa, but we think different, don't we Mrs Trevett?

She nodded emphatically. 'We do, Mr Parkin.'

He rose to his feet, shaking first one leg and then the other. 'I'm a bit stiff these days,' he said by way of explanation. 'Rheumatics caused by the damp.' He continued his strange dance until he seemed satisfied that he could move without too much difficulty. 'Now then, miss. If you've finished your tea, I'll show you back to the library. I'll come and fetch you when it's time for dinner. We eat earlier than Sir Hedley.'

'A young lady who is good with books ought to eat in the dining room,' Mrs Trevett said, refilling her cup with tea. 'Would you like another, my dear? I'm sure Parkin will give you a minute or two.'

Charity stood up. 'No, thank you, Mrs Trevett. That was just what I needed, but I'd better get back to work. I'll see you at dinner.'

That night, in a small attic bedroom with Mrs Trevett's snores penetrating the wall that separated them, Charity fell asleep despite the storm that lashed the house with rain and gales that threatened to rip the tiles off the roof. She dreamed she was in a sailing ship that was being tossed about on mountainous waves. She clung to the rails, too terrified to go below, and the vessel lurched, prancing like a Lipizzaner stallion as they were flung against a huge rock. Drenched and terrified, Charity looked up and saw the marble mermaid come alive. Her long tresses billowed about her white face and her cold lips curved in a smile. She beckoned to Charity, luring her ever nearer. Then a wave crashed over her and she awakened to find rainwater pouring through a gap in the ceiling directly above her head.

She tumbled out of bed, landing in a heap on the bare floorboards. A flash of lightning was followed almost immediately by a crash of thunder and the door to her small room burst open. In the guttering light of a candle she saw the outline of a male figure. She opened her mouth to scream.

Chapter Fourteen

'Charity?' Harry knelt down beside her. 'You're the last person I expected to see here. Are you all right?'

The scream had frozen in her throat and she could only nod her head. The nightmare still held her in its eerie clutches, and the shock of seeing Harry had temporarily rendered her speechless. He helped her to her feet. 'You're soaked to the skin. I don't know who put you in this room but they should have known better.' He took off his jacket and wrapped it around her.

The warmth of his body still clung to its folds and the familiar scent of him reminded her of her birthday when he and Wilmot had taken her out to dinner and the theatre. 'You're always giving me your jacket,' she murmured. 'But I'll make it wet.'

'Let me worry about that. Let's get you somewhere warm and dry and you can tell me how you came to be here.'

She did not argue as he led her down the back stairs to the kitchen. He pulled a chair close to the range and made her sit down while he raked the embers into life. 'I know where Mrs Trevett keeps the cocoa,' he said, grinning. 'A cup of something hot will soon warm you up.'

Huddled in his jacket with the warmth seeping into

her chilled bones, she had the feeling that she was still in the middle of a dream. 'I thought you'd gone abroad.'

'I did, and I spent some time in France, but I returned a week ago and went to visit my mother in Devon.' He took a jug of milk from the larder and poured some into a saucepan, placing it on the hob.

'Then why all the secrecy? Why didn't you tell anyone that you'd come home? Or are you still hiding from your creditors?'

'I went to Paris to try to recoup some of my losses, but I should have known better. I lost more than I won.'

She shook her head. 'You aren't a stupid man, so why do you continue to gamble when you know very well you'll lose in the end?'

'I don't know,' he said humbly. 'I suppose I live in hope.' He made the cocoa and placed a brimming cup on the table in front of her.

'I'm sorry, but you ought to know better, and it's very selfish behaviour. You've left your family to pick up the pieces.'

'They're better off without me. Anyway, I'm leaving first thing in the morning. I only stopped by to collect some of my clothes, and then I'll be off again. I might not return for some time.'

Her anger evaporated as she sensed his distress even though he was attempting to disguise his emotions behind an outward show of bravado. 'I don't understand why you don't get on with your father. He's a difficult man, but he was kind enough to allow us to stay in his house.'

'You're the first person to call him kind,' he said, chuckling. 'Maybe we're too alike to get on together.' His smile faded. 'Are you feeling better now? You're still very pale.'

'I'm almost dry and I'm nice and warm.'

'What on earth were you doing sleeping up in the servants' quarters in the first place? I don't understand why Mrs Trevett didn't put you in one of the guest rooms?'

'I am a servant, Harry. I work for your father in return for my board and lodging, as do Violet and Dorrie.'

'I didn't think he'd use you as slave labour. I don't suppose the old devil has paid you a wage.'

'He hasn't paid any of the servants for a long time. They stay out of loyalty and because they can't afford to leave.'

He met her angry gaze with a rueful smile. 'I suppose you think it's my fault.'

'Yes,' she said, looking him in the eyes. 'I do. I don't think that running away solves anything.'

'I wouldn't be much use if I were locked up in jail.'

'Then why don't you get a job and earn some money? That's what other people do.'

'There's very little I could do.' He held out his hands, palms upwards. 'I was born a gentleman, not a navvy.'

'That's no excuse. Your father is desperate to raise funds. He asked me to go through his library and select the books that would raise the most money.'

'He must be in trouble if he's willing to part with even one of his precious collection.'

She hesitated for a moment, unsure as to whether

or not to tell him the real reason for his father's sudden decision. She took a deep breath. 'Sir Hedley is in a panic because he thinks that you want to have him declared incompetent and that he'll be locked away in a lunatic asylum.'

Harry's dark eyebrows snapped together in a frown. 'That's simply not true. I've never done anything to hurt the old man. He's not the best parent in the world, but he's still my father and I can hardly blame him for mishandling the family fortunes when I'm just as bad.'

'Then who's spreading these lies? Why would anyone want to discredit you or Sir Hedley?'

'I'm sure he has a theory of his own. Hasn't he told you anything about our family?'

'He told me a little about your mother.'

'When I visited my mother in Devonshire I learned that my stepfather had been killed in a hunting accident two months ago, and that she had handed the running of the estate to Wilmot. Dan protested, of course, thinking that he was Sir Philip's son and heir, but he's under age and there's nothing he can do about it until he reaches his majority.'

'I don't understand.'

'My mother told me the whole sordid story. For years she's been living a lie and at last she's admitted the truth.'

'I can tell by your expression that it must have been something upsetting.'

'This is strictly between us, Charity. I want you to promise not to tell anyone.'

'Cross my heart and hope to die.'

'Mother left us when I was just three. She persuaded my father to grant her a divorce so that she could marry Sir Philip, but what she didn't tell Sir Philip was that she was already expecting a child.'

'Are you saying that Sir Hedley is Dan's father?'

'That's exactly it. My mother was in quite a state when she told me about the deception. I urged her to tell Father the truth, but she refused. She said that Sir Philip had always thought that Dan was his son and she saw no reason to tell the world that she had deceived him.'

'Daniel should know. It doesn't seem right to keep it from him.'

'I'll tell my brother when I think the time is right, but I suspect that Wilmot is manipulating both my mother and Dan for his own ends.'

'What could he hope to gain?'

'If Father were declared incompetent, and if I were in exile, Dan would be next in line to inherit this estate, as well the house in Nevill's Court.'

Charity shivered even though they were bathed in the warm glow of the fire. 'Do you think this has something to do with the stories of the Bligh treasure?'

'I think Wilmot is a greedy and ambitious man. If he married my mother he would gain control of his late brother's estate, and as Dan's stepfather he would have a say when it came to making decisions about Bligh Park until Dan comes of age.'

Charity's head was spinning with this tale of ambition and avarice. 'But surely it's illegal for Wilmot to marry his brother's widow?' she said, grasping at the one flaw she could see in the whole sorry business.

'I think it is illegal, but I know that many people ignore the law. They get married in Scotland or London and live together as man and wife. I just hope that Wilmot has genuine feelings for my mother.'

'You know he is here, digging up the ten-acre field.'

'Parkin told me what's been going on, but I don't think the excavation of Roman ruins is going to save Bligh Park from bankruptcy. Wilmot has his eye on something more and I need to warn Dan not to be taken in by him.'

'Then you ought to stay here. Clear your name and don't run away, leaving your father and brother unprotected.'

'I can't prove anything, Charity. It's my word against Wilmot's, and who would believe a man who can't honour his debts?'

'Tell Sir Hedley. Tell him everything and maybe together you can put a stop to Wilmot's game.'

'You know my father well enough to realise that he wouldn't listen to anything I had to say. If I stay I'll be caught and arrested, but as a free man I might have a chance to put things right.'

'Where will you go?'

'Ned Loveless is going to take me across the Channel. It's better if you don't know where I'm going.'

'How will you live?'

'I'll do what you said I should do and try to find work. Maybe I'll turn into an honest citizen if I keep away from temptation.'

She seized him by the hand. 'You are a good man; you've just taken the wrong path. I wish I could help you as you helped me.'

His eyes darkened and he dropped his gaze. 'You make me feel even more ashamed of myself. I've done exactly as I pleased all my life with no thought for the consequences or the fact that I was frittering away a fortune. You had nothing but you've struggled on, and I admire you for that.'

'Don't be so hard on yourself, Harry.' She raised his hand to her cheek. 'Thanks to you I still have my books, but when I return to London I'll sell them. Any money I raise I'll send to you.'

'That is the most generous offer I've ever had, but I couldn't let you do it.' He rose to his feet. 'You must put yourself first for once. Never mind me. I'm perfectly capable of looking after myself in my own ramshackle way.'

She shrugged off his jacket and handed it to him. 'You will write to me when you're settled, won't you?' She was close to tears, but somehow she managed to control her emotions.

'It's almost dawn and I need to see my brother before I go. I think you're right and I should tell him the truth before I go away.' He leaned over and brushed her forehead with a kiss. 'I will write to you and that's a promise. Look after yourself.' He snatched his coat and hat from a nearby chair and picked up a carpet bag. 'Goodbye, Charity.' He let himself out into the darkness.

She leapt to her feet and ran to the window. The

storm had abated and there was a pale glimmer of light in the east. Harry was shrugging on his coat as he walked off in the direction of the archaeological excavation, and then he was swallowed up in the darkness. The only sign that he had been in the house was the chair where he had been sitting, only now it was tilted on its back legs, leaning against the pine table. She righted it with a sigh. Harry had come into her life briefly, but his presence had had a profound effect on her and now he was gone. If his suspicions about Wilmot were well founded and Sir Hedley was locked away in Colney Hatch, she might find herself homeless yet again.

She went to her room and found to her relief that her clothes were dry, even though the bed was soaked. She dressed quickly, and acting on impulse she decided to seek out Daniel and tell him the truth about Wilmot. Harry might not be able to convince his brother that Wilmot was not an honourable man, but if she told Daniel how he had propositioned her he might think differently.

'You're wrong,' Daniel said in a low voice. He glanced over his shoulder at Wilmot who was standing several yards away deep in conversation with one of the archaeologists. 'You shouldn't have listened to Harry. What he said about Wilmot is nonsense. He's resigned his position at the university in order to help my mother run the estate, and he's a good man who has my best interests at heart, even though he knows the truth about my birth.'

She stared at him in amazement. 'So you knew that Sir Philip wasn't your father?'

'Mama told me soon after the funeral.' Daniel ran his hand through his already tousled hair. 'As to Wilmot, you shouldn't believe everything Harry says. My brother lives by his wits and he's desperate to get someone on his side. Not that you could do anything to help him, unless, of course, you have some influence with our father.'

'I don't think he was making it up, Dan. He genuinely believes that Wilmot is plotting to gain control of the estate.'

'Mama is fond of Wilmot, but she loved Sir Philip, and so did I. He might not have sired me, but he raised me as his son. He was my real father, and I trust Wilmot.'

'Sir Philip sounds like a marvellous man.' She lowered her voice to a whisper. 'But there are things about Wilmot you don't know.'

'How can you say that, Charity? How can you turn against him when he offered to further your education and enrol you in his classes at the university? You could have worked hard and bettered yourself, but you chose to throw his generosity back in his face.'

'That's not how it happened. If that's what he told you then he's lying. He wanted me to be his mistress.'

Daniel stared at her in patent disbelief. 'I don't believe that for a moment. You've been taken in by Harry's lies and now you're adding to them. Wilmot is my friend and mentor. He loves my mother and he only wants the best for me. I don't want anything to do with Sir Hedley, or Harry if it comes to that. I never want to see either of them again.' He stalked off to join Wilmot.

Charity resisted the temptation to run after him. She knew she had handled the situation badly but she was at a loss to know what to do for the best. She was about to return to the house when she saw Sir Hedley striding across the field towards them. She glanced over her shoulder, wondering if she ought to warn Dan, but it was too late. Sir Hedley's shabby overcoat flapped about him as he quickened his pace, and he looked like an ungainly scarecrow that had suddenly acquired the ability to walk. 'Wilmot Barton, is that you?'

Wilmot turned his head slowly. 'What can I do for you, Hedley?'

'What are you doing on my land?' Sir Hedley advanced on them, puffing and panting.

Charity hurried towards him, alarmed by his high colour and laboured breathing. 'We should get you back to the house, sir.'

He pushed her aside. 'Mind your own business, girl.' He pointed a shaking finger at Daniel. 'Who gave you permission to work with the archaeologists? I sanctioned a dig run by the university and that didn't include you or your uncle.'

White-faced and visibly upset, Daniel stepped forward shaking off Wilmot's restraining hand. 'He's not my uncle, Father.' He stressed the last word, bringing Sir Hedley to a sudden halt.

'Are you being funny, boy?'

'No, sir. I think it's time someone told you the truth.'

'This isn't the time or place, Dan,' Wilmot hissed.

Ignoring Wilmot, Dan faced up to his father. 'Mother told me the truth after Sir Philip died. I am your son. It pains me to admit such a thing but I have as much right to be on this land as anyone.'

'You're a liar.' Sir Hedley clutched his hand to his chest. 'Your mother left me for Philip Barton. You're not my son.'

'I wish it were a lie. No one in their right mind would want a man like you to be their father.'

Charity leapt forward to clutch Daniel's arm. 'Please don't say any more. Can't you see this is upsetting him?'

'Keep out of this.' He pushed her away and she fell against Sir Hedley, who staggered, lost his footing and crumpled to the ground.

She went down on her knees beside him. 'I'm so sorry. Are you all right?' She attempted to raise his head, but his eyes bulged in their sockets and he gasped for breath. She sent a pleading look to Daniel. 'Get help.'

He shook his head. 'He's play-acting. There's nothing wrong with him.'

'Not this time, Dan.' Wilmot dragged Charity to her feet. 'He's finished. You can't do anything for him. Go back to the house.'

'No. I won't leave him,' Charity said on a sob. 'I've seen men die on the streets and he doesn't deserve to end his life in a muddy field.'

Wilmot beckoned to two of the diggers who had been looking on with interest. 'Don't just stand there – carry him to the house.'

'He needs a doctor,' Charity said urgently. 'Please, Dan. Go to the village and find a physician.'

'Why should I? He's nothing to me.'

'He's your father,' Charity whispered. 'You were cruel to him and that's not like you. I know you better than that.'

Wilmot stood aside while the men lifted Sir Hedley's now inert form. 'I think it's too late for a doctor,' he said with a malicious grin. 'Perhaps an undertaker would be more appropriate.'

Charity faced him angrily. 'You are a despicable person. You brought this about with your plotting and scheming.'

'You've been listening to Harry's idiotic ranting. You shouldn't believe everything that he tells you, my dear,' Wilmot said, curling his lip. 'A man who refuses to use his father's name is not my idea of a devoted son. Harry has left the country and I'll make certain he never returns. All this belongs to Dan now.' He encompassed the estate with a sweep of his hands. 'And you are dismissed. Your services are no longer needed.'

'That's a bit harsh, Wilmot.' Daniel bent down to retrieve his father's spectacles, which had fallen from his pocket. He wiped the mud off the lenses, and handed them to Charity. 'You can stay on at Nevill's Court until you find yourself another position.'

'I wouldn't be so generous,' Wilmot said angrily. 'She's a troublemaker, Dan. Get rid of her and close the house in London until everything is settled. You can't afford to pay the servants.'

Charity felt a surge of pity for Daniel. He looked young and defenceless in the face of Wilmot's determined attempt to gain control of the situation. 'Leave him alone. Haven't you done enough harm? You might not have struck the lethal blow, but you are responsible for Sir Hedley's death.'

He raised his hand and caught her a stinging blow across the cheek. She would have fallen to the ground if Daniel had not caught her. 'That was uncalled for, Wilmot,' he said angrily. 'If anyone is to blame it's me. I goaded the old man and he suffered a seizure. I killed my own father.'

'Don't talk rubbish, boy. Take her back to the house and send her on her way.' Wilmot's voice was harsh with suppressed anger, but he seemed to realise that he had gone too far and he forced his lips into a smile. 'You'll see things in a better light when you've had time to think, Daniel. This is a heaven-sent opportunity to go through the old pile of bricks and mortar with a fine-tooth comb. By the end of the week we could be travelling back to Devon with the Bligh treasure and you'll be a wealthy man.'

'Don't listen to him, Dan.' Clutching her hand to her sore cheek, Charity backed away from them. 'You may not have liked Sir Hedley but you should have some respect for the dead.'

'You're going too fast, Wilmot,' Daniel said slowly. 'Charity's right. Whether I like it or not he was my father. I'm going back to the house to make sure that he receives the treatment he deserves.' He walked off with his shoulders bent as if he were carrying a heavy load.

Charity made to follow him but Wilmot caught her by the sleeve. 'Leave the boy alone, you little trollop. You'll go back to London today and be out of the house in Nevill's Court by the end of the week. I can't say fairer than that, but if you try to cross me or make any attempt to stir things up with Dan, I'll make you very sorry, and that's a promise.'

She pulled free from his grasp. 'I'm not afraid of you.' She walked off without giving him the opportunity to retaliate.

A blood-red sun was struggling over the horizon as she followed Daniel across the rutted field, but she did not make any attempt to catch up with him. She sensed the turmoil in his breast and she knew that he needed time to get over the shock of what had just happened. She hesitated when she reached the lane that separated the parkland from the farm, and the salt-laden breeze coming off the sea seemed to beckon her like a siren. There was just a chance that she might catch Harry before he set sail for the Continent. She lifted up her skirts and ran.

She arrived in the village just as the last boat was leaving the harbour. She came to a halt, panting and breathless, but there were only a few small crabbers in the sheltered waters of the cove, and the gigs that took the pilots out to larger ships were hauled up on the beach. The scent of pipe tobacco made her turn to see an old man seated on an upturned lobster pot, mending a net. She went up to him, clearing her throat to attract his attention. 'Excuse me, sir.'

He looked up, squinting through a haze of blue smoke that curled up from the pipe clenched between his teeth. 'Yes, maidy. What can I do for you?'

'Do you know Harry Elliott? You might know him better as Harry Bligh?'

He nodded his head. 'Aye, I've known Master Harry since he were a boy.'

'Did you happen to see him today?'

He nodded again, exhaling a cloud of smoke as he took the pipe from his mouth. 'Aye, maidy. He left on the *Mary May*. Gone fishing for bass so they say, but word has it that it's a one way trip for Master Harry.' He tapped the side of his nose with the stem of his pipe and grinned. 'You ain't one of his creditors, are you?'

She smiled. 'No, sir. That I'm not.'

'You'd have to ask Ned Loveless, the skipper of the *Mary May*, as to his destination. I can't say nothing more because that's all I knows.'

'Thank you. That's very helpful.' Charity could see that this was all the information she was going to get, and she made her way slowly back to the house.

Parkin was in the kitchen, comforting a tearful Mrs Trevett. They looked up as she entered the room and Mrs Trevett's face crumpled as tears rolled down her cheeks. 'The master has gone, miss.'

'Yes, I know and I'm very sorry.' Charity met Parkin's agonised look with a sympathetic smile. 'It was very quick. He didn't suffer.'

Parkin helped Mrs Trevett to a chair. 'I'd better go and see if Master Daniel has any orders for me.'

'Yes, Mr Parkin. Of course you must.' Mrs Trevett buried her face in her hands. 'What will become of us now? This is a bad day for Bligh Park.'

There was nothing that Charity could say that would be of comfort and she busied herself tending to the fire. She was still in a state of shock after the events at the excavation, and occupying herself with mundane tasks kept her mind focused on the immediate present. What would happen to them in the future depended on how much latitude Daniel was prepared to allow Wilmot when it came to making decisions for him. She made a cup of tea for Mrs Trevett, adding two lumps of sugar and a tot of brandy, which she found on a shelf at the back of the larder. She suspected that Parkin would benefit from the same medicine when he returned, and she put the pot to keep warm on the range.

A bowl of bread dough had been left to prove. Charity turned to Mrs Trevett. 'What should I do with this? I'm no cook and I've never made bread in my life, but I'm willing to try.'

Mrs Trevett raised herself from her seat. 'That's my job, miss. I'll see to it.'

'If you're sure.'

'Heaven knows what will happen to us now the master's gone, but I won't allow good food to go to waste.' Mrs Trevett rolled up her sleeves and plunged her hands into the dough. Her cheeks were flushed and her eyes red and swollen, but she attacked the task as if her life depended upon it. 'Sir Hedley was partial to a slice of fresh bread and a slab of cheese for his midday meal,' she said, working the dough with vigour. 'He was particularly fond of my green tomato chutney.'

Charity could think of nothing to say that would not upset the delicate balance of Mrs Trevett's emotions, and she was relieved when Parkin walked into the room. 'What's happening, Mr Parkin?' She filled a cup with tea, added a measure of brandy, and placed it on the table. 'You look as though you could do with something a bit stronger than just tea,' she said softly.

He drank greedily and two spots of colour appeared on his ashen cheeks. 'The master is laid out in the morning parlour and Jackson has gone to fetch the doctor and the undertaker. This is a bad day for us, miss. A very bad day.' He sat down suddenly, as if his aged bones had given way beneath him. 'I nearly forget to say that Master Daniel wants to see you, miss. He's in the library. Can you find your own way there?'

'I'm sure I can, Mr Parkin. Is he on his own, or is Mr Barton with him?'

'Mr Barton went to the stables, miss.'

Charity hurried from the room and reached the library without losing her way. She tapped on the door and waited for a response.

Chapter Fifteen

Daniel was standing by the table, flicking through the pages of one of the rarest volumes in the library as if it were a penny dreadful. Charity only just stopped herself from scolding him for treating a priceless book in such a cavalier fashion. 'You wanted to see me?'

He closed the book and looked up. His expression was grave. 'I shouldn't have spoken to you like that, Charity. You are the innocent party in all this sordid business.'

'When am I to leave?'

'I'm not sure, but I'd like you to stay on for a day or two and continue your work here.'

She stared at him in surprise. 'Really?'

'Wilmot is leaving for Devon shortly. He wants to tell Mother in person.'

'Shouldn't you be doing that, Dan?'

'Perhaps, but I'd rather he did it to be honest. I can't stand to see a woman cry.'

'Do you think she'll be upset? I thought there was no love lost between your parents.'

'Who knows? I'm baffled by the whole business, to tell the truth. All I know is that Harry's gone, and I've been stuck with responsibilities that I never sought and don't want.'

Once again she experienced a wave of pity for him. 'Why didn't you tell Wilmot how you felt? Or if you can't talk to him you should speak to your mother. Maybe you could persuade her to pay off Harry's debts and then he could return and sort out the estate. You don't have to do this, Dan. Stand up for yourself.'

'That's just it. Mother will do anything that Wilmot says.'

Charity shook her head. 'I can't help you if you won't help yourself.'

'I don't know what to do. Mother is convinced that the Bligh treasure is somewhere in the house or the grounds. I'm certain that's why she chose to tell me that Sir Hedley is my real father.'

'Maybe you can find the treasure.'

'I don't believe it exists. I just want to live my own life, Charity. I want to be an archaeologist and go to Egypt and spend my time excavating ancient tombs. I don't care about money, and I don't want to see my brother facing ruin.'

'You told me you wanted nothing more to do with Harry.'

'That was for Wilmot's benefit, and I was angry with Harry for running away and leaving me to deal with all this.' He glanced round at the book-filled shelves. 'If you can find anything of value I'll be happy to see it sold and the proceeds used to pay off my brother's debts. I want him to come home and claim what's rightfully his.'

'All right, Dan. I'll do anything I can to help, and there might be a way to find out where Harry is now.'

His eyes lit with hope and he grabbed her by the hand. 'How?'

'I went to the village after you left the dig this morning. I hoped I might be in time to stop Harry leaving, but I was too late. He'd sailed on a boat called the *Mary May* and the skipper is a man called Ned Loveless.'

'I know Loveless.' Dan's sombre expression was replaced with a wide grin. 'He used to take us fishing when we were boys . . .' He broke off, releasing her hand as Wilmot strode into the library.

'What's all this?'

Dan hid his hand behind his back as if he were a small boy expecting to be caned for misbehaving. 'I sent for her, Wilmot.'

'You were holding her hand.'

'He was saying goodbye,' Charity said calmly. 'I was just leaving.'

'That had better be the truth. She's trouble, Daniel.'

'I'm dealing with it.'

'I couldn't find Hedley's man, but I left word for him to report to you as soon as the fellow turns up. I'm leaving now, but I'll be back within a few days. In the meantime you can make arrangements to dispose of the old devil, and then you can start tearing this place apart. We'll find the Bligh Park treasure even if we have to pull the old ruin down brick by brick.' Wilmot uttered a hollow laugh. 'It's in such a derelict state that I doubt if anyone will notice the difference.'

'I'll do my best, Uncle.'

'I'm not your uncle, boy. I fully expect to be your stepfather by the time I return from Devon.'

'My mother might have something to say to that,' Dan said angrily. 'I won't allow you to bully her.'

Charity held her breath. For a moment she thought that Wilmot had been pushed too far, but he cast a pitying glance in Daniel's direction. 'I know how to handle a woman, Dan, my boy. Myrtle will do exactly as I say and love me the more for being strict with her.' His laughter echoed round the room after he had gone.

Daniel made to follow him but Charity barred his way. 'Let him go,' she said in a low voice. 'It amuses him to see you lose your temper. He's like a cat tormenting a mouse.'

'You told me to stand up to him,' Daniel said sulkily. 'I won't have him say things about my mother.'

'Let's forget him for the time being. I've already found some books that should fetch a tidy sum, but I'm not an expert.'

'Do what you can and I'll make a start in the house, although it seems like a hopeless task. People have been looking for the Bligh Park treasure for a hundred years or more. Wilmot could raze it to the ground and still find nothing.'

Charity ran her fingers over the tooled-leather book cover. 'Perhaps you'd do better to look for Sir Hedley's will. If he left everything to Harry there's not much Wilmot could do about it.'

'Splendid idea. Why didn't I think of that?' Daniel made for the door but he came to a sudden halt, turning to Charity with a thoughtful frown. 'I suppose I ought to see the undertaker first to make arrangements for a decent send-off for the old man. I can't mourn for him as a son, but I'll make sure that he's treated with respect. It's the least I can do.'

By mid-afternoon Charity had found at least a dozen books that might fetch a tidy sum at auction. She was covered in dust and her head ached from staring at the various types of print; the light was fading as storm clouds rolled in from the west, making it difficult to see. She was about to go in search of Dan when the door opened and he burst in, looking very pleased with himself. He waved a document under her nose. 'I found it at last,' he said triumphantly. 'Sir Hedley's will. He's left everything to Harry, as I knew he would. Wilmot won't like that, and Mama won't be best pleased, although she could hardly expect him to include me when he didn't even know I existed, at least not until it was too late.'

'It's even more important for us to find Harry. The will should go to probate; I know that much from when Jethro passed away. Dr Marchant helped me then and now he's gone, poor man. It seems that everyone who helps me comes to a bad end. I'm bad luck.'

Dan slipped his arm around her shoulders. 'Come on, Charity. That's superstitious nonsense and you know it. Your grandfather died of drink and the doctor caught typhoid in the slums. Jethro was a sick man and Sir Hedley was getting on in years.'

She managed a smile. 'I suppose so, but it seems

like an unlikely string of coincidences. I'm like the angel of death.'

'You needn't worry about me,' he said, chuckling. 'I'm only twenty and Harry is twenty-three. I think we'll be around for some time to come.'

'We need to find Harry and bring him home,' Charity said thoughtfully. 'And you should send the will to the probate registry in London before Wilmot gets his hands on it.'

'You're right, although I hate to admit it. I've always been fond of Wilmot but there's never been any love lost between him and Harry. I'll send Jackson back to London and he can take the will and the books you've earmarked for auction.'

'The servants haven't been paid for nearly a year, Dan. Perhaps you could use some of the money to look after them.'

'How did you come to be so wise, kid?'

The teasing note in his voice reminded her forcibly of Harry and her eyes filled with tears. She looked away. 'The dust has made my eyes sore and I'm gasping for a cup of tea. I don't think I can do any more today.'

Ha laid his hand on her arm. 'This isn't your problem, Charity. My family has imposed on you enough.'

'I would be homeless if it hadn't been for Harry and your father,' Charity said, dashing her hand across her eyes. 'It's in my best interests to help you. If we're turned out of Nevill's Court we won't have anywhere to go.'

'I won't let that happen, so stop worrying.'

'Perhaps I ought to take the will to London. I would

make sure it went to the right place and I could take the books to an auction house. It's not that I don't trust Jackson, but he wouldn't know how to set about it.'

'You're right, I suppose, although I don't fancy being left alone in this creepy old house.'

'It's not creepy, it's just unloved. It needs someone to take care of it and bring back the laughter. It must have been a happy home once.'

'Maybe, but the sooner I find my brother the better. I'll seek out Ned Loveless and find out where he took Harry.'

'I wish I could stay and help you, but we'll need money if we're to go looking for him.'

'Does that mean you'll come with me? He might be anywhere.'

'I have a feeling that if he's landed in France he'll head for the nearest casino. Harry was full of good intentions but if he's short of funds he won't have much choice.'

'You're a remarkable girl, Charity Crosse.' Daniel's eyes were filled with admiration. 'You're young and yet you know so much.'

'It comes from begging on the streets. When you're the lowest of the low you see the world from a different angle. I know what it's like to be cold and hungry. I never want to suffer that again, and I wouldn't like to see Harry made destitute because of the greed of someone like Wilmot.'

'Are you in love with my brother?'

The question, coming from nowhere, startled her and she felt herself blushing. 'No, of course not. I'm not sure I even like him, but I'm in his debt and I hate injustice. Harry might be foolish but he's got a good heart and to me that's all that matters.'

'He's lucky to have you for a friend.' Dan walked to the door and opened it. 'I'll send for Jackson.'

She hesitated. 'Perhaps I ought to stay until after the funeral?'

'That wouldn't be a good idea. My mother and Wilmot will almost certainly arrive in time to put on a show for the villagers. Mama always says she looks her best in black.'

Charity returned to London next day. It was late afternoon when she arrived, bruised and exhausted after a long and uncomfortable journey. Jackson carried the crate of books into the house and set it down in the entrance hall. He straightened up, fixing Charity with a hard stare. 'I need money, miss. The horse has to be fed and so do I, come to that. Sir Hedley used to pay me once a month.'

'I haven't a penny to my name, Jackson.' She saw by his expression that she had been too frank. 'But we will have funds when the books are sold. It's too late to take them to the auction house now, but we'll go there first thing tomorrow.'

He tipped his hat. 'We can only last a few days, miss. It'll be the knacker's yard for the animal if we can't keep him fed.'

Charity walked through to the kitchen and was met with cries of delight from Dorrie and Violet and a sombre-faced Mrs Diment.

'We wasn't expecting you yet,' Dorrie said, hugging Charity. 'We missed you something chronic.'

'I'm so glad you're back.' Violet put her arms around both of them and her eyes filled with tears. 'We did miss you.'

'Where's the master?' Mrs Diment demanded angrily. 'It's all right for him to go off like that but I've had the tradesmen knocking on the door demanding to be paid. We've got almost nothing in the larder and I can't conjure up meals out of thin air.'

Charity eased herself free of Dorrie's clutching hands. 'You'd best sit down, Mrs Diment. I'm afraid I've got bad news for you.'

Mrs Diment flung up her hands and collapsed onto the nearest chair. 'Don't say he's backed yet another loser. There's precious little left to sell, at least nothing of any value. It'll be the bed curtains next and then the bedding. Soon we'll all be sleeping on the floor.'

'The master had a seizure,' Charity said gently. 'He never recovered.'

'He's dead?'

'I'm afraid so. It was very sudden.'

'Where's Master Harry? He'll sort things out.'

'He can't help at the moment, Mrs Diment. He had to go away on business.'

Mrs Diment's eyes narrowed to slits. 'You mean he's cut and run? What will we do now?' She covered her head with her apron and sat rocking to and fro.

Dorrie burst into tears and Violet sank down on a chair at the table, holding her head in her hands. 'I knew it was too good to last. We'll be out on the streets.'

'No,' Charity said firmly. 'That won't happen, because I've brought valuable books from Bligh Park and I've got Daniel's permission to sell them.'

Mrs Diment peered at her through a hole in the grimy cotton apron. 'What's Master Daniel got to do with all this? He's the son of that woman and her fancy man.'

'Apparently not.' Charity took off her bonnet and hung it on a peg followed by her shawl. 'Mrs Barton lied and passed him off as Sir Philip's son, but Sir Hedley was his real father. It's come as a shock to him, but he's doing everything he can to set matters to rights.'

Mrs Diment slid the apron off her head. 'The sly cat. Who would have thought it?'

'What does it mean for us?' Violet asked anxiously. 'Will Daniel allow us to remain here?'

'You mustn't worry, Vi. Everything will be all right, you'll see.' Charity gave Dorrie an encouraging smile. 'Why don't you make us all a lovely cup of tea? That's if there is any left in the caddy.'

Mrs Diment rose stiffly to her feet. 'I've been drying the leaves and re-using them time and time again. We can't go on like this. Something must be done or we'll all end up in the workhouse.'

The following morning Charity took Sir Hedley's books to the sale room, but the next auction was not until the beginning of April and she knew they could not last that long without some form of income. She returned to the house and found Violet in the tiny front garden chatting to their next door neighbour's parlour-maid. One look at Charity's face was enough to make Violet put an abrupt end to her conversation and follow her into the house. 'What's up?'

'The sale isn't for another ten days. We need money now.'

Violet clasped her expanding belly with her hands as if protecting her unborn child. 'What will we do?'

'We can't wait for the auction. We've got to do something quickly.' Charity made for the library with Violet waddling after her.

'We can't eat books,' Violet said crossly. 'Haven't they caused us enough trouble already?'

Charity flung the door open and was enveloped in the familiar musty smell she had come to love. 'This is where they start paying their way,' she said, rushing over to the shelves that she had only recently organised. 'We need to get hold of a costermonger's barrow and we'll set up as street traders. We'll start with my books and some of Sir Hedley's less valuable volumes.'

Violet stood arms akimbo. 'I agree with the idea of selling them, but where will we get a barrow?'

'I don't know. We'll beg, borrow or steal one if it comes to that.'

'Steal?' Violet cried in alarm. 'You mustn't do anything silly, Charity.'

'Don't worry, love. This is where the years I spent begging on street corners will come in useful. I know someone who might be able to help.'

'Where are you going?' Violet demanded.

'Back to the streets where I grew up,' Charity said with a wry smile.

'Then I'm coming with you.' Violet followed her into the echoing entrance hall. 'Wait there. I'll fetch our bonnets and shawls.' She hurried off, swaying from side to side like a galleon in full sail.

'You're a born mother, Violet Chapman,' Charity murmured, smiling as she sensed an answering echo from the deep shadows in the wainscoted entrance hall. It felt as though the house was willing her on, or perhaps it was Sir Hedley's spirit begging her to save his beloved home from falling into Wilmot's hands. Fond as she was of Daniel, Charity was aware of his failings. She was afraid that his mother, urged on by Wilmot, would bully or cajole him into giving her control of the estate, and Harry would return to find nothing left of his inheritance. She would not allow that to happen. 'I will find a way,' she whispered, gazing into the darkness at the top of the wide staircase. A breeze wafted from the upper floors, brushing her cheeks like a cool caress, but she was not afraid. The old house no longer held any terrors for her. She turned with a start as something cold touched her fingers and she looked down to find Sir Hedley's wolfhound gazing up at her with limpid brown eyes. 'You must miss him, Bosun,' she said out loud and the dog wagged his tail in response. She patted his head. 'Don't worry, old chap. We'll look after you.'

'Who are you talking to?' Violet demanded, hurrying towards her with Charity's shawl draped over her arm and her bonnet dangling by its strings. She glanced at the dog. 'That's the first time he's left his bed for days. He must know that his master's passed away.'

'You're on guard, Bosun. You must look after us now that your master is no longer here.' Charity patted his head and he wagged his tail as if agreeing with her.

'Talking to the hound won't put food on the table,' Violet said, rubbing her belly. 'Me and the little 'un need vittles. We can't exist on bread and water, and there's only enough flour left for one loaf, so Mrs Diment says.'

Charity rammed her bonnet on her head and tied the ribbons without bothering to look in the mirror. She wrapped her shawl around her shoulders. 'Come on then. We'll walk round to the mews and Jackson can take us in the carriage.'

They found Jackson standing on the pavement amidst a pile of battered pots and pans, a blackened kettle and a couple of bulging sacks.

'What's happened?' Charity demanded. 'What's all this?'

'This here is the sum total of a man's life, miss. All me worldly possessions you see here on the pavement.'

Charity and Violet exchanged puzzled looks.

His shoulders sagged and he sighed heavily. 'The stables was only rented, miss. No rent, no stables. The carriage is locked inside and will be kept in lieu of back rent if we can't pay up.'

'What about the horse, Jackson?' Charity knew the answer even before he spoke. His whole demeanour was that of a defeated man.

'Collapsed and died last night, miss. The poor old nag got us home as was his wont, and then he breathed his last. I was hoping he'd live out his days at Bligh Park, but it weren't to be. I looked after him since he was a colt and now we're both done for.'

Charity took him by the hand. 'Don't say that, Jackson. I'm truly sorry about the poor horse, but I'm sure there's work for you at Bligh Park. Master Daniel will see that you're taken care of.'

He stared down at the objects scattered around on the paving stones. 'This is all I got,' he murmured.

'Violet will go with you to the house, Jackson. Mrs Diment will look after you until I return and then, when you're rested, we'll talk again.'

'I can't let you go wandering round the streets on your own,' Violet protested. 'I should come with you.'

'I know my way around so you needn't worry about me. Take care of Jackson and I'll be home before you know it.' Charity picked up the kettle and thrust it into Violet's hand. 'I expect the tea leaves that Mrs Diment has used and reused will do for one last brew.' She walked off, leaving them to manage on their own.

Although it was over a year since Charity left Duck's Foot Lane for the last time, she found that little had changed. The costermongers she met on the streets were familiar faces but not many of them recognised her. It was only now that she realised how much she must have changed since her grandfather's death had precipitated her into the world of books and commerce. She might still be shabbily dressed compared to the people she had met through Daniel and Wilmot, but she was no longer a skinny waif dressed in rags.

She held her head high and walked on as if in a dream. She stopped to pass the time of day with an elderly flower seller, but there was no responsive flicker in the woman's eyes as she offered her a bunch of violets in return for a penny. They had once, not so long ago, sat on the steps of St Paul's Cathedral and shared a cup of tea, but all Charity received was a mouthful of abuse when she confessed to being too poor to buy a single bloom. Shaken by the unfriendly reception, she walked on despite a sudden shower that fell from a previously cloudless sky. She walked past a coffee stall and the scent of baked potatoes soaked in butter made her mouth water, but she would have to go hungry until she returned to Nevill's Court, and even then there would be only weak tea to wash down the bread and scrape. Mrs Diment's hens had stopped laying and would shortly end up in the pot, even though they were nothing but skin, bone and feathers.

The rain became heavier and within minutes she was soaked to the skin. She took shelter in a doorway but was elbowed out by an irate woman who smelled strongly of jigger gin, an odour that Charity remembered from the days when her grandfather had drunk to excess. She apologised and retreated onto the wet pavement. She walked on, hoping to meet at least one of the costermongers who had befriended her in the old days, but there were new faces everywhere and the few who acknowledged her were unable to help. She had been counting on seeing Sal Sprat, the young woman from Billingsgate who plied her trade from a handcart, but either it was not the sprat season or Sal had changed her route. By mid-afternoon Charity was cold, wet and exhausted. She had not had a proper meal since she left Bligh Park, and she was faint from hunger as she retraced her steps, heading back in the direction of Fetter Lane. She was dispirited and desperate but even more determined not to be beaten, and at least the rain had ceased and the sun had come out. Her damp clothes steamed and dried on her back and as the chill left her bones her spirit of optimism began to return.

She was walking along Fleet Street and had just passed Hind Court when she heard someone shouting her name. She hesitated, glancing over her shoulder, and to her horror she saw Bert Chapman seated on the driver's seat of the brewery dray. He stood up in the well, waving his fists and calling out. She broke into a run.

Chapter Sixteen

Bert's shouts rang in her ears and she could hear him cracking the whip over the heads of the sturdy dray horses, but their way was obstructed by the heavy traffic in Fleet Street and Charity took the opportunity to duck into Red Lion Court. The narrow alley led out into Fetter Lane and it was only a short distance to Nevill's Court. She ran all the way, arriving at the house breathless and dishevelled. Dorrie answered her frantic hammering on the doorknocker and her mouth dropped open in surprise. 'What's up, miss? You look like you've seen a ghost.'

Charity stumbled into the hall and slammed the door, leaning against it while she fought to catch her breath. 'I'm all right,' she murmured. 'Fetch Violet. I need to speak to her.' She sank down on the nearest chair, fanning herself with her hand.

Violet came running as fast as her condition would allow. 'What's the matter? You scared Dorrie to death.'

'Your dad. I saw him driving the brewer's dray in Fleet Street.'

Violet's face paled to ashen and her eyes widened with fear. 'Did he see you?'

'Yes. He called my name, but I ran. I don't think he followed me because of the traffic in Fleet Street, but he knows we must be somewhere in the vicinity. We have to be very careful from now on, Vi. He might give up or he might come back and try to find us.' Alarmed by Violet's pallor, Charity rose unsteadily to her feet. 'You'd better sit down.'

'What will we do? We've got to go out in order to sell books.' Violet sank down on the chair, fanning herself with her hand. 'He'll kill me if he sees me like this.'

'You mustn't venture outside the court.'

'But he's seen you and I know my dad; he won't give up easily.'

'Then I'll have to be extra careful.' Charity adjusted her bonnet, retying the strings that had come undone during her flight. 'I didn't have any luck finding a cart, but there's a bookshop in the Strand. They may be interested in buying a couple of volumes. We have to have some money or we'll go to bed hungry.'

Violet reached up and caught her by the hand. 'Don't go. My dad might still be around.'

'He was doing his deliveries. I don't think he'd risk losing his job by hanging around.' She gave Violet what she hoped was an encouraging smile. 'I'll pick a few of the best editions and see what I can get for them.'

'Take Jackson with you. You'd be safe with him at your side.'

With Jackson trailing behind her like a faithful hound, and Bosun straining on his lead, Charity visited the bookshop and met with a modicum of success. She came away with half a crown, and even though the books in question were worth several times that amount she had the satisfaction of knowing that they would eat that night. On the way home she purchased two ounces of Darjeeling tea, a pat of butter and the final extravagance, hot meat pies from a street vendor.

When they had finished eating Jackson went outside into the yard to smoke his last pipe of baccy, and Mrs Diment put her feet up by the desultory fire. 'That was a lovely supper, Charity, but what will we do tomorrow and the next day? Now we've got a man to feed as well as ourselves, I don't know how we'll manage.'

'Jackson can have some of my food.' Dorrie stood on tiptoe to put a plate she had just dried in its place on the dresser. 'I'm not very big and he's enormous.'

Violet and Charity exchanged amused grins as Dorrie indicated Jackson's size with a dramatic sweep of her arms. 'No one will give up anything for anyone,' Charity said firmly. 'I couldn't find a cart or a barrow but that doesn't mean we can't sell the books in a street market. With Jackson's help I'll hawk the books like any other street vendor. With a bit of luck we'll be able to keep going until the auction sale.'

'Unless my dad puts his oar in,' Violet said, splashing about in the sink as she washed the last cup and saucer.

Mrs Diment had begun to doze off but she was suddenly alert. 'What's that about your dad, Violet? From what you told me when you first came here he's a nasty bit of work.'

'He saw me walking along Fleet Street,' Charity said, lowering her voice. 'I escaped through Red Lion Court and I'm sure he didn't follow me, but we'll have to be careful in future. Vi shouldn't go far from the house until after the baby is born.'

'Dad mustn't find out where I am.' Violet pulled the plug from the sink and stood back, wiping her reddened hands on her apron. 'He's a violent man, Mrs Diment. And he had his eye on Charity from the start. I know all about him and his way with women. He can put on the charm if he chooses, and he can change in a flash and start using his fists. I dunno how Ma has put up with him all these years.'

'Men have it all their own way. Your ma wouldn't have had much choice, young Violet.'

'I'm not going to get married,' Dorrie said, sniffing. 'I'm going to be like Charity and sell books for a living.'

Mrs Diment heaved herself out of her chair. 'I never had much time for books myself, and I never imagined that Sir Hedley's collection would be of any use to the likes of me, but I'm going to my bed with a full stomach, so I say thank goodness for them.' She picked up a chamber candlestick and lit the candle from the one on the table. 'That's the last of the coal,' she added, pointing to the copper scuttle. 'You'd best bank up the fire before you go to bed, or we won't be able to enjoy a nice hot cup of tea in the morning. After that it'll be cold water from the pump and like it.' She left the kitchen and her footsteps echoed on the bare floorboards as she made her way to her room.

Dorrie covered her mouth with her hand and yawned. 'I'm tired too, but I ain't going up them stairs on me own. I still think there are ghosts lurking round corners in this old house. I can hear the creaks and groans when you two are asleep.'

'It's a very old house, that's why it makes those noises,' Charity said in an attempt to allay Dorrie's fears. 'Will you take her upstairs, Vi? I'll see to the fire and make sure the doors are locked.'

'I'm ready for bed too.' Violet hesitated in the doorway. 'Don't forget that Jackson is still outside. I don't suppose he'd relish sleeping in the hen house. Come on, Dorrie, we'll go up together. If there are bogeys we'll scare them off.'

'Ooh, don't say that,' Dorrie whispered as she followed Violet out of the room.

Charity had felt the creepy atmosphere herself but she was not going to admit such a thing to either Violet or Dorrie. The old house held the secrets of the past in its lath and plaster walls, and many generations of the Bligh family had lived, loved and died there. At night when the wind whistled through the cracks in the windowpanes she could imagine that voices from the past were whispering to her, and it was as if they were pleading with her to save their beloved home.

She banked up the fire and went to the back door to call Jackson. She could see him standing outside in the moonlight with curls of smoke billowing from his pipe as he puffed on the last scraps of tobacco from his pouch. She called out to him and he turned, walking slowly towards her. 'It's a fine night, miss.' He stopped and tapped the bowl of his pipe on the wall, sending a shower of sparks and dottle floating to the ground. 'That will have to last me,' he said, sighing, as he entered the kitchen followed by Bosun, who seemed to have adopted him as his new master.

She closed the door and locked it. 'Bosun seems to have taken a fancy to you.'

'Aye, he knows we're two of a kind. Neither of us has a master or a home. We've lost our way.'

She reached for the teapot and poured the last drops into a mug. 'Here, drink this. It's not very hot and probably stewed, but it's a pity to waste it.'

He took the cup and slumped down in Mrs Diment's chair with Bosun curled up at his feet. 'What shall us do, miss? Will the shop take more of the master's books?'

'I doubt it, but I have other plans and they include you.' Charity pulled up a chair and sat down. 'I'm going to try the street markets. I couldn't find a barrow or a handcart, but I thought we could carry quite a few books between us and set up somewhere, perhaps on the steps of a church. I'll be like the barker in a fairground and hawk them round one at a time while you stand guard over the rest so that the street arabs don't steal them.'

'A barrow, miss? Is that all you need?'

'Do you know where I can get one?'

He grinned, revealing broken teeth yellowed with nicotine. 'There's one in the coach house. It ain't been used for donkey's years and it's probably worm-eaten, but I know where I can lay hands on it.'

Her expectations were dashed in a moment. 'But you've been locked out of the stables.'

He put his hand in his pocket and pulled out a key.

'They kicked me out but they forget to ask for this. If a barrow is what you need, a barrow you shall have.' He downed the tea in one thirsty swig and rose to his feet. 'Come along, Bosun, old boy. You can keep me company.' He reached for his top hat. 'I'll be back soon. This won't take long, miss.'

By moonlight the barrow looked to be in a reasonable condition, but next morning in full sunlight Charity could see that it was in a sorry state. Worm-eaten and with several spokes missing in one of its wheels, the contraption must have lain abandoned in the stables for many years. 'Don't worry, miss,' Jackson said, rolling up his sleeves with a pleased grin. 'Give me an hour or two and I'll have this little beauty ready for the road.'

'I'll go and sort out the books.' Charity did not want to discourage him, but she thought he was being over-optimistic. She went back into the house and headed for the library to sort out editions that might sell to the general public, and that meant sacrificing the stock she had brought from Liquorpond Street as these were mostly novels, school primers and a box of penny dreadfuls. Jethro had refused to have them on his shelves but she had soon realised that they were popular and sold well. She would have no difficulty in shifting them, she just needed a site where she could set up and attract customers.

With the books sorted into neat piles she returned to the yard and found Jackson standing back surveying his work. 'All done, miss,' he said proudly.

'It should do the job well enough, providing we don't overload it.'

'You've worked miracles. It looks like new.' She ran her fingers over the smooth woodwork. 'If you'll give me a hand we'll load up and be off.'

Dorrie appeared in the doorway, her eyes sparkling with excitement. 'May I come too, Charity? I could help you.'

'Not today, love. Maybe tomorrow, but we'll see how it goes.' Charity smiled and gave her a brief hug. 'Violet needs you to help her, but when I get back with lots of lovely money you can come with me to buy what we need for dinner, and if I do really well you can have some toffee.'

Dorrie uttered a gasp of pleasure. 'I ain't had a toffee since the doctor died. He kept a tin on his desk and he let me take one every evening when I brought him his cocoa.' Her eyes filled with tears. 'I'm still sad that he's gone.'

'And so am I, but he would want the best for you, Dorrie. I'm going to see that you get what you deserve.'

'Toffee?'

'Yes, if that's what you really want. I'll work hard to earn enough to buy you some toffee.'

'You won't earn nothing unless we go now,' Jackson said gloomily. 'It's no good going out at midday and expecting to find anyone with money to spare for luxuries like books. Most of them in the streets can't read anyway.'

'We'll see about that.' Charity looked from Dorrie's flushed and happy face to Jackson's bewhiskered expression of doom. 'I might read out loud to attract customers. Everyone loves a good yarn and I've got plenty of those. Come along, Jackson. We'd best hurry.'

'That's what I just said,' Jackson grumbled as he followed her into the kitchen. He grabbed Bosun's lead off its hook. 'We'll take the dog with us. He'll see off anyone who tries to take advantage of you, miss.'

Charity was excited but also nervous as she set off with the laden barrow. She instructed Jackson to follow at a discreet distance, in case his tough-looking appearance put off nervous customers or encouraged others to pick a fight. Brawling in public was common enough and there were some men who only needed to take a dislike to another man's looks to start throwing punches.

Selling books on street corners in the City was not a common practice. Charity tried to ignore the taunts of ragged street urchins and catcalls from costermongers as she searched for a suitable pitch. In the end she set up close to the Old Lady of Threadneedle Street, hoping that clerks on their way to and from work in the financial institutions and counting houses might stop to browse and then make a purchase, but her hopes were dashed when a police constable told them to move on. Jackson's lantern jaw hardened and he looked mutinous, but the last thing she wanted was for him to start arguing with an officer of the law. It was a pity, Charity thought, but perhaps they would do better in a more commercial area.

Despite a few tussles with stall holders in Leadenhall

Street, she managed to find a space close to the market, and they set up once again. Encouraged by the sale of three penny dreadfuls, Charity selected a copy of *Black Bess; or the Knight of the Road*, and began reading excerpts of the tale romanticising the exploits of the notorious highwayman Dick Turpin. It was snatched up by a young servant girl, who had no doubt just received her quarterly wages and should have been putting the money towards a new pair of boots, judging by the state of the ones she was wearing. But Charity was in business and she knew what it was like to sleep on the floor beneath the shop counter. She also knew what it was like to be hungry; her stomach rumbled for want of anything to eat since a slice of bread and scrape at breakfast, and she knew from experience that escaping into a world of fiction was sometimes the only way to deal with the harsh realities of life.

She selected another cheap edition and announced the title in a loud, clear voice, and in moments had an audience. By late afternoon the entire contents of the box of penny dreadfuls had been sold and Charity had two and fourpence in her purse, which was not far short of the half-crown she had received for two of the expensive volumes from Sir Hedley's library.

'That's where the money is,' Jackson muttered as they walked homewards. 'But you ain't gonna make your fortune by selling them cheap books, miss.'

'I know that,' Charity said, glancing nervously at the heavy rainclouds that were billowing in from the west. 'But we can eat again tonight and we'll stop on the way to buy a hundredweight of coal.'

'With all due respect, miss, you can't eat coal.'

Jackson's lugubrious expression made her laugh for the first time that day. 'I know, but I promised to take Dorrie out to buy our supper. I told her that she could have some toffee for staying at home and helping Violet.'

'You spoil that nipper.'

'She's just a little girl with no family of her own. I know what that feels like.'

He shot her a sideways glance. 'You look done in with all that there reading and shouting. Let me take the barrow now. We'll get home all the quicker, and it's going to pour down any moment now. I don't reckon there's much call for soggy books.'

Charity accepted his offer without a murmur. She took Bosun's lead and they walked on in silence, but every time she heard the sound of heavy horses and the rumble of cart wheels she could not help glancing over her shoulder in case it was the brewery dray driven by Bert Chapman.

They ate well again that evening but next morning Charity awakened to the sound of rain beating against the windowpanes, and it was midday before they were able to go out. Trade was slow and she thought they might have to go home empty-handed, but at the last moment a clerical gentleman wandered over to the barrow and purchased a copy of *The Bride of Lammermoor* by Sir Walter Scott, and the ninepence it cost him paid for a meagre supper of bread and cheese and a marrow bone for Bosun.

Each day was a challenge but somehow they managed

to exist on the few pennies that Charity managed to earn, and although she hoped the auction sale would bring a substantial sum she was not over-optimistic. She wished with all her heart that Harry had not been forced to flee the country. Despite his reputation for being a rake and a gambler, there was something about him that made her feel safe when she was in his presence. There had been no news from Bligh Park and she wondered how Daniel was coping with the responsibility that had been unexpectedly thrust upon him. She knew little of what happened when a will went to probate, but it seemed certain that Harry would be named as Sir Hedley's heir. The estate might be virtually bankrupt but if, in Harry's absence, Wilmot gained control of Bligh Park until Dan came of age, he would also have his eye on the house in Nevill's Court. If that happened they would all be evicted, including Mrs Diment and Jackson. They were existing in a fragile bubble that might burst at any minute, but that was a secret she must keep to herself until such a time when it became necessary to share it with the others. It was a heavy burden to carry but they depended on her and she must not let them down.

The auction was just two days away but trade had dropped off and she was lucky if she sold a single book. She had tried all the shops in the area without success and they were down to their last crust of bread. One of the hens had ended up in the stew pot with the addition of rotten vegetables that Dorrie had plucked from the gutter outside Covent Garden market.

The old boiler had kept them from starvation for the last few days, but now the pot was empty and if Charity failed to make a sale that day the remaining hen would go the way of her sister and that would leave the skinny old cockerel to crow for nothing. He would be next and, as Jackson said, there was probably more meat on a sparrow. Bosun's ribs were showing through his thick coat and he stalked the cockerel daily, with a glint of expectation in his brown eyes. In response, the cockerel fluttered onto the roof of the hen house, crowing in a mocking way that made Jackson threaten to wring his neck before the day was out. Mrs Diment mourned the loss of her favourite hen and ran out into the yard every time she heard the cock crowing, flapping her apron and shouting at the dog. 'Lord help us,' she said as Charity prepared to go out on her rounds, 'if you don't make a sale today we'll have to eat the old bird raw, because there's no fuel for the fire. I can't even make a pot of tea.'

'Don't worry, Mrs Diment,' Charity said with more confidence than she was feeling. 'I've packed the barrow with the sort of books that the university students used to buy, and I plan to stand outside University College all day if necessary. Maybe some of them will remember me from the shop.' She did not add that she was taking a risk by returning to an area close to Liquorpond Street, doubling her chances of running into Bert Chapman. But they were all desperate and she could not bear to see Dorrie with stick-thin arms and legs, and Violet hollow-cheeked and pale in the late stages of her pregnancy.

She set off early but without her usual bodyguards. Jackson was unwell, having eaten the last of the chicken soup, which had smelled so rank even Bosun turned his nose up when it was offered to him. She could not manage the dog and the cart and she left on her own, pushing the barrow through the busy streets as she made her way to Gower Street. It was a long walk but she arrived just as most of the students were going in to attend their lectures. They hurried past her without giving her a second glance, and she could not help envying them their seemingly carefree existence.

Brisk footsteps behind her made her turn her head in the hope of seeing a prospective customer, but to her dismay the man walking purposefully towards her was none other than Wilmot. He seemed equally surprised as he came to a sudden halt. 'By God, it's Charity.' His expression changed subtly as he took in her shabby appearance and the barrow laden with books. 'So you've come to this, have you? You were a beggar maid when I first clapped eyes on you and you're little better now.'

'I'm not doing anything wrong,' Charity protested. 'These books are mine to sell. Jethro left them to me in his will.'

'Have you got a street vendor's licence?'

She eyed him doubtfully, shaking her head. 'I didn't know I needed one.'

'And does the bailiff know that you helped yourself to the stock that should have gone to pay the back rent?'

'It's none of your business,' Charity said angrily.

He leaned towards her with a wolfish smile. 'But it is if you're living rent free in my house.'

'But the house in Nevill's Court belongs to Harry. I'm sure that Sir Hedley would have left everything to him.'

'Harry is a wanted man. He's in exile abroad and that makes Daniel the legal heir.'

'Dan gave us permission to stay in his house.'

'Daniel has not yet reached his majority. As his stepfather I take full responsibility for him and will look after his interests until he is of age.'

'You're his stepfather?'

'I wouldn't want tongues to wag and sully the good lady's name. We were married by special licence a week ago.'

'You weren't so concerned about my good name when you propositioned me,' Charity said with feeling. 'I suppose I don't count.'

'You're no lady, Charity my dear.'

'I was too much of a lady to be bought by you, Mr Barton.'

His eyes flashed angrily although his lips were stretched in a grim smile. 'You'd best move on or I'll call a constable and have you arrested for trading without a licence and for passing on stolen property.'

'You are a despicable person,' she said through clenched teeth. 'I hope that Dan finds the Bligh Park treasure and cuts you off without a penny.' She seized the barrow and was about to walk on when Wilmot's hand shot out and he grabbed her by the arm.

'What do you know about the treasure? What romantic nonsense did that boy tell you?'

'Do you really think it's a secret?' She faced up to him even though she was quaking inwardly. 'I should think the whole village knows about it by now. They also know that the Blighs have been searching for it for centuries, if it ever existed in the first place.'

He released her, wiping his hands together with an expression of disgust. 'You are a common little slut and I'd advise you to keep your pretty mouth shut. If I discover that you've been spreading malicious rumours about the family I'll see to it that you end up in prison where you belong.'

Shaken but determined not to let him see that she was upset, Charity walked away, pushing the cumbersome barrow as fast as she could over the cobblestones. Despite her vow to keep away from Liquorpond Street she found herself walking towards Jethro's former shop. Her mind had been occupied with Wilmot's threats, and the knowledge that she had been trading illegally had come as a total shock. It was not until she stopped to gaze into the shop window that she realised it was still open for business. The bailiffs had not closed it down and there were new books in the window. She was mortified and angry to think that the rent collector had lied to her. If someone had taken over the premises it was obvious that the building was not going to be razed to the ground. She left her barrow outside and marched into the shop.

A tall thin man of indeterminate age stood behind the counter. He had a book open in front of him and was intent on reading but he looked up when the bell jangled and peered at her through the thick lenses of his spectacles. 'Good morning, miss. May I be of assistance?'

Anger roiled in her belly. 'Who are you? Why is the shop still open?'

He brushed a thin strand of hair back from his forehead in an attempt to cover his bald pate. His fingers were ink-stained and she noticed that his hand shook. 'I'm sorry, miss. I don't understand.'

'This was my shop,' she said furiously. 'I was tricked into leaving it and told that the whole building was going to be knocked down, but you're here and you're selling my books.'

'Come now, miss, there must be some mistake.'

She wrenched the door open and dragged the barrow into the shop. 'These were part of my inheritance from Mr Dawkins. He took me in and trained me as his assistant. These books were on the shelves over there.' She pointed to the section which had not yet been filled.

'It had nothing to do with me, I can assure you of that.' He emerged from behind the counter. 'I just bought the lease and paid extra for the stock. I was told that the person who was here before was a fly-by-night who left owing money and took what didn't belong to them. Was that you, by any chance?'

'Was it a man called Seth Woods who told you all this?'

'It was Mr Woods, yes.'

'He forced me out, threatening me with the bailiffs,

and these are some of the books I took because they were mine. Woods is a bad man and you need to watch him or he'll do the same to you.'

'But you owed rent, miss. That was why he acted as he did.'

'He doubled the rent at a time when he knew I couldn't raise that much cash.'

The man's face crumpled into worried lines. 'Seth is my brother-in-law,' he said, glancing nervously over his shoulder in the direction of the kitchen. 'My wife will be very upset to hear you speaking ill of her brother.'

'Who's there, Frank?' The kitchen door opened and a tall, broad-shouldered woman stepped into the shop. 'I heard raised voices. Do I have to stop what I'm doing to sort out all your problems?'

'No, my dear,' Frank said hastily. 'It's all right. The customer returned some books but we've come to a mutually satisfactory arrangement.'

'I'll have words with Seth when I see him. That's the second time this week this sort of thing has happened. Take a bookshop, he said. It will make your fortune, he said. Well, I beg to differ. I'll speak very sternly to Seth when he comes for the rent.' She retreated into the kitchen, slamming the door with such force that the windows rattled.

'What do you want from me?' Frank seemed to have shrunk into his oversized black frock coat when his wife appeared, but the moment the door closed on her he peered over the starched points of his shirt collar, eyeing Charity with a scared look on his pinched features. 'I need you to go quickly.'

'Ten shillings the lot,' Charity said boldly. 'Give me ten bob and you can restock the shelves and keep your wife happy.' She picked up a text book. 'Students will buy these for their courses when they start next year. You'll soon make your money back.'

He scuttled behind the counter and produced the cash box that had once belonged to Jethro. He took out two silver crowns and pressed them into her hand. 'Take it and leave the books.' He glanced at the kitchen door which remained firmly closed. 'Anything for a quiet life. You're sure these will fetch a good price?'

Charity unloaded the books, piling them on a table beside the counter. 'They will, and if I were you I'd stock plenty of penny dreadfuls. They'll fly off the shelves.' She made for the door, opened it and manoeuvred the empty barrow out into the street. 'Good luck, Frank.' She walked off with the coins jingling in her pocket. It seemed like a small fortune and she felt ridiculously happy. Ten shillings would keep them until after the auction and they would have coal, candles and hot food. The old cockerel would be saved and Bosun would be fed.

The problems that had weighed her down since their return to London had been lifted, even if temporarily, and she had not lied to Frank. He could do well in the shop if he had the right stock and as long as he could earn enough when business was brisk to carry him through the dark days after Christmas.

She was so deep in thought that she had not noticed that the brewery gates were open, nor the pair of dray horses that were champing at their bits. She heard a shout and looked up to see Bert Chapman rise from the driver's seat and raise his whip. The loud crack caused the animals to shy and lunge forward. She started to run but one of the barrow's wheels caught in a rut and it tipped over, flinging her to the ground. Winded and unable to move, she looked up, and saw several tons of horseflesh rearing above her.

Chapter Seventeen

Even as Charity fought to get air into her lungs she had the sensation of flying through the air, clasped in a pair of strong arms, and then, with a sudden jolt, the world righted itself. She opened her eyes and took a few faltering breaths.

'Are you hurt?'

She found herself looking into the face of a young man. His curly, reddish-gold hair flopped over his forehead and his grey eyes were filled with concern. She wondered vaguely if he was an angel who had rescued her from certain death, or perhaps she had died and gone to heaven. But as she tried to move she felt a stab of pain in her right ankle and she realised that she was very much alive. Every bone in her body had begun to ache and she was suddenly conscious of the crowd of people that had gathered around them.

'Are you all right? You took a nasty tumble.'

'It weren't my fault.' A horribly familiar voice cut into Charity's consciousness and she struggled to a sitting position.

'You tried to run me down, Bert Chapman,' she said breathlessly. 'You could have killed me.'

Bert tucked his thumbs into his wide leather belt,

turning to the onlookers with a cocky grin. 'She must have hit her head when she fell. She don't know what she's saying.'

The young man, who had apparently braved the horses' hooves to save Charity from being run down, looked up at Bert with a frown creasing his smooth brow. 'That's not what I saw. Your actions were quite deliberate. You might have killed this young woman had I not seen what was happening and come to her aid.'

Bert stared at him and his brazen attitude was replaced by a sheepish grin. 'I'm sorry, your reverence. It weren't intentional, I can assure you.' He tipped his cap and backed away. 'If the young lady ain't taken harm I'll go on me way.'

'I think you owe her an apology.'

'Yes, vicar. Sorry, miss. I never saw you until it was too late.' Bert retreated to the dray where his mate was holding the horses' heads. He hauled his large frame onto the driver's seat. 'C'mon, Charlie. We'll be behindhand all day if we don't get a move on.' He barely allowed his helper time to get on board before driving off.

Charity turned her head to look at her rescuer. She had not noticed the clerical collar he was wearing at first, but that would account for the sudden change in Bert's demeanour. 'Thank you, sir,' she said, making an attempt to stand and wincing as a sharp pain stabbed her ankle.

He helped her to her feet. 'You're hurt. Do you think you can walk?'

'Where's my barrow?' Leaning on his arm she saw the shattered remains scattered over the road. 'It's broken,' she said, stifling a sob.

'Better the cart than you.' The young parson turned to the crowd. 'There's nothing more to see. I'll look after the lady and see she gets home safely.' He waited until the curious onlookers had dispersed before turning to Charity with a rueful smile. 'It's a bit late for formal introductions, but my name is Gideon Raines. I'm the curate at St Pancras New Church.'

'Charity Crosse. You saved my life, vicar.'

'I just happened to be in the right place. Anyone would have done the same.'

'I don't think so, but thank you anyway.' She made an attempt to walk but the pain was too great.

'Where do you live, Miss Crosse? I'll hail a cab.'

The mere thought of what it would cost made her shake her head. 'No, thank you, I'll be all right in a minute or two. I just need to rest, and then there's my barrow. I can't leave it there.'

He looked round and catching sight of a group of small boys who were picking over the rubbish in the gutter, he called them over. 'Now then, boys, if you'll clear up the wood you'll be doing a kindness for this young lady.'

The oldest and boldest stepped forward. 'What's in it for us, guv?'

'If you bundle it up you can sell it for kindling, and you'll be doing a good deed into the bargain.' Gideon turned to Charity with an apologetic smile. 'That is all right, isn't it? I mean it's not fit for anything else.'

'Yes, of course,' she murmured, although she would have liked to take it home. It would have helped keep the fire going for days, but her pride would not allow her to admit this to the young man who had saved her life. In the old days, when her grandfather was still alive, she had come across many well-meaning churchmen who wanted to save the souls of the men and women who lived on the streets. Some of them had grown cynical and world-weary in the knowledge that their efforts would come to nothing, but others, the young men newly graduated from ecclesiastical college, were fresh-faced and confident in their ability to restore hope to the down-trodden and spiritual healing to those who had fallen by the wayside. Charity knew instinctively that Gideon Raines was one of the latter. She could feel his enthusiasm for life and sense the optimism radiating from his conviction that he could help his fellow men. He was also very good-looking, which seemed like a waste in someone who had dedicated his life to good works.

'I'll see if I can find a cab,' he said cheerfully. 'You won't get far with a twisted ankle.'

'I'd really rather walk, if you don't mind.'

He gave her a searching look. 'Where do you live?'

'Nevill's Court off Fetter Lane. Really, it's not far.'

'Isn't that the Bligh family's London home?'

She stared at him in surprise. 'Yes. Do you know Sir Hedley?'

'I grew up in Sutton Pomeroy. My father is rector of St Michael's. Harry and I used to roam the countryside together as boys, although I haven't seen much of him recently. I was in my last year at university when Daniel started, so you might say we're old friends. How do you know the family, Miss Crosse?'

'It's a long story,' she said vaguely.

'And you've just had a nasty fright. We must get you home.' He stepped out into the road and hailed a passing cab. 'Nevill's Court, please, cabby.' He climbed in and sat beside Charity. 'I'm sorry about your barrow.'

'It really doesn't matter.' She could not bring herself to tell him that it did matter very much. 'I'm truly grateful for what you did.'

'You're quite a long way from home. How did you come to be pushing a barrow in this part of town?'

Suddenly the need to confide in someone was overpowering. By the time they reached Nevill's Court she had explained how she had become involved with the Bligh family. She had told him about Harry's plight, and the fact that he and Dan were brothers. The cab rumbled to a halt. 'I must pay my part of the fare,' she said, putting her hand into her pocket.

'I was coming this way,' Gideon said quickly.

She met his earnest gaze with a smile. 'I thought that men of the church were supposed to tell the truth at all times.'

He grinned. 'It was a white lie, and now I've heard your story I feel quite justified in seeing you safely home. Harry would never forgive me had I abandoned you in Liquorpond Street.'

'I wasn't looking for sympathy. I don't know why I

told you all that, because we're managing well enough, and it will be even better after the auction.'

He stepped down from the cab and helped her to alight. 'I admire your fortitude, Charity. You're a brave young woman.'

'Thank you, but you're quite wrong. I muddle through the best way I can.'

'Even that takes courage.' He took a card from his inside pocket. 'I know you're not one of my parishioners, but this is where I live. If you need help at any time, don't hesitate to call on me. After all we have mutual friends so we're not complete strangers.'

Charity took it from him and tucked it in her pocket. 'Thank you, sir.'

'Gideon, please.'

'Thank you, Gideon. Thank you for everything.' She turned and limped into the narrow alleyway, heading into the darkness. She did not look back. He was a good man but he was Dan's friend, not hers. People in her position did not have friends amongst the clergy. She emerged into the sunlit square, where spring had come at last and the gardens were bursting into bloom. Sparrows were squabbling over crumbs that one of their neighbours had thrown out, and the tabby cat belonging to the two maiden ladies who lodged in the sea captain's house crouched ready to kill. Charity clapped her hands and the birds flew up in the air twittering in protest, and the cat arched its back, glaring at her with malevolent yellow eyes. She felt suddenly light-hearted for no reason at all other than that she had money in her pocket and she had received kindness and understanding from a man of the cloth.

She made her way to the house, silently rehearsing a tale that would explain her dishevelled state and the loss of the barrow. She had no intention of telling them that it was Bert Chapman who tried to run her down, and the unpleasant encounter with Wilmot Barton was best forgotten. She would just give them the good news that she had earned ten shillings from the sale of the books. She lifted the brass knocker and rapped on the door. The sound reverberated throughout the house coming back to her in staccato echoes. She fixed a smile on her face when Dorrie opened the door. 'Good news, Dorrie. I sold all the books.'

Dorrie looked her up and down. 'Lawks, Charity. What happened to you? You look like you was dragged through a hedge backwards.'

Charity stepped inside. 'I had a bit of an accident, but it was nothing really.'

On the day of the sale Charity was about to leave for the auction house when Violet came slowly down the main staircase with her shawl draped around her shoulders and her bonnet in her hand. 'I'm coming with you,' she said firmly. 'I've been a blooming prisoner since we come here. If I don't go out I swear I'll go mad.'

Charity shook her head. 'No, it's not a good idea, Vi.'

'Why not?' Violet demanded crossly. 'I'm not due for a month or two. It's not fair to keep me cooped up like one of Mrs Diment's hens.'

Charity could not give a reason without scaring Violet, who was already nervous and jumping at the slightest sound. Perhaps it would do her good to go out for an hour or two. 'All right,' she said grudgingly. 'But if you get tired or feel unwell you must come home.'

'Yes, I will. Don't worry about me.'

Charity opened the door and found Gideon Raines with his hand raised as if he were about to knock. He doffed his hat. 'Good morning, Miss Crosse.'

'What are you doing here, Mr Raines?' Charity stiffened as she felt Violet's breath on the back of her neck.

'Who is it?' Violet whispered. 'Why has the vicar come to call?'

Charity thought quickly. 'Mr Raines was kind enough to see me home after my little mishap with the barrow.'

'I'd hardly call it a little mishap, Miss Crosse. You were nearly killed by that oaf . . .'

She stepped outside, taking him by the arm. 'It's very kind of you to call, Mr Raines, but as you see I'm quite recovered and Miss Chapman and I are off to the auction sale.'

He met her anxious gaze with a nod of his head. 'Miss Chapman, of course.' He held out his hand to Violet. 'How do you do?'

She blushed and giggled, shaking his hand as if it were the pump handle at the kitchen sink. 'Pleased to meet you, I'm sure.'

'What are you doing here?' Charity demanded in an undertone.

'I've never been to an auction sale. You told me that

it was today and I thought you might allow me to accompany you.'

'That's ever so kind of you, vicar.' Violet treated him to a bright smile. 'You're sure to bring us good luck.'

'I've never been thought of as a lucky charm,' Gideon said, laughing. 'Shall we go, ladies?'

'Lady,' Violet whispered in Charity's ear. 'He called me a lady.'

'Behave yourself, Vi.' Charity managed a smile, but inwardly she was quaking. If Gideon let slip about the cause of her accident she would have to tell Violet everything and risk upsetting her. She had to wait until she was seated next to him in the auction room before she had a chance to speak privately. Violet had gone to buy a programme and had joined a long queue. 'Please don't mention what happened in Liquorpond Street,' Charity said urgently. 'Violet is terrified of her father and with good reason. If he were to see her now there's no knowing what he would do.'

'I suppose there's no chance of the baby's father stepping up to the mark?'

'None at all.'

'And do you intend to support Violet and her child?'

She shot him a sideways glance, annoyed by his assumption that he could criticise her actions simply because he wore a clerical collar. 'I think that's my business, vicar.'

'I'm sorry. I didn't mean to offend you, Charity. But you're very young to have taken on such a responsibility. You have your own life to lead.'

'I suppose you think I should abandon Violet and Dorrie.'

'I didn't say that. All I meant was . . .'

She silenced him with a glance. 'They are my family now. We may not be blood-related, but we support each other. Please don't say any more – Violet is on her way back and the sale is due to start any moment now.'

Violet sank down on the seat beside Charity and gave her the programme. 'Isn't it exciting? I never been to a sale before. Come to think of it I never been nowhere much. That's what happens when you have to look after younger brothers and sisters and don't get out and about.'

'Shh,' Charity said, putting her finger to her lips. 'It's starting.'

The sale of Sir Hedley's books raised the princely sum of five guineas, but after the commission was deducted it was still not enough to provide money for food and fuel as well as the servants' back wages.

'That's splendid, isn't it?' Gideon said when Charity received a chit authorising her to collect the money next day.

'Yes, of course.' She did not tell him that it was nowhere near as much as she had hoped for. Sir Hedley might have paid vast sums for his collection during his lifetime but its value had diminished. Dan would have to find another way to keep the estate from bankruptcy and she would have to find work, as would Violet once the baby was born. Dorrie would have to act as nursemaid. Their future depended upon what Dan intended to do with the house in Nevill's Court, but if Wilmot had any say in the matter they would once again find themselves homeless.

'You don't look very pleased,' Violet said chirpily. 'It's a fortune if you ask me.'

They stepped outside onto the pavement and Gideon took Charity's hand and tucked it in the crook of his arm. 'I think this calls for a small celebration.'

'I don't think so, cully.' Bert Chapman emerged from a shop doorway. He barred their way, but when he spotted Violet in her advanced state of pregnancy his mouth dropped open and his eyebrows knotted together over the bridge of his nose. 'You little slut! You're a bloody disgrace, flaunting your shame for all to see.' He raised his hand as if to strike her, but Gideon stepped in and grabbed him by the wrist.

'What sort of man would strike a pregnant woman?'

'An outraged father, that's who.' Bert pushed him away. 'Vicar or no vicar, I'll not allow you to interfere in family matters.'

'No, Dad,' Violet cried, clinging to Charity. 'Don't start a fight.'

Bert grabbed her by the hair. 'You're coming home with me, my girl. We'll see what you have to say when your interfering friends aren't around.'

'What's all this?' A police constable strolled up to them, wielding his truncheon in a way that did not invite argument.

'It's a family matter, constable,' Bert said gruffly. 'This here is my daughter and I'm taking her home.

She's fallen in with a bad lot and look what come of it.' He jerked his head in the direction of Violet's swollen belly. 'A good girl she was until she got in with that young madam.'

'How dare you?' Charity stormed. 'Don't touch her, you brute. I've been taking care of this girl, officer. That man may be her father, but he'll beat her senseless when he gets her home.'

'That's a lie,' Bert roared. 'And if I want to chastise me daughter that's up to me.'

Violet began to sob hysterically as her father tried to pull her away. 'Don't let him take me!'

Gideon faced up to the constable. 'Officer, you can see that the young lady is distraught. I beg you to intervene and allow her to return home with her friend.'

'I can't interfere in a domestic matter, vicar. You should know better than to ask, if you don't mind me saying so.'

'I do mind, as it happens.' Gideon took a swing at Bert and caught him a hefty punch on the jaw. Bert was a big man and the blow was not hard enough to knock him down, but it caught him off balance and he staggered, letting go of Violet as he blundered into a group of people who had just emerged from the saleroom.

'Run,' Gideon shouted above the raised voices as people demanded that the constable stop the fracas. Bert lunged at Gideon and the constable swung his baton, hitting out at both of them.

Charity seized Violet by the hand and ran.

* * *

Violet had been put to bed with a stone bottle filled with hot water at her feet, and although she was shaken and upset she seemed none the worse for the headlong flight from the auction house. Charity was in the kitchen drinking a cup of tea, which was Mrs Diment's panacea for all ills, and Dorrie had been set to peel vegetables to add to the beef bones that were simmering on the hob.

Mrs Diment sipped her tea, relating gory accounts of miscarriages that had been brought about by quite trivial incidents, but Charity tried not to listen. She was more worried by the fact that Bert must have found out where they lived, and she knew that an altercation with the police would not be enough to stop him coming for Violet at the first possible opportunity. He must, she thought, have followed her home, or perhaps he had made enquiries in the area and someone had recognised her description. In the end it did not matter how he had discovered their whereabouts; the problem was what to do next.

'When will we get the five guineas?' Mrs Diment asked, having apparently exhausted her supply of horror stories relating to childbirth.

'I'll collect it from the counting house tomorrow morning.'

Mrs Diment's wrinkles creased into a wide smile. 'What a relief. It will keep us fed for weeks and we won't have to kill Bessie.'

Dorrie dropped the potato she had been peeling and it rolled across the floor gathering a furry coating of dust. 'Who's Bessie?'

'My hen, dear. Some folks think it silly, but I always give them names. Poor Hettie was the one we ate, although I could hardly force down a morsel without choking.'

Dorrie shot a wary look at the blackened saucepan on the hob. 'Do you think the cow had a name?'

'No, of course not,' Charity said hastily. 'Mrs Diment's hens are a different matter altogether.'

'Why?' Dorrie asked plaintively. 'They'll all animals, aren't they?'

Charity rose to her feet. 'I think I heard someone knocking on the door. Stay here, Dorrie. I'll go.'

'D'you think it's him?' Mrs Diment asked anxiously.

'I hope not.' Charity hurried from the kitchen. Her heart was hammering against her ribs and she could hardly breathe. 'Wh-who's there?'

'Gideon. I've come to see if you and Violet are all right?'

She opened the door. 'Yes, thank you. I'm fine and I hope Violet will be when she's got over the shock. Come in.' She stepped aside and he crossed the threshold, taking off his hat.

She closed the door quickly. 'You weren't followed, were you?'

'The constable told Chapman to go about his business or he'd be arrested for breach of the peace. Of course he protested, but that only made it look worse for him. I got off with a caution, but the crowd were on my side. I even got a cheer as I walked away.'

'You're hurt,' Charity said, noticing for the first time that he had a cut above his right eye and a bruise was already forming. 'Come into the kitchen. I think Mrs Diment has a bottle of arnica on the dresser.'

He hesitated. 'I really should be getting back to my duties.'

'Nonsense. I'm sure that God wouldn't expect you to go to work with blood trickling down your face, or begrudge you a nice hot cup of tea.'

'I hadn't thought about it in those terms,' he said, laughing, which caused him to wince with pain and hold his hand to his head. 'Perhaps a short break is in order. Since I've been playing truant this morning anyway, it's not going to make much difference.'

'I don't suppose you'll go to hell because you took a morning off to help a friend.' Charity walked off in the direction of the kitchen. 'Come along, vicar. You can meet Dorrie and maybe you can explain why we humans make pets of some animals and are happy to kill and eat others.'

Luckily Dorrie had forgotten about the fate of poor Hettie, and she showed off her prowess in making a pot of tea while Mrs Diment bathed Gideon's cut and Charity searched for the arnica.

'I could get used to this,' he said when it was done and Dorrie handed him a cup of tea.

'It was the least we could do after you stood up for us against Bert Chapman,' Charity said with a grateful smile. 'Things would have turned out very differently if you hadn't been there. Goodness knows what Bert would have done to her when he got her home.'

He shook his head. 'It's a bad business, but I'm afraid

there are too many men like him, and the law turns a blind eye to the way they treat their families, especially when they're drunk.'

Dorrie stared at him in horror. 'Then I ain't never going to get married.'

'All men aren't like that,' Charity put in quickly. 'Remember the doctor, and how good and kind he was?'

Dorrie's blue eyes brimmed with tears. 'Don't keep reminding me that he's gone. I never had a father, nor a mother come to that, but if I could choose someone it would have been Dr Marchant.'

Gideon rose to his feet, placing the cup and saucer back on the table. 'That was the best cup of tea I've ever had, Dorrie. And Charity is right: we aren't all monsters. I'm quite a nice chap when you get to know me.'

'But you got into a fight,' Dorrie said, pointing at his injured face. 'You use your fists too.'

'Violence is always wrong, but occasionally we have to resort to it in order to protect others. I didn't want to hit him, but I couldn't allow him to hurt Violet. Can you understand that?'

Dorrie's solemn expression melted into a wide grin. 'I'd have punched him too. I wouldn't let no one hurt Vi and her baby.'

'Quite right too.' Mrs Diment rose to her feet, holding out her hand to Gideon. 'I'd like to shake your hand, vicar. I don't go to church as often as I should, but I might attend more regularly if the parson was like you.'

Gideon held her hand, smiling down at her. 'I'm flattered, ma'am. But I doubt if the rector would approve of my actions today, however justified. Thank you for tending to my needs, but I really must be on my way.'

'I'll see you out,' Charity said, but as she made a move towards the door it opened and Violet barged into the room. 'He's outside. I heard him shouting my name. Me dad's out there and he's bellowing like a bull in the slaughterhouse.'

Chapter Eighteen

Mrs Diment leapt up from her seat and seized Violet by the shoulders. 'Sit down, dear. You mustn't upset yourself.'

'I'll have a word with him.' Gideon headed for the door, but Charity ran after him and caught him by the sleeve.

'No, please don't. It wouldn't do any good.'

'But the man must be stopped. He must be made to see reason.'

'My dad don't know the meaning of the word,' Violet sobbed, burying her face in her hands. 'Belt and fists is all he knows, and I had the benefit of both when I was living at home.'

'If we ignore him he might go away.' Charity looked to Gideon for confirmation but he shook his head.

'He'll come back again and I won't be here to protect you.'

She smiled despite the ice-cold claws of fear that gripped her insides. 'It isn't your problem, Gideon.'

He covered her hand with his. 'I'm making it my problem, Charity. Is there anywhere you and Violet could go until her child is born?'

Violet raised a tear-stained face. 'I got nowhere else to go. Ma's parents disowned her when she married my dad, and he was raised in an orphanage.'

'What about me?' Dorrie's bottom lip trembled ominously. 'You can't run away and leave me, Charity.'

'Of course not,' Charity said stoutly. 'We're in this together, but I think Gideon is right. We can't stay here now that Bert Chapman has found out where we live.'

'Oh dear.' Mrs Diment clutched her hands to her breast. 'Don't say you're leaving me and Jackson to fend for ourselves. What will become of us now that the master is dead and gone?'

Gideon looked from one to the other, frowning thoughtfully. 'Am I correct in thinking that Daniel owns this house now?'

'Harry should be the legal heir.'

'But he's left the country and is unlikely to return.'

'So Wilmot says, but Harry doesn't know that his father is dead.'

'I'm just thinking about the here and now, Charity. Daniel is your friend, and it was he who sent you back to London.'

'Yes, that's true.'

'He's a good fellow and I'm certain he'll help you.'

'There's no real reason why he should. It was Sir Hedley who employed me, and I daresay the contents of both libraries will be sent to auction in order to raise funds.'

'I used to work for the old master when he lived in Bligh Park,' Mrs Diment said, sighing. 'Those were the days.'

The sound of Bert's hammering and shouting was growing louder by the minute and Gideon shut the door. 'As I see it the only solution is for you all to pack up and go to Bligh Park. Tell Dan how things stand and let him decide what's best to be done.'

'You're right about Mrs Diment and Jackson,' Charity said slowly. 'But I've no claim on the family and I wouldn't want to impose on my brief friendship with Dan.' She turned to Mrs Diment with what she hoped was an encouraging smile. 'I agree with Gideon.'

Mrs Diment eyed her doubtfully. 'But what will happen to you girls?'

'I don't know. We can't stay here, that's for certain. I'll think of—'

Charity's words were cut shot by a loud scream from Dorrie. She pointed a shaking finger at the kitchen window and Charity spun round to see Bert's face pressed against the windowpane. He hammered his fists on the frame, shouting at them to let him in.

Charity ran to the window. 'Go away or I'll send for a constable.'

He was purple in the face as he used his elbow to shatter the glass in one of the small panes. Violet leapt to her feet but the colour drained from her face and she would have fallen to the ground in a dead faint if Gideon had not caught her in his arms. Charity backed away from the window, torn between fear of what Bert would do and her need to look after Violet. Dorrie cowered in Mrs Diment's arms as Bert's shouted obscenities echoed round the room. He picked up a brick and was about to smash his way in when Jackson came up behind him and lashed out with a horsewhip. Bosun threw himself at Bert growling ferociously, and in a flurry of raised hackles and flying paws the dog knocked Bert to the ground.

'See to her. I'll go outside and help your man.' Gideon set Violet down on a chair and headed for the back door, leaving Mrs Diment and Dorrie to care for her.

Charity hurried after him. 'What are you going to do?' she demanded as he stepped out into the yard.

'Go inside and let us deal with this.'

She had no intention of hiding away like a frightened schoolgirl and she stood her ground watching as Gideon went to Jackson's aid, although by the look of things Bosun and his new master had the upper hand. Bert lay on the ground looking nervously up at the dog's bared fangs, and Jackson stood over him, whip in hand. 'Get up and fight like a man,' he said through clenched teeth. 'You're very brave when it comes to bullying women and children. Let's see how you go on with someone your own size.'

Bert lay motionless. 'Call the bloody dog off.'

'Here, boy.' Jackson beckoned to Bosun and with wagging tail the dog came to heel.

'I'll do for that creature. A poisoned lump of meat will sort him out.' Bert shuffled to a sitting position, leaning against the wall.

'Come near any of us and you'll feel the full force of this.' Jackson raised the whip and was about to strike when Gideon caught him by the arm.

'Don't sink to his level.' He turned to Bert. 'Get up and go on your way or I'll have you arrested for breaking and entering.'

Bert scrambled to his feet. He shot a malevolent glance in Charity's direction. 'She's the one to blame for all this, and I'll get even with her if it's the last thing I do.'

'Touch her and I'll slit your gizzard,' Jackson said grimly.

Bert adjusted his clothing with a defiant scowl. 'I ain't afraid of you, old man. You just got one over on me, cully, but that ain't gonna happen again. You'd best watch out for yourself.' He turned to glare at Gideon. 'You too, vicar. I owes you one and your dog collar ain't going to save you.'

Gideon took a step towards him, hands fisted at his sides. 'I'm not afraid of your threats, Mr Chapman. You're the one who's going to end up in front of the magistrate. I'd advise you to go now and keep well away from here in future.'

Bert snatched up his cap, which had come off in the skirmish. 'As for that little trollop standing there, looking as if butter wouldn't melt in her mouth, I could tell you things about her that would make you change your mind.' He stalked off and Jackson followed, brandishing the whip.

Charity hurried to Gideon's side. 'I must get Violet away from here,' she said urgently. 'We must find a place where I can get work.'

'One thing at a time,' he said thoughtfully. 'I think I might have a solution, but I can't say at the moment.' He took her hand in his, looking into her eyes. 'Will you trust me, Charity?'

'Of course, but I don't see what you can do.'

'I have an idea, but I don't want to say anything in

case it doesn't come off. Go indoors and don't let anyone in, except Jackson, of course. I'll return tomorrow when I hope I'll have some good news for you.' He squeezed her fingers, smiling. 'Don't look so worried. Everything will be all right, I promise.'

She watched him walk away, and even though she could not share his optimism, she returned to the kitchen with a smile on her face. 'Jackson has seen Bert off, and Gideon has promised to help us.' She went to kneel beside Violet, who was sitting in Mrs Diment's chair sipping a glass of water. 'Are you all right, Vi?'

'I think so.'

Mrs Diment sank down on a chair at the table. 'What a to-do. I'm sure I don't know what will happen next.'

Charity rose to her feet and slipped her arm around Dorrie's shoulders. 'Bert won't return tonight. We'll make sure everything is locked and I'll get Jackson to board up the broken window.'

'We can't lock ourselves in forever.' Mrs Diment shook her head. 'What a state of affairs.'

'No, of course not.' Charity made an attempt to appear confident. 'Tomorrow morning, as soon as the auction house opens, I'll collect the money. Jackson and Bosun will accompany me, and I don't think Bert will risk another set-to in public, but if he should turn up again I won't hesitate to summon the police.'

Charity returned to Nevill's Court with what was left of the five guineas after the auction house had taken their commission. Jackson and Bosun followed close behind her, but there had been no sign of Bert. She entered the kitchen holding up her reticule, shaking it so that the coins jingled. 'It's all here,' she said triumphantly. She came to a halt, looking from one to the other. Mrs Diment, Violet and Dorrie had on their bonnets and shawls, and there was baggage piled up by the door.

Gideon rose from his seat at the table. 'I take it that all went well.'

Jackson tipped his cap. 'Aye, sir. No sign of the wretch.'

'What's going on?' Charity demanded. 'Where are we going?'

Mrs Diment beamed at her. 'I'm going home. Gideon is going to take us to Bligh Park.'

Charity turned on him, frowning. 'But I told you that I wouldn't impose on Daniel.'

'Nor will you. I quite understand your position, and last evening I sent a telegram to my father. I received a reply by return.'

'I still don't understand.'

'I'm taking Mrs Diment to Bligh Park and then we'll go on to the rectory at Sutton Pomeroy.'

'That's your home, Gideon,' Charity said slowly. 'Why would you take us there?'

'My father lives on his own apart from his housekeeper and a maidservant. I sent him a message to say that I was bringing three friends to stay for a while.'

Charity shook her head. 'But what happens then? What would we do in the country?'

'I think it's a good idea,' Violet said eagerly. 'We'd be safe there.'

'I'd like to see a cow,' Dorrie added, grinning. 'I ain't never been to the country.'

'You'd be near to Bligh Park, dear. It's walking distance from the rectory.' Mrs Diment glanced round the room with a misty expression softening her features. 'I'll miss my kitchen, and I suppose I'll have to put up with Polly Trevett bossing me around, but it will be lovely to be back home again.'

Gideon met Charity's worried gaze with a smile. 'My father loves company, and he'll be delighted to have someone to talk to after dinner. He is a great reader so you'll have a lot in common.'

The notion that she might share an interest with someone of the rector's education and standing came as something of a revelation to Charity, but ghosts from the past continued to haunt her. She was still the same girl who had begged and occasionally stolen in order to make a living.

Dorrie rushed up to her and grabbed her hand. 'Oh, please say yes. I don't want to stay here with the spooks and that horrible man making faces through the window.'

Charity turned to Jackson who had been standing behind her with Bosun sitting patiently at his side. 'What do you say, Jackson?'

He shrugged his shoulders. 'Seems to me that I'd best stay here and keep an eye on the house.' He patted Bosun's head. 'I got a sister living in Hoxton. She'll make sure we don't starve, and I can always earn a penny or two as a rat catcher. Sir Hedley wouldn't thank me for leaving the place to be broke into and vandalised.'

'Are you sure?' Charity gave him a searching look.

He nodded. 'Yes, miss. Quite sure.'

'Then Daniel must be told and it's up to him to see that you get paid for your trouble.'

Jackson tipped his cap. 'I'd be grateful for that, miss. Now, if you don't need me no more I think I'll go out and see if there's an egg in the hen house. I quite fancy a boiled egg for my dinner.' He left through the back door with Bosun at his heels.

'Well,' Mrs Diment said, shrugging. 'He always was a cantankerous old curmudgeon, and he'll be better off on his own. He'll think he's the king of the castle if he has the whole house to hisself.'

'Are we agreed then?' Gideon looked to Charity for an answer. 'If we go now we can catch the midday train from Waterloo.'

She glanced at the eager faces surrounding her and she knew that she was beaten. It made sense to leave London, for a while at least, and Violet's health and that of her unborn child were her main concern. 'Are you coming with us?' she asked warily.

'Of course. I checked with the rector and I'm due for some time off, besides which I haven't seen my father since Christmas, so it's a long overdue visit. I'll go to find a hackney and we'll be on our way.'

It was almost dark by the time they reached Sutton Pomeroy, having stopped briefly on the way to drop Mrs Diment off at Bligh Park. The carriage that Gideon had hired at the station drew to a halt outside the rectory and he alighted first, holding out his hand to help Charity from the vehicle. She surveyed the scene with mounting optimism. The mellow red brick of the Georgian house seemed to glow in the fading light and the trees that surrounded it melted into purple shadows. An oil lamp had been placed in the window closest to the front door, and its welcoming beam illuminated the gravel path leading up through a garden heady with the scent of hyacinths and narcissi. Even before Charity opened the gate in the picket fence the front door was flung open and an elderly gentleman came out to greet them. Gideon paid the driver and hurried to meet his father, throwing his arms around him in a fond embrace. 'It's good to see you, Father.'

'And you, my boy.' The Reverend Philip Raines peered over his son's shoulder. 'And these are the young ladies you told me about.'

Gideon released him, turning to hold his hand out to Charity. 'May I introduce Miss Charity Crosse?'

Charity bobbed a curtsey. It did not seem appropriate to shake the hand of a distinguished gentleman of advanced years. 'How do you do, sir?'

'How do you do, Miss Crosse. Welcome to Sutton Pomeroy.'

Violet and Dorrie had hung back, but Gideon drew them forward. 'Miss Violet Chapman and Miss Dorrie – I don't know your last name, Dorrie.'

'Fisher, sir. It's Dorrie Fisher.' She made an attempt to copy Charity's curtsey and almost toppled over.

'I'm delighted to make your acquaintance,' Philip said, smiling. 'Come inside. It's chilly out here.' He linked his arm through Gideon's and led the way into the wide entrance hall, and at once Charity was struck by the homely atmosphere in the rectory. An overcoat had been left carelessly draped over a chair and a pair of galoshes had been discarded as if the wearer had simply stepped out of them. The polished floorboards smelled of lavender and beeswax, which brought back memories of home to Charity. A vision of her grandmother making the polish in the small kitchen in Chelsea brought a smile to her lips, but it froze as she met the contemptuous gaze of a woman who stood at the foot of the stairs. 'Who are these people, Philip?'

The rector turned to her with a benign smile. 'These young ladies are Gideon's guests, Jane.'

'Aunt Jane.' Gideon hurried forward to plant a kiss on her cheek. 'I didn't know you were here.'

'I only arrived this morning,' she said coldly. 'Are you filling your father's house with your charity cases again, Gideon?'

Dorrie sniggered, but instantly realised her mistake and covered her mouth with her hand. 'Sorry,' she murmured.

'What do you find amusing, child?' Jane spun round to glare at Dorrie, who blushed to the roots of her hair.

'I think it was the word charity,' Gideon said hastily. 'May I introduce Miss Charity Crosse, Aunt?'

Charity met Jane Raines' hard stare without blinking. 'How do you do, ma'am.'

Jane acknowledged her with the briefest of nods, looking her up and down with obvious distaste, but when she turned her gaze to Violet her winged eyebrows shot up to her hairline. 'I see you're giving shelter to whores as well as street urchins, brother.'

Philip's smile faded into a frown. 'That was uncalled for, Jane.'

'I see no wedding ring.' Jane sniffed and turned away as if offended by the sight of Violet's swollen belly.

Violet's mouth drooped at the corners and she backed towards the door. 'I ain't staying here to be insulted by the likes of her, the stuck-up cow.'

'Did you hear that, Philip?' Jane clutched the newel post, closing her eyes. 'I feel quite faint.'

Charity sent a warning glance to Violet. 'I'm sorry if my friend offended you, Miss Raines, but we've had a long and trying day. We're all tired and we would be most grateful for something to eat and a bed for the night, but we'll leave first thing in the morning.'

'There's no need for that,' Gideon protested. 'I think you owe Violet an apology, Aunt Jane. She's a respectable young woman who was taken advantage of and needs our help and compassion, not condemnation.'

'You can say what you like, Gideon. You too, Philip, so don't look daggers at me. I've heard it all before, but when you take on such people they invariably disappoint you. I refuse to sit at table with them, and I'll take my meals in my room while they're here.' She ascended the stairs with her head held high despite Gideon's protests.

'Let her go,' Philip said wearily. 'Jane will come round if we leave her on her own.' His tired face creased into a smile. 'In the meantime, I apologise on my sister's behalf, and I suggest we all go into the drawing room and have a glass of sherry before supper.' He headed towards a door on the far side of the hall, motioning them to follow him.

Violet hung back. 'I dunno. I'd rather go and stay with Mrs Diment, if it's all the same to you, sir.'

'You mustn't take any notice of my aunt,' Gideon said with an apologetic smile. 'It's just her way. She'll come round.'

Violet did not look convinced, and Dorrie's eyes were bright with unshed tears. Charity drew Gideon aside. 'I know you brought us here with the kindest of intentions, but it's clear that we're upsetting your aunt and your father.'

'You'll upset my father more if you insist on leaving now, and anyway there's nowhere to go at this time of night. Join us for supper and we'll talk again in the morning.'

Charity could see that Violet was exhausted and Dorrie was likely to burst into tears at any moment. She forced herself to smile. 'Come along, you two. We mustn't upset Gideon's father by refusing his hospitality.' She followed Gideon into the drawing room, with Violet and Dorrie lagging several steps behind. However, they both seemed to brighten when they entered the room and saw a log fire blazing up the chimney, and their mood changed subtly when an aged maidservant brought in a tray of milk and biscuits for them to share.

Charity sat down by the fire and sipped a glass of sherry. The taste was sweet and nutty and she began to relax, but Jane's cold reception was still fresh in her memory. This was just a temporary measure, she told herself, gazing round the room. It would be easy to think of this lovely old house as home, with its comfortable armchairs covered in chintz and the jewel-coloured Persian rugs scattered over the polished floorboards. A vase filled with daffodils and narcissi filled the air with their sweet scent, and velvet curtains moved gently in the draught from two tall sash windows. Watercolour paintings of country scenes brightened the white walls and framed daguerreotypes were carefully arranged on an escritoire beneath a painting of a pretty young woman. With her red-gold hair and large grey eyes, the likeness to Gideon suggested that this might be his mother, but she did not like to ask. He followed her gaze and smiled. 'That lovely woman is my mother. She died ten years ago but sometimes I can feel her presence in this house.'

Philip cleared his throat noisily. 'The scent of spring flowers always brings her to mind. Christina loved them.'

Charity could see that they were both deeply moved at the mention of her and she said nothing, although she thought that they were lucky to have such fond memories when she had none of her own mother. She sat and listened while Gideon and his father made conversation. It would be so easy to imagine herself living in a home like this, but she must not fall into that trap. Tomorrow she must find work, even if it meant doing the most menial tasks. She had allowed her attention to wander, but was brought sharply back to the present by the appearance of the maid to announce that dinner was served.

'Thank you, Jennet.' Philip rose with some difficulty, refusing a hand from his son. 'I can manage, thank you. My old bones get set in one position and then I have to shake them around a bit in order to get them moving again, but once I'm on my feet there's no stopping me.' He teetered towards the doorway. 'Come along, ladies. You must be very hungry after all that travelling.'

Gideon took Charity's arm and led her into the dining room with Violet and Dorrie trooping dutifully behind them like schoolchildren on an outing. They took their places at the table but Jane was noticeable by her absence. Jennet served vegetable soup followed by collops of mutton in caper sauce and boiled potatoes, and once again the conversation revolved around parish matters, most of which Charity suspected held little interest for Gideon, but he listened politely and made the right noises. Charity had grown used to eating sparingly and she was full even before Jennet brought in the apple pie and custard sauce, but she managed to eat a little as she did not want to offend her host.

When the meal was over the housekeeper, an elderly white-haired woman called Mrs Simms, led them up to their rooms on the first floor. The rectory was a rambling house intended originally to house a large family, and as Philip had remarked at dinner, he and the servants rattled round in it like peas on a drum. Charity had her own room with a luxurious feather bed which she did not have to share with anyone. A fire had been lit in the grate and she was lulled to sleep by the whisper of the wind as it rustled the branches of the trees at the back of the house. She lay in solitary state imagining how Violet and Dorrie must be feeling in the room they had opted to share. Mrs Simms had offered to put Dorrie in the old nursery on the top floor, but she had made such a fuss that Violet allowed her to share her bed. There was no sound from their room next morning when Charity went downstairs to find Gideon, but as luck would have it she entered the dining room to find Jane seated at the table.

'I'm sorry,' Charity said nervously. 'I was looking for Gideon.'

'As you can see he's not here, and it would be more appropriate if someone of your station in life were to address him as Mr Raines.' Jane's tone was scathing and she turned her back on Charity, taking out her spite on a boiled egg. The top flew off and landed on the polished surface of the rosewood table. She clicked her tongue against her teeth, tut-tutting in annoyance. 'Go away, girl. I want to have my breakfast in peace. You should eat in the kitchen with the servants.'

Mortified and angry, Charity stepped back into the hall. She stood for a moment, wondering what to do next. She had a feeling that she might not be too welcome in the kitchen, and as she had no idea as to Gideon's whereabouts she decided to take a walk in the garden. She looped her shawl around her shoulders and let herself out through the front door. Standing on the doorstep she found herself faced with the full splendour of a spring morning in the country. More accustomed to smelly streets strewn with hay and horse dung, and buildings crammed together with not an inch to spare between them, she took in the view of verdant lawns and flowerbeds overflowing with daffodils, narcissi, hyacinths and pools of sunny primroses with a feeling of delight. A vista of rolling hills dotted with sheep stretched out above the hedgerows, which were bursting into life. The beauty of it all was quite overwhelming, and taking deep breaths of the wine-clear air made her feel as if she had drunk a glass of the rector's sherry in one long, greedy gulp. She raised her face to the sun and felt its gentle warmth caress her cheeks.

'It is a beautiful day, isn't it?'

She opened her eyes with a start and saw Gideon walking towards her. He was dressed in riding breeches and a hacking jacket, an outfit which, she thought, suited him much better than his clerical garb. He looked almost as dashing as Harry. 'Good morning, Mr Raines.' She averted her gaze quickly. She had tried to put Harry out of her thoughts, but despite their short acquaintance she could neither forget him nor could she stand by and see him lose everything that was dear to him.

'Mr Raines?' Gideon said, chuckling. 'Why the formality?'

Reluctantly she met his amused gaze. 'Your aunt scolded me for calling you by your Christian name.'

'And I suppose she told you that your place was in the kitchen with the servants?' He shook his head.

'Dear Aunt Jane; I'm afraid she'll never change, but she's not so bad when you get to know her.'

Charity faced him squarely. 'Gideon, this won't work. The girls and I can't stay here. It was a wonderful gesture and I'm very relieved to be away from London and Bert Chapman, but as I told you yesterday we can't impose on your father. We have to find accommodation quickly and I must look for work.'

'I do realise that you're in a difficult position, but you mustn't worry about Father. He is only happy when he's helping people and he won't let Aunt Jane spoil things for you. However, for your sake it can only be a temporary measure and I thought we'd ride over to Bligh Park this morning to see if Daniel has any ideas.'

'Ride?' Charity stared at him in horror. 'Do you mean ride a horse?'

He laughed. 'Well, I certainly don't mean you to ride a camel or an elephant. We don't have too many of those in Sutton Pomeroy.'

'I can't,' she said nervously. 'I've never sat on a horse in my life.'

'Then now is as good a time as any to start. We'll have breakfast and then I'll take you to the stables and introduce you to Nellie. She was my mother's horse and she's the gentlest, quietest animal you'll ever meet. You'll pick it up in no time.'

Chapter Nineteen

Charity was not afraid of horses. There were plenty of them in London, but riding one was another matter. With the aid of a mounting block and help from Gideon, she managed to settle herself on the side-saddle and found it surprisingly comfortable. The rector's groom led the animal out of the stable yard at the back of the house and into the lane.

'How does that feel?' Gideon asked, drawing his mount alongside hers.

'It's a long way to fall,' Charity murmured, clutching the pommel as she tried to adapt to the motion of the horse's gait.

'You won't fall off,' Gideon said confidently. 'We start off slowly and when you feel more confident we'll trot.'

Charity said little, staring between the horse's ears and hoping desperately that she would not fall off and make a fool of herself, but after a while she began to feel less scared and was beginning to enjoy herself. It was wonderful to be able to see over the hedgerows and feel the cool breeze ruffling her hair. Her bonnet had slipped off and hung by its ribbons, but there was no one other than Gideon to see her dishevelled state and he was grinning widely.

'You're getting the hang of it. You're a born horsewoman, Charity.'

She turned her head to look at him, thinking he was teasing her, but there was no hint of mockery in his grey eyes. 'Do you really think so?'

'I wouldn't say it if I didn't mean it. Would you like to go a bit faster?'

'Yes. I think so.'

He urged both horses to a trot and Charity bumped up and down on the saddle, but gradually she accommodated to the motion and when Nellie broke into a canter she was not afraid.

'Mama would have been proud of you,' Gideon said as they entered the gates of Bligh Park. 'She loved Nellie and she was an excellent rider.' His voice broke and he turned his head away.

'What happened?' Charity hardly dared ask the question.

'It was a hunting accident. She was riding an Irish hunter that belonged to Sir Hedley, and she was thrown at a particularly difficult fence. There was nothing that anyone could do to save her. Sir Hedley had the animal shot, and after that he rarely visited Bligh Park; hence the state of disrepair.'

'He must have been very fond of your mother.'

'Everyone loved her. Mama was a wonderful woman and I still miss her, and so does Father. It was ten years ago but the feelings are still as raw as the day it happened.'

'I'm so sorry, Gideon.'

He shot her a sideways glance and she saw tears in

his eyes. 'She would say "well done" if she could see you now. Mama was sweet and gentle but she was also strong and she never gave up on anything or anyone. Father hasn't been the same since her passing.'

There was nothing that Charity could say and they rode in silence until they reached the stable yard. Gideon dismounted and helped her from the saddle. He tossed the reins to the groom. 'Good morning, Tapper. Is Master Daniel at home?'

Tapper deftly handled both horses. 'I think so, sir. He hasn't asked for the carriage or his horse.'

'What about Mr Barton?'

'Mr and Mrs Barton left for Devonshire yesterday, sir.'

'Thank you, Tapper.' Gideon turned to Charity with a relieved smile. 'That's one less thing to worry about. Let's find Dan and see what he has to say.' He slipped her hand through the crook of his arm and they walked towards the house.

'Have you met Wilmot?' Charity asked as they left the mews.

'Never had the pleasure, but to tell the truth I never got on well with Daniel's mother, although of course I wouldn't dream of saying anything against her in his hearing.'

'Wilmot is a snake. He pretends to be one thing to hide the real person lurking beneath a show of charm and good manners.'

'We'll go round to the kitchen,' Gideon said thoughtfully. 'If Dan's at home I think that's where he's most likely to be. Mrs Diment always spoiled us as boys and I doubt if she's changed despite the fact that we're grown men.'

They skirted the house, following the gravel path, but as they reached the gardens Charity tugged at Gideon's arm. 'I can see him. He's in the garden with the mermaid.'

'Daniel.' Gideon's voice rang out loud and clear. 'Dan.' He waved his hand and Daniel looked up. His sombre expression was replaced by a grin and he strode towards them, stepping over the box hedges in his haste.

'Gideon. This is a pleasant surprise. And Charity too?' He held both her hands, looking into her eyes with a sheepish smile. 'I'm sorry I was so rude to you when we last met. I had no right to speak to you like that.'

'You were upset, Dan. I didn't take offence.'

He raised one hand to his lips. 'Thank you.' He turned to Gideon with a friendly smile. 'I didn't realise you two were acquainted until Mrs Diment told us what had been going on in London. She gave us a blow by blow account of your encounters with Chapman.'

'You'd have done the same if you'd been there.' Gideon slapped him on the back. 'It's good to see you again.'

Charity watched them with a smile hovering on her lips. 'It was pure chance that we got to know each other, but Gideon's been wonderful. I don't know what we'd have done if he hadn't come to our aid.'

'Let's go and sit by the mermaid,' Daniel said eagerly. 'We can talk without being overheard. With Mrs Trevett and Mrs Diment reunited it's like listening to a couple of magpies chattering in the kitchen. Poor old Parkin has to flee to the butler's pantry if he wants a bit of peace and quiet.' He led the way between the low hedges to the centre of the garden, where the mermaid rested on the mountain of blackened slabs that were alleged to have been salvaged from a wrecked ship.

'These are so strange,' Charity said, sitting down and picking up one of the unexpectedly heavy brick-shaped objects.

'It's always been assumed this was a mixture of lead and some other metal used as ballast,' Daniel said casually. 'Or perhaps it was cargo to be sold and melted down to manufacture pots and pans or swords. I know nothing about metallurgy.'

Gideon sat down beside Charity. 'We've come to ask for your help, Dan.'

'I didn't think it was a social visit.' Daniel cocked his head on one side. 'You're welcome to come back here and work in the library, Charity. I won't be able to pay you at first, but I'm still hoping to find the treasure. The dig is going well and we've found a tessellated pavement, which is exciting, but won't make my fortune.'

Charity felt the metal taking on the warmth of her hand and she began rubbing it with her sleeve. 'If this was cargo and not ballast it would have some monetary value. Has anyone tried to find out?'

Daniel shook his head. 'Not to my knowledge. I don't suppose it's worth much.'

Charity continued to polish the smooth surface. 'I've

seen plenty of rusty iron railings in London. This is as smooth as silk and it's beginning to shine.'

'Must be lead then,' Daniel said casually. 'Hardly worth the trouble of taking the thing apart, besides which the mermaid is part of our family history. It's supposed to be bad luck if we disturb her resting place.'

'She's just a statue, Dan.' Clutching the metal brick in her hands, Charity rose to her feet. 'I must go and see Mrs Diment and Mrs Trevett. They'll be most offended if I neglect them.' She had had an idea but she did not want to say anything until she was sure of her facts. She walked briskly in the direction of the kitchen, breaking into a run when she was out of sight. If what she suspected was true it would be the answer to Dan's problems and they would be able to raise enough money to pay off Harry's debts and bring him home. She entered the kitchen to find Mrs Diment and Mrs Trevett deep in conversation. They looked up and smiled when they saw her. Mrs Trevett leapt to her feet. 'You look as though you could do with a cup of tea, my dear.'

'Thank you, but I need your advice, ladies. This is something that only you will know.'

Mrs Diment angled her head. 'You look excited, Charity. What's that you're holding in your hand?'

Charity placed it on the table. 'Tell me how to clean silver.'

Mrs Trevett put the kettle on the hob and returned to the table, peering at the blackened brick. 'Baking soda dissolved in hot water with a little soap, and I'll add some vinegar to make the solution stronger.' She looked up at Charity with a glimmer of hope in her eyes. 'Do you really think this is silver?'

'I started rubbing it and it began to shine. If the ship that sank was carrying a cargo of silver bullion then most of it is right here under our noses.'

'The villagers use these as doorstops. You've seen them, haven't you, Fanny?'

'Yes, Polly.' Mrs Diment nodded emphatically. 'Ma and Pa had one for years. It's probably still in the cottage.'

'Which has been empty since they passed on,' Mrs Trevett added knowingly. 'The old place has gone to rack and ruin, and there's been no one to take up the tenancy.'

'Silver or no silver, that could be the answer for you and the girls,' Mrs Diment said eagerly. 'Master Daniel is in charge now and I'm sure he won't object.'

Charity turned to Mrs Trevett. 'Have you got baking soda and vinegar, Mrs Trevett? We need to clean this ugly piece of metal and make it beautiful.'

Mrs Trevett waddled over to the larder and went inside, re-emerging seconds later with a bottle of vinegar and a stone jar filled with white powder. 'I haven't done this for years. Fanny will remember the days when Sir Hedley and that woman he married threw parties for the local gentry. We spent hours cleaning the silver and polishing the crystal wine glasses, but all that went to auction bit by bit and now there's only the library that's untouched, and if Mr Wilmot has his way all the books will be sold and the house too.'

'It's true.' Mrs Diment's mouth turned down at the corners and her bottom lip wobbled ominously. 'He wants to sell up and spend the money on Mrs Barton's estate in Devonshire. The house in London will go too.'

Charity stared at them, horrified. 'But it belongs to Harry. Daniel is only taking care of things until his brother returns.'

'Master Daniel won't stand up to his mother and Mr Wilmot.' Mrs Trevett produced a large bowl and began mixing the ingredients, largely ignoring the advice given by Mrs Diment. Charity submerged the brick in the liquid and waited, hardly daring to breathe. Slowly, bubble by bubble, the black coating began to dissolve, leaving the ingot gleaming in the bottom of the bowl. 'It is silver,' Charity gasped. 'Ladies, we've found the Bligh Park treasure.'

Daniel and Gideon stared at the shiny ingot in disbelief. 'Silver,' Daniel said slowly. 'Do you mean to say that my family has been sitting on a fortune quite literally for a hundred or more years?'

'Mrs Trevett tells me that the villagers have been using them for doorstops,' Charity said with an excited laugh. 'There's one in the old keeper's cottage where Mrs Diment grew up.'

Daniel took the ingot from her, cupping it in his hands as if it were the Holy Grail. 'This is unbelievable. You're a wonder, Charity.'

'It seems like a miracle,' Gideon murmured. 'And I remember the keeper's cottage. Mrs Diment's mother used to bake gingerbread, and if we were lucky she'd give us a piece each. That cottage hasn't been inhabited for years.'

Charity met his smiling gaze with a flash of understanding. 'But it might be made habitable with a bit of elbow grease.'

'My thinking exactly,' Gideon said enthusiastically.

Daniel picked up as many of the heavy ingots as he could manage. 'We'll need a wheelbarrow to start collecting these and taking them into the kitchen. If they're pure silver, we really have found the treasure of Bligh Park.' He gave Charity a sheepish smile. 'I should say that the credit goes to you. I would never have thought of cleaning one of these things in a million years.'

'There is something you might be able to do for me, Dan.' Charity studied his expression carefully; he was not good at masking his feeling and she would know instantly if the plan did not meet with his approval. 'Do you think we could take a look at the keeper's cottage? And if we can make it habitable would you allow us to live in it until I can find work elsewhere?'

Daniel stared at her as if she were speaking another language. 'What are you talking about? I said you could have your job back sorting the library.'

'You won't have to sell all those beautiful books now, and Violet's baby is due in a few weeks. The cottage might be the answer to our problems.'

'Of course you can have it, if that's what you really want, although you could live here and be much more comfortable.'

'I don't think Wilmot would approve.'

Daniel's expression darkened. 'Perhaps you're right. Of course you can have the cottage, and instead of rent you can help clean all these hundreds of ingots. I'll pay you a proper wage as soon as I'm able. We'll be rich.'

Charity could have kissed him, but she did not want to embarrass him in front of Gideon. 'Thank you, Dan. Might we have a look at the cottage before I leave today?'

'I don't see why not.' Daniel glanced at Gideon. 'It's up to you, old chap.'

'It's fine with me. Let's make a start on this.' Gideon bent down to pick up more ingots.

Charity hesitated. 'You won't forget your brother, will you, Dan? You do want Harry to come home, don't you?'

'Of course I do. I never wanted to run the estate anyway, and if the silver fetches a high price it will enable me to do what I want. I'll go to Egypt and join Petrie on his archaeological excavation.'

Gideon tapped him on the shoulder. 'Where's this wheelbarrow you were talking about?'

They invaded the kitchen to Mrs Trevett's obvious annoyance, and after Daniel broke a mixing bowl, spilling the cleaning fluid on the floor, she shooed them all out of the room. 'Leave the cleaning to those who know how to do it,' she said crossly. 'This is a job for experts, not clumsy boys.'

'I'm sorry about the basin, Mrs Trevett,' Daniel muttered, hanging his head.

'You'll have to send Tapper into town to fetch more

baking soda and vinegar, Master Daniel,' Mrs Trevett said crossly. 'And a new mixing bowl to make up for the one you just broke.'

'Yes, Mrs Trevett.' Daniel made his escape, followed by Charity and Gideon.

Charity looked from one to the other, giggling. 'You look like a pair of naughty schoolboys caught scrumping apples in the orchard. You're supposed to be the master of Bligh Park, Dan. You should stand up to her.'

He shrugged his shoulders. 'That's easy for you to say. You weren't brought up by a nanny who ruled you with the proverbial rod of iron. Mrs Trevett is a good sport just as long as you don't get on the wrong side of her.'

'Never mind, Dan,' Gideon said with a sympathetic smile. 'At least we've proved that we're useless in the kitchen and that gets us out of cleaning the ingots. Let's concentrate on collecting them up and bringing them into the house. If word gets round that they're valuable you'll have every rascal in the county looking for them.'

'I'm sure there must be another wheelbarrow in the potting shed.'

'I'll help,' Charity said eagerly. 'And then we can go and take a look at the cottage.'

The keeper's cottage was concealed beneath a cloak of dark green ivy, and the garden was a tangle of brambles and bindweed. Anyone unfamiliar with the area could be forgiven for driving past without realising that there was a dwelling place hidden beneath the encroaching woodland. Daniel had to force the gate open and the rusty hinges gave way, sending the rotting wood to rest on a bed of nettles. 'I'm afraid the building itself might be in the same condition as that gate,' he said as he made his way towards the front door. He produced a bunch of keys and began trying each one in the lock until he found one that fitted, and the door opened with a groan of protest. He stepped inside, tugging at a frond of ivy that had somehow managed to squeeze through the gap between the lintel and the door. Charity could barely wait to see the interior, but the smell of damp and dry rot was not encouraging.

It was gloomy inside due to vegetation excluding most of the light, and the windows were grimed with an accumulation of dirt. There seemed to be one large room downstairs with a small lean-to at the rear of the cottage. Gideon opened the back door and a trickle of sunlight revealed a flagstone floor, a deal table and a stone sink beneath the window. Dead leaves blew in from the garden but the waft of fresh air dispelled some of the mustiness. 'What's out there, Gideon?' Charity asked, peering over his shoulder.

'Nothing much, other than a rusty old mangle and a pile of dead leaves. The roof leaks, but I'm sure it could be fixed without too much trouble.' He turned his head to give her an encouraging smile. 'I've seen worse in the back streets of Whitechapel.'

'The place is uninhabitable,' Daniel said, shaking his head. 'I couldn't allow you girls to live here. It wouldn't do at all.'

Charity was not going to be put off. 'I've slept in shop doorways and under railway arches in the middle of winter. This will be paradise compared to sleeping under the counter in Jethro's shop.'

'Better you than me,' Daniel said, pulling a face. 'Let's check upstairs before we come to a decision. For all we know there might be a hole in the roof.'

They made their way up the narrow, twisting staircase to a narrow landing, off which were two bedrooms. The ceilings were festooned with cobwebs and there were a few damp patches where slates had fallen off the roof, but if they were replaced there was nothing that could not be sorted out by soap and a scrubbing brush. 'It's fine,' Charity said firmly. 'We can make ourselves very comfortable here.' She glanced anxiously at Daniel. 'You did say you wouldn't charge us rent, didn't you?'

He threw back his head and laughed. 'I ought to pay you for putting the place in order. It's yours for as long as you like, and maybe Violet and Dorrie will help to clean the ingots. I expect Mrs Trevett will allow females into the kitchen. It's just us chaps who are banned.'

'You'll need some furniture.' Gideon gazed round with a worried frown. 'And you'll need bed linen and all manner of things.'

'We've got rooms filled with furniture and cupboards overflowing with linen,' Daniel said cheerfully. 'Take what you want, Charity. You've more than earned it.'

Charity reached up to kiss him on the cheek. 'Thank you, Dan.' She turned a smiling face to Gideon. 'Would it be possible to bring Violet and Dorrie over to see the cottage in the morning? We could start cleaning it up straight away.'

'Of course it will. I'm afraid I'll have to return to London at the end of the week, but I'll gladly do all I can to help in the meantime.'

Charity hurried downstairs to take one last look at the living room. She tried to memorise all the details so that she could tell Violet and Dorrie what to expect, but she knew they would be thrilled at the prospect of having a home of their own no matter how much hard work it entailed. She clapped her hands in delight. 'I can't wait to start scrubbing the floor. We'll need buckets and mops and dusters and . . .'

Daniel laid his hand on her shoulder. 'Stop, you're making my head spin. Just tell Mrs Trevett what you want and she'll sort it out for you. I'm going to spend tomorrow going round the estate to make sure there are no more silver ingots being used as doorstops.' He glanced round. 'I don't see one tucked away here.'

Gideon went to open the back door. He stepped outside and returned holding two lumps of blackened metal in his hands. 'I thought I'd noticed something propping up a mangle,' he said, laughing. 'Here are two more to add to the collection.'

Daniel held his hands up, shaking his head. 'Take them, old chap. Get them cleaned up and use the money to restore the church roof, or to help families in need.'

'That's very generous of you. I'll give them to my

father and he can decide what to do with the money they raise.'

'Tell you what,' Daniel said thoughtfully. 'I'll travel up to London with you. We'll hire a carriage and I'll take the ingots that have been cleaned to a bullion dealer.'

Charity eyed him curiously. 'Why the hurry?'

'To be perfectly frank, I don't like the way Wilmot has been behaving since he married my mother, and I think that both Sir Hedley and I should have been told the truth long ago. I love Mama, but neither she nor Wilmot is entitled to a share in the Bligh Park treasure.'

'We must find Harry,' Charity said firmly. 'He'll stand up to Wilmot.'

'I agree, but I need to raise funds first.'

'Do you know where he is?' Gideon asked.

'Ned Loveless was a bit vague but I assume he must have put Harry ashore on the coast near St Malo. If I know my brother he'll have headed for the casinos in Paris.'

'I don't think so,' Charity said, shaking her head. 'He wanted to clear his name.'

'I think it's time we set off for home.' Gideon moved to the door and opened it. 'You'll be able to pass on the good news to Violet and Dorrie.'

'Yes,' she said, making an effort to sound cheerful, but the pleasure and excitement of finding a home was dimmed by the fear that Harry might not have kept his word. He was nothing to her, of course, but if it weren't for him they would have been in a sorry state.

She realised that both Gideon and Daniel were staring at her and she forced her lips into a smile. 'Let's see if I can remember how to ride.'

Next morning Violet and Dorrie travelled to Bligh Park in the rector's trap with Gideon driving, and as there was not room for all of them Charity opted to ride Nellie. She had quickly developed an understanding with the fifteen-year-old mare and was eager to gain more riding experience. Gideon applauded her enthusiasm and made sure she was safely seated before he climbed up onto the driver's seat. Violet and Dorrie were bubbling with enthusiasm, and as she rode behind the trap Charity could hear their excited chatter punctuated with gusts of laughter.

The cottage, despite its dilapidated condition, was an instant hit. Both Violet and Dorrie were delighted with everything. Dorrie said it was like the illustration of the bears' cottage in a storybook that the doctor had given her for her eighth birthday. Violet was more prosaic and said it needed a thorough clean before she would even think of sleeping there and then she burst into tears, which she assured everyone were tears of happiness. 'My baby will be born in a proper house,' she said, mopping her eyes with Gideon's handkerchief. 'But we haven't even got a bed and she'll need a crib and all sorts of things.'

Gideon slipped his arm around her shoulders. 'Don't cry, Violet. I think my old cot is in the attic at the rectory. I'm sure that father would be only too happy for you to have it.'

'I bet Miss Jane wouldn't,' Dorrie said in a stage whisper.

Charity hushed her but Gideon did not seem put out. 'It has nothing to do with my aunt, Dorrie. She won't have a say in the matter.'

'We mustn't waste time,' Charity said, gazing round at the accumulation of dust and dirt. 'I think I saw a besom in the lean-to. We can start by sweeping the floor, and perhaps you could go to the big house with Gideon, Vi? Mrs Trevett has promised to let us have buckets and mops and all the things we need to clean this place up.' She turned with a start as someone hammered on the door. She ran to open it and found Tapper standing on the path loaded up like a tinker. Pots and pans dangled from strings looped around his shoulders and in each hand he held a bucket filled with scrubbing brushes, dusters, cleaning cloths and a bar of lye soap.

'With Mrs Trevett's compliments,' he said gruffly. He peered over Charity's shoulder. 'And Mrs Diment said the young lady called Violet must come to the house and give them a list of your needs.'

'I'll take her in the trap,' Gideon said easily. 'I should be there giving Dan a hand anyway.'

Tapper dumped the buckets on the ground and doffed his cap. 'Thank you, your reverence.' He slid the pots and pans from his shoulders and laid them at Charity's feet.

'It's just Gideon, Tapper. I may wear a dog collar now, but you taught me everything I know about horses.'

'You was a quick learner, Master Gideon. I wish I could say the same for Master Daniel. Now Master Harry was another matter. He could ride almost afore he could walk and he had no fear. It were a bad day when Ned Loveless set him ashore on that little island.'

'What island?' Charity gave him a searching look, wondering if the old man's mind was wandering.

Tapper dropped his gaze. 'I weren't supposed to say nothing.'

'You can trust us, Tapper,' Gideon said gently. 'Where did Ned take Master Harry? We want to find him and bring him home, but we can't unless you tell us where he is.'

Chapter Twenty

Tapper stared down at his boots. 'I weren't supposed to say nothing, sir.'

Charity seized his hand. 'Please, Mr Tapper. We must find him and bring him home.'

Tapper raised his head and his eyes were filled with hope. 'If Master Harry returns we'll see the back of that man Lady Hedley married.'

'Yes, indeed we will.' Charity squeezed his calloused fingers. 'Where did Ned Loveless take Master Harry?'

'I weren't supposed to say, but it was one of the smaller Channel Islands, miss. I can't exactly remember the name of it but Loveless knows.'

She released his hand with a grateful smile. 'Thank you, Mr Tapper. You won't regret this, I promise.'

He mumbled something beneath his breath and shambled off along the path to where he had left his barrow. He hesitated, glancing over his shoulder. 'There's more to come. I'll bring it later.' He walked off in the direction of the big house.

Charity turned to Gideon. 'Harry didn't go to Paris. He didn't break his word.'

He met her excited gaze with a heavy sigh. 'I thought perhaps I stood a chance, but now I see that I was mistaken.'

'I don't understand.'

'I was deluding myself, Charity. I sensed that there was something between you and Harry, but I hoped it was just my imagination. I can see now that it was not.'

She knew she was blushing furiously and she looked away. 'Harry was kind to me, that's all, and I owe him a lot. There was never anything romantic between us.'

'Are you sure of that?' Gideon picked up the buckets and took them indoors.

Charity stepped outside, taking deeps breaths of the cool air. Gideon had jumped to the wrong conclusion, she thought, fanning her hot cheeks with her hand. It was madness to think that a man like Harry would be interested in someone with her background, and she was stunned to think that Gideon had feelings for her. He had been kindness itself, but he had never given her cause to think that he was anything but a friend. She could not look him in the face when he emerged from the cottage with Violet.

'I'm going to the big house to help Mrs Trevett sort out the bed linen,' Violet said apologetically. 'I don't like leaving you to do all the work.'

'You've got an even more important task,' Charity said with an attempt at an encouraging smile. 'Cleaning is the easy part. It's up to you to bring back the things we need to make ourselves comfortable.'

'Come along, Violet.' Gideon strode off towards where he had left the trap.

'Don't worry. I'll be as quick as I can.' Violet hurried

after him, leaving Charity to return to the house and supervise Dorrie.

'Right,' she said briskly. 'I think there's a well in the back garden. Let's go and fill the buckets.'

Charity saw little of Gideon during the next few days. He accompanied Daniel on his hunt for the remainder of the silver ingots, and she was kept busy in the cottage. At first it was simply a matter of brushing the cobwebs down and sweeping the floors. She managed to get a fire burning in the small cast-iron range, which Dorrie had cleaned and blackleaded so that it looked almost new, and they were able to heat water and begin scrubbing the floors.

Tapper fixed the roof and brought cartloads of furniture from the big house. He hefted the brass bedsteads from the old servants' quarters up the stairs to the first floor. After that came two pine chests of drawers and several clean, but faded, rag rugs. Mrs Trevett had been generous with bedding and kitchen utensils and at the end of the fourth day the cottage was ready for habitation. The garden was still a wilderness but that did not matter. They now had a home of their own.

Their parting with the rector and his household was tearful but they promised to visit often, and Philip demanded the privilege of baptising Violet's baby when she arrived. Violet was certain that her child was a girl and had already chosen her names, which she kept to herself, as she said, 'just in case it happens to be a boy, although I know it won't be'.

There had been no sign of Miss Jane when they left,

but Charity looked back and saw a pale face peering out of an upstairs window. Gideon drove off with Violet and Dorrie in the trap and Charity flicked the reins to encourage Nellie into action, resisting the temptation to wave to Jane and let her know that she had been spotted. During the last few days there had been signs that frosty Miss Jane was thawing a little towards them, but she was a great one for keeping her dignity. Charity blew a kiss to the rector and another to Mrs Simms and Jennet as she urged Nellie into a brisk trot. She was genuinely sorry to leave the comfort of the rectory; she knew she would miss the cosseting and the many kindnesses she had received, but she was eager to start afresh in a place she could call home.

Daniel and Mrs Diment were waiting for them at the cottage with a fire burning in the range and a pot of rabbit stew simmering on the hob. One of Mrs Trevett's freshly baked loaves was on the table, which was set for three, together with a dish of butter and a hunk of cheese. A bowl of oranges on the dresser made Dorrie shriek with delight when she saw it and Mrs Trevett hastily attributed the gift to Daniel, who received a rapturous hug. 'I only tasted an orange once,' Dorrie said, licking her lips at the memory. 'Dr Marchant put it in me Christmas stocking with a handful of walnuts and a bar of chocolate. He were ever such a lovely man.' She clapped her hand to her mouth. 'And so are you, Mr Daniel. So are you.'

He tugged playfully at one of her pigtails. 'I hope you enjoy them, Dorrie.' He glanced at Charity and smiled. 'We'll be leaving for London tomorrow. I'll be staying with Gideon at his lodgings and I plan to visit the bullion dealers as soon as possible.'

Gideon nodded. 'We'll be leaving first thing.'

'There are still plenty of the wretched things to clean,' Mrs Diment said, sighing. 'My hands are red raw from dipping them in that dratted mixture.'

'Perhaps you'd like to drive Mrs Diment home in the trap, Dan,' Charity suggested before Gideon could offer. 'I'll ride Nellie.'

Gideon shook his head. 'If Tapper doesn't mind looking after her, I'll leave Nellie for you to ride, Charity. She needs the exercise and she gets none at home. Father only keeps her for sentimental reasons.'

'Thank you,' she murmured, averting her eyes. She had felt uncomfortable in his presence since he hinted that his feelings for her went deeper than friendship. She had been touched and flattered, but she could not allow him to harbour false hopes. It was only when he made her face up to the truth that she realised it was Harry who occupied her thoughts and dreams, even though she knew it could never come to anything. The mistress of Bligh Park with its restored fortune would need to be a lady of good breeding. It was a sad fact, but she knew that her early misfortune, and the way she had survived by begging and petty theft, would come back to haunt her. She was a criminal in the eyes of the law, the only difference between her and a prisoner in Newgate was that she had not been caught.

'Come along then, Mrs Diment,' Daniel said, proffering his arm. 'Let's go home. The aroma of that stew is making me feel hungry.'

'There's plenty where that came from, sir. Mrs Trevett knows that you're very partial to one of her stews.' She paused in the doorway. 'I'll see you tomorrow, girls. There are still some ingots to be cleaned and polished, but you'd best remain here, Violet. You look ready to drop at any moment.'

Violet's face reddened and she clasped her hands around her belly. 'Not in front of the gentlemen, Mrs Diment.'

Daniel opened the door. 'Don't worry, Violet. I didn't hear a thing.' He propelled Mrs Diment outside into the garden. 'Don't loiter, Gideon. We've an early start tomorrow morning.'

Gideon turned to Charity. 'Come and say goodbye to Nellie.'

It was more of a command than an invitation and to refuse would draw attention to herself. Violet and Dorrie were forever teasing her about her two handsome suitors, both of them convinced that Daniel was also sweet on Charity. She hurried after him. 'I'm very grateful,' she said hastily. 'It was a kind thought, but won't your father be upset if you leave Nellie here?'

'It was his idea, Charity. He admires you greatly, as do I.'

'Please don't say any more, Gideon. I'm very fond of you, of course, but . . .'

'But you don't love me.'

She raised her eyes to his face, shaking her head. 'I'm sorry. I wish I felt differently, but it wouldn't be fair to take advantage of you.'

'You would make a wonderful vicar's wife. We could

work wonders together in the East End. You of all people would understand my parishioners' needs.'

'You mean a girl from the streets would know how to treat others like her.'

'No, I didn't mean that at all. What happened to you was through no fault of your own. All I meant was that your past experiences have made you a more understanding person. You're brave and you face up to adversity. You don't allow it to crush you.'

'You deserve a wife who loves you deeply. I could never be that woman.'

'Harry Bligh is not the man for you,' he said angrily. 'He might have inherited a baronetcy and a fortune, but he's a gambler and always will be. He'll run through the money and leave you to handle his debts and his estate. You'd do better with Daniel if your heart is set upon joining the Bligh family.'

'I thought you were his friend.' Stung by his words and the tone of his voice, she met his angry gaze with a toss of her head. 'That was a cruel thing to say, and unfair. I'm not a fortune hunter, nor am I so heartless that I would marry simply to better myself in the eyes of the world. I'd rather remain a spinster all my life than commit myself to a loveless marriage.'

A soft whicker from Nellie broke the moment of silence that hung between them. Gideon turned on his heel and taking the bridle led the horse away without a backward glance.

Charity resisted the temptation to run after him and make things right between them, but she knew instinctively that he needed to be alone. He would realise his mistake one day and thank her for being honest. She went into the cottage, closing the door and shutting out the rest of the world.

Dorrie was already seated at the table and Violet was about to dish up the stew. 'Isn't this lovely?' Violet said, smiling happily. 'Our own home. We'll be safe here.'

'Yes,' Charity said, sinking down on one of the kitchen chairs brought over from the big house. 'Quite safe.'

That night, despite the comfort of her new bed and the peaceful silence of her own room, Charity could not sleep. Thoughts of Harry filled her mind and she knew that the time had come when he must be found, despite the fact that seeing him again would tear her heart in two. He must be persuaded to come home and secure his estate from Wilmot and Myrtle's grasping hands. She loved Daniel, but only as a brother, and she knew his weaknesses; he would be no match for the combined efforts of his mother and Wilmot. The money raised by selling the silver ingots would surely pay off Harry's debts, and then he could claim his title and his estate.

She fell into a troubled sleep and was up at crack of dawn next morning. She went downstairs in her night-gown and stepped outside in the pearly May morning, walking barefoot across the dew-spangled grass to draw water from the well. Through gaps in the fence she could see the carpet of bluebells in the woods that surrounded the cottage on three sides, and the air was filled with birdsong. It was, she thought, the sort of morning when it felt good to be alive, and with a newly found feeling of optimism she knew that it was up to her to set things right. She could not wait until Daniel returned from London; he was full of good intentions but he would dither and there was no time for that.

She went inside and spent several minutes encouraging the sleepy embers in the grate to burst into flames. She filled the kettle and placed it on the hob before taking a quick wash at the sink. The cold water refreshed and revitalised her and she hurried upstairs to get dressed. Having breakfasted on a slice of bread and butter and a cup of tea she put on her bonnet and shawl, let herself out of the house and set off at a brisk pace. As she neared the avenue of trees leading up to the main house she saw the brougham driving off through the gateway. She came to a halt, bending over to catch her breath. She had planned to tell Daniel of her plans, but it was too late. He was on his way to London to find a bullion dealer, leaving her on her own, and she was suddenly nervous and unsure of herself. Even now, assuming that news had travelled fast and that he had heard about the treasure from one of his cronies at the archaeological excavation, Wilmot might be making arrangements to return to Bligh Park. She dreaded to think what he might do should he get his hands on any of the money, and she broke into a run, heading for the stable block. She found Tapper in the tack room, munching bread and dripping. He rose swiftly to his feet, wiping his lips on his sleeve. 'Good morning, miss.'

'Good morning, Mr Tapper. I'm sorry to interrupt

your breakfast but I need to go to the village urgently. I wonder if you'd saddle up Nellie for me?'

He gave her a shrewd look. 'You'll be going to Ned's cottage.'

It was a statement and not a question. She nodded. 'That's right.'

'You'll need more than words to make him talk, miss.' Tapper's button-bright eyes twinkled, reminding Charity of a cheeky London sparrow.

'I take your meaning, Mr Tapper.'

He moved to the back of the tack room and opened a cupboard. She uttered a gasp of surprise when she saw its contents. 'Where did you get those?'

He lifted out an ingot and handed it to her. 'They've been there for years, miss. No one knows who put them there or why. I've used them for all manner of things, but never thought they was of any value. Now I know different and here they'll stay until the master comes home. You can tell him that when you see him.'

'I will,' she said, smiling. 'Thank you.'

He shrugged his shoulders. 'I'll go and saddle up Nellie. You do your best, miss. We need Master Harry here where he belongs. You tell him that too.'

Charity dismounted outside the cottage where Ned and his family lived. Small children were playing in the tiny garden and in the lane. One of the older boys volunteered to hold Nellie's bridle and she tipped him a halfpenny, which was all the money she had in her pocket. She knocked on the front door and waited. Eventually it opened and Mrs Loveless stood there with a baby in her arms and a grubby toddler clinging to her skirts. 'Yes, miss?'

'Is your husband at home, Mrs Loveless?'

A look of suspicion crossed the woman's weary features. 'What d'you want?'

'Some information, that's all. I'll make it worth his while.'

'Ned.' Mrs Loveless backed into the living room. 'There's a young lady to see you. Says she wants some information.' She retreated into the house.

Moments later Ned Loveless stood in the doorway. His eyes narrowed when he saw Charity. 'I told Master Daniel all I know.'

Charity was not going to be intimidated by his surly expression. She stood her ground. 'I think you might have a little more information to give, Mr Loveless.' She produced one of the ingots from the leather pouch that Tapper had given her.

He stared at it and burst out laughing. 'That lump of lead? I got two of those already, miss. Everyone in the village has at least one. Bloody good doorstops they make too.'

'They'll make even more than that if they're cleaned and polished, Mr Loveless. Daniel is on his way to a bullion dealer in London as we speak. These ingots are solid silver and worth a small fortune.'

He scowled at her. 'You're pulling my leg. That ain't silver.'

'It is. I'm not joking.'

He snatched the ingot from her and began rubbing it with his sleeve. 'It's some kind of metal but it can't be valuable. These things have been knocking around for as long as I can remember. They was here in my grandfather's time and even before then.'

'You need to clean them with a mixture of baking soda, warm water and vinegar. I'm sure that your wife will know how to make it.'

He turned his head. 'Martha, come here.'

His wife joined them with the baby at her breast. 'Can't you see I'm busy, you stupid man?'

He repeated what Charity had just told him, but Martha Loveless did not look convinced. 'It's a joke. That stuff is worthless. She's trying to hoodwink you, Ned.'

'Please just try it,' Charity said in desperation. 'Master Daniel has taken some of these to London. He wouldn't do that if he didn't believe the ingots were silver bullion.'

'Bring it in here then, Ned.' Martha glared at Charity. 'You stay there. The house ain't in a fit state for visitors.'

Charity waited on the doorstep for several minutes with the younger Loveless children staring at her, sucking their thumbs, and their older brothers ignoring her presence as they played tag or wrestled on the ground like playful puppies.

Ned reappeared and his expression was deferential. 'What did you want to know, miss?'

'What was Master Harry's destination? I know it was one of the Channel Islands and I'll pay you to take me there.'

He gave her a calculating look. 'How many of these is it worth?'

'I'll give you one to take me to this island and another if you bring us back safely.' She knew that she was being reckless with the Bligh fortune but she had seen the greedy look in Ned's eyes when he realised that the ingots were valuable.

'It's a deal.' Ned spat on his hand and held it out to her.

She shook hands. 'How soon can you take me?'

'We'll have to wait for the tide, but we could go tonight if you're brave enough to sail in a fishing boat. There ain't no conveniences for a young lady and it can be a rough crossing, especially when we hit the Alderney Race.'

'What time will we leave?'

'Be down at the harbour at midnight. With a favourable wind we'll get there before nightfall tomorrow, but it could take longer.'

The voyage to Herm was something that Charity would rather forget. She was not, she discovered, a very good sailor, and the sea was choppy. Ned and his eldest son, Joe, went about their duties in silence with the assistance of an old man called Nobby, who chewed tobacco and spat streams of brown juice overboard at regular intervals. The voyage seemed to last for an eternity and Charity made herself as small as possible, huddling in the bows beneath a pile of sacks that stank of fish. She slept eventually in between bouts of nausea, and just when she thought she could bear it no longer she heard Joe's shout of 'Land, ho'.

She emerged from her smelly cocoon to peer into

the dusk. She could see the dark shapes of the islands rising up out of the moonlit sea, and there was a sudden flurry of action on deck as Ned expertly manoeuvred the vessel alongside the granite harbour wall. She struggled to her feet, clutching the wooden gunwales for support. Ned secured the wheel and made his way towards her. 'Well, miss. We're here, and that's my part done.'

'Only half of it,' she reminded him quickly. 'You said you'd wait and take us home.'

'Aye, I did. We can't sail until the tide is right anyway. Me and the boys are going to get some sleep.'

'What about me?' Charity demanded. 'I must find Harry.'

Ned shrugged. 'I just dropped him off here, miss. I dunno where he went next. That's your problem. As for me, I'm going to the pub to have a few beers before I get my head down.'

Charity could see that she was not going to get any more help from Ned, and she did not want to spend another night on board. 'All right, but I'll come with you. This seems to be a very small island. Someone is sure to know where I can find Harry.'

'Suit yourself, miss. But it ain't exactly the place for a young person such as you.'

'Let me worry about that.' She shook out her skirts and patted her tumbled hair into a semblance of order. 'I'm ready when you are.'

The pub was in reality a barn belonging to an old farmhouse where the farmer's wife served beer and cider straight from the barrel. Quarrymen and farmers sat cheek by jowl on wooden forms set around trestle tables. The air was heavy with tobacco smoke and the fumes from oil lamps, which all but masked the pleasant scent of the straw bales piled up against the walls. Heads turned and men stared curiously at the newcomers. The farmer's wife smiled at Ned but when her eyes rested on Charity she shook her head. 'This isn't the place for you, my dear.' She turned on Ned with a frown puckering her brow. 'You should take your daughter away from here, mister.'

Ned bridled. 'She ain't my daughter. She's on her own.'

'No she isn't.' A figure rose from the far end of the furthest table. 'She's with me.' Harry strode across the straw-covered floor to take Charity by the arm. He propelled her outside in a none-too gentle manner, leaving Ned staring after them.

Caught by surprise and unable to speak she could only stand and stare at this person who sounded like Harry, but looked like a stranger. Dark stubble covered his chin and above it his face was tanned, as were his bare forearms. His eyes were no longer underlined by bruise-like shadows and he had lost the louche, world-weary look with which she was so familiar. He was leaner, and the workman's clothes he wore made him appear to have grown in stature. He gave her a shake. 'What d'you think you're doing? Why did Ned Loveless bring you here?'

'I have bad news for you, Harry.' She wrenched her arm free. 'Stop glowering at me and I'll tell you.'

He released her with an apologetic smile. 'I'm sorry. It was a shock seeing you here.'

'There's no easy way to say this, Harry. Your father has passed away and you're needed at home.'

He was silent for a moment, staring up into the starlit sky as he absorbed the news. 'If I'd wanted to return to England I'd have done so before now. You know why I can't go home.'

'But everything has changed. We've found the Bligh Park treasure and you'll never guess where it was.' She shivered as a cool breeze wafted off the sea, ruffling her hair and tugging at the salt-stained hem of her skirt.

His stern expression melted into one of concern. 'You're cold. We can't talk here.'

'I'm not going back to the boat. I don't want to spend another night sleeping under sacks that reek of dead fish.'

A reluctant smile curved his lips. 'You were mad to make the journey, but let's get you into the warmth.' He took her by the hand and strode off into the darkness of a narrow lane with the beach on one side and fields on the other. As they rounded a bend she saw the welcoming lights from a small terrace of cottages. He opened the door of the first one and ushered her inside. 'This has been my home for the past couple of months.'

She stepped over the threshold and found herself in a small room lit by the warm glow of a fire in the ingle nook. A cooking pot sat on a metal trivet placed over the burning peat, its contents simmering gently. She glanced round, casting off her bonnet and shawl. 'You've made yourself comfortable. Do you live alone?'

He pulled up one of the only two chairs in the room. 'Sit down and have something to eat. You must be starving.'

'I am, but you haven't answered my question.'

He moved across the floor to a crudely made pine dresser and returned with bowls and spoons. 'I live here entirely alone, and before you ask, I've spent all my time on the island with only a couple of trips to St Peter Port when I needed to purchase necessities.' He ladled soup into one of the bowls, added a spoon and placed it within her reach on the table. 'I'm still learning how to cook but this won't poison you.' He served a portion for himself and sat down.

'I wasn't going to cross-examine you.' Charity tasted the soup and smiled. 'This is very good.'

'There's no need to be polite. I know it isn't up to Mrs Diment's standards or those of Mrs Trevett, but at least it's edible.' He gave her a searching look. 'You'd better start at the beginning and tell me what's been going on at home, and what's all this about treasure?'

'You're right,' she said, taking a fishbone from her mouth. 'This would be lovely without the bones.'

'Don't change the subject, Charity. I want to know everything. You can't turn up out of the blue and tell me I can go home without an explanation.'

'Don't you want to come home?'

'Of course I do. I've been supporting myself by labouring in a granite quarry and I haven't made too bad a job of it, but I don't want to spend the rest of my life holed up in this cottage, away from those I love.'

Her heart seemed to do a somersault inside her breast and she was finding it difficult to breathe. 'People you love?'

'I've thought about nothing else since I left you. I told myself that I could forget you and that you were better off without me. What woman in her right mind would want to be tied to a compulsive gambler? But forgetting you was probably the hardest part of being exiled even to such a splendid place as this.'

'Y-you love me?'

'From the first moment I saw you, but you were an innocent young girl and too good for me.'

'I can't believe you would even think that, Harry. You know my history.'

'I know what happened to you, but that's not what you are, Charity. Despite the way you'd been forced to exist you were and are an innocent. I chose my way of life.'

'But I love you too, and I can see that you've changed. All you need is a new start.'

'Put me within a hundred yards of a gaming club and I know I'd be back at the tables in a flash. You say that the Bligh Park fortune has been found, but I doubt if it would take me long to go through it.' He laid his hand on hers. 'I couldn't risk your happiness by going back to my old life. Can you understand that, darling?'

Chapter Twenty-One

The term of endearment was something that she had longed to hear coming from Harry's lips, but now it sounded like the death knell to all her hopes and dreams. She wrapped her fingers around his hand and clasped it to her heart. 'I won't let you give up so easily, Harry Bligh.'

He smiled wearily. 'You're forgetting that I use my mother's maiden name.'

'I'm not forgetting a thing. You are Sir Harry Bligh now, and you have a responsibility for all those left who depend on you. Are you really willing to allow Wilmot to take over the estate? If you don't return he'll ruin Bligh Park and sell the house in Nevill's Court to the highest bidder. If you don't care about your brother and his dreams of becoming an archaeologist, think of Mrs Diment and Mrs Trevett, Jackson and Parkin and Tapper, and the home you grew up in.'

He raised her hand to his lips and kissed it. The caress was as gentle as the touch of a butterfly's wings, but then he seemed to regret his romantic action and stood up, helping her to her feet. 'You must get some sleep. There's a reasonably comfortable bed upstairs.' He made for the door.

'Where are you going?'

'I'll sleep in the barn. This is a tiny island and your reputation would be in shreds if word got round that we'd spent the night in the together.'

'But that's ridiculous.'

'Maybe, but that's how it is. Don't worry about me, my love. I'll have a glass of Mr Ogier's excellent cider and that will send me straight into the arms of Morpheus.'

'But you haven't given me your answer. We'll have to sail on the morning tide or Ned will go without us.'

'I need to think this through, Charity. It's your future I have to consider as well as those of Dan and the servants.'

'I can look after myself,' she said stoutly.

He smiled. 'I don't doubt it, but you've saddled yourself with a pregnant woman and a child.'

'That's my problem, not yours,' she said angrily. 'I want you to come home for your sake as much as mine, and you don't have to feel responsible for me.'

'It's a responsibility I would be privileged and honoured to accept, but I'm afraid I'd let you down. I have to battle with my own particular demons.' He walked out into the night, leaving a gust of salt-laden air in his wake.

Charity sat for a long time, staring at the slow-burning peat. The astonishing and wonderful revelation that Harry loved her was tempered by fear that he would refuse to return home. Eventually, overcome by exhaustion, she made her way up the steep staircase to the bedroom and huddled beneath the coverlet, still fully dressed. She fell asleep drugged by the scent of him that lingered on the pillow and in the sheets.

She was awakened by the sound of someone calling her name, and when she realised that she was no longer dreaming and that it was Harry's voice, she tumbled out of bed, snatched up her boots and raced downstairs. 'You've decided to come with me?'

'You were right, Charity,' he said slowly. 'I've been awake all night struggling with the dilemma, but I came to realise that I was being a coward.'

'No!' she cried angrily. 'Never say that.'

'It's true, sweetheart. I was running away from myself.' He held up his hand as she took a step towards him. 'But what I said about us still stands. I'm a gambler and probably always will be. Everything depends on whether I'm strong enough to avoid temptation.'

'I'll help you. I'll do everything I can to stop you sliding back into your old ways.'

'One step at a time, I think.' He smiled, and the tender look in his eyes made her want to throw her arms around him, but she resisted the temptation and sat down to put on her boots.

They walked, hand in hand, down to the jetty but Ned's boat had gone, as had all the other fishing boats that had been moored alongside. Harry went to enquire at the harbourmaster's cottage and returned minutes later, frowning angrily. 'Apparently there were reports of a big shoal off Alderney. All the fishermen left on the tide and they aren't expected back until tonight or tomorrow. In fact, knowing Loveless, I wouldn't be surprised if he took his catch to St Malo and sold it there.'

'So we're stranded here until he remembers us.'

He met her worried gaze with the beginnings of a smile. 'That's not such a bad thing, is it, Charity? It means we have some time to ourselves. I'll show you my island, for that's how I've grown to think of Herm.'

Her first thoughts were for Violet and Dorrie, but then she realised that they had only to ask Mrs Trevett or Mrs Diment for help and it would be given wholeheartedly. She smiled up at him. 'I don't suppose Dan will return home for a few days, and now that Vi and Dorrie are in the cottage . . .'

He laid his finger on her lips, shaking his head. 'Stop worrying about everyone else. Whatever happens in the future, this time has been given to us so let's not waste it.' He slipped his arm around her shoulders. 'I suggest we go to the pub. I happen to know that Rozelle Ogier serves a wonderful breakfast. I've eaten there almost every day since I've been here.'

They enjoyed a tasty breakfast of buttered eggs and toasted fruit bread, which Mrs Ogier explained was called gâche, made from a traditional Guernsey recipe. 'I was a Guernsey girl,' she said proudly. 'My family had a farm in Vale and I met my husband in the market where I was selling the first strawberries of the season.' She placed a dish of creamy yellow butter on the table in front of them. 'You should eat plenty of our good food while you're here,' she added, aiming the remark at Charity. 'Men like their women to have a bit of flesh on them.' She chuckled and moved off to a table where a group of quarrymen were just finishing their meal.

'You're perfect as you are,' Harry said, grinning. 'Rozelle is the motherly sort who is only happy when she's looking after people. That's the secret of her success, as most of the men who work in the quarries have come from far away.'

Charity sipped her tea. 'She's a very good cook, but I can't manage another mouthful.'

'Then we'll slip away while she's busy with my workmates. I've told the foreman that I won't be in today.' He stood up and held out his hand. 'It's a beautiful May morning; just right for seeing the island.'

Charity discovered that the island of Herm was only a mile and a half long, and it seemed like a tropical paradise to a girl brought up in the teeming filth of the East End streets. The white sandy beaches and sheltered coves were beyond her imaginings. 'It's like Treasure Island,' she said, leaning against Harry's shoulder as they sat side by side on the sands of Belvoir Bay. 'I expect to see the *Hispaniola* moored out there and Long John Silver limping across the beach.'

Harry kissed her tenderly on the lips. 'You and your books, Charity. Reading was never one of my pastimes. I liked to be active when I was a boy.'

She smiled. 'You don't know what you're missing. When I was in the shop I used to read by candlelight. It was the only way I could stand being alone at night, except for the cockroaches and the rats, but I don't count them.'

'I want to make it up to you, Charity. I've never forgotten the first time I saw you. It was a bitterly cold day and Wilmot insisted on stopping in at a bookshop in Liquorpond Street, and he introduced us. I suppose I should be eternally grateful to him for that.'

'It was my birthday and you and he took me out to dinner and the theatre. You stood up for me when Wilmot said hateful things, and you made the cabby stop so that we could get out and leave Wilmot to travel on alone. You took your coat off and wrapped it around me because I was shivering.'

'I felt the need to take care of you then, as I do now.' He stroked her cheek. 'Don't frown, darling. I know you're a capable and independent young woman, but that doesn't stop me wanting to give you everything that was denied to you when you were growing up. I know it's selfish but I want you to be with me for the rest of my life.'

A fluffy white cloud passed across the sun, sending shadows across the silvery sands, and a breeze rustled the leaves of the trees on the cliff top. Charity felt a shiver run through her even though it was a warm day. She twisted round so that she was facing him. 'But it's not as easy as that, is it, Harry?'

It was his turn to frown. 'I don't understand. I thought that's what you wanted. I was the one who had doubts.'

'You've inherited the land and the title and now you're a rich man. You have a position to keep up and that doesn't include a girl from the slums of the East End.'

He stopped her protests with a kiss that blotted out reason and made time stand still. 'I'll hear no more of that talk,' he said gruffly when they drew apart. 'You were born to a better life despite the misfortunes that were forced upon you. I love you and you love me. Nothing else matters.' He held her in his arms and Charity allowed herself to relax and enjoy the moment. There was silence except for the gentle sound of the waves lapping on the shore and the beating of their hearts.

She lost all track of time as they sat together on the warm sand. There was no need for words. They were the only two people in the world and this was their island, safe from intruders and far away from the problems that awaited them at home.

The rest of the day passed like a wonderful dream. Charity put all thoughts of home firmly out of her mind. Even if they only had this precious time together she would be grateful for the rest of her life. They returned to the old barn to eat their midday meal but there was no sign of the fishing boats and no one seemed to expect them before nightfall at the earliest.

Charity slept alone again that night, but she went to bed feeling happier than she had ever felt in her whole life. Harry had quashed her misgivings, setting them aside as if they were of no importance. He had promised to put his old ways behind him, and she was certain that he would keep his word. When they returned to Bligh Park it would only be a matter of having the banns read and then they would be married. She fell asleep hoping that Ned would haul in a huge catch of fish and that he would not return for another day at least. She realised that this interlude on the idyllic island was precious and once gone would never return. It was like a jewel that she would wear close to her heart for the rest of her life. 'Just one more perfect day,' she whispered as she drifted off to sleep.

Ned's boat returned to harbour in the early morning of the third day. He was unapologetic. 'I couldn't let up on a chance like that,' he said, grinning. 'Sold the lot in St Malo and made enough money to see me through next winter, if I'm careful.'

Charity had expected Harry to be angry, but he merely laughed and slapped Ned on the back. 'When do we sail for home?'

'Six o'clock this evening, unless the weather breaks. It's set fair at the moment, but I got a feeling there's a storm brewing to the west.'

'Perhaps we ought to postpone sailing until we know it's safe,' Charity murmured. She was not afraid, but the seasickness she had suffered on the crossing was still fresh in her mind.

'You'll be safe with me. I'm the best there is when it comes to boat handling.' Ned swaggered off towards the pub.

'He's right,' Harry said with a rueful smile. 'And my meagre wages have almost run out. Let's hope that Dan has had some luck with the bullion dealers.'

Charity linked her hand through the crook of his arm as they walked away from the harbour, heading towards his cottage. 'You know it came as a total shock to him when he found out that Sir Hedley was his father too.'

'It's not something I would boast about,' Harry said grimly. 'I still love my mother, but I think she played a dirty trick on my father, and perhaps I should have given him more of a chance to prove himself to me. I allowed her to turn me against him and that was wrong.'

Charity squeezed his arm. 'It wasn't your fault. Neither you nor Dan were to blame for your parents' actions.'

'We'll be home soon, but I can face anything as long as I have you at my side.' He stopped and drew her into his arms.

Their homecoming at Bligh Park was met with tears of joy from Mrs Trevett and Mrs Diment and grim satisfaction from Parkin and Tapper. No doubt Jackson would react in a similar stoical manner when news filtered through to Nevill's Court. Daniel had not yet returned from London, but at least there was no indication that Wilmot had been alerted as to the existence of the bullion.

Charity went back to the cottage and found that Violet and Dorrie were coping very well without her, although they were delighted to see her and welcomed her with hugs and demands to hear all about her travels. Violet, who was very close to her time, had stopped going to the big house to help clean the ingots, but Dorrie had been happy to take her place. Charity accompanied her each morning, essentially to complete her task in Sir Hedley's library, but it did not take much persuasion from Harry for her to abandon the books and spend time with him. He had wanted to announce their engagement the moment they arrived home, but she had persuaded him to keep their relationship secret until Dan's return.

She suspected that it was already common knowledge in the village, but she also knew that if that particular piece of news were to reach Wilmot's ears he would double his efforts to prevent Harry from claiming his inheritance. Harry had told her that his claim to inherit his father's baronetcy could not be officially recognised until his name appeared on the Roll, which seemed unlikely while the shadow of bankruptcy and even prison loomed over him. They would have to wait for Dan to return with the money raised from the sale of the bullion before Harry could begin paying off his creditors.

In the days that followed he threw himself into matters concerning the estate. He spent most of the time riding round the various farms and smallholdings, reacquainting himself with the tenants whom he had known in his youth. Charity accompanied him on Nellie whenever possible and she saw yet another side of Harry's character. He had a natural gift for conversing with people no matter what their station in life. He was a good listener and she could see that he was deeply shocked by the rundown state of some of the smaller farmhouses and their outbuildings. He never made rash promises but he seemed to have the ability to instil confidence in his tenants, and they trusted him to make their lives more bearable. Each day she learned a little more about the man she loved and what she saw made her love him even more, but a sense of foreboding still lingered in the recesses of her mind. Sometimes she awakened in the middle of the night, snapping to a sitting position in her narrow bed as she escaped from a bad dream where she had been cold and frightened, begging once again for pennies on the streets of London. Gnarled fingers had reached out at her from the shadows, threatening to drag her down into a world inhabited by sewer rats and toshers; desperate people who sorted through the filth and excreta looking for valuables that had been lost down the drains. It took her several minutes to realise that the nightmare had passed and she was safe in her own bed, but the fear would not quite go away, even in broad daylight.

They had been home for almost two weeks and Charity was in the kitchen helping Mrs Diment to clean the last of the ingots, waiting for Harry to return from visiting one of his tenants who had suffered a fall while mending a barn roof and broken his leg. Mrs Trevett had sent a jar of calf's foot jelly and a dozen eggs to the family, and Harry had gone to see if there was any more practical help that could be given until the farmer was well enough to work again.

'That's the last one,' Mrs Diment said with a satisfied sigh. 'At least, as far as I know. They seem to keep popping up in unexpected places.'

Charity was about to answer when the door flew open and Daniel breezed into the kitchen with a triumphant grin on his face. He held out his arms. 'Charity, you look blooming. The country air suits you.'

Mrs Diment and Mrs Trevett exchanged knowing looks that were not lost on Charity, but she chose to ignore them. She gave Daniel a welcoming smile. 'It's good to see you. How did it go in London?'

He produced a heavy leather pouch from his coat pocket and thumped it down on the table. 'Put it this way – we're no longer poor. The dealers will take all the bullion we can find and give us good prices.'

Charity picked up the pouch, weighing it in her hand. 'That's wonderful. You've done well, Dan. You must be tired after the journey.'

'Of course he is.' Mrs Trevett bustled over to the range and put the kettle on the hob. 'Are you hungry, Master Daniel?'

He smiled, shaking his head. 'I had breakfast at an inn, but a cup of tea would be very welcome.' He looked round at the sound of the door opening and his smile faded when he saw Harry. 'I didn't expect to see you so soon,' he murmured, glancing nervously at Charity.

She had already sensed his unease and she was ready to intervene if necessary, but Harry crossed the floor and embraced his brother. 'Welcome home, brother.'

'I'm so glad to see you, Harry.' Daniel loosened the strings and opened the pouch. 'There's enough there to pay off your debts and more. When I've recovered from the journey I'll take the rest of the ingots to the bullion dealer.'

'You've done enough for now, Dan. I'll take them to London. I have legitimate business there.'

'Are you sure?' Daniel asked anxiously. 'I mean, is it wise to show your face in the city before you've had a chance to settle matters?'

'My creditors will welcome me with open arms when they realise that I can settle my debts.'

'Why don't you take your tea into the study?' Charity suggested hastily. 'I'm sure you have a lot to talk about.'

'I think this calls for something a little stronger.' Harry turned to Mrs Trevett. 'Where's Parkin? I haven't seen him this morning.'

'He's in the kitchen garden,' Mrs Trevett said, pursing her lips until her mouth resembled a wrinkled prune. 'It's not right that a man of his age has to tend the vegetable beds.'

'I agree entirely, and that will be rectified in the very near future.' Harry held out his hand. 'We won't disturb Parkin. If you'll give me your keys I'll go down to the cellar myself.'

Mrs Trevett unclipped a large bunch of keys from the chatelaine she wore around her waist, and handed them to Harry with a look of disapproval. 'It's Parkin's job,' she muttered.

'Don't be such an old stick, Polly.' Mrs Diment moved to the range and picked up the teapot. 'We'll have a cup of tea. It won't go to waste.'

Harry shot a casual glance in Charity's direction. 'I have some papers I'd like you to sort, Miss Crosse.'

'Yes, of course, sir.'

'Come along, Dan.' Harry paused as he reached the doorway. 'We'll discuss matters over a glass of Madeira, unless Wilmot has drunk the cellar dry.' He strode off in the direction of the study, giving Charity and Daniel little option other than to follow him.

'How did you find him?' Daniel whispered. 'I doubt if he came home of his own accord.'

Charity had to quicken her pace in order to keep up with his long stride. 'He didn't need much persuading,' she said smiling. 'Spend some time together, Dan. Get to know each other properly.' She hurried on and caught up with Harry just as he was about to enter the study. 'Give me the keys and I'll go down to the cellar. I'm sure that you and Dan will have a lot to talk about.'

'Have you ever been down to the cellars?'

'No, but I'm sure I can find my way without too much difficulty.'

Reluctantly he handed her the keys. 'All right, but be careful. It's pitch dark down there and the floor is uneven. If you can't find anything come straight back.'

'What's going on?' Daniel demanded.

Charity snatched the keys and left Harry to talk things over with Dan. She was not keen on venturing into the cellars, but she wanted the two brothers to have time on their own. She stopped to light a candle before venturing down the stone steps that led to the cellar. A strong smell of damp and must assailed her nostrils and an involuntary shiver ran down her spine as she made her way between the wine racks, most of which were festooned with cobwebs but otherwise empty. She walked further and further into the depths of the vaulted caverns beneath the house, glancing round nervously at the odd sounds of scuffling that seemed to come from all corners. She knew that it was more than likely to be rats, but that was hardly a comforting thought and she had to force herself to continue her search.

The cobwebs grew thicker, hanging like lace curtains between the rows. She shuddered to think of the spiders that were lurking in them but she pressed on, focusing her thoughts on searching for something with which Harry and Dan could toast their future. She had reached the end of the extensive cellar complex and was about to give up when she found a couple of crusty bottles at the bottom of the last rack. She bent down to read the labels, and out of the corner of her eye she saw the glint of metal. A closer look revealed a pile of ingots reaching up to the ceiling. Stunned and hardly able to believe her eyes, she ran her fingers down the smooth and slippery surface of the blackened silver. The candle guttered and she held it steady, praying that it would not go out and leave her in Stygian darkness. She snatched up a bottle and headed back the way she had come.

She arrived at the cellar steps and almost dropped the crusty bottle of Madeira when a figure loomed up in front of her. 'My God, you gave me a fright, Charity.' Harry wrapped his arms around her. 'You've been gone for such a long time I thought something must have happened to you.'

She breathed a sigh of relief. 'You scared me too.' She held up the bottle. 'But I found what you wanted. It was at the very end of the cellars, and I discovered something else too. Come with me and I'll show you.'

'What's going on?' Daniel demanded when they walked into the study. 'I sensed it the moment I saw you two together.'

Harry slipped his arm around Charity's waist. 'Is it that obvious?'

'It is to me,' Daniel said, chuckling. 'I'm sure that the two ladies in the kitchen have your measure too.'

'I wanted to tell the world that I'd fallen in love with a wonderful woman, but Charity insisted that we kept it a secret.' Harry's smiled faded. 'There was never anything between you two, was there, Dan?'

'No.' Charity and Daniel spoke as one.

'Of course not,' Charity added. 'I love Dan as a brother.'

Daniel nodded in agreement. 'That goes for me too, but Gideon is going to be doubly disappointed.'

'Gideon?' Harry gave Charity a questioning look. 'You told me that he'd helped you, but that was all.'

'And so it was,' she said hastily. 'I like Gideon and I think a lot of him, but that's all it was on my part.'

'She turned him down, and he was pretty cut up about it. He talked of nothing else all the way to London.' Daniel took the bottle from Charity. 'We need a corkscrew.'

Charity met Harry's troubled gaze with an apologetic smile. 'I would have told you, Harry, but it didn't seem important. I was grateful to him for all his help, but I never knowingly gave him any encouragement. He's a good man and he deserves better than me, as do you.' She held her hand up as Harry was about to speak. 'There, I've said it and it's out in the open. I've been allowing myself to think that we might have a future together, Harry, but it was wishful thinking.'

He seized her by the shoulders and twisted her

round so that she was facing him. His dark eyes flashed with anger. 'That's arrant nonsense. I love you and you love me. What more could anyone want?'

She drew away from him, shaking her head. 'Ask your brother if he thinks that I would be well received as your wife.' She turned to Daniel. 'Tell him, honestly.'

Daniel's cheeks burned with spots of colour. 'It has nothing to do with me.'

'This is ridiculous, darling,' Harry said angrily. 'I don't give a damn what other people think. I love you and I want to marry you.'

'Even if it were possible, that must be the most unflattering proposal any woman ever received.' Charity pushed past him. 'I'm going to the cottage. Vi wasn't feeling very well this morning. I want to make sure she's all right.'

'We need to talk this through.'

She spun round to face him. 'I want some time on my own, Harry. We've been living in a make-believe world and now it's time to face reality.' She stormed out of the room, leaving the door to slam behind her.

She did not want Mrs Diment or Mrs Trevett to see her in such a state. They would only have to take one look at her to realise that something was wrong, and she would be overwhelmed with cups of hot sweet tea and bombarded with questions. After all this time she knew the house well enough to find her way out through the conservatory without getting lost, and she headed off across the fields towards the cottage.

Violet's screams of agony rang out even before Charity had reached the front door. She let herself in and raced up the stairs to find Violet lying on her bed, her face contorted with pain and Dorrie silently weeping as she held her hand.

'Why didn't you send for me?' Charity demanded angrily.

'I dunno what to do,' Dorrie murmured through her tears. 'She won't let go of me hand.'

Charity moved swiftly to the bedside. 'Let her go, Vi. I'm here now. Everything will be all right.'

'The baby's coming,' Violet gasped. 'It hurts something awful. I'm being punished for my wickedness.'

'I'll stay with you while Dorrie runs to the house and fetches Mrs Diment. She'll know what to do.'

'I need a doctor.' Violet let go of Dorrie and reached out to grab Charity's hand. Her face contorted with pain as another contraction racked her body.

Charity stroked Violet's damp hair back from her forehead. 'On second thoughts, Dorrie, go to the rectory and ask Mrs Simms where the doctor lives. Tell her that Vi's baby is coming.'

Dorrie backed out of the room and Charity heard her footsteps pounding on the stairs followed by the opening and closing of the front door. She tried to keep a semblance of outward calm, but inwardly she was quaking. She had not the slightest idea what to do and only the vaguest notion of what happened when a woman gave birth. She assumed a smile. 'You'll be fine, and soon you'll have a lovely baby girl to put in the crib that Mr Raines gave you.' Her last words were drowned by Violet's screams.

There was little that Charity could do other than try

to keep Violet calm. It was stifling in the room beneath the eaves and Violet was sweating profusely. Charity managed to prise her hand free and hurried downstairs to fetch a bowl of water and a clean towel. She tore off strips and used them to bathe Violet's brow. She kept up a monologue, talking about anything and everything in an attempt to distract Violet, but time passed so slowly that the clock might as well have been going backwards. The pains were getting closer together. Charity prayed silently for someone to come who knew something about birthing babies, and in the middle of a particularly painful contraction, when Violet's screams reached a crescendo, Charity realised that someone was knocking on the front door. 'Come in,' she shouted. 'It's not locked.'

But the hammering continued and Charity was forced to leave Violet, promising to return instantly. She ran down the stairs and opened the front door. 'Oh,' she said, fighting back tears of disappointment and distress. 'It's you.'

Chapter Twenty-Two

Jane Raines stepped over the threshold, clutching a black leather medical case. 'I'm a fully trained Nightingale nurse,' she said briskly. 'Dorrie turned up at the rectory in a state of near collapse, poor child.' She headed for the staircase. 'Bring me hot water and clean towels.'

Charity stared after her, too surprised to move. Violet's screams echoed throughout the small cottage, but the stern tones of Jane Raines seemed to have a calming effect. Gathering her scattered wits, Charity set about making up the fire before going outside to fetch water from the well. Violet's agonised cries seemed less frequent, and Charity could only think that the sudden appearance of Miss Raines must have shocked her into silence.

She was about to mount the stairs carrying a clean towel and a kettle filled with hot water when she heard the sound of a baby crying. She uttered a sigh of relief and took the stairs as fast as her long skirts would allow.

The room was filled with sunshine and Violet was propped up on pillows cradling the swaddled infant in her arms. 'It's a girl,' she announced proudly. 'I told you it would be.'

Jane folded a pile of bloodied bedding into a bundle. 'I'll take these to the rectory. I'm sure Mrs Simms won't mind if I ask Jennet to put them in the copper on washday. I don't suppose you have the luxury of a washhouse in such a small cottage.'

Charity met Jane's cool gaze and saw the beginnings of a smile in her ice-blue eyes. 'Thank you, Miss Raines. I don't know what I'd have done if you hadn't taken over.'

Jane shrugged her shoulders. 'I've lost count of the births I've attended. This one was quite straightforward.'

'That's easy for you to say, miss,' Violet muttered, rubbing her cheek on the baby's downy head. 'You wasn't at the receiving end.'

'Perhaps it will teach you to be more careful in future.' Jane looked down her long nose at Violet. 'You must learn to say no, at least until you have a husband to provide for you and your offspring.'

Violet's eyes welled with tears and Charity placed herself firmly between nurse and patient. 'May I offer you a cup of tea, Miss Raines? It seems little enough thanks for what you've done for us today.'

'A happy mother and a healthy baby is my reward.' Jane picked up her bag. 'But a cup of tea would be most welcome.' She shot a stern glance in Violet's direction. 'Follow my instructions and we'll have you up and about in no time.'

'Thank you, miss.'

'I'm returning to my position at St Thomas' Hospital at the end of the week,' Jane said, moving towards the doorway. 'But I'll call in before then to make sure that everything is as it should be.'

She left the room and Charity moved closer to the bed. 'What are you going to call her, Vi?'

'Alice Charity Dorrie Chapman. Isn't she beautiful?'

'She most certainly is. She's perfect.' Charity stroked the baby's velvety head with the tip of her forefinger. 'I'll go downstairs and make Miss Raines some tea, and I'll bring you a cup. Would you like me to put Alice in her crib so that you can have a rest?'

'Not yet,' Violet said sleepily. 'In a while maybe.'

Charity felt almost envious as she went downstairs. The sight of Violet holding her baby in her arms had touched her deeply, and she wondered if she would ever know the joy of having a child of her own. It was something she had never considered in the past, but now it brought an ache to her heart.

She found Jane seated at the kitchen table, tapping her fingers impatiently. 'I should be getting back to the rectory. Philip insists on punctuality at mealtimes, as I'm sure you'll remember.'

'The kettle is boiling. It won't take long to make tea.'

Jane watched in silence while Charity warmed the pot, added three spoonfuls of Darjeeling and poured in the boiling water. She set the pot on the table to brew while she took the cups and saucers from the dresser.

'I see that you've made yourselves comfortable here,' Jane said at length.

'Yes, indeed.' Charity filled the cups, but did not choose to elaborate, even though she could see that Miss Raines was curious.

Jane sipped her tea. 'My nephew is very fond of you.'

'I don't know what we would have done without his help.'

'He is a good man and he could go far in the church.'

Charity put her cup down on its saucer with a clatter. 'Please say what you came to say, Miss Raines. I can see that you're leading up to something.'

'If that's the way you want it, Miss Crosse, I am only too happy to oblige. It's quite obvious to me that Gideon is infatuated with you, and it will not do.'

Charity met her angry gaze with a cool look. 'I've never done anything to encourage his attentions,' she said wearily. It was becoming tiresome to have to keep repeating such an obvious truth.

'Maybe not intentionally, but if Gideon were to marry beneath him it would ruin his chances of advancement in his calling. Do you understand?'

Charity rose to her feet. 'I may be a common girl, but I am not stupid, Miss Raines. I would never do anything that would hurt Gideon.'

'That isn't an answer. I want you to promise me that should Gideon be foolish enough to propose, you will refuse his offer of marriage.' Jane reached for her bag and stood up.

'I make no promises to you, Miss Raines. What passes between Gideon and me is our business.'

Jane snatched up the bundle of washing. 'Don't take that tone with me, young lady. If you were one of my nurses I'd have you punished severely for such insolence.'

Charity filled a cup with tea, adding a lump of sugar. She headed for the stairs. 'Goodbye, Miss Raines.

Thank you once again for looking after Violet. I am truly grateful, but I'm sure you can find your own way out.'

Dorrie returned an hour later, laden with gifts from the rectory and from Bligh Park. She flew into the cottage, pink-cheeked and breathless. 'Mrs Simms gave us a fruit cake and a meat pie, and Mrs Diment sent some eggs and butter. She said that Violet needed good food to build her up.'

Charity took the basket from her. 'That was very kind of them.'

'Can I see the baby now?'

'I think they're both asleep, so maybe you should wait until Alice wakes up. You'll soon hear her; she has a fine pair of lungs.'

'Alice is a nice name.'

'And she's called after you too.'

Dorrie's eyes sparkled. 'She's named after me?'

'She is Alice Charity Dorrie Chapman. Perhaps Violet will ask you to be one of Alice's godmothers.'

Dorrie flopped down at the table, repeating the word godmother again and again. 'It makes me sound like a fairy,' she said at last. 'I could be a fairy godmother.'

Charity laughed and the strain she had felt since her uncomfortable talk with Jane seemed to evaporate. Dorrie had reminded her that they were a proper family. They might not be related by blood but their ties were just as strong.

'I wonder if Mrs Diment and Mrs Trevett will be godmothers too,' Dorrie said, eyeing the fruit cake hopefully. 'Mrs Simms would be a good one because she makes lovely cakes. D'you suppose we ought to have a taste? We don't want it to give Vi belly ache.'

Charity cut her a slice and put it on a plate. 'I think it's up to Vi who she wants to stand up for her daughter, but I'm sure you'll be her first choice.'

'Does a baby have a godfather too?'

'Yes, I believe so.'

Dorrie frowned, munching a mouthful of fruit cake. 'Then I suppose that would have to be Mr Daniel now that Mr Harry has left.'

'Left?' Charity dropped the knife and it clattered onto the flagstone sending crumbs flying in all directions.

'Mrs Diment said he left for London, sudden-like. She said it took them all by surprise.'

Charity felt as if the air had been sucked from her lungs. 'There's something I forgot to do at the big house. I want you to stay here and look after Vi and the baby. You don't have to do anything except maybe take her up something to eat and drink if she asks. Can you manage that, Dorrie?'

'Of course I can.' Dorrie puffed her chest out. 'I'm nearly nine. I dunno exactly when my birthday is, but Dr Marchant said it was probably some time in June. He used to give me a new pair of boots for me birthday and a new dress.'

'I'm sure we can manage something better than that.' Charity reached for her bonnet and shawl. 'I won't be gone long.'

* * *

Daniel was in the study, sitting in the padded leather chair with his feet up on the desk and his eyes closed. He opened them with a start when Charity burst into the room. 'What's the matter?' he demanded sleepily. 'Is the house on fire?'

'Why did Harry leave so suddenly?'

'Why do you think? You made it clear that you didn't want to marry him, and anyway he had to take the rest of the ingots up to the dealers.'

'It's not that I don't want to marry him, and he knows that. There was no need for him to go flying off without speaking to me. What am I to think?'

Daniel swivelled round to place his feet firmly on the floor. 'You told him there was no hope. If a girl I loved said that to me I think I'd feel pretty bad about it too.'

'But you must understand why I said those things.'

'No. To be honest I don't.' He stood up and stretched. 'I think you're putting obstacles in the way for some reason best known to yourself. You'd make him a splendid wife. Who cares what other people think?'

'You're as bad as he is,' Charity said angrily. 'Harry is an important person in this part of the world.'

'And he loves you, you goose.' Daniel walked round the desk and hooked his arm around her shoulders. 'Can't think of anyone I'd like better as my sister-in-law.' His smile faded. 'You aren't thinking of tying yourself to Gideon, are you? He's a good chap and all that, but he's not for you.'

'So I've just been told by Miss Raines,' Charity said with a rueful smile. 'Everyone seems to think they know what's best for me.'

'Harry would have something to say if he thought Gideon was making advances to you. He said he was going to look him up when he reached London.'

'I'm sure Gideon wouldn't say anything untoward, but I just hope his aunt doesn't try to interfere.'

'When did you see that awful woman? I thought she was away working as a nurse in one of the big London hospitals.'

'About an hour ago. When I got home I found Vi in labour and I sent Dorrie for help. She went straight to the rectory and Miss Jane turned up on the doorstep. She took over and I was very glad she did. Vi has a lovely baby girl and both of them are doing well.'

'That's wonderful.'

'It was afterwards I had to suffer a cross-examination. I felt as if I was up before the beak.'

He grinned. 'I've only met Miss Raines once and that was enough: I bet she puts the fear of God into her patients. She certainly scared me.' He pointed Charity towards the door. 'Let's go and see what Mrs Trevett has prepared for luncheon. I'm starving.'

'I'm not very hungry, and I need to get back to the cottage in case Vi needs me.'

'A few more minutes won't make much difference, and you must eat.'

Mrs Diment and Mrs Trevett plied Charity with food and kept asking questions about Violet's labour until Daniel protested that he was eating, and it wasn't a fit subject to discuss in front of an unmarried man.

Mrs Diment pursed her lips and Mrs Trevett sighed. 'Tell us more about little Alice. Is she a bonny baby?'

'Has she any hair?' Mrs Diment added eagerly. 'Is it fair or dark?'

Parkin had been sitting at the table, getting on with his meal, but at this he raised his head. 'Will you women please stop prattling on about an infant? They all look the same – like wizened monkeys. I don't know what the fuss is about. She's just another mouth to feed.'

Mrs Trevett's lips worked in a soundless protest and Mrs Diment pointed her knife at Parkin. 'That's a wicked thing to say, Mr Parkin. All babies are a gift from God.'

'Not all of them,' Daniel whispered in Charity's ear.

Mrs Diment shot him a suspicious glance. 'I'm sure that Nanny would have told you that it's rude to whisper, Master Daniel.'

He smiled and nodded. 'Quite right, Mrs Diment. But I'll reach my majority very soon and I left the nursery a long time ago.'

Mrs Diment flushed uncomfortably and Parkin made a noise in his throat that sounded suspiciously like 'Hear! Hear!'

Mrs Trevett opened her mouth as if to remonstrate but the sudden appearance of Tapper cut short any remarks that she might have made. She rose to her feet. 'Whatever's the matter, Tapper? You look as though you've seen a ghost.'

He dragged his cap off his head and clutched it to his chest. 'Not a ghost, Mrs Trevett. Mr and Mrs Barton have just arrived. I saw them getting out of their carriage as I crossed the yard.'

As he spoke the bell marked *Front door* jangled noisily on its spring and Parkin rose stiffly to his feet. He hobbled out of the kitchen, mumbling beneath his breath. Daniel pushed his plate away and stood up. 'I'd better go and greet them.'

'And I'd better go home and check on Vi and the baby.' Charity stood up, leaving half her meal untouched.

'Don't run away,' Daniel said, smiling. 'I think it's time you met my mother.'

'No, really it's not a good idea,' Charity protested. 'I mean, they've only just arrived and they'll be tired after their journey from Devonshire. Perhaps another time.'

Daniel caught her by the hand. 'If I allow you to go now you'll find excuse after excuse for keeping away.'

'Go on, dear,' Mrs Diment said in a low voice. 'You'll have to face her one day so it might as well be now.'

Charity could see that she was outnumbered, but a quick introduction should be enough to satisfy Daniel, and then she could make her escape. She followed him through the corridors to the entrance hall where a liveried footman was staggering beneath the weight of several heavy suitcases, portmanteaux and band-boxes. The double doors were open and she could see Wilmot outside on the carriage sweep giving instructions to his coachman.

'Mama, how lovely to see you.' Daniel embraced his mother, receiving a look of overt disapproval in return.

Myrtle Barton straightened her perky little hat,

which was embellished with a ridiculously large ostrich feather. 'Don't be so boisterous, Daniel. A kiss on the hand would have sufficed.' She flicked a casual glance at Charity who was hovering in the background. 'You may take the bandboxes up to my room and start unpacking, girl. My maid is travelling behind with the rest of our luggage.'

'Charity is not a servant, Mama,' Daniel said, blushing to the roots of his hair.

'That's exactly what I am, ma'am.' Charity bobbed a curtsey, keeping her gaze lowered. 'I am in Mr Bligh's employ, but not as a maid. I work in the library, cataloguing the collection of books.'

'A servant is a servant. Do as I bid and don't answer back.' Myrtle turned her supercilious gaze upon her son. 'I can see that we arrived not a moment too soon. You have a lot to learn, Daniel.'

He bowed his head. 'But, Mama, you don't quite understand . . .'

'Nonsense. Anyone can see that you've allowed the servants too much leeway. From now on things will change.' She pointed to the pile of candy-striped hat boxes. 'Take those upstairs first, girl.'

Charity eyed her with a sinking heart. She knew instinctively that this person would never accept her as one of the family. Myrtle Barton was a handsome woman, and must have been a beauty in her youth. Her golden hair was as yet untouched by strands of silver and her fine skin glowed with health. Her large blue eyes were undoubtedly her most arresting feature, fringed with impossibly long dark lashes, and if the downward turn of her well-shaped mouth gave her a petulant expression, it vanished the moment she smiled, which she did when Wilmot strode into the building. She held her hands out to him. 'I'm just going to my room, darling. Will you send Brown to me the moment she arrives? In the meantime I'll have to make do with this girl.'

Wilmot barely glanced at Charity, who had backed into the shadows and kept her head down. 'Yes, of course, my love. Go upstairs and rest.' He slapped Daniel on the back. 'Good news travels fast, boy. The Bligh Park treasure has turned up at last.'

'Yes, sir,' Daniel said, holding out his hand to Charity. 'Thanks to my good friend.'

She sent him a warning look, shaking her head, but it was obvious that Wilmot was not listening. He was gazing round the oak-panelled entrance hall with a satisfied smile. 'We'll invest some of the money in renovating this old pile. I'll have plans made up and we'll agree them together, although I'm sure that your dear mama will have ideas of her own.'

Myrtle inclined her head graciously. 'Of course I will. A woman's touch is what is needed here, and always has been. Hedley hated change and refused to allow me to touch a thing, but now we'll transform Bligh Park into the magnificent dwelling it was meant to be.' She beckoned to Charity. 'Why are you loitering there, girl? I told you to take my bandboxes to my room.'

'Charity isn't a housemaid, Mama,' Daniel said firmly. 'I'll instruct Mrs Diment to have your room made ready, and Parkin will bring some refreshments if you would like to wait in the drawing room.'

'Charity?' Wilmot spun round, his expression darkening as he recognised her. 'What in hell's name are you doing here?'

Daniel stepped in between them. 'Charity is here at our invitation, Wilmot.'

'You and who else?' Wilmot demanded suspiciously.

'Harry, of course. He is the master here now, not I.'

'Harry?' Myrtle swayed on her feet. 'But Harry was hounded from the country by his creditors. Surely he hasn't been foolish enough to return?'

Wilmot put his arm around her. 'Don't upset yourself, my love.' He glared at Daniel. 'Are you a complete idiot? Do you want to inherit or do you want to see everything frittered away by your brother?'

'Harry is the rightful heir to the baronetcy and the estate.'

Wilmot fixed Charity with a stern look. 'You're at the bottom of this. You were trouble from the first.'

'What is going on?' Myrtle demanded. 'Who is this girl who looks like a skivvy and talks as if she were mistress of the house?'

'She's the woman that my brother loves and wants to marry.' Daniel nodded to Charity. 'Tell them.'

'You needn't worry, ma'am,' Charity said firmly. 'I know that I'm not good enough for your son, and I rejected his offer.'

Myrtle moved away from her husband's sheltering arm. 'I don't care who you are, maidservant or not, you will come upstairs with me. I want to get to the bottom of this.' She turned on Wilmot with narrowed eyes. 'I'll deal with you later. You've been keeping things from me and I won't have it.'

'Mama, please leave Charity alone.' Daniel took a step towards his mother, but she stopped him with a single movement of a dainty hand.

'Keep out of this, Daniel.'

'None of this is her fault and she did refuse Harry; I can vouch for that. We wouldn't have found the silver bullion if it hadn't have been for Charity's sharp eyes.'

'No doubt fuelled by self-interest.' Myrtle turned her head to give Charity a calculating look. 'Perhaps we will go to the drawing room after all.'

'I'll come too,' Wilmot said hastily. 'She'll tell you a pack of lies.'

'Have you something to hide?' Myrtle's tone was scathing, and, for once, Wilmot seemed at a loss for words. He strode out of the house, shouting instructions at the footman.

Myrtle rounded on Daniel. 'Make yourself useful and tell Mrs Trevett to send a tray of tea and cake to the drawing room. I'll speak to you on your own after I've dealt with this little fortune hunter.'

'This is most unfair, Mama,' Daniel protested, but his mother had marched off in the direction of the drawing room.

'I can look after myself,' Charity said stoutly. 'Don't worry about me, Dan.'

Myrtle threw herself down on one of the threadbare sofas, where Bosun's doggy smell still lingered and his hairs were intertwined forever within the fabric. She looked around the room with obvious distaste. 'My former husband had no idea when it came to elegant living.' She stared at Charity with raised eyebrows. 'Do you really think that a maidservant could raise herself to the position of Lady Bligh? You can forget any ideas you may have harboured about marrying my son and becoming mistress of Bligh Park. I won't allow that to happen.'

'I never had any aspirations beyond my station in life, Mrs Barton. I didn't want to fall in love with Harry, but I couldn't help myself.'

Myrtle curled her lip. 'Really? I'm afraid I don't believe you. I want you to be gone from this house before nightfall, and I want you to promise to keep away from both my sons in future.'

'If you think that I'll stand by and see you and that hateful man you married, cheat Harry out of his inheritance and make Dan's life a misery, you're quite wrong.'

'Nobly said, but impossible to accomplish.' Myrtle leaned back against the odd assortment of cushions. 'Daniel doesn't come of age for almost two months, and I wouldn't want Harry to inherit a single penny because he will only gamble it away. Harry takes after his father, but Daniel is more malleable and sensitive. He will be guided by us and this estate will recover from years of mismanagement and neglect.'

'I think you've underestimated both your sons, Mrs Barton,' Charity said calmly. 'They are grown men with minds of their own, and you've married a devious man who will take everything from you.' She held up her hand as Myrtle opened her mouth to protest. 'I've had my say and now I'm leaving. You won't be bothered by me again.' She swept out of the room, almost bumping into Parkin who was carrying a tea tray.

She managed to avoid Wilmot who was in the entrance hall, directing the servants who had just arrived with the rest of the Bartons' baggage. It looked to Charity as though the couple planned a long stay, which made it even more important to find Harry and warn him of their intentions.

She found Daniel in the study with a glass of Madeira in his hand. 'That won't solve anything,' she said crossly. 'You have to stand up to them, Dan.'

'I've tried,' he said, taking another sip of wine. 'But you can see what my mother is like, and backed by Wilmot she is truly formidable.'

'Only because you still allow her to treat you like a child. In two months' time you'll be of age and neither of them can tell you what to do. Can't you see that they're desperate to gain control of Bligh Park and the estate, as well as Nevill's Court? Even if they managed to discredit Harry to such an extent that his inheritance was lost to him, do you really think that they would treat you more fairly?'

'I don't care about the land or the houses. You know what I want, Charity.'

'I'm going to London to find Harry, and tell him what's going on behind his back.'

'I'm coming with you.'

She shook her head. 'That's not a good idea. If you

do that Wilmot will follow us and make things difficult. You must stay here, and if you can't face up to them then you must use delaying tactics. Think of Egypt and what it will be like to join Flinders Petrie's expedition. You could have all that, but only if you refuse to allow your mother and Wilmot to bully you.'

Daniel frowned thoughtfully. 'Harry took most of the ingots to London. Wilmot won't be able to get his hands on the money.'

'There, you see. That will be your best defence.' She hesitated. 'I'll need money to get me to London and I haven't any.'

'I can give you as much as you need.'

'There's just one other thing.' She treated him to a persuasive smile. 'Will you keep an eye on Violet and Dorrie for me? If Mrs Diment could go and stay there while I'm away it would put my mind at rest.'

'I'm sure she'd be delighted.' Daniel drained his drink and stood up. 'When do you want to leave?'

'I'd like to make sure that the girls are all right before I go. Perhaps Tapper could drive me to the railway station first thing tomorrow morning?'

Chapter Twenty-Three

The house in Nevill's Court was shuttered and silent. At first she thought that Jackson was not at home, but then one of the neighbours, Miss Lettice Creedy, an elderly spinster whose house was home to dozens of stray and feral cats, put her head over the garden fence to inform her that she had seen Mr Jackson not half an hour earlier, and he had given her two eggs, which she planned to boil for her supper.

Charity was about to go round to the back of the house and see if Jackson was in the yard when the door opened. His stony face registered neither surprise nor pleasure. 'Miss Charity. Come in.'

'See!' Miss Creedy mewed with satisfaction. 'I told you he wasn't far away. Thank you for the eggs, Mr Jackson.' She was still thanking him when he closed the door.

'You have an admirer,' Charity said, chuckling.

'Her and her bloody cats.' Jackson peered out of the window. 'I daresn't let Bosun out at night in case them kitties are on the prowl.' At the sound of his master's voice Bosun appeared as if from nowhere, almost knocking Charity over with an enthusiastic greeting.

'Bosun wouldn't harm a fly,' she said, patting the dog's great head.

'I ain't worried about him. Them cats is like wild animals. Bosun come in one night bleeding from scratches on his nose and close to his eyes. I can't abide cats.'

Charity put her bag down at the foot of the stairs. 'I was hoping that Master Harry might be staying here, Jackson. Have you seen him recently?'

Jackson's surprised expression was answer enough. He shook his shaggy head. 'No, miss.'

She had been pinning her hopes on the fact that Harry might not have anywhere else to stay, but perhaps he had found the house locked and assumed that everyone had left. It was a disappointment, but she would find him. She realised that Jackson was staring at her. 'What's the matter, Mr Jackson?'

'I got nothing for our dinner, miss. The money ran out some time ago and me sister's been feeding me and Bosun when we visit her in Hoxton. It's lucky you arrived when you did because we was about to set off.' He glanced down at the dog who was looking up at him with adoration in his large brown eyes. 'Wasn't we, old man? Us is good pals, ain't we, mate?'

Bosun wagged his tail in answer and his pink tongue lolled out of his mouth as he waited for his master to give him instructions.

'I've brought money,' Charity said hastily. 'I can give you your back wages and tomorrow I'll go to market and get provisions.' She met his anxious gaze with a smile. 'If your sister won't mind, perhaps you'd care to share a dinner with me at a chop house? I haven't eaten since I left Bligh Park this morning.'

Jackson's deep-set eyes twinkled appreciatively. 'I'm sure she won't mind, miss. She's got ten nippers to feed and a husband who labours in the Gaslight and Coke Company all hours of the day and night.'

'I'll take my bag up to my old room and tidy up, and then we'll go.' She went upstairs, grimacing at the layer of dust that lay everywhere like a fluffy grey blanket. Mrs Diment would have a fit, she thought, as she trailed her fingers along the balustrade.

The room she had shared with Violet and Dorrie was stuffy in the heat of the late afternoon and flies buzzed lazily against the windowpanes. She opened one of the sashes and allowed them to fly free. A cool breeze floated in, bringing with it the all too familiar noxious city smells that she had happily forgotten during her stay in the country. She took off her bonnet and brushed her hair, tying it back with a length of blue ribbon that Dorrie had left on the dressing table. A quick look in the fly-spotted mirror revealed smuts on her nose and cheeks and she wiped them away with a clean hanky. Satisfied that she looked reasonably presentable, if a little travel-stained, she went downstairs to find Jackson seated by the range, smoking a clay pipe. He leapt to his feet, knocking the remains of the tobacco into the fire. 'I'm sorry, miss. I ain't allowed to smoke indoors, but I got used to it in Mrs Diment's absence.'

'That's quite all right, Mr Jackson. I don't mind at all. My grandfather smoked cigars in the old days, but he became accustomed to smoking a pipe. It was one of his few comforts in life towards the end.' She felt tears stinging the backs of her eyes as she recalled her grandfather's tragic death, but this was not the time to wallow in the past. She must be positive and think of the future. 'I know a very nice chop house close to the Gaiety Theatre. It's not too far to walk.'

Jackson picked up his battered bowler hat. 'I ain't fit to be seen with a young lady like you.'

'Nonsense,' she said firmly. 'It's not every day a girl has a chance to be escorted by a fine figure of a man like you, Mr Jackson.'

She could have sworn that he blushed, but he turned away quickly and shambled to the door. 'After you, miss.'

It came to Charity in the middle of the night. She had assumed that Harry would return to Nevill's Court, but Jackson had not seen him. Dan had said his brother intended to contact Gideon, and there was a good chance that he might know Harry's whereabouts. It was so blindingly obvious that she wondered why she had not thought of it sooner, but then she remembered her last encounter with Gideon. Their easy-going relationship would never be the same again after his declaration of love. She lay back against the pillows, smiling ruefully into the darkness. Proposals from two highly eligible bachelors must be the stuff that dreams were made of for some young women, but not for her. It was a cruel blow of fate that had thrown her into the path of two such men; one whom she loved, and the other for whom she had a great fondness, but she was not a fit partner for either of them. She would have to face both Gideon and Harry, and she must see this matter through to the end. After that it was up to her to make a life for herself, Violet, baby Alice and Dorrie. She closed her eyes. Early tomorrow morning she would walk to St Pancras New Church. There must be someone there who could tell her where to find Gideon.

The lodging house was in a side street not far from the church, and Gideon's landlady wore the world-weary expression of a woman who was accustomed to opening the door and finding distressed parishioners on the step. 'Mr Raines is out visiting the poor.' She had a duster clutched in her hand and she began polishing the brass doorknocker as if her life depended upon it. 'He won't be back for ages.'

Charity smothered a sigh of relief. She had not been looking forward to her meeting with Gideon, but at least she was spared an embarrassing encounter. 'Is Mr Bligh staying with you? Or he might be going under the name of Elliott.'

'This is a respectable house, miss. I don't harbour gentleman who use aliases.'

'I have some very important information that I must pass on to either Mr Raines or Mr Bligh.'

'I don't doubt it, miss. Try the church or come back another time. I haven't got all day to stand here talking to the likes of you. I have work to do.' The landlady was about to slam the door but Charity put her foot over the threshold.

'My name is Charity Crosse and I'm staying at the house in Nevill's Court. It's really urgent that I speak to one of them, but Mr Bligh in particular. I'd be very much obliged if you would pass on that message.'

'Get your foot off my doorstep, miss.'

Charity's foot was wedged in between the door and the jamb, causing her considerable pain and she had little option but to remove it. 'Please pass on the—' The door slammed in her face.

She limped down the steps to the pavement and stood for a moment, glaring at the house, where not a speck of dirt had been allowed to linger. The windows gleamed and winked in the sunlight and Charity had a vision of the tenants being dusted and polished as they sat down to eat their meals. The rest of the street had a far more relaxed atmosphere. Housemaids leaned on iron railings, chatting to their counterparts next door. Charwomen holystoned the front steps and swept the pavements, although none of them matched the standard set by Gideon's fearsome landlady. Butchers, bakers and fishmongers pushed barrows from house to house, while others drove carts along the street shouting their wares. There was no sign of either Gideon or Harry and Charity had no idea where to start looking.

She went first to the church and left a message with the warden, giving the address in Nevill's Court, and then she set off for the market to buy food. It might, she thought, be worth a visit to the bullion dealer in Hatton Garden. Daniel had given her the address and it was just possible that they might know where she could contact Harry. Cheered by the thought, she was on her way to market when she heard a deep voice calling her name. She stopped and turned to see Bert Chapman standing in the well of the brewery dray. 'Stop,' he shouted above the noise of the horses' hooves and the rumbling of cart wheels. He drew the animals to a halt and handed the reins to his mate. 'Don't run away from me, girl.' He leapt to the ground.

Charity broke into a run, dropping her basket in her attempt to dodge a couple who were walking arm in arm and a woman who was pushing a wooden cart which seemed to be overflowing with babies and toddlers, all of them crying in a pathetic chorus.

'Stop that girl. She's me daughter,' Bert shouted breathlessly, and a male passer-by put out his foot to trip Charity up. She fell headlong, winding herself. Bert dragged her to her feet and gave her a shake. 'Where is she?' he hissed. 'Where's that wanton little bitch Violet?'

'I'm not telling you,' Charity gasped.

He twisted her arm behind her back. 'You will or I'll break every bone in your body.'

'She's somewhere you won't find her.' She yelped as he put even more pressure on her arm. She felt as though her shoulder would dislocate at any moment, but she was not going to tell him. Then, just as she felt she could stand no more, Bert released her and she fell to her knees. In a flurry of fur and bared teeth, Bosun brought Bert to the ground and stood over him.

'Get that bloody animal off me,' Bert demanded, cowering.

Jackson strode up to them. He helped Charity to her feet, ignoring Bert's angry cries. 'Are you hurt, miss?'

Shaken and in pain, she shook her head. 'No. I'm all right, thank you.'

'Shall I let Bosun finish the brute off, miss?'

An interested crowd had gathered round them and someone at the back applauded. 'I'll bet a crown on the dog to win.'

Bert covered his head with his arm. 'Call a copper. I'm about to be savaged by this brute.'

Jackson leaned over and grabbed Bosun by the collar. 'It's all right, old chap. We won't finish the bugger off this time, but if he so much as comes near Miss Charity again you can have him for your dinner.'

Bosun wagged his tail and licked Jackson's hand, which sent a ripple of amusement round the onlookers, but Bert was not amused. He struggled to his feet, wiping the dust from his clothes. 'You haven't heard the last of this.' He strode back to the dray and climbed up onto the driver's seat, swearing volubly.

The crowd melted away as swiftly as it had gathered and Jackson took Charity by the arm. 'Where to next, miss? I think you need a bodyguard from now on.'

She reached out to stroke Bosun. 'Thank you both. I don't know what would have happened if you hadn't come along when you did.'

'I guessed you was out looking for that vicar chap you told me about after supper. He seems the best bet while you're looking for your man.'

Charity let this pass. She was not in the mood to argue. Now that Bert had discovered her presence in London she knew he would not give up until he had her cornered. It was even more important to find Harry now. 'I was going to market and then on to the bullion dealer in Hatton Garden.'

"We'll try there first and the market on the way home. I take it that that fellow was Violet's dad. I've met his type afore and he ain't exactly the salt of the earth, if you get my meaning.'

'Yes,' Charity said simply. 'I know exactly what you mean.'

The bullion dealer remembered Harry. 'My business with the gentleman is completed, and I don't know where to contact him.' He smiled knowingly. 'People find me. I don't need to go looking for them.'

'Can you tell me when you last saw Mr Bligh?' Charity asked anxiously.

'It must have been at least two days ago, miss. I'm sorry I can't help you further.'

Disappointed and frustrated, Charity left the gloomy premises in Hatton Garden, emerging into bright sunlight. Jackson was leaning against a lamp post, smoking a cigarette, which he stubbed out beneath the heel of his boot as she approached. Bosun wagged his tail and licked her hand as if sensing that she was upset.

'No go then?' Jackson straightened up. 'What next?'

'I don't know.' She shook her head. 'Perhaps he's left for home, in which case he'll find out soon enough what's been happening in his absence.'

'Then it's off to market, miss. We got to eat and I'm feeling hungry. Bosun could do with a tasty meal and a nice juicy bone.'

'You're right, of course.' Charity tucked her hand through the crook of his arm. 'I'm afraid I lost my basket. I'll have to buy another one.'

They returned to Nevill's Court, having stopped at Jackson's request to eat a dish of eel pie and mash swimming in liquor. Bosun carried a marrowbone in his mouth, growling ominously at anyone who looked as though they might take it from him. Charity blinked as they emerged from the darkness of the alley into the sunlit court. The cottage gardens were filled with roses and honeysuckle clambered over brick walls and wound itself around railings vying with the wild convolvulus. She could hear voices and recognised the shrill tones of Miss Creedy, and the meowing of several of her feline friends. Shading her eyes she saw that Miss Creedy's latest victim was none other than Gideon.

He looked round and smiled. 'Charity, I came as soon as I got your message.'

'I told him that you would be back soon,' Miss Creedy said, picking up a fluffy tortoiseshell cat and wrapping it around her shoulders like a shawl. 'We've been having a lovely conversation about cats.'

'Yes, indeed.' Gideon gave her a courtly bow. 'Thank you, ma'am. I've learned a lot about our feline friends today.'

'You must come again,' she said, reaching out to grab him by the hand. 'You must come to tea one afternoon. My cats and I so rarely have visitors.'

'Thank you, that's very kind of you.' Gideon withdrew his hand gently.

'Come inside, sir,' Jackson said, putting down a basket of groceries to take a key from his pocket. He placed it in the lock and it turned without protest. 'You'll be here all day and all evening if she has her way.' He tipped his bowler hat to Miss Creedy. 'Good day to you, miss.'

'Yes, thank you for keeping my friend company.' Charity shot a quick smile in Miss Creedy's direction and hurried into the house, followed swiftly by Gideon. Jackson had already made his escape, accompanied by Bosun, who was cowering away from a gang of cats who were stalking him with their green eyes fixed on the bone.

'Come into the parlour, Gideon.' Charity led the way to the small, sunny room on the far side of the entrance hall. She snatched the dust covers off two of the chairs and motioned him to sit down. 'Thank you for coming,' she said shyly. 'After our last meeting I wasn't sure of my reception.'

'You should know me better than that, Charity.' He took off his hat and sat down. 'Of course we're still friends. I wouldn't want it any other way and I've accepted the fact that I'm not the man for you, even though I wish it were different.'

She took a seat opposite him, folding her hands tightly in her lap. 'I must find Harry.' She raised her head to look him in the eyes. 'It's not for me. I know there can never be anything between us.'

He frowned. 'Why not? He loves you.'

'He told you that?'

'We're old friends, and he was devastated when you rejected him.'

'Harry needs a wife from his own class. A girl with my background would never fit in – his mother made that perfectly clear.'

'His mother? You've met the beautiful Myrtle?'

'She is lovely, isn't she? And she must have been stunning when she was young. I could never live up to the standard she set as Lady Bligh.'

Gideon leaned forward to cover her hands with his. 'Are you comparing yourself to the woman who tricked Sir Philip into thinking that Daniel was his son?'

'Yes, well, that's not the point,' Charity said lamely. 'She's a society lady and they behave differently.'

'My point exactly. Many of our so-called betters behave exactly as they wish without a thought for anyone else. They don't think of themselves in the same way as the rest of the world, but you are a good person, Charity. You're loyal and brave and you would make any man a wonderful wife. Harry would be lucky to have you.'

She met his earnest gaze with a rueful smile. 'Try telling that to his mother.' She held up her hand. 'Don't say any more on the subject, Gideon. The most important thing is to find Harry and tell him that Mr and Mrs Barton have moved into Bligh Park, with every intention of remaining there. I don't know what pressure they can bring to bear on Daniel, but it seems that they are after a share in the money.'

'Harry has been pursuing his claim to the baronetcy. He's required to produce his birth certificate and the marriage certificate of his parents, as well as his father's death certificate and that's just the beginning of the procedure.'

'And I suppose he needs to remain in London while this is in progress?'

'That's what I would think, but it's Harry you must ask.' Gideon gave her a long look. 'He's staying with me, so what shall I tell him when I see him this evening?'

'Your landlady denied all knowledge of him.'

Gideon grinned and tapped the side of his nose. 'She would charge me double if she knew I had a guest sleeping on my sofa.'

'Does he spend every evening with you?'

'He hasn't returned to his old ways, if that's what you mean.'

She breathed a sigh of relief. 'He made me a promise when we were on the island. I didn't know whether he would be able to keep it.'

Gideon rose from his seat. 'Only he can answer that, but if I were a betting man, I'd put my money on Harry.' He picked up his hat and tucked it under his arm. 'I must go now, but would you be happy to see him this evening? I doubt if I would be able to prevent him from rushing round here the moment he knows you're in town.'

'Yes, of course. I must see him as soon as possible.'

Charity was on edge for the rest of the afternoon, and although she prepared supper for herself and Jackson she could not eat a thing. If Jackson noticed he said nothing, nor did he comment when she put her plate of food on the floor for Bosun to finish off in several greedy gulps.

'I'm going to the pub,' Jackson said, getting up from the table. 'Will you be all right on your own?'

'Of course,' she said confidently. 'I'm expecting visitors and they'll keep me company.'

Jackson nodded. 'C'mon then, Bosun. We'll stretch our legs afore we goes for a pint.'

Charity set about clearing away the dishes and washing them in the stone sink. It helped to keep her hands busy, but she kept glancing at the clock on the mantelshelf. It was a warm summer evening but there was a damp chill in the parlour and she lit a fire before taking off the rest of the dust covers. It was still light outside but the wainscoting made the room appear dark and she lit candles. She sat down to wait. She tried to read a book, but she could not concentrate and she put it aside. She rose from her seat by the fire and paced the floor. The ormolu clock had long since stopped working and according to the hands on its pale face the time was stuck at a quarter to twelve. She went to the kitchen to look at the clock on the mantelshelf, but less than an hour had passed since she last checked the time. She filled the kettle and placed it on the hob.

She returned to the parlour but she could not settle. She walked up and down, rehearsing what she would say to Harry, but she was unaccountably nervous. She began to think he was not coming and that his feelings towards her had changed.

The sound of the doorbell made her jump and her heart started to pound. For a moment she could not move but she took several deep breaths and forced herself to walk slowly to the front door. She opened it with a welcoming smile which froze on her face when she saw Bert Chapman standing on the doorstep. He forced his way in and pinned her against the wall. She opened her mouth to scream for help but he clamped his huge hand to her face and strange-smelling fumes filled her lungs. She struggled for breath but darkness enveloped her and she felt herself sinking into a swirling eddy of oblivion.

Chapter Twenty-Four

She opened her eyes and at first she could see nothing. She was lying on her side, facing what appeared to be a brick wall which was running with damp, and the rank air was thick with the smell of stale beer and must. Every bone in her body ached. She tried to roll onto her back but then she realised that her hands were tied, as were her ankles. She had not eaten since breakfast and she was tormented by thirst. She lay still for a moment, exhausted and chilled to the bone. The sound of a movement behind her made the hairs on the back of her neck stand on end. 'Who's there?'

'So you've come back to the land of the living, have you?' Bert moved to her side, and she was blinded by the light of a lantern swinging over her head. 'I thought I'd overdone the chloroform and killed you. Not that you'd be any great loss, but I wants to know where you've hid me daughter.'

'I can't breathe like this,' Charity murmured. 'Sit me up.'

'You'd better mind your Ps and Qs if you wants to stay alive for a bit longer. I could leave you here in this rat-infested cellar and no one would find you until you was a mass of bleached bones.'

'Please sit me up,' Charity said through clenched teeth. 'If you kill me you'll never find Violet.'

He reached out and dragged her to a sitting position by her hair. He held the lantern very close to her face. 'There now. I ain't going to repeat the question. Have you got an answer for me?'

She turned her head away. 'Why do you want to find Violet?'

'She's me daughter and I love her.'

'No, you don't. You treated her like a slave.'

He grinned, revealing blackened teeth, and his breath reeked of alcohol and stale tobacco. 'That's what daughters are for, my girl. Someone should have taken the strap to you long ago and knocked some of the cockiness out of you.'

'Violet is happy where she is. You should be thankful that you have one less mouth to feed.'

He put the lantern down and grabbed her by the ear, twisting it until she cried out with pain. 'Less of the lip, girly. Answer me this, has she given birth and is it a boy or a girl?'

'Let go of me and I'll tell you.'

'Where's that little word?'

She shot him a sideways glance. It was obvious that torturing her was giving him pleasure. 'Please let go of my ear.'

He thrust his face closer. 'And you'll tell me?'

She nodded and with a last spiteful tweak he released her.

'She has a lovely baby girl.'

'I got a customer for that nipper. A poor woman

whose child died in infancy and she can't have no more of her own. I'll be doing me civic duty in providing the grieving parents with a substitute and now my Violet has provided me with one.' He scrambled to his feet. 'You'll take me to her.'

Charity stared at him in disgust. 'You'd sell your own flesh and blood, never mind breaking your daughter's heart?'

'She ain't got no heart. Poor folks like us can't afford to be sentimental. Violet should think herself lucky that her old pa is willing to get her out of this scrape. She don't stand a chance of finding a husband if she's got a nipper tied to her apron strings. I'm giving her the opportunity to make good her mistake.'

'You can't take Vi's baby. I won't let you.' Charity turned her head away, expecting to receive a blow from his raised hand, but he let it fall to his side, shrugging his shoulders.

'You'll change your mind, sweetheart. Let's see what a night alone with the rats and cockroaches will do.'

'Where am I?' she demanded angrily. 'You can't keep me here. My friends will be looking for me.'

'Let them look. There's no one knows that you're here. This place was a pub years ago. It was on my delivery round so I knows every inch of this cellar.'

'The police will have been informed.'

'This building is due for demolition tomorrow. You'd better make up your mind quickly.' He picked up the lantern and walked towards the steps. 'I'll be back first thing and you'd better be ready to tell me what I want to know or it'll be the worse for you.'

'At least leave me a candle,' Charity cried urgently, but all she received in answer was a mocking laugh that echoed round the cellar walls after he had gone. She was left in almost complete darkness, and she was close to panicking when she saw a glimmer of light coming from the street above. For a moment she was puzzled, and then she realised that she was in a pub cellar, and the sliver of light was coming from trap doors which would have opened to allow barrels of beer to be delivered down a chute. She forced herself to remain calm, subduing the fear of the dark that had haunted her since childhood. It was late evening and if there was light outside it must come from a street lamp, which meant that the former pub was in a thoroughfare. She strained her ears, listening for the sound of footsteps and passing traffic. If she could work her way free from her bonds she might be able to attract the attention of a passer-by. She tried shouting for help, but there was no answer to her frantic cries.

She struggled, but the ropes chafed her wrists and ankles and tore at her skin, forcing her to stop. She rested for a while, trying to ignore the crippling pangs of hunger and increasing thirst. As her eyes became more accustomed to the darkness she could make out the shape of a table and what looked like a bottle that Bert must have forgotten to take with him. Driven by desperation she threw herself onto her side and rolled across the filthy floor, scattering cockroaches and crushing those that were not quick enough to make their getaway.

She could not see where she was going and she came to a sudden halt as she crashed against the table. She heard the bottle topple and it fell to the floor, shattering into shards, the largest of which reflected the sliver of light from above. If she could just get her hands free she could untie the rope that bound her ankles, or at the very least slice through it with a piece of broken glass. She rocked sideways in an attempt to raise herself to a sitting position. It took several tries but eventually she managed to sit upright, and then she began the process of freeing her hands. The pain was intense but she gritted her teeth and persisted until the bonds slackened. She rested for a few minutes and then began again until she could slip her hands free.

The rope burns hurt but she had no intention of giving up until she was free. She reached down and attempted to untie Bert's knots. When this failed she picked up a shard of glass and began sawing through the tight cords. Eventually, with blood pouring from her cut fingers, she managed to slice through the last few strands and she uttered a cry of relief. Tearing a strip off her petticoat she made a rough bandage for her right hand. The cuts were superficial but painful, and the numbness in her feet was replaced by pins and needles. She reached up to hold on to the table and pulled herself into a standing position, stamping her feet in an attempt to bring them back to life. It was only then that she realised how quiet it was. The traffic had ceased and she could no longer hear the sound of footsteps on the pavement. It must be the middle of the night, but time did not seem to mean anything in this subterranean world. She was exhausted and there was nothing she could do until morning, but she had the uncomfortable feeling that she was not alone in the dank cellar. She could hear the patter of small feet as the resident rodents circled around her. She had heard horrific stories of people attacked by rats, and she dragged the table over to the far wall and climbed onto it. She lay down and curled up, making herself as small as possible in order to retain some of her body heat. She closed her eyes and imagined herself back in the bedroom at the cottage with Violet and Dorrie sleeping in the next room. In her mind's eye she could see Alice sleeping peacefully in her crib and she vowed that she would protect Violet's baby with her life if necessary.

She was awakened by the rumble of traffic overhead and the sound of footsteps as people walked over the trap doors. The events of last evening came back to her in a terrifying flood and she knew that Bert would return. What would happen then did not bear thinking about; she sat up and she swung her legs over the side of the table. The cuts on her hand were the least of her worries but they stung painfully and her stomach contracted with pangs of hunger. She slid off the table and made her way carefully towards the chute, stepping between the scattered slivers of glass. She looked around, hoping to see a stick or a broom that was long enough to tap on the doors above her head, but it was too dark to see into the corners of the cellar. She shouted until she was hoarse, but no one seemed to hear her. She made an abortive attempt to walk up the chute but it was damp and slippery and she could not get a foothold.

Feeling along the walls she found the cellar steps and made her way to the door at the top. It was locked, but she had expected that and she banged on it with her fists, calling for help, but still no one came. She returned to the cellar and dragged the table to the foot of the chute, climbed onto it and stood with her hands cupped around her mouth, calling for help. On one occasion the footsteps slowed down and she shouted even louder, but whoever it was walked on, and she could have cried with frustration. She was growing ever more desperate. A beating would be the least of the methods Bert might use to drag the information out of her when he returned and she refused to give him the information he demanded. She called out again, and this time she heard a familiar sound that made her heart race. Above her head the thin sliver of light was dimmed and she could hear snuffling and the scratching of claws on wood. 'Bosun! I'm here!'

The scrambling grew louder, followed by the heavy tread of booted feet. With a creak and a groan of hinges the trapdoor was lifted and daylight flooded into the cellar. Charity shielded her eyes. 'Jackson, is that you?'

He leaned over, peering down at her with Bosun at his side. 'Hold on, miss. I'll have you out of there in two ticks.' He motioned the dog to sit. 'On guard, Bosun.' He disappeared and Charity slumped down on the table, tears of relief pouring down her cheeks. She wiped them away on her sleeve at the sound of the cellar door being kicked until the lock shattered and it flew open. She leapt from the table and ran to the steps, meeting Jackson halfway. He grabbed her by the hand. 'Come along, miss. There's no time to lose. Workmen are clearing the street and they're going to start knocking the place down.'

'How did you know where to find me?' Charity held on to him as he led her out through the derelict building, stepping over clumps of fallen plaster and wall tiles.

'You got Bosun to thank for that, miss.' Jackson lifted her over a fallen beam and set her on her feet the other side. 'Are you all right?'

His words were echoed by Harry, who was standing outside on the pavement with Bert held in an arm lock. 'Are you all right, Charity?' His voice shook with suppressed emotion and white lines etched the sides of his mouth. Dark shadows underlined his eyes and he looked like a man who had endured a sleepless night.

Her heart did a massive leap inside her chest, making her feel faint, but she managed to nod her head, and was suddenly conscious of the sight she must look. In broad daylight she could see that her skirts were blood-stained and filthy and her hair hung loose about her shoulders. 'Harry,' she murmured. 'You came.'

'Very touching,' Bert sneered. 'Don't tell me you got your eye on this cove, you slut. D'you think a gent like him would want you for anything other than a . . .' His words were lost as Harry spun him round and sent him hurtling down the chute.

'He had it coming to him.' Gideon slapped Harry on the back.

Harry leaned over the open trap door. 'I've a good mind to shut you in and let them bring the building down round your ears, you miserable bastard.'

Bert shook his fist. 'You've broke me arm. I'll have you up before the beak for assault.'

'Tell that to the police when they arrive,' Harry shouted above the noise of the workmen who were advancing on the building with picks and shovels. 'I think kidnap and false imprisonment carry a longer sentence than a punch on the nose.' He turned to Charity, holding out his hand. 'Are you really all right? If he's hurt you I'll go down there and beat him to a pulp.'

'I'll help you,' Gideon added angrily. 'You look very pale, Charity. We'd best get you home.'

Bosun licked her hand, and Charity stroked his head. 'Thank you for finding me, Bosun.'

'He's a good dog,' Jackson said proudly. 'We've been out all night looking for you, miss. I'd never have thought of the Old Three Tuns if Bosun hadn't taken up the scent.'

Harry placed his arm protectively around her shoulders. 'Are you able to walk, my love? We're not far from home.'

She met his concerned gaze with a tremulous smile. 'Never mind me, Harry. You must go home to Bligh Park. The reason I came to London was to tell you that you're needed there.'

He nodded. 'Gideon told me what's been going on, but you're more important at this minute. The rest can wait.'

'I agree.' Gideon glanced into the cellar where Bert was making his way up the steps. 'Chapman's trying to escape.' He beckoned to two burly workmen. 'There's a villain in the cellar. Keep him here while I go for a constable, and be careful, he's extremely violent.'

The elder of the two rolled up his sleeves, exposing muscular forearms. 'Leave it to me, vicar. I ain't one to stand by and see a woman beat up.' He cast a sympathetic glance in Charity's direction, confirming her suspicion that she was not looking her best.

She leaned on Harry's arm. 'Take me home, please.'

The smell of something savoury wafted from the kitchen and Charity stopped, turning to Jackson with a questioning look. 'I didn't know you could cook.'

He let Bosun off his lead and the dog bounded across the hall, gambolling joyfully around Mrs Diment as she came bustling towards them. 'Get out of the way, you stupid animal,' she said, flapping her apron at him. 'Are you all right, Charity? We've been out of our minds with worry.'

Harry stepped aside as Mrs Diment rushed over to embrace Charity. 'It was good of you to come at such short notice.'

Dazed and weak, Charity looked from one to the other. 'How long have I been away?'

'Too long,' Harry said fondly. 'I can't take credit for sending for Mrs Diment. You have Jackson to thank for that.'

Jackson took off his hat. 'I took the liberty, miss. I sent a telegram to Bligh Court yesterday, and Fanny caught the next train to London.'

'I'd had enough of playing second fiddle to Polly Trevett. She was always the bossy one when we were kitchen maids.' Mrs Diment tossed her head, very nearly dislodging her spotless white mobcap. 'This is my home and it's where I hope I'll end my days.' She gave Harry a meaningful look. 'Anyway, that's enough talking. You should go to your room and change out of those filthy rags, miss. I'll bring up a jug of hot water and a clean towel. I daresay everything has gone to rack and ruin since I've been away, and you can make yourself useful, Enoch. Fetch some coal for the range and fill a scuttle for the parlour in case the master wants a fire. It might be summer but that room always feels damp and cold.'

Jackson and Bosun slunk off towards the kitchen, followed by Mrs Diment, who seemed determined to make sure that both of them did as they were told.

Charity waited until they were out of earshot before turning to Harry. 'Enoch? I never knew that was Jackson's first name.'

Harry took her in his arms, smiling. 'Neither did I, come to that. But never mind them, I've got you safely home and that's all that matters.' He bent his head and kissed her on the lips. It was a sweet and gentle caress, devoid of passion but filled with longing. Charity felt herself floating as if she were weightless, but then he drew away with a worried look. 'Are you really all right? If he harmed you in any way I'll see that he goes to prison for the rest of his life.'

'A few bruises, that's all. I cut my hand while I was sawing through the ropes with a piece of broken glass.'

He held her closer. 'He won't hurt you again. I'll make sure of that.' He was about to kiss her again, but she laid her finger on his lips.

'Not now, Harry. I must go to my room before Mrs

Diment catches me dawdling, but first I must beg you to go home as soon as possible.'

'I will, my darling, but only when I'm satisfied that you are all right.'

'I'm fine, but I'm worried for Dan's sake. I don't know how much he told you, but Wilmot is determined to get a share of the Bligh treasure, and your mother seems to think that Bligh Park is her rightful home. They arrived with a retinue of servants and enough luggage to last a year.'

He traced the frown lines on her forehead, wiping them away with a touch of his forefinger. 'You mustn't worry, my darling. I can handle Wilmot and my mother. She's not a bad person, Charity. She's easily led and no doubt Wilmot is trading on her weaknesses, but I'll set her straight. You will be mistress of Bligh Park, not Mother.'

His words made Charity's heart sing and her head spin, but a small voice in her head advised caution. 'I love you, Harry, but you know it's not that simple. I've only met your mother once but she made it very clear that I must keep my place. I can't help feeling that she's right. She's well versed in the ways of the world.'

'And she's created more scandals than she cares to mention. Mama might act like a dowager duchess but she's a practical woman at heart. She'll come round eventually.'

'She was just being realistic, and I agree with her. You're Sir Harry Bligh from now on, and you have a position to keep up.' She stepped away, indicating her dishevelled state. 'This is what I am – a bruised apple fallen from a costermonger's barrow to end up in the gutter. I would drag you down to that level.' She backed towards the staircase. 'I'm going to change my clothes but I can't change what I am.'

He frowned. 'That's arrant nonsense, and I won't listen to such talk. You are the finest person I've ever met, and I love you with all my heart.' He was about to kiss her again but was interrupted by the appearance of Mrs Diment.

'There's a fire in the parlour because that room always feels chilly, despite it being the middle of summer, and I filled a decanter with sherry wine, Sir Harry,' she said, emphasising his new title. 'The old order is restored and we can resume our rightful place in the world.'

'I'll go upstairs and make myself presentable,' Charity said, smiling. 'I'll be as quick as I can.'

Washed, dressed in clean clothes and with her injuries tended to by Mrs Diment, Charity made her way downstairs to the parlour to find Harry seated by the fire with an untouched glass of sherry on the table at his side. He stood up and his smile enveloped her like a warm caress. 'You look beautiful.'

She felt her resolve weakening, but she was determined to stand firm. 'You must go home, Harry. You know very well that Dan isn't strong enough to stand up to your mother, let alone Wilmot. That man is a bully beneath all that outward show of charm.'

'I can't leave London for a day or two. I still have

some formalities to go through, but once my name is on the Official Roll no one can dispute my claim.'

'Wilmot will find a way round that if he can. Don't underestimate him.'

'Even so, I'm sure that Dan's birth certificate will state that his father was Sir Philip, even though it's untrue.'

'So he couldn't inherit the land or the title?'

'I suppose he could put in a claim if I were to die suddenly.' Harry reached out to take her hands in his. 'But I think murder would be a step too far for Wilmot. He's greedy, but he's not stupid.'

She stared down at their intertwined fingers. 'I think that Wilmot knows you'll be generous to your brother, and that he'll do his best to make Dan surrender whatever share of the fortune you decide to allow him. You know how easy-going and good-natured Dan is – he'll agree to anything for a quiet life and he wants to see your mother happy.'

'You are wise beyond your years, my darling, and I love you more than ever. I'll go home as soon as possible, and in the meantime I'll do my best to persuade you to change your mind about us.' He kissed her on the forehead. 'I'll propose to you properly when all this is settled. All I ask is that you don't let anyone or anything come between us. It's our future that counts and damn the rest of the world.'

She looked into his eyes. 'I promise,' she murmured.

He released her hands and wrapped his arms around her, holding her close so that she could feel his heart beating in time with her own. She laid her head on his shoulders and breathed in the scent of him, which she knew she would carry in her memory for the rest of her life even if they were to part now and never meet again.

The sound of the doorbell made them move apart and seconds later Gideon burst into the room. 'He got away,' he said breathlessly. 'The workmen held Chapman captive until the police arrived. They arrested him but he gave them the slip.'

'He's desperate to get hold of Vi's baby,' Charity said urgently. 'He said he'd found a couple whose baby had died and they were prepared to pay him good money for . . .' she could not finish the sentence and she sat down suddenly as her knees gave way beneath her. 'He'll be looking for Vi.'

Gideon sat down beside her. 'She should be safe at Bligh Park.'

'He's clever in his own way.' Charity knotted her fingers together in attempt to stop her hands shaking. 'He found me here and he must know that you own a country estate.'

'The police will be on the lookout for him, my love,' Harry said, frowning.

She shook her head. 'He'll be on his way there now. He'll find Violet and take her baby. We have to stop him.'

Chapter Twenty-Five

Harry leapt to his feet. 'I'll go to the police station and tell them all we know. They won't let him get away.'

Charity shook her head. 'Bert is too cunning to be caught. He'll bide his time and hide in the shadows until he thinks he's safe. He's a violent man and he'll stop at nothing to get what he wants.' She stood up, shaken but determined. 'I'm going to catch the next train to Dorset. I have to warn Vi and get her to a place of safety.'

'You're putting yourself in danger, and I won't allow that.' Harry seized her by the shoulders. 'Let me do as I said and inform the police.'

'Do what you like, but I'm going to Sutton Pomeroy. You can stay here and sort out your title and all that's important to you, but I'm going.'

'That's not my main reason for delaying.' Harry let his hands fall to his sides. 'I've paid off all my gambling debts but one, and this person would be delighted to see me ruined. I've pinned him down to a meeting this evening when I'll settle with him and then I'm a free man.'

Gideon rose to his feet. 'We don't know for certain that Chapman will head for Bligh Park, Charity. Even then he won't know where to find Violet and her baby.'

She spun round to face him. 'You don't know him

like I do. I suffered at his hands when I was at the bookshop. I didn't dare go into the back yard at night in case he attacked me. He's a brute and he'd have taken pleasure in torturing me if Bosun hadn't found me in time.'

'I can't leave until tomorrow morning at the earliest,' Harry said with a worried frown. 'If you'll just wait until then . . .'

'Damn your title and the bloody Official Roll or whatever it's called and this person who's playing some devious game with you. I'm leaving now and you can't stop me.' She ran to the door and wrenched it open.

'Charity, wait.' Harry followed her into the entrance hall. 'This is ridiculous. I'll go to the police station right away and tell them everything. Leave it to them.'

She headed for the stairs. 'Leave me alone, Harry. I'm going to get my things. If you want to help you can find a cab to take me to Waterloo.'

'I'll go with her,' Gideon said hastily. 'You do what you have to do, and I'll see that no harm comes to her.'

Charity paused with one foot on the bottom stair tread. 'Perhaps we could take Violet and her baby to the rectory. They'd be safe there.'

'I'm sure that Father would be only too happy to give them shelter.'

'I would come with you if I could, but I'll join you tomorrow,' Harry said firmly. 'You do understand, don't you, Charity?'

She gave him a searching look. 'You aren't playing the tables again, are you?'

'I gave you my word and I've kept it. You have to trust me.'

'I'll go and hail a cab,' Gideon said hurriedly. 'Perhaps you could get a message to the rector, Harry. You could say that I've been called away on an urgent family matter.'

'Of course.' Harry slapped him on the shoulder. 'It's the least I can do.'

Charity hurried to her room, returning minutes later with a hastily packed valise. 'I'm ready. Let's hope we don't have to wait too long for a train.'

Harry thrust a leather purse into her hand. 'You'll need this. I'll be with you as soon as possible.' He turned to Gideon with a grateful smile. 'You're a good friend. I know you'll look after her.'

Dusk was falling by the time they reached the cottage. Charity could barely wait for the driver to rein in his horse before she leapt from the trap. She ran to the front door and finding it unlocked she went inside. She could have cried with relief when she saw Violet sitting by the range, suckling her baby, while Dorrie busied herself tidying away the remains of their evening meal. She gave a cry of delight and threw her arms around Charity. 'You came home.'

'Of course I did.' Charity smiled down at her. 'I'm glad to see that you've been looking after Violet and the baby.'

'I've done everything Vi asked,' Dorrie said proudly. 'But we missed you.'

'And I missed you.' Charity turned her head to give Violet a questioning look. 'Are you all right, Vi?'

Violet smiled dreamily. 'Of course I am. I couldn't be better. We've been managing very well without Mrs Diment, haven't we, Dorrie?'

Dorrie released Charity and did a twirl. 'I'm learning to cook, and I've been a great help.'

Violet smiled and shifted the baby to her other breast. 'We've muddled along together.'

Charity jumped at the sound of the door opening. She knew it was Gideon even before she looked round but her nerves were on edge. Violet moved her shawl to cover her naked breast. 'We wasn't expecting visitors,' she said, blushing.

Gideon drew Charity aside. 'You haven't told them then?'

'What's going on?' Violet demanded, looking from one to the other. 'You're as edgy as a cat, Charity. There's something you're not telling us.'

'There's no easy way to say this, Vi.' Charity went to sit beside her. She gave a brief account of the happenings in London, trying not to frighten them too much, and failing.

Dorrie buried her face in her hands and tears trickled out between her fingers. 'I don't want to leave. This is our home.'

Violet was deathly pale. 'You say he wants to sell my baby?'

'I'm sorry, but it's true,' Charity said, rocking Dorrie as if she were the baby. 'It's only for a few days. The police have been informed and they'll be on the lookout for him. He's already a wanted man, and when they catch him he'll go to prison.'

'What will Ma and the nippers do?' Violet's eyes brimmed with tears. 'They'll end up in the workhouse for sure.'

Gideon cleared his throat. 'Might I suggest that you pack the things you'll need for a short visit to the rectory? The driver is waiting outside and we ought to be on our way.'

Charity lifted Dorrie to her feet. 'You can help me. We'll go upstairs and you can decide what you want to take with you. It'll be lovely seeing Mrs Simms and Jennet again.'

Violet hoisted the baby over her shoulder and patted her tiny back, which resulted in a satisfactory burp. 'You're right, Charity. I know me dad. He won't stop at nothing when he sees a way of making money. Not that he'd ever spend it on us – it'd go on beer and baccy.' She rose to her feet and handed the sleepy baby to Charity. 'I'll sort out what we need. You can get to know my Alice.' Violet shooed Dorrie up the stairs.

'That was easier than I thought,' Charity murmured, cradling the baby in her arms. 'I do hope that your father won't mind, Gideon.'

'Don't worry about that. My father is the most generous, kind-hearted man I've ever known.'

'And his son comes a close second,' Charity said, smiling. She held out her hand. 'Thank you for this, Gideon. I'm truly grateful.' He held it briefly and he was smiling but there was regret in his eyes and she knew she had touched on a painful subject. 'I wish things were different, but you must understand how it is,' she added.

'Of course I do, and I wouldn't be human if I didn't

envy Harry his good fortune, but I'll always be your friend and his.'

'Thank you,' she said softly. 'That means a lot to me.' She held Alice close. 'How could anyone think of selling this child? It doesn't bear thinking about.' She looked up, putting her finger on her lips to hush Dorrie as she came bounding down the stairs with a carpet bag in her hand. 'Don't wake her.'

Dorrie grinned. 'She'd sleep through a thunderstorm when she's got a full belly. Ain't she just a little pearl?'

Gideon glanced anxiously out of the window. 'It's time we were on our way. There won't be room for all of us in the trap, but I'll come back for you, Charity. Will you be all right here on your own?'

The memory of her last encounter with Bert and the night spent in the dank cellar was still fresh in her mind. Charity shook her head. 'I'll walk to Bligh Park. Harry will have sent them a telegram telling them I'm on my way, so they'll be expecting me.'

'It's almost dark. Please wait until I return.'

'I know a short cut through the fields. Even if Bert had discovered the whereabouts of the cottage he'd be lost in the countryside.'

Gideon did not look convinced. 'You'd be safer here. Lock the doors and make sure all the windows are closed and I'll return within the hour.'

Charity could see that he was not going to give in easily, and she nodded. 'All right, but please go now. I'll douse the fire and make everything secure, but please hurry.'

* * *

They had gone and she was alone. Charity had always felt safe in the cottage but the atmosphere had changed subtly and she was on edge. Every creak of the timbers and every small noise made her stop in her tracks and cock her head on one side, listening for the sound of footsteps on the gravel path. She went round locking doors and securing windows. She drew the curtains and instead of dousing the flames she added a few more lumps of coal to the fire. Having tidied up, she had nothing to do other than sit and wait. The minutes ticked by and she wondered if they had reached the rectory. She was tempted to leave the cottage and follow her original plan to walk across the fields and through the spinney, but she knew that Gideon would worry if he returned and found her gone. She would have to wait for his return.

An hour passed and she was growing impatient. Soon it would be too late to go to Bligh Park. She knew that they kept country hours and that Parkin would lock the doors soon after ten o'clock, and everyone would retire to bed. Daniel would wait up if he was at home, but if he wanted to keep out of his mother's way he might be sleeping in the camp at the excavation site. The thought of hammering on the door and arousing Wilmot, or disturbing him from a pleasant evening with his wife, was not encouraging. She rose from her chair and began to pace the floor, wondering what could be keeping Gideon. Perhaps the horse had lost a shoe or there had been an accident on the road. Travelling by night was always a hazard, especially in the narrow country lanes where it was impossible for two vehicles to pass each other. Her imagination was running riot when she heard the crunch of a footstep on the path outside. Without thinking she ran to open the door.

'So this is the right place.' Bert loomed up in front of her with a triumphant grin. 'I enquired at the railway station and the porter told me where the young ladies were living. I thought you'd hotfoot it here to warn my girl. Where is she?'

Charity slammed the door in his face and shot the bolts with trembling hands. She leaned against it until the vibration of his booted feet kicking the panels made her move away.

'Open up or I'll break the door down.'

'I'm expecting someone at any moment. Go away, Bert Chapman. Your daughter isn't here.'

'You little bitch; you can't help interfering, can you?' Another mighty kick on the door sent splinters of wood onto the flagstones but the panels did not give way. Charity thought about escaping through the back door but decided against it. Gideon would arrive at any moment. On his own he would be no match for Bert's brawn, but the driver of the pony and trap was a big fellow who could probably outmatch Bert in height and muscle. She breathed a sigh of relief when Bert abandoned his attempt to break down the door, but then he turned his attention to the windows. He shook the casements until the handles rattled, but they remained firmly in place, and the lattice panes were too small for him to put his hand through even if he managed to break one of them. She could hear his heavy tread as he stomped round to the back of the house.

There was a sudden silence and she held her breath. Perhaps he had gone away after all. She had told him that Violet and the baby were not here and maybe he had taken her at her word. She sat very still, hardly daring to move. The minutes ticked by and still there was no sign of Gideon, but all was quiet outside. Then, just as she was beginning to think that Bert had given up, the sound of splintering wood and breaking glass from upstairs was followed by a string of expletives. He came thundering down the stairs. 'You was telling the truth. Where've they gone? Violet and the babe – where are they?' He crossed the floor and grabbed her by the hair. 'I should have done for you when I had the chance.'

Her eyes watered with pain as he dragged her head back so far that she thought her neck would snap. He thrust his face close to hers. 'I could finish you off with a flick of me fingers, but you're no good to me dead. You'll tell me where they are or I'll make you sorry you ever drew breath.'

He released her suddenly and rushed to the door. 'Someone's coming. You come here and tell them you're not at home to visitors.' He strode over to her and grabbed her by the arm, pulling her off the chair.

'Charity, it's me, Gideon. Let me in.'

'So it's the parson you got in tow, is it?' Bert leered at her. 'Answer him, girl. Ask him what he done with me daughter.'

'She's safe from you.' Charity spat the words at him.

'I'd die before I'd let you get your hands on Vi or her baby.'

'Charity, who's with you? Are you all right?' Gideon rattled the latch. 'Let me in.'

'I can't,' she shouted in desperation. 'Bert's here. He broke in.'

'I got your woman here, parson.' Bert dragged her to the door. 'Tell me where you took my Violet and the babe.'

'No, don't tell him anything.' Charity uttered a cry of pain as Bert twisted her arm behind her back.

'Don't hurt her.' Gideon's voice cracked with emotion. 'Tell me what you want and I'll see what I can do, only let her go. She can't help you.'

'I already told you, mate. Bring me daughter and her brat here and you can have this one.'

'Give yourself up, Chapman. The police know you're here. Make it easier on yourself.'

'The cops ain't here.' Bert snorted with laughter. 'I ain't falling for that one. Go away, parson. Don't come back unless you bring them as what I asked for. Miss Crosse stays with me until I have what I want.'

'Have I your word that you won't hurt her?'

'I ain't a gent so me word don't count, but if you fail to satisfy my demand I'll wring her pretty little neck or stick a chiv into her breadbasket. I got nothing to lose.'

'I want to hear from Charity.'

'Tell him you're all right,' Bert growled.

'I'm not hurt.' Charity raised her voice. 'I won't tell him where Vi is and you mustn't either.' She winced and bit her lip to prevent herself crying out as Bert twisted her arm.

'You got until dawn, mate. I ain't saying no more.' Bert pulled up a chair. 'Sit down and don't utter so much as a squeak.' He snatched a couple of drying cloths from the wooden clothes horse and tore them into strips. 'This will keep you out of mischief while I find something to eat.' He knotted the strips together and bound her hands and feet before tying her to the chair. 'Get out of that if you can.'

'I'll be back.' Gideon's voice was hoarse. 'Don't be afraid, Charity. We'll have you out of there in no time.'

'That's what he thinks,' Bert said with a satisfied grin. He lumbered over to the cupboard where they kept their supplies and took out a loaf, a slab of cheese and a dish of butter. 'Them country folk eat well,' he said, taking a seat at the table. 'All I need now is a pint of ale and I'd be a happy man.' He stabbed the loaf with the bread knife. 'That's what you'll get if you misbehave.'

She could do nothing but sit and watch him stuff food into his mouth. Eventually, when it seemed that he could not manage another mouthful, he sat back in his chair and belched. 'I was ready for that,' he said, grinning. 'You led me a merry dance, girl. But now I got the upper hand.' He stood up and grabbed the bread knife.

Charity closed her eyes. He was going to finish her off now, but the blow never fell and she opened her eyes again to see him hacking through the material that bound her to the chair. 'Get up them stairs,' he said gruffly.

She sat motionless, staring at him in horror. He seized her by the arm and dragged her to her feet. 'Don't worry, it ain't your body I'm after tonight. I need some kip if I'm to pit me wits against the police in the morning.' He gave her a shove towards the staircase. She stumbled up the stairs with Bert following so close that she could feel his hot breath on the back of her neck. When they reached the narrow landing he thrust her into the girls' room and slammed the door. She heard the key turn in the lock.

It was hard to believe that Bert was going to allow her to rest. He must be tired, she thought dazedly, or he would have done more to prevent her from attempting to escape. She ran to the window and opened it, peering into the darkness. It was raining and below her she could just make out the tangle of undergrowth that they had not yet managed to clear. The intention had been to make a kitchen garden where they could grow vegetables and soft fruit, but now such hopes seemed like pipe dreams. Their idyll in the cottage looked as though it was going to end in disaster.

A flickering beam of candlelight emanated from the broken window of the room where she had always slept, and she could hear Bert moving about. Then the candle was extinguished and the bed groaned beneath his weight. She leaned out of the window to see if it was possible to jump to safety, but it was a sheer drop and there did not appear to be anything to give her a foothold. The tree that Bert must have climbed in order to break in through her bedroom window was too far away to be of any use. She could leap into the unknown and risk breaking bones or she could remain where she was and try to snatch a few hours' sleep in the hope that Gideon would return with the police at daybreak.

She moved away from the window and stood looking round the small room. The two single beds were separated by a pine chest of drawers and Alice's crib stood at the foot of Violet's bed. The solution came to her in a flash of inspiration, and she heaved the flock-filled mattresses off the beds and eased them out of the window, one at a time. She climbed onto the sill and squatted down, clutching the window ledge with both hands as she lowered her body until she was hanging by her fingertips. She let go and landed with a dull thud.

She lay sprawled on the damp mattresses with the rain trickling down her face and soaking her cotton frock. The shock of the sudden impact had taken her breath away but she was not hurt. She scrambled to her feet, hoping that the sound of her fall had not roused Bert, and made her way through the undergrowth, snagging her skirts on brambles and the clutching thorns of dog roses. It was too dark to see where she was going, but she had often walked this way in daylight and she headed across the fields, in the direction of Bligh Park. She did not feel safe until she reached the shelter of the spinney. Even if Bert awakened and found her gone he would not find her here. She stopped, leaning against the slim trunk of a silver birch; her one thought was to get to the safety of the house she had come to think of as home. It came as a shock to realise how much she had grown to love the eccentricities of Bligh Park. She had been happy to settle into the cottage for the sake of the girls, but in her heart of hearts she knew now that she would never love anyone but Harry, and Bligh Park was a part of him that he had yet to acknowledge.

A sudden breeze sent a shower of rainwater from the leafy branches, bringing her abruptly back to her senses, and she hurried on. She had reached the dense thicket that separated the open parkland from the home farm when she heard a rustle in the undergrowth and a shadow became a reality.

Chapter Twenty-Six

Her cry of fright was muffled in the folds of a man's greatcoat and strong arms held her in a vice-like grip. 'What the hell are you doing wandering around at this time of night?'

Charity pushed him away with a burst of strength fuelled by shock. 'Harry. You frightened me to death.'

He drew her more gently into his arms and held her. 'What happened? Where is Chapman? Gideon came to the house on his way to fetch the police. I'd only just got home and he told me that Chapman had taken you prisoner.'

'I jumped out of the window.' A gurgle of laughter escaped from her lips. 'I escaped, Harry.'

'Are you hurt? Did he harm you? I'll kill the brute if he so much as touched you.' He hooked her arm around his shoulders. 'I'm taking you home. The police can deal with Chapman.'

'I'm all right. But I thought you were staying on in London.'

'Explanations later.' He lifted her off her feet. 'I think you have something in common with our little mermaid. I always seem to find you soaked to the skin.'

* * *

Mrs Trevett was in the kitchen. She was wearing her wrap and her grey hair was tied up in rags, giving her the appearance of an elderly child. For a moment she seemed overwhelmed by relief, but she quickly recovered and became her usual bossy self. She sent Parkin to fetch a blanket and made Charity sit by the fire, pressing a cup of hot sweet tea laced with a generous measure of brandy into her hands. 'You poor child,' she murmured, rearranging the folds of the blanket around Charity's knees. 'What a terrible time you've had. Master Harry has told us all about your dreadful experience in London, and now you've gone through it all again. Violet's father should be locked up in prison for what he's done. The rector's son should have alerted the constabulary by now and I hope they catch Chapman and give him what for.'

Harry laid his hand on Charity's shoulder. 'Will you be all right if I leave you for a while?'

'Why? Where are you going?' she asked anxiously. 'You still haven't told me how you got here so quickly.'

'There are some things more important than money and title. I realised that the moment you left with Gideon, so I went straight to the police and travelled with them on the train. I'm going to see to it that Chapman is put away for a very long time.'

'So you didn't settle your debt. You risked losing everything to save me.'

'You are the most important person in my life. How could I do anything else?'

'But you'll be ruined.'

'I sent Jackson with the money. It would be a brave

man who would argue with him, and if Lord Chetwin carries out his threat to put it about that I reneged on a debt of honour, so be it. I'm done with that world forever.'

He leaned over and dropped a kiss on her damp curls. 'I'm riding over to the rectory. I want to make sure they're all safe in case Chapman has given the police the slip yet again.'

'I don't understand why they came from London for a petty criminal like Bert.'

'Apparently it wasn't Chapman's first brush with the law. He's been involved with one of the lesser known street gangs for some time, but they moved south of the river when it became too hot for them in Whitechapel. Chapman decided to carry on where they left off and now he's going to pay for his crimes. He'll go away for a very long time.' He kissed her again. 'Get some rest, sweetheart, and don't worry about Violet and the baby. They'll be safe in the rectory.' He left the kitchen without giving her a chance to argue.

'It's bed for you, my dear. I've put you in one of the best guest rooms this time.' Mrs Trevett took the cup from Charity's hands and placed it on the table. 'Come along now. You won't do any good by sitting there worrying. Master Harry will make things right. He's come home at last.'

Charity had only intended to catnap, but when she opened her eyes the sun was streaming through the window and the warm air was filled with birdsong.

In London she had grown accustomed to the chattering of sparrows and the raucous noise of the cockerel's attempts to be heard above the rumble of traffic and the sound of horses' hooves. She sat up with a start as she recalled the events of the previous evening. She tumbled out of bed and dressed hurriedly in one of her old print frocks, brushed her hair and tied it back with a ribbon and slipped on her boots which were still damp after her flight through the rain-soaked fields.

Downstairs in the kitchen she found Parkin eating his breakfast and Mrs Trevett sitting at the table drinking tea. 'Any news?' she asked anxiously.

'None as yet, my dear. Why don't you sit down and have something to eat?'

'Thank you, but I must find out what's happening. I'll ask Tapper to saddle up Nellie and I'll ride over to the rectory.' She looked from one to the other. 'Have you seen Daniel this morning? I'm surprised that we didn't wake him with all that commotion last night.'

Parkin exchanged meaningful glances with Mrs Trevett. 'Master Daniel stays at the camp with the archaeologists these days, miss.'

'He doesn't get on very well with the master,' Mrs Trevett added.

'The master?' Charity looked from one to the other. 'Do you mean Mr Barton?'

'We've been told to call him that. I don't think he was expecting Master Harry to return so soon.' Mrs Trevett sent a warning glance to Parkin. 'It isn't up to us to criticise our betters.'

'Things will be different now, Polly.' Parkin's stony expression did not change but there was an optimistic note in his normally sepulchral voice. 'Sir Harry will take his rightful place and Bligh Park will come alive again.'

'Mrs Barton has her eye on the fortune. She was always trouble, that one.' Mrs Trevett tossed her head, sending her mobcap askew. 'She'll wheedle and scold and have a fit of the megrims until she gets her own way. I've seen it all before.'

Charity made her escape, leaving them to continue their discussion uninterrupted. She found Tapper in the stables, grooming Wilmot's horse. He stopped what he was doing and at her request saddled Nellie. 'She could do with the exercise, miss,' he said as he helped Charity onto the saddle. 'Mrs Barton prefers to ride in the carriage.' His tone implied that he had little time for Myrtle Barton and Charity was not surprised. None of the servants seemed pleased to have their old mistress back in residence, and after only a brief acquaintance with Myrtle she did not find this surprising.

'Good girl, Nellie,' she said, patting the animal's sleek neck. 'Let's go.' She rode out of the stable yard, but instead of heading towards the village she guided Nellie towards the excavation site. She found Daniel outside his tent stripped to the waist, washing his hands and face in an enamel bowl. She called out to him and he looked up with a start.

Flicking water from his eyes he grabbed his shirt and shrugged it on as he hurried to meet her. 'Charity, it's good to see you. When did you get back?' She leaned towards him, lowering her voice so that the curious onlookers could not hear. She gave him a brief account of events and told him why she was on her way to the rectory. 'Hold on for a few minutes and I'll come with you,' Daniel said firmly. 'If that fellow is as desperate as you say he might get away and come after you as well as Violet.' He called to one of the students. 'Fitzroy, lend me your mount, there's a good chap.'

'Hold on, Dan. I was going into Dorchester this morning. We need supplies.'

'That will have to wait. This is a matter of life and death, quite literally.' He winked at Charity. 'That may be an exaggeration, but Fitzroy enjoys a bit of drama.

'All right. I suppose my trip can wait.' Fitzroy marched off to where several horses were tethered in the shade of an oak tree.

'I'll put my jacket on and then I'm ready for anything.' Daniel hooked his coat off a hawthorn bush and slipped it on. 'I love living in camp,' he said, grinning. 'It's better than being under my mother's thumb. Life in the house became unbearable with Mama and Wilmot nagging me about the inheritance.'

'What did they want you to do?' Charity asked curiously.

'After you'd gone to London Wilmot produced a document drawn up by his solicitor. He wanted me to give him power of attorney over my affairs until I reach my majority.'

'You didn't?'

'No, of course not. I'm no fool and I'll be twenty-one in less than two months. I knew that had I given in Wilmot would have appropriated most of the money, or at least compelled me to give Mama a generous allowance, which no doubt he would have enjoyed spending.'

'Would you have done that?'

'No. Well, maybe. I don't know, Charity. Anyway, now that Harry is here everything will be settled and they'll leave me alone.' He looked round as Fitzroy arrived, leading his horse. 'Thanks, old man. I'll return the favour.'

'You'd better.' Fitzroy held the horse while Daniel mounted.

'I'll take good care of him,' Daniel promised as he took the reins. He turned to Charity with a roguish smile. 'I'll race you to the crossroads.'

They arrived at the rectory to find Mrs Simms and Jennet in a state of near hysteria. 'Oh, thank goodness it's you, sir,' Mrs Simms cried, clutching Daniel's arm. 'We are so frightened. The rector, Sir Harry and Master Gideon left over an hour ago, soon after the policeman arrived to tell them that the villain had escaped. He got out of the window and climbed down the tree while it was still dark. He could be outside right now, lurking in the bushes.'

Charity's hand flew to her throat in an involuntary gesture. 'Where are the girls?'

'Hiding in the old nursery at the top of the house,' Jennet said, looking round nervously as if she expected to see the house surrounded by a dozen Bert Chapmans. 'That man is like Spring-heeled Jack. I read about him in a penny dreadful, and he was seen again in Aldershot Barracks ten years ago. My mum said there was an account of it in the *News of the World*, so it must be true.'

'Don't be silly, Jennet,' Mrs Simms said crossly.

'But it was near London and that man come from there.' Jennet crossed her arms beneath her large bosom, nodding her head wisely. 'Who's to say that Chapman ain't a reincarnation of the devil?'

Charity laid a comforting hand on Jennet's arm. 'I don't think that Bert Chapman is anything other than a very wicked man, but that doesn't mean we should take chances. Daniel will stay with you and I'll go upstairs to see Violet and Dorrie, if that's all right with you, Mrs Simms?'

'Certainly, miss. Of course, you must do that.' She turned to Daniel with a motherly smile. 'May I get you some refreshment, sir?'

Charity did not wait to hear Dan's answer. She raced up two flights of stairs to the nursery and knocked on the door. 'Violet, it's me, Charity. Let me in.'

Moments later after hugs and tears, Charity sat on a threadbare nursing chair with Dorrie at her feet while Violet huddled on the bed with Alice sleeping peacefully in her arms. 'I can't believe that me dad was mixed up with the gangs,' she said sadly. 'If he goes to prison it'll be the workhouse for Ma and the little 'uns.'

'I'm sure we can do something to help her.' Charity

stroked Dorrie's hair. 'We'll survive this, as we've survived everything else You mustn't worry.'

'You won't leave us, will you, Charity?' Dorrie clutched her hand, holding it to her cheek. 'I'm not scared when you're here.'

Charity was about to answer when a commotion from the front garden made her leap to her feet and run to the tiny dormer window. She looked out and saw Bert standing in the middle of the road, shouting and storming at the village men who had surrounded him. She opened the window. 'I know they're here somewhere,' Bert roared. 'My daughter has been abducted by the parson. He's going to ruin her and I want her returned to the bosom of her loving family.'

Violet slid off the bed, clutching Alice to her bosom. 'What's he doing out there? What lies is he spreading?'

'I'll go down,' Charity said, closing the window. 'Stay here, both of you. Let me and Daniel handle this until the police arrive. Harry should be with them so they can't be far off.'

She let herself out of the room and ran downstairs to find Daniel in the entrance hall. 'Don't go out there,' she pleaded. 'Wait for the police.'

Mrs Simms clutched her hand to her heart. 'I can feel my palpitations coming on. If only the rector had stayed at home instead of rushing off to the cottage with Master Gideon and Sir Harry.'

Jennet peered out of the window. 'That man is saying terrible things about Master Gideon. I'm going out there to give him a piece of my mind.'

Charity caught Jennet by the apron strings as she

was about to open the front door. 'Don't. You'll just play into his hands. No one in the village will believe his lies. We have to wait and hope that Harry and the police come quickly.'

'I'll go out and tell them he's a wanted criminal.' Daniel reached for the door handle, but Charity barred his way.

'Don't. You'll only make matters worse. If anyone goes out there it should be me. I'll tell the men what he did to me and what he intends to do to his own flesh and blood.' She opened the door and slipped out before Daniel had a chance to argue. Unnoticed by the crowd she walked down the garden path and opened the gate. 'Brave words, Bert Chapman, but they're all lies.'

A sudden silence fell and all heads turned to stare at her. She pushed her way through the throng until she came face to face with Bert. 'This man is a gang leader from London. He's wanted for numerous crimes including abducting a young woman and keeping her prisoner. He plans to take his daughter's baby and sell her for the highest price he can get. Do you want to allow this villain to go free?'

'Don't listen to her,' Bert roared. 'She's a slut from the East End who sells her body to any man with a penny to spare. She wouldn't know the truth if it bit her on the bum.'

Someone in the crowd sniggered and was immediately shushed.

'None of that is true.' Charity held her head high, projecting her voice so that it rang out loud and clear.

'This man is a criminal. Your wives and daughters aren't safe when he's around.'

'What Miss Crosse says is the truth.' Daniel had left the safety of the house to stand beside her. 'You all know me, and I say arrest this man. Hold him until the officers of the law arrive.'

There was a sudden scuffle as Bert attempted to push his way to freedom but he was no match for men who earned their living by muscle power and brawn. He lay on the ground with one man's foot pressed on his back and another holding his feet. The sound of horses' hooves and police whistles shattered the sudden stillness and Harry arrived, followed by Gideon and the police with Philip Raines bringing up the rear.

Harry leapt from the saddle and rushed to Charity's side. 'Are you all right, darling?'

'I am now,' she said, smiling.

'Albert Chapman, I'm arresting you in the name of the law.' The police sergeant from London dragged Bert to his feet. 'You won't get away from us this time.'

Bert shot a malevolent look at Charity. 'I'll make you pay for this, you bitch.'

'Don't worry, miss,' the sergeant said, grinning. 'He'll be going away for a long time.' He gave Bert a none too gentle shove, sending him into the arms of one of the constables who slapped handcuffs on him with obvious satisfaction. Bert was led away still proclaiming his innocence.

'I've never come across such a slippery customer,' the sergeant said, mopping his brow. 'The streets of London will be safer when he's locked up.'

Harry shook his hand. 'Might I suggest that you and your men take some refreshment at the village inn before you set off for London? At my expense, of course.'

'Thank you, sir. But with a character like Chapman I think it best to get him on the train as soon as we can. I want to see him locked in the guard's van with two of my most able constables.'

'I quite understand.' Harry turned to Charity with a tender smile. 'Let's get you home. I think we've all had enough excitement to last a lifetime.'

Charity shook her head. 'I must go and tell the girls first, and the cottage needs some repairs before we can live in it again.'

'Come inside, all of you,' Gideon said firmly. 'We all need some sustenance after that experience.' He took his father by the arm. 'I was never so proud of you as I was today, Father.'

'I had a powerful ally.' Philip smiled and cast his eyes heavenward.

'Tea is what you need, sir,' Mrs Simms said, seizing Jennet by the arm. 'If you'll make yourselves comfortable in the drawing room we'll bring refreshments.' She hustled Jennet back into the house, and was met in the doorway by Dorrie and Violet. Dorrie flew at Charity and clung to her like a burr.

'Has he gone? Has the bad man been taken away?'

'He won't trouble any of us again,' Charity said gently. 'Everything will be all right.'

Violet shook her head. 'For us maybe, but not for Ma. I'll have to go home and help her look after the young 'uns.'

Dorrie uttered a muffled shriek. 'You mustn't leave me, Violet.'

Violet rocked Alice in her arms as the baby opened her eyes and began to whimper. 'What choice do I have? You can stay with Charity.'

Charity turned to Harry, who had remained at her side, holding her hand. 'What can we do?'

He gave Violet an encouraging smile. 'You mustn't worry. We'll think of something.'

Gideon paused in the doorway. 'In the meantime Violet and Dorrie are more than welcome to stay here until the repairs are carried out at the cottage.' He lowered his voice. 'It would give Mrs Simms something to think about other than fussing over Father's health. It drives him mad but he's too soft-hearted to tell her so.'

'Thank you, sir.' Violet bobbed a curtsey. 'You're very kind.'

He shook his head. 'Not at all. You would be doing me a favour, Violet. I have to return to London as soon as possible and I know that Father enjoys your company.'

Dorrie stared hard at Violet. 'You're blushing, Vi.' She turned her attention to Gideon. 'You should marry her, sir. Vi can cook a lovely rabbit stew and she's already got a baby, and I could be Alice's sister. You'd have a family ready and waiting for you.'

Violet stared at her in horror. 'Hush, Dorrie. You don't say such things to a gent like the reverend.' She rocked Alice in her arms in a desperate attempt to silence the baby's howls.

Gideon threw back his head and laughed. 'Thank you for the suggestion, Dorrie. I'll give it my earnest consideration.' He held his hand out to Violet. 'Come indoors and allow Mrs Simms and Jennet to make much of the baby. Have you thought about having her christened?' He led Violet into the house and Alice immediately stopped crying.

'See,' Dorrie said triumphantly. 'They was made to go together, just like you two.' She skipped on ahead, leaving Charity and Harry to follow.

'She's right,' Harry said, smiling. 'We were destined to meet and fall in love. I'm never going to let you out of my sight again, Charity Crosse.'

'Your mother won't approve. She hates me, Harry.'

'Nonsense. Give her time and she'll grow to love you as I do.'

'Over my dead body.' Myrtle Barton paced the floor, wringing her hands. 'I won't allow it, Harry. You can't marry a girl from the slums. A pretty face won't help when she's ostracised by society. You'll bring the family name into disrepute.'

Harry threw back his head and laughed. 'That's rich coming from you, Mama. Did you consider the Bligh name when you left my father for Sir Philip?'

'That was different.' Myrtle stopped, facing him angrily. 'I fell in love with Philip. My marriage to your father was arranged by our families. There was no love lost between us.'

'And yet he never remarried, Mama. And he never said a word against you that I recall.'

Charity cleared her throat nervously. 'I should go to my room. You ought to discuss this in private.'

'No.' Harry's tone did not invite argument. 'I am going to marry you, and my mother will have to get used to the idea.'

Wilmot moved swiftly to Myrtle's side. 'You can't speak to your mother like that, Harry. You're the one who's dragged the family name through the mire. Marry the girl if you want to bed a slut, but give up your claim to the land and title. Allow your brother to inherit and accept an allowance from the estate, which you can fritter away at the gaming tables while your wife peddles books in the market or sells her body in order to make ends meet.'

Harry made a move towards Wilmot but Charity placed herself between them. 'That's enough,' she said angrily. 'You are a disgusting man, Wilmot. You were quick enough to proposition me when I was destitute and yet you accuse me of being a wanton.'

'He did what?' Harry and his mother spoke in unison.

'It's true,' Charity said hastily. 'He'll deny it, of course, but it is true.'

Myrtle turned on her husband in a fury of flailing hands and bared teeth. 'You brute. You utter cad.'

He grasped her by the wrists. 'It was before I fell in love with you, my darling. I admit that I offered the girl a home, but she misunderstood my meaning. What can you expect from a child of the gutter?'

Harry seized him by the shoulders, twisted him round and pinned him against the oak panelling. 'If you ever go near Charity again I won't be responsible for my actions.' He released him, wiping his hands together as he faced his mother. 'You married a scoundrel, Mother. I hope you'll find some happiness with him, but I want you both out of this house by tomorrow morning at the latest, and that's being generous.'

'You're throwing your own mother out of her rightful home?' Myrtle's lovely eyes welled with tears and her perfectly shaped mouth drooped at the corners. 'How can you speak to me like that?'

'Don't try that with me,' he retorted angrily. 'I'm no longer a child, and I can see through your ruses. I love you, Mama, but I love Charity even more and she will be my wife, if she'll have me after all this.' He held his hand out to Charity. 'You've seen the worst of the Bligh family; do you think you could bring yourself to make an honest man of me?'

She slipped her hand into his. 'I do,' she said simply.

'Bah!' Myrtle flew at Wilmot, beating him once again with her fists. 'This is all your fault. You brought me to this. I was happy in my Devonshire home but it wasn't enough for you. You wanted the Bligh Park estate as well.'

Wilmot brushed her off as if she were an irritating insect. 'Spare me the histrionics, my dear. You are as avaricious and grasping as I am. We'll do very well together, but I know when I'm beaten.' He marched her towards the doorway. 'We'll leave tonight. I won't stay where I'm not welcome.'

Safe in the circle of Harry's arms Charity could hear her future in-laws arguing all the way up the stairs until the sound of their voices faded away. She looked up at him with a question in her eyes. 'Did you mean that? Do you really want to marry a beggar maid?'

'More than anything else in the world.'

She slid her arms around his neck and closed her eyes as he claimed her mouth with a kiss that made her heart sing with joy.

Daniel burst into the dining room, coming to a halt with a broad grin on his face as he saw Charity and his brother seated side by side, gazing into each other's eyes. The table was laid and set for three. 'Wonderful,' he said enthusiastically. 'I'm in time for dinner, and you two have obviously resolved your differences as I knew you would.'

'Come and sit down, Dan.' Harry raised Charity's hand to his lips. 'You can be the first to congratulate us.'

Daniel slapped him on the back. 'I'd have been the first to give you a good hard kick if you hadn't proposed to the girl.' He leaned over and kissed Charity on the cheek. 'I couldn't have wished for a lovelier sister-in-law, or a more courageous one. You're a lucky dog, Harry.' He sat down and shook out a starched white napkin. 'I noticed that Wilmot's carriage had gone from the coach house, so I take it they've left.'

'I told him to go in no uncertain terms, but I hope he makes her happy nonetheless,' Harry said seriously. 'She's still our mother no matter what she's done in the past.'

'Mama is a survivor,' Daniel said, helping himself to a bread roll. 'She'll bounce back and lead Wilmot a terrible dance, which is exactly what he deserves. I'll go and see her when I've sorted out my trip to Egypt.' His smile faded. 'You will fund me, won't you, Harry? I mean I know the money belongs to you, but you wouldn't begrudge a little of it to your brother, would you?'

Harry flicked a piece of bread roll at him. 'It will be worth it to get a bit of peace and quiet, old chap.'

'Of course he will,' Charity said firmly. 'And I, for one, will miss you. I'll re-read Miss Edwards' book about her trip up the Nile and think of you in all those exotic places.'

'Maybe we'll join you one day.' Harry looked round as the door opened and Parkin ambled in carrying a soup tureen. 'Thank you, Parkin. We'll serve ourselves, and tomorrow we'll have a chat about employing more staff. I can't have you and Mrs Trevett run ragged. There'll be a few changes made, but they'll all be for the good.'

'Thank you, sir.' Parkin's face split into a semblance of a grin and Charity could swear that there was a spring in his step as he left the room. She rose to her feet and began serving the savoury-smelling stew.

'We must help Violet's mother,' she said, placing a plate in front of Harry. 'And there's Nevill's Court lying empty and neglected.'

He looked up at her, eyebrows raised. 'You're not thinking of filling it with little Chapmans, are you?'

She passed a steaming plate to Daniel. 'Not exactly,

but it might be a good thing to bring them to Sutton Pomeroy. I'm sure there must be a vacant cottage on the estate and you just said you were going to employ more servants. Mrs Chapman is a hard-working woman used to working in a laundry. Maybe we can find something for Violet as well.' She ladled stew into another plate and set it in front of Harry before serving herself.

Daniel swallowed a mouthful of bread and butter. 'I know almost nothing about these things,' he said slowly. 'But I think Gideon has rather a soft spot for Violet. I wouldn't be at all surprised if he spent a bit more time visiting his pa, or if he put in for a transfer to the parish when Mr Raines retires. The old man can't go on forever.'

Charity stared at him in amazement. 'I think you might have something there. Who would have thought it?'

'Stop matchmaking, you two,' Harry said, laughing. 'You'll have Dan waiting for young Dorrie to grow up next.'

'Now that is ridiculous.' Daniel picked up the piece of bread roll and tossed it at his brother. 'I'll marry a girl who shares my love of archaeology and doesn't mind roughing it.' He shot a sideways glance at Harry. 'How soon can we settle matters? We've just about finished the dig here and found nothing more than a tessellated pavement, which isn't going to add to the Bligh fortune, even if it does attract the interest of academics and people who have nothing better to do than roam the country looking for antiquities. Anyway, I'll soon be at a loose end.'

'I'll see my solicitor and he'll advise me on the best way to handle my finances. I'm not going to fritter away the Bligh Park fortune.' Harry reached out to hold Charity's hand. 'I think we should travel up to London tomorrow and spend a few days in Nevill's Court. I have to decide what to do with the old place.'

'You don't want to live there, do you?' Charity asked anxiously. 'I mean, I wouldn't mind at all and I love London, but you don't have to give up everything for me.'

He smiled. 'I've had enough of the high life. I want to settle down and be a country squire with you at my side. We'll raise our family here in Bligh Park and restore the old house to its former glory, but as to Nevill's Court, I'm at a complete loss and yet I don't want to sell it.'

Charity laid her spoon down and faced him eagerly. 'I had an idea for the house while I was living there. The library is filled with wonderful books, as is the one here. It seems such a waste to keep all that knowledge and learning locked away.'

'Dash it, Charity.' Daniel stopped eating to stare at her. 'You don't mean to open another shop, do you?'

She laughed and shook her head. 'No, of course not. Nor do I intend to hawk them round the streets as I did when we were desperate for money.' She turned back to Harry with a persuasive smile. 'I thought we could open up some of the rooms and start a free lending library so that the poor could have access to books that they could never hope to afford. We could use volunteers who would be willing to coach people who can't read, or children who are slow at learning. Maybe wealthy benefactors will donate money to help with the running costs, and most important of all it would mean that Mrs Diment, Jackson and Bosun have a permanent home.'

Harry raised her hand to his lips. 'Am I going to spend the rest of my life doing good works?'

'No, I don't expect miracles,' she said, chuckling. 'I love you just as you are.'

Getting to know

Dilly Court

Read on for an insight into *The Beggar Maid*, an interview with Dilly and an exclusive extract from Dilly's next book

Dear Reader,

Starting a new book is like the beginning of an adventure – you never know quite where it will take you or what characters you'll meet on the way.

This was particularly so with *The Beggar Maid* and the trials that beset young Charity Crosse who had begun life in a comfortable middle-class home, only to lose everything when she was orphaned and had to struggle to exist on the streets of Victorian London.

Her encounter with the crippled bookseller, Jethro Dawkins, came as much a surprise to me as it did to young Charity. Characters come into my head, fully formed and with a back history that is all their own. My inspiration for this unfortunate man might have come from the time I worked as a medical secretary in a large orthopaedic hospital in Shropshire. I witnessed the enormous bravery of young children who had been born with similar disabilities, and I was filled with admiration for the courage they exhibited while undergoing treatment. Modern medicine and the skill of the surgeons gave them chances in life that were denied to poor Jethro. It's no wonder he was not the kindest of men, but he loved his books, and he gave Charity a chance to better her lot.

Dear Reader

I like to have a picture in my head of the area where I set my stories and I work from old street maps and old photographs of London. I based Sir Hedley's ramshackle London home on a photograph of what had once been a splendid late seventeenth-century merchant's house' in Nevill's Court, off Fetter Lane. Sadly, this magnificent building, together with the other houses in the alley, all of which had survived the great fire of London, were swept away in 1929 to create a new road.

Altogether *The Beggar Maid* was an exciting journey and, of course, I had to fall in love (a little) with my hero, but I have a soft spot too for all my characters, even the nasty ones, although some are nastier than others. And lastly, the magical mermaid and the silver bullion – it was rumoured that many years ago such a treasure was washed ashore on Portland, but was so blackened that many islanders thought it valueless and used the lumps of metal as doorstops. I can't say if this is true, but it makes a good story.

I hope that you have enjoyed reading about Charity and the people she met along the way to a happy ending. Anyway, now I can start on my next book, and I wonder where that will take me?

With my very best wishes,

Dilly Court

Dilly Court grew up in the suburbs of north-east London. Her imaginary childhood friends soon became characters in stories that she made up to amuse her cousin, Clive. She wrote her first book aged nine, very much under the influence of Enid Blyton, and continued to scribble stories and plays all through her schooldays.

Her first job was with Associated Rediffusion, London's original commercial television company, where she began as a secretary and graduated to writing advertising copy. During her first marriage to a merchant navy officer, she lived in various parts of the country, giving up work to raise her son and daughter – who are now her best friends and have given her four beautiful grandchildren.

She now lives by the sea in Dorset, on the beautiful Jurassic coast with her most excellent husband, John. Her hobbies are gardening, cooking, oil painting and knitting things for her family.

1. What made you want to become a writer?

It's something I've done ever since I can remember. I was making up stories before I had learned to write.

2. Describe your routine for writing and where you like to write, including whether you have any little quirks or funny habits when you are writing.

I write every day, starting in the morning after getting my granddaughters off to school. I go into the engine room, as my husband calls my office (which is part toy cupboard, part working space) and I write until lunchtime. I'm very much a morning person.

3. What themes are you interested in when you're writing?

Relationships between the characters, and these change as I get to know each character a little better.

4. Where do you get your inspiration from?

That's a difficult one – I suppose from life and the places I have visited.

5. How do you manage to get inside the heads of your characters in order to portray them truthfully?

The moment a character appears they develop a life of their own. Of course it's in my imagination, but I see them and listen to them as they tell me their stories.

6. Do you base your characters on real people? And if not, where does the inspiration come from?

That would be very dangerous – I don't think my family or friends would speak to me again if I did.

7. What's the most extreme thing you've ever done to research your book?

I'd like to say bungee-jumping, but that wouldn't be true. I'm afraid it's much more boring than that – I have books on most subjects and I use Google.

8. What aspect of writing do you enjoy most? (i.e. plot, character development)

The plot develops as I get to know the characters.

9. What's the best thing about being an author?

Getting positive feedback from my readers.

10. What advice would you give aspiring writers?

Persevere. Write every day even if it's only a few lines and learn to take constructive criticism and turn it to your advantage.

11. What is your favourite book of all time and why?

That would have to be *Gone with the Wind*. I admire Scarlett's courage and determination and it's a real page turner from start to finish.

12. If you could be a character in a book, or live in the world of a book who or where would you be?

I think the character I would like to be is Jo in *Little Women* and the sequels *Good Wives* and *Jo's Boys*. She was an author too.

Dilly's new book will be out
12 February 2015

Born out of wedlock when her mother was only fourteen, Lucy Pocket has spent all her life in the care of her disreputable but charming grandmother, Eva. They dodge from one poor lodging house to another, always in debt and resorting to theft in order to exist.

Until her wealthy paternal grandfather buys her from Eva, determined to bring Lucy up to be a lady. When her grandfather dies, his despicable nephew cheats Lucy out of her inheritance, except for a run-down lodging house in Whitechapel, where she is forced to look after his three illegitimate children.

Jilted by her would-be fiancé, Lucy is determined to make a life for herself and the children. And to search for her long lost grandmother, creating the family she has always longed for.

Read on for an exclusive extract . . .

Chapter One

Aldgate, London 1871

The strange gentleman was there again, sitting in a brougham drawn by a sleek black gelding. The coachman sat as still as a dummy in a shop window, with his caped greatcoat pulled up to his chin and a striped woollen muffler covering the lower part of his face. He stared straight ahead, neither looking to left nor right.

Lucy Pocket shot a sideways glance at the man in the carriage, and was met with an unblinking stare. He had been in the same spot yesterday, and the day before. His eyes were a piercing blue, set wide apart beneath satanic-looking black brows and he was clean-shaven, but his hair was long, reaching his shoulders in curls that gleamed like silver. She looked away quickly. There was a coat of arms in the lozenge on the carriage door, but heraldry was as unfamiliar to her as the languages spoken by foreign sailors from ships that arrived daily at St Katherine docks. The man was obviously a toff, but the business which brought him to such a rough area as Nightingale Lane was anyone's guess. The romantic name of the road belied the fact that it was, and always had been, an area where the police worked in pairs, and ordinary people walked in fear.

Lucy quickened her pace, concealing the bundle she carried beneath her ragged shawl as she headed towards Cat's Hole buildings where she and her grandmother had been living for the past six months. They never stayed anywhere for long; they had to keep moving, but they had so far managed to steer clear of the law and the gangs who demanded protection money.

She sidled along the high brick wall which separated St Katharine docks from the London dock, glancing over her shoulder to make sure she was not being followed, but the carriage had gone, vanishing into thin air, or so it seemed. She tightened her grip on the bundle beneath her shawl and hurried on until she reached Burr Street and Cat's Hole, an aptly named building pinched between a tobacco warehouse and the King George pub. She was jostled by a large woman wearing a cloth cap, with a clay pipe firmly gripped between her teeth. 'Look where you're going, you stupid little cow.' The woman, who reeked of jigger gin, thrust open the pub door and a gust of warm air laden with tobacco smoke and the smell of unwashed bodies, stale beer and pickled onions slapped Lucy in the face. The noxious odours in the street were little better; the stench of the mud on the riverbank and night soil waiting for collection almost completely overpowered the rich aroma of molasses, tobacco and roasting coffee beans exuded in belches of steam from the manufactories and warehouses. Lucy sidestepped a soot-encrusted chimney sweep whose head was bent beneath the weight of his brush-filled sack as he cannoned along the road. She let herself into the building and closed the door.

The passageway was narrow, damp and dark. A shaft of light from a window at the top of the stairs helped her find her way to the first floor, and the back room where she laid her head at night. Ten feet square and bare of anything other than an iron bedstead, a deal table and two wooden chairs, it could not even with a stretch of imagination be called a home. Lucy tossed her bundle onto the table and looked round, playing the game: in her mind's eye she saw a comfortable living room, furnished with chintz-covered armchairs, an inviting sofa and a rosewood table, on which stood a silver vase filled with red carnations. The clove scent of them filled her nostrils, momentarily blotting out the stink of the outside privy, which was used by all the occupants of Cat's Hole. There were pictures on the walls in her dream home. Sometimes she allowed herself the luxury of examining them individually, and they changed from day to day. On rare occasions, when she was dipping pockets in Trafalgar Square, she allowed herself time to visit the National Gallery and wander through its great halls, gazing at the great masters' works. She crossed the floor, her imaginary new boots barely sinking into the thick pile of the Chinese carpet, and her silk petticoats swishing beneath her merino gown. She drew back the wine-red velvet curtains, but the material seemed to dissolve at the touch of her fingers and the dream faded into reality; she was left holding a scrap of moth-eaten cotton. She looked down at her feet encased in boots where the uppers had come away from the soles, and the heels were worn down to almost nothing. She lifted her skirt to reveal a red flannel petticoat that hung limp and mud-stained ending well above her ankles, and she sighed.

'What's up, Lucy?'

Eva Pocket breezed into the room carrying a wicker basket which she placed on the table. She eyed her granddaughter with her head on one side. 'You was playing the game again, wasn't you?'

Lucy nodded and her bottom lip trembled. 'Sorry, Granny. I know it's silly, but I can't help it.'

'Come here, my duck.' Eva held her arms outstretched and Lucy walked into her warm embrace. Cuddled up against Granny's generous bosom she felt like a child again, although at the age of ten, very nearly eleven, she considered herself to be a young woman. She had worked the streets since she was six and could sell matches or bootlaces with the best of them. She had toiled in a laundry and she had scrubbed floors, washed dishes and done all manner of jobs. She had even set herself up as a shoeshine, working outside Bishopsgate station, but she had been seen off by a group of boys who were plying the same trade. She was a grown-up now and able to take care of herself, but Granny's hugs were always welcome.

Eva released her, giving her a searching look. Nothing missed Granny's sharp eyes. 'Come on, love. Out with it.'

Lucy took off her shawl and laid it over the back of

a chair. 'He was there again, Granny. That strange man was watching me, I'm sure of it.'

Eva discarded her faded blue bonnet and tossed her head so that her mass of curls floated about her pointed face like a cloud of spun gold. At forty-two she was still a handsome woman, not exactly beautiful but her large, almond-shaped eyes brimmed with intelligence and their unusual shade of blue-green seemed to change with her mood. People said that Lucy looked just like her grandmother, but she could not see it herself. Eva turned away, unbuttoning her mantle. 'I'm sure it's just a coincidence, poppet. Maybe he's looking for someone, but it's not likely to be you or me. What would a gent want with a pair of guttersnipes like us?' Her merry laugh made the room seem bright and sunny and she spun round to tweak Lucy's curls so like her own.

'Maybe he's looking for Ma,' Lucy murmured.

'Well he won't find that one here, now will he? Christelle is goodness knows where, singing her heart out and hoping to become the next star of the Paris Opera.'

'Is she very beautiful, Granny? I can't remember what she looks like.'

'You were only two when she took off with her fancy man, darling. She is a beauty, there's no two ways about it, and she has a lovely voice, but she has no sense when it comes to blokes. She never did or you wouldn't have come into the world when she was only fourteen.'

'I won't let that happen to me,' Lucy said firmly. 'I'm going to make something of myself.'

'Of course you will, love.' Eva smiled and sat down at the table. 'I walked miles today and my dogs are barking. Anyway, that's my problem. How did you do?'

Lucy unwrapped her bundle. 'A few silk hankies and a wallet, but there's no money in it, Granny – just a few letters and some visiting cards.'

Eva examined it carefully. 'Peccary leather, this must have been expensive. Where did you get it?'

'A gent came out of a shop in Burlington Arcade and it fell out of his pocket.'

'Fell out?' Eva raised a delicate winged eyebrow.

'It did, honest. I wouldn't have the nerve to take it. Dipping for silk hankies is one thing, but lifting wallets is beyond me.'

'You could have given it back to him,' Eva said, frowning. 'He might have offered you a reward.'

'And he might have accused me of taking money from it, even though it was empty.'

Eva stared at the hankies with a practised eye. 'There's a couple of bob to be had for those, although Old Pinch is getting meaner by the day, and more particular in what he's prepared to take.' She opened the wallet and took out a deckle-edged visiting card. 'I don't believe it. This belongs to Linus Daubenay, Esquire.'

'Do you know him, Granny?'

'He used to be one of the mashers who hung around the stage door when your ma was in the chorus. She was only thirteen, but she looked older, especially with all that greasepaint on her face.'

'Was he my father?' Lucy clasped her hand to her chest in an attempt to still her racing heart.

'My Christelle wouldn't have anything to do with a man like that. She was flighty but she wasn't daft.'

'One day I'll find my dad, and then I'll know who I really am.'

'Sweetheart, you know who you are.' Eva reached out to clasp Lucy's hand. 'You're the best girl in the world.'

'But you won't talk about him. You must have known him, Granny.'

Eva frowned. 'He was a toff, that's all I'll say. He walked out one day, leaving my girl all alone in Peckham Rye, and you only a few weeks old.'

'Why did he go away? What happened to him?'

'He was killed in a duel, that's all I know. But he broke my girl's heart and set her on the path to ruin. I just wish I could have given you a better start in life.'

'You've given me everything, and I love you.' Lucy slipped her arm around her grandmother's shoulders.

Eva patted her hand. 'And I love you, sweetheart. But let's be practical, we need money and I had a bad day. I knocked on so many doors looking for any sort of work that my knuckles are raw.' She scanned Lucy's face, shaking her head. 'It's time we thought of a better way to earn our bread, and one that's on the right side of the law for a change.'

'You're tired and hungry, Granny.' Lucy bundled up the hankies. 'I'll take these to Old Pinch, and I won't allow him to fob me off with a few pence.'

Eva turned her attention to the wallet, taking out folded slips of paper and opening them. Her expression brightened. 'You said there wasn't any money, but these are like cash in the bank.'

'I don't understand. What are they?'

'These are IOUs made out to Daubenay, and he's owed close to three hundred pounds.' She held up the slips of paper with a triumphant smile. 'Returning these to their rightful owner should entitle you to a generous reward.'

'Do you really think so?'

'I do indeed.'

'I'll go now, and I won't take no for an answer.'

'It'll be dark in an hour and I don't want you wandering the streets on your own. Take the wipes to Old Pinch and get what you can and then we can eat. Tomorrow morning we'll go to Half Moon Street together.'